SPOUSE
TRAP

Also by Cynthia Hamilton

SPOUSE TRAP

A NOVEL

CYNTHIA HAMILTON

First Published 2013
Woodstock Press

ISBN: 978-0-9776278-4-4 (paperback)
ISBN: 979-8-9852621-3-1 (hardcover)

Formatting and cover design by Six Penny Graphics
Editing by Gail Prather
Proofreading by Amy Orozco

This book is dedicated to my
husband, with love and gratitude

I wish to thank the following
people whose generous support
made this print edition possible:

Rodger Boots, Delia Cunningham, Oliver Dixon, Justine and Josiah Hamilton, Alison and Glenn Leopold, Emma and Dave Malina, John M. McNamara, Dennis Peterson, Trevyn Pless, Melanie Rose, Margaret and Richard Walker, Brad Wathen, and Bob Young. You all have my undying gratitude.

PROLOGUE

Madeline Ridley opened her eyes with a start. Her mouth was dry and an unpleasant taste lingered on her tongue. Her head felt heavy and it ached as she moved. Reflexively, she flung out an arm, seeking the reassuring comfort of her husband's body. Instead, she encountered the cool starchiness of unfamiliar bed linens. *Where am I?*

She sat bolt upright, her heart and head throbbing in unison. Either she had been in the throes of a disorienting dream, or she really was in a strange room. Not knowing where she was terrified her.

The only illumination came from the meager predawn seeping through the French doors at the far end of the room. Her left hand groped the side table for the lamp switch.

The light temporarily blinded her, making her wince. She looked around, quickly searching for any object that would ground her to her life. She was not in either of her bedrooms, or any of the guest rooms. She sat tentatively on the edge of the bed, breathing hard. By the furnishings and the layout she figured she was in a hotel room. But where?

Grabbing the phone, she recognized the familiar logo of The Edgecliff Hotel across the top. *The Edgecliff, right. Steven and I were here for the fundraiser,* she thought. *Okay.* This recollection made her feel less shaky, but it didn't explain how she'd ended up in this room. *Did we drink too much and decide to get a room?*

She glanced at the other side of the bed. The sheets were flung back, indicating it had been occupied at some point.

"Steven?" she called out. "Steven?" As she got up from the bed, she caught sight of the dress she'd worn to the ball. She reached for it and the bra and panties she had been wearing only hours earlier fell to the floor. She stooped to retrieve them, discovering the dainty lace articles were in tatters.

"Steven!" she cried out, trembling as she wove her way to the bathroom on unsteady feet. "Steven?" She flipped on the light switch, and squinting through the glare, found the room empty. She backed out into the hallway, checking the closets for clues of her predicament.

Why am I in a room at The Edgecliff? she asked of her reflection in the hall mirror. All she saw was tousled hair, smudged lipstick and bloodshot eyes. Her hand traveled down the side of her neck to her clavicle, where three bright red scratches stretched toward her left breast. She turned away from the mirror, panting as she forced herself to recall how she had gotten there. And whose nails had made those marks on her.

Images of last evening began filtering across her mind's eye. She recalled stepping out of the Maserati at the hotel entrance and walking with Steven to the main ballroom. He had been in a foul mood; she clearly remembered that. She could hear the harsh tone in his voice, could see the anger in his eyes as he laid into her. *What was he mad about?* Madeline shook her head. She couldn't figure it out.

But she did recollect walking fast to catch up with him as he stormed off toward the lobby—him turning around, calling her a filthy whore under his breath. She remembered the sting of tears in her eyes and the feeling of disbelief as she watched him drive off, leaving her there on the curb.

With shaking hands, Madeline struggled into the red lace Valentino gown. She recalled the dark-haired man coming toward her...two glasses of champagne in his hands. His consoling words...*Don't worry, I'll make sure you get home...*

Madeline's throat closed, making it impossible to breathe. Her eyes teared up, but the cries couldn't escape. *This did not happen! This did not happen!* she thought, though it was obvious she had been in a hotel room with someone, and the odds were it wasn't her husband.

She sank into a chair as she pleaded with herself to remember how she had gotten to this room. Panic set in. Her hands flew to her earlobes; she went limp with relief when she felt the teardrop diamond earrings still in place. But where were her diamond watch and bracelet? And her wedding ring?

She frantically looked around and spotted her handbag, itself a pricey investment. She opened it hastily and found her jewelry, along with her cell phone and credit cards. She had not been robbed, at least. But what happened? Who had been here with her?

As she looked for cash in her tiny bag, she discovered the key to the beach house. She had put it in at the last minute, just in case she and Steven drank too much and didn't want to drive back up the hill. She clutched the key tightly in her hand; it was her salvation.

She found her shoes and carried them in one hand and hiked up her gown with the other. With the first tinges of daybreak coloring the sky, she crept out the French doors and followed the pathway. She crossed out of The Edgecliff grounds and headed down the steps to the sand. In less than ten minutes, she had made it to the beach house without seeing a soul.

ONE

"That was quite the haul," Madeline said into the phone distractedly, as she scanned through her emails.

"That's putting it mildly! It's the largest amount we've ever raised. Twice as much as last year's event," Carla Dickens reported with effervescent glee, clearly enjoying their triumph over the previous co-chairs' fundraising efforts.

"That's fantastic," Madeline agreed, but she had a hard time putting any real feeling into her words. Carla didn't seem to notice. It had been a fairly lopsided conversation from the start, which was fine with Madeline. She had far more pressing matters on her mind.

"I got an email from Katherine Broadhurst, the national chairwoman for the NHDF, congratulating me—us—on our success. She thought the 'Open Your Heart' Valentine's Ball was ingenious. I had to tell her it was *your* brainchild. She said she's going to institute it nationwide next year. She said her mind was just 'whirring' with the potential of a campaign based on that slogan."

Madeline had not heard these last bulletins at all; her mind had been completely distracted by the sight of Steven's car pulling up out front. It was only 10:30. He must have forgotten something.

Since the fundraiser fiasco on Saturday night, and the uneasy détente that had ensued since their phone conversation Sunday morning, she and Steven had been polite and reserved around each other, outwardly civil, but still tentative with one another.

After thoroughly showering at the beach house Sunday morning, Madeline had racked her brain for clues to the previous night's unraveling. The most she could come up with was that Steven's dark mood had further blackened when she danced with the dark-haired stranger. Beyond Steven leaving her standing on the sidewalk like a fool and taking the glass of champagne from the mystery man, she couldn't remember a thing.

On the assumption that jealousy had sparked Steven's bizarre behavior, Madeline bridged the divide and called him. To cover for the missing hours of her memory, she told him she had walked to the beach house when the ball was over, as she'd been too upset to stay in the same house with him. Only the fear of facing what had happened in that hotel room allowed her to keep her cool.

"I know we should be basking in our success right now, but I've had a couple ideas that could make next year's event even more successful," Carla was saying as Steven walked through their bedroom headed straight for Madeline's sitting room.

"Carla…I've got to call you back," she said, scarcely hearing Carla's response as she ended the call.

"Hi…" Madeline said cautiously as Steven approached. Her hesitant smile vanished when Steven took several 8 x 10 glossy photographs from a manila envelope and splayed them across her desk. Steven's face was rigid with rage, his eyes filled with contempt.

"What…?" Madeline's heart began to pound as her eyes focused on the subject matter in the accusatory photos.

"You filthy, disgusting slut!" Steven spat, picking up the photos and shoving them at his wife.

She stared at the amber-lit images of herself naked, in the tangled embrace of who she suspected was the stranger from the fundraiser. Photo after photo graphically depicted the two of them engaged in the act of sex. Madeline's hand shot to her mouth as a weak groan escaped. Her nightmare was far from over.

"Where did you get these?" Madeline sputtered, as she rose awkwardly from her seat, trying to distance herself from the pornographic images.

"That's your response? I show you pictures of you having sex with another man, and you want to know where I got them?" Steven yelled at her. "The fact that I now know what a cheap, disgusting whore you are doesn't worry you. No, you're only concerned about where this trash came from."

Madeline's face became a pale mask of trepidation as Steven ranted at her. She tried to speak, but no words came out. Her inability to answer for her crimes further infuriated him. He stood there, sheaf of damaging photos in his hand as he fumed, his face contorted with loathing.

"Who else have you slept with?" Steven demanded, taking a menacing step towards her. "How many times have you cheated on me, Madeline? Did you think you could get away with having an affair in a town this small? Or have you, and I'm just the last to know?"

"I've never cheated on you," Madeline said, her voice quavering. Steven barked out a harsh laugh that made his features more menacing. Suddenly, the wrath in his eyes was replaced by despair, and his voice broke when he spoke.

"It was the only thing I ever asked of you, the only thing you promised—*swore*—you'd never do…" Steven held his hand over his face to hide his pain.

"Steven…I swear I didn't do anything—" Madeline said, taking a step closer to him.

"How can you say that?" he said, throwing the photos at her. "How can you stand there and *lie* to me like that? Just like you lied to me Sunday morning—telling me you stayed at the beach house. You didn't, did you? Obviously not." Steven turned away, his anger causing him to wander indecisively.

Even though she was being accused of infidelity, Madeline couldn't stand to see Steven so anguished. She moved toward him, but his anger flared and froze her to the spot. "Stay away from me! I hate the sight of you."

Tears landed with loud plops on the photographs as Madeline bent down to gather them up. The drops left streaks on the glossy paper as she wiped them away.

"Do you have any idea how potentially damaging this could be for me?" Steven railed, as loss took a backseat to bitterness. "My credibility would be shot if this filth fell into the wrong hands. Think of the scandal this could cause." Madeline held the photos against her chest as Steven began to pace.

"Twelve years I've been faithful to you. *Twelve years!* I've given you everything you've ever wanted. I've treated you like a princess! You would've been nothing without me. Look at you! Look at your life! And this is how you repay me?" A truck from a local nursery pulled up on the drive. Voices could be heard as the gardener conferred with the driver.

"I'm leaving for Dallas tomorrow. I want all your things out of here when I get back on Saturday," Steven said, cutting off Madeline's attempts to persuade him of her innocence. "I'll have Hughes take your things to the beach house. You can stay there until the divorce is final. Or shack up with your new boyfriend, I don't care which," he said contemptuously.

"Steven—please don't go! I swear I don't know what happened…" Madeline sank back into her chair, completely devastated, as she watched her distraught husband walk out of the room. Moments later, she heard his car start, the low purring diminishing as he headed down the drive. She burst into tears as her heart broke in half.

❖ ❖ ❖

Madeline sat there, unaware of time, a wad of soiled tissues clutched in her hand as her mind raced over the events of the last few days. Somewhere in the missing hours of memory, she had broken her vows and destroyed her marriage.

But why? Why would she do something like that? She had never once been tempted to cheat on Steven. Never. When he walked out on her at the ball, she had no thoughts of retribution. She had been baffled and hurt, but surely not vengeful. Besides, she was the fundraiser's co-chair; she had duties to perform.

Her iPhone chimed, reminding her of a tennis game at 2:00. She scrolled down through the messages that had continued to flood in while she sat there helplessly, unable to move from the spot where her life had been suddenly wrenched away from her.

She stared at the messages uncomprehendingly, as if they were written in a foreign language. They might as well have been; she had no interest in anything right now but in trying to salvage her marriage. It couldn't be over just like that. Twelve years of marriage didn't end at 10:30 one day without any warning.

Steven was hurt. That was understandable. She couldn't fault him for his reaction or his feelings of betrayal. He was definitely the injured party here. But something inside her made it impossible to resign herself to the role of unfaithful spouse, despite the lurid photos proving otherwise.

Every time she replayed their conversation, she shook her head in disbelief. It simply wasn't in her makeup to cheat on her husband. There was something wrong with this scenario. And the damning photographs.

Madeline moved the envelope to uncover the pictures. It made her feel sick all over again, but she forced herself to look at all seven of them. If she hadn't found herself alone in a hotel room with her lingerie in shreds, she'd have dismissed this evidence as a photo-shopped attempt at character assassination.

She took a closer look. It was her, alright. She recognized the room, but the man—what she could see of him—could've been anyone. She shuddered and stuffed the photos into the manila envelope. But even in her distressed state, something didn't make sense.

She removed the photos and carefully scanned each one. Her profile was clear, but it was impossible to read her expression, except to speculate that she was so enraptured by her lover that her eyes were closed in bliss. Each photo was the same.

Madeline's heart raced as she laid the photographs side by side. Maybe *they* hadn't been altered, but *she* clearly had. It was all starting to add up: the man—Italian, she vaguely recalled—who she'd never seen before; the glass of champagne; the complete memory loss.

She sprang out of her chair, her mind spinning with the sickening realization that someone had planned this. To discredit her? What would be the purpose of that? It was not conceit to say she was well liked. As far as she knew, she was the darling of Santa Barbara society. Even if someone were jealous of her wealth and position, it seemed extremely unlikely they'd go to all this trouble to destroy her. But what about Steven?

Do you have any idea how potentially damaging this could be for me? My credibility would be shot if this filth fell into the wrong hands. Think of the scandal this could cause. Recalling his words sent chills down her spine.

Yes, that had to be it. Someone was trying to get at Steven. They wouldn't even need to know that infidelity in a spouse was Steven's Achilles' heel. Horrible pictures like these could be used to smear anyone's reputation.

The blood drained from Madeline's face when it occurred to her these hideous photos could be all over the Internet by now. She rushed to the bathroom and threw up.

As she stood in front of the sink, consulting her reflection for answers, she realized she had to share her suspicions with Steven. If she could explain everything to him, he would have to listen—he would have to know that she hadn't been unfaithful to him. Not willingly, at least.

Once she had her resolve, Madeline shifted into high gear. She sent a text to Jane canceling their tennis game, pleading exhaustion. She took a quick shower, then took pains with her hair and makeup. She wanted to present the image of a calm, pulled-together ally. She wanted Steven to see her as an asset again, not as the enemy.

She carefully chose her clothing, going for non-flashy neutrals, elegant but understated shoes, gold earrings and bracelets instead of diamonds. She looked the epitome of style and grace as she rang Hughes and told him she was going out and would need him to bring the car around—the BMW sedan, not her Porsche Carrera. She was going to appear upstanding and irreproachable in every manner. Her marriage was riding on it.

TWO

Madeline slowed down as she scanned the lot behind Steven's building for a parking place. All were taken, as she feared. She crept further down the street, spotting a space on the opposite side of the one-way street. She pulled forward and reversed into the spot.

Once parked, she drew a deep breath and silently rehearsed her plea one last time. *Steven, I need you to hear me out—I need to tell you what happened to me after you left The Edgecliff Saturday night. I believe someone is deliberately trying to ruin our marriage or your reputation, and I think these photos are proof... Steven, I think I was raped...*

This last thought made Madeline perspire all over. She turned the key in the ignition and cranked the A/C to full blast. She drew in the cool air and tried to fight back the tears. The possibility of having been drugged and raped had been completely overshadowed by Steven's rash conclusions.

Ordinarily, being the victim of a sexual assault would've out-ranked other worries. But making Steven see that she'd never cheat on him, under any circumstances, was her top priority. If she could get through that, maybe she could face what she didn't have the courage to accept now. But that would have to wait. Saving her marriage was the most immediate challenge.

"Okay," she said, nervously inspecting her makeup in the visor mirror and steeling herself for battle.

As she was checking the passenger's side-view mirror for traffic, she spotted Steven standing in front of the back staircase. Just as Madeline was about to seize the moment, a man crossed the street to join him.

As Madeline craned around to get a better look, both men glanced discreetly up and down the street before Steven pulled a slim envelope from his jacket pocket and handed it to the man, tapping him lightly on the shoulder. The man skimmed through the contents quickly, then offered his hand to Steven.

After a brief handshake, the man started up the street and Steven went up the rear staircase.

Madeline waited for the man to pass, watching as he made his way up the street. She had been anxious to go after Steven, but the exchange she just witnessed struck her as highly unusual. As the man darted across the street ahead of the traffic, Madeline put her head down.

Once the man reached the sidewalk a couple cars ahead of her, Madeline slid out of the driver's seat and casually began to follow him at a safe distance, her footsteps absorbed by the sound of passing traffic. When he turned left at the corner, Madeline rummaged through her large handbag, keeping her face down until the man was out of sight. She waited a few seconds before following him down Sola Street.

She was half a block behind him when he paused to let traffic pass before crossing Anacapa Street. Once he turned left and was out of her sight, she started running, only slowing as she neared the corner. She reached it just in time to see the man slip a key into a lock and disappear through the door.

Madeline stepped behind a tree for cover as she snuck glances at the old Craftsman home-turned-office. Her heart stopped as she read the business name emblazoned across the plate-glass window: Russell Barnett, Licensed Private Investigator.

A wave of heat rushed over Madeline as her brain registered this news. She took a couple backward steps, but she couldn't pull her eyes away from the building. *What is happening?* she thought, as she gasped for air. She found herself unable to think or move. She felt rooted to the spot, as if what she had witnessed had turned her to stone.

A shrill horn blast brought her back to reality just in time to see Russell Barnett exit his office. Madeline ducked behind a van and inched her way toward the front in order to observe the P.I. With casual alertness, Russell scanned the block before getting into a silver Honda Accord.

Madeline edged toward the rear of the van, staying completely out of sight as the Honda pulled out of the small lot and headed down the one-way street. As soon as his vehicle cleared the intersection at Victoria Street, she turned to flee to the safety of her car, where she could sort through the implications of what Steven's involvement with a P.I. meant.

By the time she reached the BMW, there was no room for doubt: Steven was paying a man for a job completed. She had run every possible scenario through her mind, searching and hoping for any other reasonable explanation for what she'd seen.

She had grudgingly shot down the desperate hope that Steven had hired this man to find out who had sent the photos to him. There simply hadn't been enough time between receiving them and the payoff. There wouldn't have been time for a meeting to examine the evidence, to go over possible suspects, to initiate a plan and secure hard evidence. Besides, she had the photos. Of course, Steven could've made copies, but that didn't really change anything.

No, the payment was for a service already rendered. And by the weakness in her knees, Madeline was sure the assignment had already been carried out, and that Steven was satisfied with the results. If she couldn't prove otherwise, she had to face the fact that her husband no longer wanted to be married to her.

For several minutes, Madeline rehashed every alternative that would justify the need for hiring a private eye, in hopes that her instincts were wrong. The type of business Steven was in required careful vetting; whether it was for financing start-ups, would-be film producers, land-rich individuals in need of private mortgages, or the investors culled to back them—everyone was subjected to in-depth background checks. Knowing who he was dealing with was of paramount concern to Steven and his group of investors.

But Steven had an in-house security team that handled everything from vetting to protection. She could think of no other reason for Steven to hire the services of a lone P.I. Not a single one, and she'd thought so hard, her head was splitting.

She suddenly felt the need to put a safe distance between Steven and herself. She started the car and pulled out into the street, driving by rote, with no destination in mind. Where could she go? She couldn't bear the thought of running into anyone she knew. She sure didn't want to be anywhere near Steven, but as long as he was at the office, she might as well take advantage of being at home, where she could think in private. She turned at Mission Street, headed for the 101 south.

Fifteen minutes later, she was winding up the steep drive to her house, her beloved home, the place she had been so happy for the last five years. Tears blurred her vision as she parked the car out front, leaving the keys in the ignition for Hughes. She entered the house unnoticed and headed straight to her sanctuary—her spacious, 20 x 20 square foot closet, her favorite room in the house. Her favorite room in the world.

As soon as she passed through the doorway, some of her anxiety began to melt away. Ever since they built the house, this room had become Madeline's fantasy hideout, nerve center and think tank. It was where Madeline felt most at home. This was hardly surprising, considering her love of fashion. But it was in this dressing room that she not only clothed herself to perfection; this was where she had invented the trendsetter who had soared to the top of Santa Barbara's social ranks with amazing alacrity. This is where she became Madeline Ridley, hostess and benefactress extraordinaire.

She eyed her reflection distractedly in one of the full-length mirrors as she kicked off her shoes, her mind roving over the events and discoveries of the last four hours. Her mental state had fluctuated from guarded to horrified, determined to devastated. As she regarded herself, she could feel the mix of all those emotions churn together, making her feel as though she might faint.

She sank to the round ottoman by her dressing table, once again trying to order her thoughts. On a gut level, she believed she had been the victim of some vile plot. No matter which way she worked it, she had been set up by someone: Steven, or someone else out to blackmail Steven.

If it was the latter, why weren't the photos accompanied by some sort of demand? What if they had been and Steven didn't tell me? What if he was trying to protect me? Madeline got up and began to pace. If Steven was trying to protect her, then he wouldn't have shown her the photos and accused her of infidelity. Or demanded a divorce. She slumped onto the chair in front of her vanity table, stymied.

If that scene had been set up at the request of the mystery man, what would the motive have been? Sending the photos to Steven without a specific threat didn't serve any purpose, except for destroying their marriage. But who would gain from that?

Intriguing question, Madeline thought, as she rose out of the chair and went to get a bottle of water from the mini fridge. She took a long drink and retrieved her laptop from her sitting room, then headed back to the dressing room.

Someone in love with Steven might want to break up our marriage, Madeline thought with a pang. Even in her hyper-susceptible state, this theory seemed a little farfetched. But everything about this situation seemed incredible.

As she returned to her dressing room, her heart stopped. There, hanging on a hook, waiting to be photographed and archived, was the red lace Valentino gown, fresh from the dry cleaners. The sight of it made her feel sick. She set down the water bottle and her computer, drawn to the dress with a mix of revulsion and curiosity.

I wish you could tell me what you saw that night, she thought as she examined it for signs of damage. Her lingerie had been demolished; she disposed of the flimsy pieces in a public trash can, possibly discarding valuable DNA evidence. But the dress looked as fresh as it did when it had arrived at the house last week. There was nothing to indicate that the wearer had been forcibly pulled from it.

"Oh, there you are, Mrs. Ridley," Erma said with a light laugh as she held her hand to her chest. "I thought I heard you come in, but when I put the dress up I didn't see you."

"Sorry, Erma—I came straight in here when I got home. I should've let you know I was back," Madeline said, trying to act as if everything was perfectly normal in the Ridley household.

"Mr. Ridley phoned. Said he tried to reach you, but he got your voicemail. Asked me to tell you he won't be home for dinner. Said he'll be going straight from work to a business dinner." Madeline nodded her head knowingly.

"That's fine, Erma. Don't worry about dinner for me. If I get hungry, I'll make a sandwich or something."

"Are you sure, Mrs. Ridley? I could prepare a piece of salmon—that won't be any trouble."

"No thanks, Erma. I'll be fine, really. In fact, why don't you take the night off—leave early for a change," Madeline said, busying herself at her computer.

"Are you sure, Mrs. Ridley?"

"I'm sure. You've been working as hard as everyone else—harder, I'm sure. And frankly, I'd love a night of doing nothing. I'm just bushed," Madeline said, slouching back in the chair for emphasis.

"I bet you are. Okay, then I'll get out of your hair, if you're sure you don't need me for anything…"

"Not a thing."

"Alright, Mrs. Ridley. I'll see you in the morning." Erma took one last glance around, making sure everything was in order before she backed out of the room.

Madeline let out a deep sigh and mulled over the latest developments. So, Steven wouldn't be coming home until late. Obviously trying to avoid her. As soon as she heard the back door close and Erma's footsteps as she walked toward her cottage, Madeline jumped up and went through the bedroom she shared with Steven to his side of the master suite.

After twelve years, Madeline knew Steven's habits down to the smallest detail. She knew which luggage he used for short business trips; she knew what suits he would likely take to Dallas in late winter, and what kind of shirts, ties, shoes, etcetera. With one glance, she could see that Steven's bag had already been packed for the trip. But it wasn't there.

From his dressing room, Madeline walked through the entry hall, past the living room and the dining room to the guest wing. Of the three guest rooms, she figured Steven would likely choose the one at the end of the hallway, the largest room with the best views, as far away from her as he could get.

Sure enough, she found his bag and a suit of clothes arranged on a hook in the armoire. His toiletries had been moved from his bathroom and stood awaiting his arrival. Simultaneously mad and hurt, Madeline left the guest room and wandered like a stranger in her own home.

In Steven's mind, their marriage was over. But Madeline wasn't prepared to see it end like this. There were far too many unknowns at this point, and there was no way she was going to let herself be painted with the brush of adultery until she could prove without a doubt that she was guilty. Or more precisely, that she wasn't.

THREE

After wandering aimlessly around her elegant home without noticing her surroundings, she found herself in Steven's study. She stood in the doorway, picturing him sitting at his desk, the late afternoon sun filtering in from the window behind him. The memory of such a familiar sight caused Madeline to choke up. Tears began to run down her cheeks as she sank into the leather chair she had occupied countless times over the years.

She wiped ineffectually at the tears as she recalled happier moments spent in this room—discussing travel plans, dinner parties, his latest achievements and her minor triumphs—all of which seemed so trivial in retrospect.

As the light grew dimmer with the setting sun, Madeline reached over and switched on the desk lamp. With the illumination came a sudden urge to snoop, something she had never been the least inclined to do in the past. She rounded the desk and sat in Steven's chair as she perused what little there was in plain sight.

Finding nothing of interest on top of the desk, Madeline tried the center drawer. Everything was orderly; just a tray of pens, blank notepads taken from hotel rooms around the globe, and an ashtray from a famous restaurant in New York, filled with assorted unlabeled keys. She tried the top drawer on the left and found it full of software discs. The large drawer below was locked. She tried the other side.

After picking through the top left drawer and finding nothing that implicated Steven in a hateful setup, Madeline tried the lower drawer. It appeared to be full of files pertaining to household expenses. She soon lost interest in the search.

She contemplated trying the keys in the ashtray to see if any might open the locked drawer, but she discovered this kind of prying didn't appeal to her. If Steven had any involvement in what transpired Saturday night, she seriously doubted he'd leave any evidence of it at home. She wouldn't know what to look for anyway.

She pushed away from the desk and idly wandered around the room, picking up photos taken of them throughout the years. They'd had so many happy times together. As she studied their wedding photo, she found it impossible to believe their marriage was about to end in divorce. Their compatibility was something she'd taken great pride in. Naturally, they'd had their disagreements, but neither of them had ever been prone to rages or fits. Both valued their unified front too much to let domestic squabbles get in their way.

That's what made Steven's behavior since Saturday night so puzzling. It was as if someone had thrown a switch and turned him into a distrustful, jealous husband. The fact that his personality change came just prior to her blackout made her even more apprehensive about the circumstances she now found herself in. The more she thought about it, the harder it was to believe the whole situation hadn't been contrived in order to extricate her from his life. What she couldn't fathom was *why?*

She caught her reflection in the glass case that protected Steven's prized first editions. It had been a hard day, emotionally speaking, and Madeline could see it in her posture. She immediately pulled herself to her full height, chin up, shoulders back. The light from the desk lamp threw unflattering shadows along her jawline, causing her to lift her head higher. This helped, but she couldn't deny that even though she was still holding up well, she was now at the age where defying gravity was a full-time job.

She had crossed the big psychological barrier—40—a few months ago. As vanity had become a necessary mechanism in her daily life, she had stepped up her efforts to rewind the effects of time. In reality, she was as fit as she'd ever been, but there were telltale signs that couldn't be excised, all of which pointed to the fact she wasn't pushing 29 any longer.

Steven had ribbed her about turning forty, but only—she thought—because she was so sensitive about it. But now, as she faced the inexplicable end of her marriage, she had to wonder: did her defamation have anything to do with Steven wanting a younger wife?

As Madeline pulled herself away from her puzzled reflection, she was left with another fact to consider: her apparent inability to conceive. A humorless laugh escaped as she realized that from Steven's point of view, she had reached the point of diminishing returns.

With an even heavier heart, Madeline returned to her private quarters in hopes of corralling all the suspicions and worries that had been rocketing through her brain the last eight hours. She grabbed a legal pad and pen—her favorite mode for capturing her thoughts—and settled in her corner chair.

She drew a line down the center and began her two separate lists:

Facts
Awoke @ The Edgecliff
My lingerie was ripped
3 scratch marks
No theft
7 photos with the Italian (?)
Hand-off to detective
S wants a divorce

Having listed everything she knew to be factual, she listed her suspicions:

Unknowns
Was I drugged?
Did S pay detective for the photos?
If so, why??
Why does S suddenly want to get rid of me?

As she read this last question, the obvious conclusion hit her like a punch in the face, making her head recoil from the jolt of it. She sat rigidly, stunned by her failure to see the obvious. Steven had the advantage of surprise on his side, she realized, as the treachery of his gambit finally hit home.

There was only one scenario that wove all these facts and question marks together, and realizing it was such a shock to her system, she was instantly filled with a white-hot hatred of the man she had married. Her hand jerking in anger, she summed up the answer to the riddle: *Adultery + prenup = no divorce settlement.*

Madeline stared at the truth behind Steven's wounded husband outrage, as she drew rings around the equation. The longer she looked at it, the more certain she became. It was really quite simple, as far as acts of treachery go.

Once Steven decided it was time to get rid of her, the plan was a cinch. It probably took all of a day to concoct and execute. Once he hired a sleazy private investigator, he only had to wait for his cue—the Open Your Heart Valentine's Ball—and seize the opportunity to storm out and leave her behind.

Madeline seethed as she continued to jot down what she now bet were solid facts. *It was such a perfect setup*, she thought bitterly as she recalled how compromised she felt by Steven's sudden exit. What could she have done? She couldn't have gone after him; the fundraiser was her baby.

"That son-of-a-bitch," Madeline hissed as her pen ripped through the paper. She threw the tablet aside and began furiously pacing her now too-confining dressing room. She felt so claustrophobic, she longed to jump in her Porsche and tear down the quiet lanes, racing to the freeway where she could really vent her fury on the open road.

But she let that fantasy die out; if she was in a war with Steven, she needed to collect her wits. Crossing her out of the picture without a penny was almost insignificant compared to what he had done to her psyche. The thought that he was even capable of such acts of cruelty and abuse made her start crying again. Unlike her earlier tears, these were hot and full of vengeance.

FOUR

As Madeline wore a path in her plush carpet, the Maserati's dulcet purr startled her back to reality. She made a lunge to turn off her lights. Just the thought of seeing Steven made her shudder. But before she heard his car door open, her survival instincts kicked in. She racked her brain for the best line of attack, deciding in the end to feign total ignorance.

In order to make Steven think she was still unaware of his part in Saturday night's betrayal, she had to act as though saving her marriage was still her highest priority. She checked her appearance in the mirror and hastily combed her hair with her fingers. She grabbed a lipstick off her dressing table and applied a light coat and pursed her lips. She definitely felt like she'd survived a day in hell, and it showed.

The front door opened and Madeline braced herself. "Okay, okay, okay," she said under her breath as she tried to steady herself. She heard Steven's footfalls as he retreated to the far side of the house. She took long, silent strides as she tried to catch him before he reached the guestroom.

"Steven," she said softly, stopping him in his tracks.

"Madeline, I've had a hard, trying day…" Steven said, sounding both weary and put upon.

"I realize that. So have I." This last comment earned her an impatient sigh.

"I don't want to get into this right now, Madeline," he said, his tone hard and implacable.

"Steven, you can't go away for three days thinking the worst of me," she said, clutching his sleeve as he turned away from her. "Please let's talk this over. This is all some sort of horrible nightmare, but I'm completely innocent—I swear to you." To add sway to her plea, she began to cry, silently, tears springing from her eyes on cue.

"I *cannot* get into this now. I've got a very early flight out tomorrow—"

"But Steven, I can't bear for you to think I cheated on you." Steven gave her a stony look before stepping into the guestroom.

"Steven, no…don't shut me out—you have to believe I would never do anything to hurt you." Madeline swallowed hard; she was so into her role, she found herself hopeful as Steven stared at her. But instead of softening, he slammed the door in her face.

This affront made Madeline quake with rage. She took three sharp breaths before resuming her performance. She was not actress enough to weep like she meant it, when really what she wanted to do was hurl obscenities at him for demeaning her in the most unimaginably hostile way. What he'd done was criminal, really. But she forced herself to focus on the task at hand and moaned pitifully through the door.

"Steven…Steven…I can't believe this is happening…" She snuffled loudly, waiting for some indication that she was getting his attention. "Steven, *please open this door! I can't stand this! I can't live without you*…Steven! Steven!" she called out, banging her fists against the door.

"Stop that this second," Steven said, yanking her into the room. "Does everyone have to know what a desperate, despicable tramp you are?" he railed. Madeline glanced off the edge of the bed, barely catching her footing. She had been a little too successful in getting Steven's attention, and the look in his eyes now gave her concern for her safety. She backed away as she murmured his name softly, beseeching him with outstretched arms.

"I'm only going to tell you this one more time, Madeline—our marriage is over. I don't care if you swear your innocence in front of God Almighty, I don't believe a word you say. And the reason is simple. I have proof—hard, cold proof to the contrary. So, you can blather away all you want, but I will never trust you again. It's as simple as that. Even if I could forgive you, I'd never be able to look at you without seeing you with that other guy."

Madeline gulped air, trying to approximate the proper emotion for Steven's dismissal of her. Steven, hands on hips, breathed heavily as he kept his face averted from hers.

"You better go now," he said, opening the door and standing back to give her ample room to pass. She tried to implore him with her eyes, but he wouldn't look at her. She took one step beyond where he was standing and stopped abruptly as he automatically tried to close the door behind her.

"I will never stop loving you, Steven. And I will never believe that I deliberately cheated on you. Maybe someday I can prove it to you." With that last proclamation, Madeline walked away. With the sound of the door closing quietly behind her, she gritted her teeth and sucked in air. *It's war now, Steven*

FIVE

The sound of footfalls crunching on the gravel drive woke Madeline from her troubled sleep. She had stayed awake most of the night, making notes to herself, trying to chart the events that led to her current situation and what her next moves should be. She squinted at her watch: 5:05. She heard a car door close and more faint crunching as she imagined Hughes walking around to the driver's side. She craned her neck and caught a glimpse of the Maserati as it glided down the driveway.

Madeline rubbed her aching shoulder as she pried herself from the chair. The legal pad fell from her lap and she stooped with effort to retrieve it. She tried to make sense of the scrawled notes, but she had made them under duress and they were too cryptic to decipher easily. She tossed the pad on the table and did a few minutes of gentle stretching while she got her mental bearings. By the time her muscles were loosened, she recalled her activities during the wee hours of the morning.

After storming away from the guest wing the previous night, Madeline had made a large highball and retreated to her side of the master suite. She had taken her computer back to her sitting room and researched prenuptial agreements and private investigators. Steven was using both of these tools to railroad her out of her marriage, so she figured she needed to retaliate in kind.

The problem was—as Steven reminded her less than twenty-four hours earlier—Santa Barbara was a pretty small town when you were part of a highly-visible couple. Finding an attorney or a private eye whom she could trust implicitly wasn't going to be so easy. The quick education she had just gotten on the *real* Steven Ridley made her understand his impeccable exterior hid a sinister, calculating heart. In her paranoid state, it was possible to imagine that his tentacles reached all through the city. Finding someone who wasn't somehow beholden to him might be impossible.

The only good news at this point was she had the house to herself for three days. It rankled her that Steven had basically ordered her off the property by the time he returned from Dallas, like she was some tawdry piece of filth not worthy of being in her own home. She should've listened to her father; he was the only one who had voiced any reservations about the "benign" prenuptial agreement Steven's attorney insisted she sign.

From this vantage point, it was clear Steven had made sure he had an out if he ever needed one. It would've never occurred to her he was capable of faking infidelity on her part. The question still nagging at her was *why?* She had a solid suspicion, but she had to find the specifics behind it. Nothing would make sense until she did.

But she had one card Steven was unaware of, and it was the only thing that was keeping her sane and coherent. Had she not witnessed the payoff to the P.I., she'd probably be suicidal by now.

Since she had Steven pegged as a bastard of the worst order, she felt she had carte blanche to deceive him right under his nose. She was pleased with her performance last night; it had just the right amount of groveling and pathetic hopefulness. She was certain Steven bought the act without picking up on her true feelings. Now that he was out of the house, she could take a breath and plot her next moves.

She did have the disadvantage of not knowing what Steven had told Erma and Hughes. But she'd use the same stoic, brokenhearted routine around them, if they brought anything up, which was doubtful. She hopped in the shower, constantly turning over each piece of the puzzle as she searched relentlessly for answers and clues she had missed.

SIX

After her shower, Madeline ventured to the kitchen for coffee. Besides getting the caffeine she desperately needed, it would give her a chance to get the lay of the land—find out how Erma and Hughes reacted to her presence. Steven had to have at least told Hughes about her imminent departure, as he was saddled with the duty of relocating her personal possessions by Saturday.

When she entered the kitchen, Erma was just unlocking the back door. Madeline had lost sight of how early it still was.

"Good morning, Mrs. Ridley. I suspect you're looking for some coffee," Erma said. Though she had affected ease, Madeline could read the discomfort in her manner. "Won't take but a couple of minutes," the housekeeper assured her, as she turned on the coffeemaker.

Erma always made sure the coffee was ready for brewing before she retired for the evening; it was one of the qualities that had so endeared her to Madeline. The thought of being ousted from her comfortable life—a life that she had put a lot of effort into—made her heart constrict painfully and the taste of bile rise in her throat.

"I'll bring it to you in your room, if you like, Mrs. Ridley," Erma offered over her shoulder. It was clear to Madeline that Erma felt uneasy around her.

"That'd be great," Madeline said, backing away.

"Would you like something to go with it? Toast and a couple fresh eggs?" Erma asked, pulling two brown eggs out of the basket she had carried in.

"Ah, maybe later," Madeline replied cheerily for Erma's benefit. As Madeline passed out of the kitchen, she felt certain Erma had been briefed by Hughes of the marital discord between her employers. Other than that, Madeline hadn't learned anything.

Madeline was continuing her research of the night before when Erma came to offer more coffee. Madeline smiled as she raised her oversize coffee cup.

"Are you sure you wouldn't like me to make you a little breakfast?" Erma asked, her face full of concern. Madeline pushed away from her desk.

"You're right, I should eat something or I'll be shaking from all that caffeine," Madeline said with a laugh. "I'd love a slice of toast and a poached egg. Maybe some fruit, too. Whatever you've got." Madeline was scanning the emails she had no intention of answering when she belatedly realized Erma was still standing there.

"Is there something else…?" Erma eyed the floor for a moment while she summoned her resolve.

"I just wanted to say that both Mr. Hughes and myself are very sad that you'll be leaving us…" Erma averted her gaze again. Madeline could see she was on the verge of tears. "I know this isn't my place, but it hurts to see you and Mr. Ridley not getting along. I've never worked for a nicer couple than the two of you. I'm just going to keep it in my prayers that you'll patch things up with Mr. Ridley. The thought of you leaving him is breaking his heart. I'm sorry—I shouldn't have said that," Erma sobbed, as she fled the room.

Madeline watched Erma's departure with her mouth hanging slack. *So that's how the bastard's spinning it,* she thought bitterly. Steven had found a way to turn her into a double villain: an unfaithful tramp *and* a fickle wife.

SEVEN

After working at her computer until her neck and shoulders began to ache, Madeline pushed away from the desk, her mind a seething jumble of information and half thought-through plans. As she stretched her kinked muscles, she decided the best way to assimilate everything she had researched was to go for a run. She changed, tied her hair back, grabbed her sunglasses and cap and jogged out the front door.

She traversed along the path, past the pool and the gardens, then let herself out the security gate that led out to the deeded trail. She turned right, angling back above her property, choosing the path that would be more challenging on the front end.

After ten minutes of a butt-burning climb, during which she thought of nothing more than putting one foot in front of the other, the trail eased to a more manageable incline. As her heartbeat stabilized, she was able to focus her attention on formulating a strategy for dealing with her underhanded husband.

As she ran, her brain started another list:

> Get referral from Cheryl for a good L.A. divorce attorney
> Contact P.I. – see list
> Set email to auto-responder
> Get money

It occurred to her she would need to withdraw a large sum of money from their joint account so she could work under the radar. She did have a separate account that she'd transferred when she relocated from Denver—her private little nest egg, so insignificant in size, she'd all but forgotten about it.

As she jogged along, it hit her that her small savings account was still in her maiden name. That was a bit of luck, she thought. Once Steven made her a signatory on his accounts, she had stopped using her own meager funds. What was $25,000 compared to the high six-figures of their joint accounts? It wasn't much, but it gave Madeline an unexpected lift to realize she wasn't entirely without assets of her own.

But while Steven was away, she needed to withdraw as much from their checking account as she could without setting off any alarms. That would be her first stop of the day, she thought, as she circled back toward home. Although exercise had been a good way to jumpstart her brain, nothing would be as reassuring as taking action. The sooner she got her artillery in place, the better she would feel. Three and a half days was not a lot of time to erect a line of defense capable of thwarting her diabolical, devious husband, but it had to be enough.

Madeline skimmed over her revised notes while she brushed her teeth. From what she had read online, it was possible to break a prenup if certain conditions existed. According to one site, "clear proof of coercion, duress, fraud, or bad intent" will void the document. If having been drugged and raped in order to be divorced without a settlement wasn't clear proof of "bad intent," nothing was. But she would need to hire her own private investigator to connect the photos to Steven. The thought of such a task made her feel empty inside.

Though she believed it wise to seek legal counsel outside of Santa Barbara, she felt it was important to hire a private investigator who was familiar with the area. After scrutinizing every local P.I. she could find online, she narrowed it down to one: Burt Latham.

There were others who offered a broad range of services and expertise, but Mr. Latham had the added benefit of being a one-man operation. This appealed to her immensely; the fewer people who knew about the trouble she was in, the less likely information would leak out. She had to be extremely cautious about who she spoke to, and knowing this made her understandably nervous.

Another bonus to choosing Burt Latham, P.I. was the location of his office, which was in the building adjacent to Saks Fifth Avenue. If Steven was going to have her tailed in his absence—and there was no reason to think otherwise—she'd have to be very cognizant of her every move.

One of the best features of Saks was the valet parking in the rear. She could go in through the back entrance and any P.I. operating alone would have no other choice but to wait for her to exit the lot or follow her around the store. All she had to do is linger on the first floor long enough to determine if someone was lurking around her. That would be a risky move for anyone trailing her. Besides, she'd have to go back to her car at some point.

She felt relatively sure no one would risk being noticed in the store. Her gut told her she'd be able to slip out the front entrance undetected and up the stairs to Burt Latham's second floor office. The only unknown would be if she'd find him in or not. But she couldn't take a chance trying to call him; for all she knew, her calls could be monitored.

She dressed in jeans and a T-shirt, ballet flats and a long, shawl-collar cashmere cardigan. She added a pair of designer earrings and several bracelets. She packed her favorite Prada handbag and steeled herself for her mission.

As she drove down East Valley Road, Madeline amended her plan to include a first stop at the post office. This would give her an opportunity to see if anyone was following her. After she angle parked, she pretended to search for something in her bag while she kept her eyes on the side view mirror, checking each vehicle that passed behind her. She was both alarmed and satisfied when Russell Barnett and his silver Honda Accord passed behind her car. She took a couple deep breaths and put her plan into action.

Though she didn't have any reason for going to the post office, she waited in the long line for fifteen minutes to purchase a book of stamps. For good measure, she walked along the storefronts, stepping inside a clothing boutique where she pretended to browse. As she suspected, the P.I. had parked several slots down from her Porsche. She caught a peripheral glimpse of him while he hid his face behind a newspaper.

From the Upper Village, Madeline drove to Bank of Santa Barbara. The bank manager jumped to attention when she walked into the lobby. Madeline asked if she could speak to him in private. He graciously ushered her into his office. Fifteen minutes later, she departed, a cashier's check for $20,000 tucked securely in her bag.

Ordinarily, she would've gotten back into her car and driven to the next stop, but as her other bank was less than two blocks away, Madeline thought it best to walk and put her tail through his paces. She arranged for a confidential meeting with the assistant manager in one of the glassed-in offices. She explained that she had an existing account in her maiden name, which she wanted to keep that way. She turned over the cashier's check for deposit and asked if she could convert her savings account to checking.

"That would be no problem," Adele assured her. "I can give you temporary checks to hold you over until some can be printed for you." This threw Madeline off for a moment. She'd have to rent a mailbox somewhere before she'd have an address to use.

"Thanks. I'll have to postpone ordering any. I'm in the process of moving," she added without elaborating further.

"That's no problem. Just give us a call and we can change the address in our system and place the order," Adele said pleasantly. "Is there anything else I can assist you with, Mrs. Ridley?"

"Yes, I need a credit or debit card for use with this account. And I'd like it to be in my maiden name. Can I get that now?"

"Absolutely," Adele said, rising from her chair. "Let me get this check deposited and I'll activate a card for this account right now. It will only take me a few minutes. Can I get you some coffee or water while you wait?"

"Water would be nice. Thank you." Once Adele left the room, Madeline stood up on the pretense of examining the painting of Butterfly Beach behind Adele's desk. This gave her the opportunity to glance around the office, see if Steven's hired spook had followed her inside. She wasn't surprised that he hadn't, but it made her feel better to know for sure.

Now that she had skimmed off a bit of pocket money, she felt a little more relaxed as she walked back to her car. It took a bit of looking, but she caught sight of the silver Honda parked a few spaces down Coast Village Road as she exited the parking lot.

She didn't bother to keep tabs on Mr. Barnett until she exited the 101 at Carrillo Street. As she stopped at the red light at De La Vina, she pretended not to notice his Honda in the right lane two cars back. She crossed Chapala and turned left into the parking lot behind Saks. Justin, the valet on duty, greeted her with his easy banter and backed her car into the closest spot, ready for a quick departure.

Though shopping really was the last thing on Madeline's mind, she had to at least make a show of browsing, if for no other reason than to make sure she hadn't been followed into the store. It had suddenly occurred to her that she didn't know for sure if Russell Barnett was a lone wolf or if he had associates he could call on to help with surveillance. After pausing to look at scarves and handbags, killing about five minutes and feeling fairly certain no one had followed her in, Madeline made her move.

She pushed through the heavy glass door to the sheltered colonnade in front of the store. She turned left and walked inside the columns until Saks ended and the neighboring building jutted out, forcing her onto the sidewalk for a few feet. The stairway up to the offices above the retail spaces came up so quickly, she nearly overshot it. She ducked in, glancing quickly at the directory to make sure she had the right location.

She walked cautiously down the narrow hallway that housed an assortment of professionals, including an architect and a website designer. Halfway down the hall, she found what she was looking for. She took a deep breath and turned the knob. The door was locked.

Having made it this far only to come up empty-handed, Madeline suddenly lost a good bit of her courage. She had already assigned Burt Latham to the role of savior and protector; it was the hope of arming herself with her own investigator that had given her the wherewithal to take up the battle against Steven's underhanded agenda. Not being able to engage an ally left her feeling as vulnerable as she did the day before, when her world collapsed and her husband turned into a sinister stranger.

She tried the handle again; no luck. She could hear the muffled voices of the other tenants and their clients, but she saw no one. She rapped on the door and waited. Nothing. She tried again. As she was about to walk away, she caught sight of a notepad and a pen tied to a string on the far side of the doorjamb. She hesitated for a moment, then took the clipboard off the crude hook.

The problem was she didn't know what kind of message to leave. She didn't want to give out her cell number, in case someone was keeping tabs.

She was about to put the notepad back when she came up with another plan. She wrote out her name, the time, stressed the urgency of needing to meet with him, and that she would return in one hour. She folded the paper and slid it under the door.

EIGHT

"We just got those in—aren't they fabulous?" the saleswoman asked as Madeline distractedly admired a pair of zebra-striped Manolo Blahnik sling-back heels. "Would you like to try them on, Mrs. Ridley?" Madeline looked at the shoe in her hand as if she didn't know how it got there. She started to put it back on the display, but changed her mind.

"Sure, Maryanne—why not? And while you're back there, I'd like to try these as well," Madeline said, handing her a jewel-encrusted silver slide.

"Good choice. They look amazing on," Maryanne said before disappearing into the back. Madeline let out a sigh and sank onto one of the leather chairs. After mulling over the situation, she realized that shopping for no reason was actually a good way to not only get back at Steven, but to lift her spirits as well. In fact, she should be going at this as though it were a competition sport, she decided, rising out of the chair to check out what other pricey delights were on offer.

As winter was winding down, two racks had been placed on the showroom floor, boasting significant savings on boots and fancy holiday shoes. Madeline was in no mood for bargains; if she was going to sock it to Steven, she should go for the most extravagant footwear available.

Besides, Madeline rationalized as she ran her eyes over the Chanel and Prada tables, high-ticket shoes like these could easily be converted to cash on eBay. This thought put her in the proper frame of mind. As soon as Maryanne returned from the stockroom, Madeline had five more decadent styles she wanted to try on.

Before now, she had never fully appreciated the notion of "retail therapy." But amplifying an urge that just came naturally gave her mood a huge lift. It was a perfect pastime, given the circumstances. If Steven bothered himself to keep tabs on her spending while he was in Dallas, then this was a very plausible display of inner turmoil.

What other choices had Steven left her with, after branding her as an adulteress, declaring he wanted a divorce, and ordering her off the property by the time he returned? He had given her zero hope of reconciliation and no means with which to prove her innocence. He had effectively taken away the ability to look to friends for consolation; those photos of her were his guarantee of her silence. He'd even jammed a wedge between her and the help.

So, faced with no other options, what could Madeline be expected to do but go shopping? She smiled as Maryanne teetered toward her with a wobbling tower of shoeboxes.

Trying on footwear with wild abandon was an expedient way to kill time. In fact, when Madeline remembered her hoped-for rendezvous, she was aghast to find that she'd overshot the clock by ten minutes.

"Oh shoot—I've got to run. You don't mind holding these for me, do you Maryanne?" she said, as she wriggled back into her flats.

"Not at all," the saleswoman replied, glancing around at the piles of boxes strewn around her feet. "Which ones?"

"All of them!" Madeline called out as she made a hasty exit.

By the time she reached his office suite, Madeline's pulse was racing. What if she had missed him? What if he hadn't returned yet? She was too anxious to even consider these possibilities. She took one ragged breath to calm herself, then tried the doorknob. It turned. She pushed the door open to find a tall, grey-haired man leaning against the front of his desk, arms folded across his chest, a mere trace of bemused curiosity on his face.

"Mrs. Ridley, I presume?"

NINE

Madeline went momentarily weak with relief. Now that the unthinkable had been avoided, she took a second to compose herself.

"That's correct. And you must be Mr. Latham."

"Call me Burt," he replied, as he beckoned for her to follow him into his private office. He casually seated himself behind the desk and motioned for Madeline to take a seat in one of the two visitor chairs. "I'm glad I popped by to get something this morning. I wasn't planning on coming into the office today."

"Lucky for me," Madeline said, easing herself into a chair.

"So, Mrs. Ridley, how can I be of help?"

Madeline felt her face grow hot as she reached into her tote for the manila envelope. She slid it across the table toward Burt Latham, but she didn't let go of it. Burt leaned forward automatically to pick it up, but stopped short, his eyes meeting hers. Clearly, she felt the need for prior disclosure. She took a couple deep breaths for courage.

"Can you give me your word that anything I reveal to you will be strictly confidential, between us and no one else?"

"I absolutely guarantee it," Burt said, sitting back in his chair, sending Madeline the message he didn't intend to rush her in any way. She relaxed a little and let go of the envelope.

"Before you look at these photos, I'd like to first give you some background." Madeline glanced around and found what she was looking for. "Could I trouble you for some water?" Burt got up and took a paper cup off the stack, filled it with tepid water and handed it to her.

"Thank you." Madeline gratefully drank the stale-tasting water as she collected her thoughts. "Last Saturday evening, my husband and I attended a fundraiser at The Edgecliff. I was a co-chair of the event, so it was a working gala for me. My husband, Steven, was in an irritable mood on the way over, but I was too preoccupied to attach any significance to it.

"Looking back, I recall that he seemed out of sorts throughout the dinner, and when the dancing started, he flat out refused to dance with me, which is totally out of character for him. I asked him if something was wrong and he snapped at me. When a man approached and asked me to dance, I did. I was happy for the diversion. I suppose this was not a wise move on my part, but given my position, I felt completely justified. It was part of my duties to keep the festivities going.

"When the first song ended, my dance partner kept me on the floor. Like I said, this was a fundraiser, and for all I knew, this man—whom I've never seen before—could've been contributing heavily to our campaign. I danced through one more number with him, then begged off tactfully.

"When I got back to our table, Steven was livid. In the twelve years I've been married to him, he'd never acted like that before. He read me the riot act for dancing with the man, called me all kinds of horrible names—just went off on me. I tried to calm him down. Honestly, I thought there might be something wrong with him. But everything I said seemed to infuriate him more.

"He turned away from me mid-sentence and stormed out of the ballroom. I went after him, but the valet had kept his car at the entrance, so he was able to drive away before I could reach it. I stood there, debating whether I should grab a cab and go after him, but I couldn't do that. I had an auction to oversee, so I went back inside.

"As soon as I reentered the ballroom, the man I had danced with appeared with two glasses of champagne and a promise to make sure I got home safely. Even at the time, his offer struck me as a little odd. But I was so rattled by Steven's departure, it didn't make that much of an impression on me. Until yesterday morning."

Madeline motioned for Burt to look at the contents of the envelope. She watched uncomfortably as the detective removed the photos and rotated them so he could see them properly. One by one, he scrutinized them, glancing up at Madeline as he compared the subject's features to those of the woman in front of him.

"From the photos and what you've told me, it appears that one of two things occurred after your husband left," Burt said, his forearms resting on the arms of his chair, his fingertips lightly balanced beside the photos. "Either you consented to have sex with this man, or you were drugged and have no recollection of what transpired prior to and during the photos."

"The latter," Madeline confirmed.

"When did you receive these?" Burt asked, leaning forward to grab a notepad.

"Actually, my husband received them yesterday, at his office."

"Was there a demand made?"

"He didn't say."

"How were they delivered?" Madeline shook her head. Burt sat back in his seat while he contemplated the direction this story was taking.

"Does your husband know that you've come to see me?"

"No."

"How did you come to be in possession of the photos?

"Steven brought them to me at home, around 10:30 yesterday morning."

"What was his reaction?"

"He was outraged and devastated. He wants a divorce. He ordered me out of the house by the time he gets back from a business trip on Saturday. He left for Dallas early this morning."

"What was your reaction to the photos?" Madeline choked on her answer. "It's okay, take your time," Burt said.

"I was absolutely horrified."

"What happened after Steven left, after the man gave you the glass of champagne?" Again, Madeline found it hard to speak.

"I don't remember. I can't remember anything after that moment. Until I woke up, just before dawn in one of the cottage rooms at The Edgecliff."

"I take it you were alone then…"

"Yes. And terrified. I had no idea where I was at first. I remember calling out for Steven, but I was alone…in bed…with nothing on." She became silent as her gaze went inward.

"Tell me anything else you can remember," Burt coaxed her.

"I remember this really awful taste in my mouth…and my head—it felt like it was going to split in half."

"What did you do once you figured out where you were?"

"I went into the bathroom, looking for Steven. I found my dress and put it on. My…my bra and panties had been torn to shreds… Um…I remember panicking about my jewelry…"

"Was any of it missing?"

"No, my diamond watch and bracelet were in my handbag, along with my credit card, driver's license and phone. And a key to our beach house."

"What did you do next?"

"I realized the key gave me a perfect cover story. I left through the French doors while it was still mostly dark out and was able to walk to our beach house without seeing anyone. I had a scalding hot shower, and around 9:30, after my head stopped pounding, I called Steven and told him I had stayed at the beach house because of the way he had walked out on me. Later, he picked me up and we went to brunch. It was like nothing had happened."

Burt sat back in his chair, his eyes fixed on a spot above Madeline's head.

"What do you think happened that night?" he asked.

"I think I was drugged. I think I was drugged and..." Madeline's bottom lip began to quiver. She bit it to keep from crying.

"Why didn't you go to the police?" Burt asked. The frankness of the question startled her. She was momentarily at a loss for an answer.

"Oh...wow...I don't...I didn't...I had no idea what had happened. I was pretty sure that I hadn't ripped my own lingerie and put these scratches on my neck," she said, pulling back her sweater for Burt to see. "But I didn't know *what* had happened. Like I said, I had a splitting headache, and I was so disoriented." She looked down at her hands while she tried to rationalize her actions.

"I guess I was afraid I had done something terrible," she said, her lip trembling again. "I didn't know what else to do. I was frightened and in shock. Nothing like this has ever happened to me before. *Nothing.* I was puzzled by Steven's behavior, but I wasn't trying to retaliate or anything. I was just co-chairing an event, like I've done dozens of times. I wouldn't pick up some guy and have sex with him, right there in the same hotel where everyone who works there would see me. It wouldn't ever enter my mind to do something like that..." she sputtered. Burt held up his hands to stem the flow of words.

"I wasn't trying to insinuate anything like that," he said soothingly. "I was trying to get a better sense of what your mindset was the morning you found yourself in that hotel room." Madeline took in shallow breaths as she tried to get her emotions under control.

"I'm sorry..." she said, taking another sip of water with a trembling hand.

"It's okay. You have nothing to be sorry about. I'm trying to get you to paint as clear a picture as possible so I'll know where I should concentrate my efforts. Are you alright?" Madeline nodded. "Okay, let me ask you this—why do you think someone would do this to you?"

"When I first saw the photos, I suspected someone was trying to get at Steven, discredit or blackmail him. Actually, it was something he said while railing at me, how if the existence of those pictures ever got out, it would irreparably damage his reputation."

"That's what he was most concerned about?" Burt asked skeptically.

"Not at first. No, Steven's greatest fear has always been infidelity. His first wife cheated on him and he never got over the pain of it. When we first started getting serious, it was very hard for him to put his trust in someone that way again. He was so wary about having the same thing happen to him again, he made me sign a prenup with an infidelity clause." Burt stiffened at hearing this.

"Yeah, I know," Madeline said with a humorless laugh. "It's taken me a little while to put the pieces together, but after Steven left the house yesterday morning, all I could think about was his emotional anguish and trying to find a way to convince him that I hadn't *knowingly* been unfaithful to him. I was totally blindsided by seeing the photos, even though I knew something awful had happened to me at The Edgecliff. I really couldn't believe I'd had sex with another man…I just couldn't bear to let my mind go there. But after going over everything in my head, all I could think about was trying to save my marriage.

"Around one o'clock, I drove to Steven's office downtown. I wanted a chance to talk to him, to tell him about what had happened after he left the fundraiser. But before I could get out of the car, I saw him on the sidewalk outside his building, handing an envelope to a man I didn't recognize. The exchange was brief, and as I watched the man head up the street, I got this sudden impulse to follow him. He led me straight to his office in the 1300 block of Anacapa. The name on the window read 'Russell Barnett, Private Investigator.'" Before Madeline could disclose the identity of the man she had followed, Burt's countenance hardened with recognition.

"I take it you know this person," Madeline said, watching his reaction carefully.

"It's a small town, especially in my line of work." Burt got up and went to stare out the window that gave view to the parking lot behind the building. Madeline took this opportunity to rack her brain for any detail she might've overlooked.

"Did you go speak to your husband after following Barnett?"

"No. I was too shaken. I couldn't think of any innocent reason for Steven to be paying off a private investigator. He's got an in-house security team, and the only explanation I could think of for needing outside help was if Steven were trying to do something on the sly. That, coupled with the photos, made me very suspicious of his motives."

"Do you think Barnett saw you?"

"No," Madeline said emphatically. "I stayed well behind him and hid once he entered his office. Besides, he's been tailing me all morning, so he probably doesn't know his cover's been blown." Burt swung away from the window.

"Did he follow you to this building?"

"No, I valet parked behind Saks. He didn't follow me into the store, so I slipped out the front entrance unseen and ducked into this building."

"Both times?" Burt grilled her. The question made Madeline blanch. She had been in such a rush, she hadn't thought to scan the street when leaving Saks the second time.

"What did you do from the time you left the note until the time you returned?

"I went back into Saks, the way I left."

"You were there the whole time?"

"Yes. I indulged in some revenge shopping," Madeline admitted. Burt grunted his approval as he retook his seat.

"Steven's having you trailed while he's gone so that he can figure out what your plan is."

"*My* plan?"

"He told you he wanted a divorce and said you had to be out of the house when he gets back on Saturday. In the three days that he's away, his stooge will report back to him every move you make so Steven will know if you plan to hire some hotshot attorney to break the prenup. That's probably his biggest worry right now." Burt stared off into space while he pieced the probable scenario together.

"He's most likely banking on you being too humiliated to show the photos to anyone. And, as far as your memory is concerned, you don't know if you willingly engaged in sex with that man or not." Madeline's hand flew to her mouth as another cold truth about her husband's scheme hit home. "So, after you followed Barnett, what did you do?"

"I went back home."

"Did you speak to anyone?"

"Only our housekeeper, and only when she came to tell me Steven wouldn't be home for dinner last night."

"Did you see him before he left for the airport?"

"Yes, I was still up when he came home last night. He'd had our butler pack his bag and put his things in one of the guestrooms. My first reaction was to turn out my lights and pretend I was asleep. But then...I don't know... I started thinking defensively after witnessing the payoff, so I decided the most convincing thing for me to do was to act remorseful and try to make him think I'd do anything to save our marriage."

"What was his reaction?"

"He was very cold. He's playing the wounded spouse to the hilt." Burt sat back as he considered the situation.

"What do you want me to do for you, Mrs. Ridley?"

"I'd like you to find out who took those photos of me—who paid for them, who set me up to be humiliated...and..." Madeline dropped her gaze. "I want to know for sure if Steven is behind all this. I guess from your point of view it seems pretty cut and dried. He's probably trying to divorce me without having to pay me a nickel. But I'd like to know that for sure. Until I have solid proof, I'll find it difficult to believe he's really capable of something like this." Burt nodded slowly as he followed her logic.

"I did a little research while I was waiting for you to return," he said, picking up his phone. "You and your husband are quite the power couple." He handed his cell phone to Madeline so she could see the picture of her and Steven as they entered The Edgecliff Saturday night. The sight of them together, arm and arm, her in the red Valentino gown, made her feel physically ill. She thrust the phone back at Burt.

"From what I was able to glean from a few minutes of searching is that your husband is the founder and CEO of RAM L.P., which as far as I can tell is some private equity management company. Is that correct?

"Yes, that's right. Ridley Asset Management."

"What does his company do exactly?"

Madeline gazed at him wryly. It struck her that being semi-oblivious to Steven's business put her at a disadvantage in their new adversarial roles.

"He finds private investors to fund a variety of ventures. He has a stable of wealthy clients looking for a good rate of return on their capital. Steven acts as sort of a middleman between people who have money and people who need it."

"What kind of needy people are we talking about?"

"People looking for loans on property or for startup companies, or to produce a film—it could be anything, really. Steven's company is set up in three divisions—one deals strictly with real estate, one handles anything to do with intellectual properties—like computer technologies or film making, and one that handles everything that doesn't fall into those two categories."

"How long has he been doing this kind of brokering?"

"For about ten years."

"Prior to that?"

"He oversaw his father's assets. Sean Ridley died about thirteen years ago, and that's when Steven got into the private loan business. He did so well with it, pretty soon he had people begging him to do the same for them." Burt looked up from his note taking.

"Can you make a list of all the participants that you know of?" he asked, pushing a clean pad of paper and pen toward her.

"Sure," Madeline said tentatively, her mind slow to conjure up the faces she'd been only marginally connected with.

"What do you need them for?" she asked as she jotted down the names of Santa Barbara's "quiet giants." Making this list made her feel like she was violating some code of ethics, though she didn't know why. She had no agreements with these people, and Steven was now her enemy. Still, some of these men were married to friends of hers. It made her resent Steven even more for forcing her into this position.

"I may need to comb through every bit of information I can find about your husband in order to piece together his motives. It could be as simple as you say—he wants a divorce without it costing him anything. One way to find out who drugged and assaulted you would be to have your dress and undergarments tested for DNA." Madeline grimaced; she had destroyed the evidence herself. Steven might've been counting on that too.

"I disposed of the lingerie and the dress has already been dry cleaned." Burt exhaled out the side of his mouth and crossed out something on his list.

"And it doesn't sound like a rape kit was performed." Madeline shook her head.

"Okay, there are other ways of finding out who was involved in this." Burt tapped his pen on the desk while he thought. "I'm not an attorney, but I do know that prenups can be invalidated if certain conditions exist. If we prove your husband was involved in having you sexually molested, obviously he would be in some serious legal trouble, and you might have grounds for voiding the clause."

Hearing someone say this out loud had a different effect than ruminating over it herself. As her heart began to thud, she understood why: it was devastating to think someone she loved was capable of doing that to her. Self-preservation had gotten her to this point, but she would need a stronger emotional rampart to survive the fallout of admitting her husband had her raped in order to dispose of her cheaply. Before she could construct a protective armor, tears started trickling down her cheeks. Burt offered her a box of tissues.

"Have you spoken to a divorce attorney yet?"

"No, I'm afraid to contact anyone here. I plan to make some discreet inquiries in the L.A. area. I don't want Steven to have any idea I know what he's up to. That's why I didn't call you ahead of time—I don't want to leave a trail for him."

"If the prenup wasn't an issue, what do you think you would stand to gain in a divorce settlement?" Madeline dried her tears, grateful for the detective's dispassionate approach.

"Several million, I would imagine. I know we have a lot of investments, but Steven handles all that. We've got a house on Park Lane and a house on Miramar Beach. And an apartment building in San Francisco. Those are the only real estate assets I know of for sure. But he's involved in several real estate partnerships."

Burt took a wad of keys from his pocket and unlocked a drawer on his left. He took out a phone and checked the battery life. He then handed it to Madeline, along with a charger.

"This phone will not be traceable back to you." Madeline studied the phone for a moment before depositing it and the charger in her tote. "And that will be the way I contact you."

"What is our next step?" she asked.

"Well, we've got to discuss my fee. I charge $100 an hour, plus $500 up front for expenses. I can't give you an estimate at this point because it all depends on the amount of hours I put in. I refund anything left over from the expense funds, but given the complexity of your case, unless we get really lucky, I can see myself spending several days on this assignment. Can you manage that?"

"Yes. I have a separate bank account in my maiden name that my husband is unaware of."

"Can I make a copy?" Burt asked as he reached for the photographs. Madeline nodded hesitantly. He picked one that wasn't showing just the man's back, though Burt doubted he'd have any luck learning his identity with so little to go on. "Don't worry, I'll cut you out," he said, as he put the photo on the copier. "Did you have a professional photographer at the ball?"

"Yes," Madeline said, instantly realizing the significance of this. "And a videographer. I haven't had a chance to look through all the photos yet. Damn, I wished I'd thought of that sooner."

"It's okay. You really haven't had much time to react yet."

"The videographer said we'd have the final cut in a few days. You don't suppose either of them would be involved in this…"

"You never know until you start digging around. In any event, tell both of them you want to see every frame they took of the event. You're going to need to go through everything thoroughly, see if you can get a good picture of this guy. That would make it a lot easier to find him. Even if no one else at the fundraiser can identify him, I can have it run through face-recognition databases. If he's got any kind of record, we've got him. Once we have him, we can find out if and how he's linked up with your husband." The thought of actually coming face to face with the man in the photos—the man who'd drugged her, undressed her and raped her chilled her to the core.

"In the meantime, I'll need a physical description of him," Burt said, pen poised to take notes.

"Oh...okay...I wish I'd paid more attention to him when we were dancing. The truth is I was too preoccupied by Steven's odd behavior."

"Just tell me anything you can remember. About how tall would you say he was?"

"We were about the same height, but I was wearing four-inch heels. So, that would make him around 5'11" or six feet." Burt scrutinized the photo.

"Seems fit," he surmised. Madeline's breathing became fast and shallow again. Burt put the photos back in the envelope and slid them across the desk. "Can you think of any other characteristics? The color of his eyes? Any scars?" Madeline tried to focus her mind on that night. She had been only inches from his face, yet she could barely recall anything at all about his features. "Did he remind you of anyone—a friend, a movie star...?"

"Oh gosh... He had dark hair, combed back, I think. He seemed attractive, but it was more about the way he carried himself than his actual features."

"So, not the kind of guy who attracts stares from the ladies?"

"No...I'd say he was average good-looking." Burt laid the pen down.

"What should I do now?" she asked after she digested the possibility of nailing Steven and his accomplices.

"I think you need to pretend everything is just hunky dory in the Ridley household. Do everything you would normally do until Steven gets back." Madeline let out a strained sigh.

"I don't think I can face any of my friends right now," she said, rubbing her neck.

"But you need to. You have access to a valuable source of information that I can't get to without raising red flags. You need to be visible, that way you can find out details of what happened during your blackout period. The more people you can connect with while your husband's away, the better." Madeline remained unconvinced.

"Maybe one of them brought the man to the event. Not that you've got much of a description to go on. But also, we can't completely rule out the possibility that your husband wasn't involved in this."

Another wave of anxiety rushed over Madeline, along with a faint glimmer of hope. All she really wanted in her heart of hearts was to have her life back, the way it was before Saturday night. But then doubt nudged this fervent hope out of the picture. Steven's behavior was too hard to explain away. Plus, even if he hadn't been involved in having her drugged and raped, she would be damaged goods as far as he was concerned.

"Since you haven't reported this to the police, I guess I should caution you to get tested for sexually transmitted diseases."

Madeline pursed her lips. It had been bad enough telling the doctor at the clinic in Ventura about her fear of having contracted an STD. Now she felt doubly humiliated. She knew her face was red because she could feel the heat of her fury all over her body.

"I took care of that on Monday," she said matter-of-factly.

"I'm sorry I brought it up," Burt said.

"Don't be. I appreciate your concern," she said. She let out a bitter laugh, shaking her head.

"What is it?" Burt asked, as she regarded him, her expression now hard and focused.

"I found out from our housekeeper this morning that Steven has already been spinning our breakup. She begged me with tears in her eyes not to leave him. I don't know who else has gotten this warped version of events." Burt gave her a dour look of sympathy.

"For now, I want you to continue playing the role of the perfect wife. I've got another case I'm wrapping up, so I'll be in touch with you later. In the meantime, go back to Saks and shop till you drop." Madeline had to laugh at his directive.

"I guess I should. I may need to convert some luxury goods to cash down the road," she said as she stood to leave. "Anything else I should be doing until I hear from you?"

"Can you get access to the guest list and a list of any additional donations that were pledged that night?"

"I should be able to."

"I want you to take a look at all the names on the lists and mark all the ones you personally know. That will help to narrow the list for me. If you can think of anyone else that was in attendance that night—like florists or musicians, whoever—see if you can get their names, too." Madeline was looking a bit overwhelmed by the assignment.

"I cast my net as far as I can in the beginning, that way I don't have to spend time running down the info later. I always overkill on fact-finding leads. You just never know which one is the key to unlocking the case."

"I see. Anything else I should be doing?"

"Keep discreet tabs on your shadow. If at any point you think Barnett has stopped following you, let me know."

TEN

Madeline left Burt Latham's office in a daze. She snapped out of it briefly as she exited the stairwell to State Street. She slipped on her sunglasses and feigned obliviousness as she scanned the area for signs of her tail. She relaxed as she reentered Saks and remembered her directive to "shop till she dropped." In spite of her dire circumstances, the echo of Burt's words made her smile.

A nervous Maryanne spotted her as soon as she neared the shoe salon. "I've got everything boxed and bagged for you, Mrs. Ridley. Was there anything else you wanted to try on before I ring you up?" she asked hopefully. Madeline regarded the four shopping bags by the register; she couldn't for the life of her remember what was in them.

"No, I think that's going to do it for now."

"Very well, Mrs. Ridley. If I could just get your card…"

Madeline had the shopping bags put in her car while she ventured on to the next department: fine jewelry. The thought of the damage she could do there made her grin wickedly.

"Well, hello Mrs. Ridley!" Leona called out from behind the display case. "I was just reading about the event at The Edgecliff Saturday night. Gorgeous photo of you and your handsome husband!" Madeline forced a small laugh. "I hear it was a great success," Leona flattered her, leaning suggestively over the counter, subtly drawing Madeline's attention to the striking enhancer dangling from a silver chain around her neck.

"Talk about gorgeous," Madeline said, happily taking the bait. Leona lifted it up to give Madeline a better look.

"Tanzanite and white sapphires," Leona informed her as she unclasped it and handed to Madeline. "Just came in this morning and I *had to* try it on. Wow, with your coloring, that is just amazing!" Madeline looked at herself in the mirror Leona was quick to supply. It was beautiful, even on a T-shirt.

"I'm not really doing it any justice with this outfit," she said, handing it back to Leona, who accepted it with disappointment.

"You should try it on with something upstairs—or take it home and try it with some of your own things," she suggested. Madeline could barely suppress a smile at her blatant salesmanship.

"Put it aside and I'll think about it," Madeline said, her eyes already on to the bracelets in the case. "I need a gift for Lauren. She's been working her tail off these last few months."

"I'm sure she'd love one of these. Does she own any David Yurman?"

"Not yet," Madeline said, toying with Leona. "Let me see that one with the peridot."

"Ooh, she'd love this," Leona said, placing it on the suede viewing square.

"So this is where successful fundraisers go to get their just rewards," Carla Dickens said as she crept up behind Madeline, making her jump. Carla laughed at her co-chair's reaction, grabbing her shoulders from behind as she gave her a playful squeeze.

"It's not for me," Madeline insisted, playing down the indulgence. "It's for Lauren, so she won't go looking for an easier job."

"She'd love it. But then I'd have to get something for my Stephanie just as expensive or *she'd* go looking for greener pastures."

Madeline mouthed to Leona to hold the two pieces for her and turned her attention back to Carla. Burt had assigned her a mission, and this was as good an opportunity as any to get an eyewitness account of her behavior Saturday night.

"What brings you in here?" Madeline asked, steering Carla away from the counter.

"We're leaving for Venice next week…"

"Oh, that's right," Madeline said, missing half a beat. *The auction item: Carla's husband must've won the bid.*

"Need to pick out some fabulous things for the trip."

"Of course. I'll come with you and get my thrills vicariously," Madeline joked as she let her co-chair lead the way.

"That was fun!" Carla said, her face beaming as she waited for Justin to bring her car around. He pulled up the Jaguar sedan and hopped out. He took the bags from Carla and deposited them in the trunk. "My schedule is packed, but let's talk before I leave next week. Maybe we can squeeze in a lunch or something." She favored Madeline with two air-kisses, tipped Justin and slid into the driver's seat.

"Oh, wait—I almost forgot! We've got the committee meeting tomorrow night. That's right—I'll see you then. Bye love."

"Bye, see you tomorrow," Madeline said, barely able to conceal her dread. Justin pulled her car up and held the door open as she rifled through her overcrowded tote for her wallet.

"I had to put some of the bags on the passenger's side—hope that's alright," Justin said as Madeleine slid a ten into his hand.

"That's fine," she said, slipping into her low-slung sports car. She fished out her sunglasses and took stock of all the loot she had acquired. Instead of giving her the customary thrill, the evidence of such useless spending dampened her mood. While pretending to make sure everything was accounted for, she checked the immediate environs for signs of Steven's P.I. She began feeling a little panicky as she started out of the lot, but just before turning right onto Carrillo, she glimpsed a silver Honda through the hedge in the public lot adjacent to Saks.

She couldn't say for sure it was Barnett, so instead of going straight down Carrillo to the freeway, she waited for the pedestrians to cross, then turned right up Chapala. While she waited for the light to turn green at Figueroa, the silver Accord exited the public lot. This made her breathe easier.

As an excuse for heading this direction, Madeline pulled up in front of the Wine Hound. After purchasing a couple bottles of wine that she didn't need, she got back in her Porsche, but not before making Barnett's sedan.

With private dick in tow, Madeline headed for the freeway. She went through the lights and merged onto 101 unaware of her actions; her mind was a seething stew of information and new concerns.

It was almost 1:30 and she was famished. Problem was, she was in too vulnerable a state and didn't want to go home. *Home*, she thought; *not for much longer.*

There was another more practical reason for not wanting to go back up the hill just yet; it went against her sense of decorum to show up at the house with her car packed with proof of her shopping extravaganza. She didn't want Erma and Hughes thinking any worse of her than they already did.

With all the worries dancing around her head, she almost missed her exit. As she sat at the stop sign waiting for traffic to pass, she got an idea better than creeping around her own home like a thief. Instead of turning left, she cranked the wheel and executed a quick right, toward Miramar Beach.

Though hiding out at the beach appealed to her desire for privacy, once she was standing in the entry, the bungalow felt far too confining. It had been closed up since the weekend and the winter sun made the place feel as though all the oxygen molecules had expired. She opened a few windows to get a cross breeze going and opened the blinds on the east side of the house to let some light in. She'd always loved this house, but the thought of living there in exile for six months made her edgy.

She needed to put her thoughts in order and digest her meeting with Burt Latham, and this was as good a place as any. But she also needed to eat. She was starting to feel lightheaded and she knew there was nothing there to eat except for some stale crackers and martini olives. She stood in the middle of the living room for another minute as she willed herself into action. She shuffled her priorities, and after stuffing her day's purchases in the hall closet, went in search of something to eat.

ELEVEN

As Madeline pulled into the breezeway of the Montecito Inn, she caught sight of friends sitting at a table by the window. *Oh damn,* she thought, tempted to keep going. But Jane had spotted her and she had no choice but to relinquish her car to the valet.

When she walked into the Montecito Café, Jane had already annexed another chair from a neighboring table to make a place for her. Madeline covered her disappointment with a bright smile and joined the party already in high-squawk mode.

"Hello, stranger," Jane greeted her, giving her a quick hug. "We've only just ordered—your timing is perfect." The waitress appeared wearing an expression of anticipation.

"Can I get you something to drink, Mrs. Ridley? A glass of Brander Sauvignon Blanc?"

"Thanks, Barbara, that'd be great. And I'll have the trout salad," Madeline replied as she circled the table and bussed all the proffered cheeks of her girlfriends.

"Hey, thanks for canceling on me yesterday," Jane snarked. "I was forced to play Amanda and she kicked my ass in straight sets." Everyone laughed except Jane.

"Is that the only reason I'm roped into our weekly games, because you hate to lose?" Madeline quipped.

"Hardly," Jane said, eyeing her with playful antagonism. "I've let you win a few times." Madeline laughed.

"You mean, *I've* let you beat *me* a few times." All the women laughed at this, including Jane, but only because she could never stay mad at her closest friend for long.

"So, where have you been hiding out?" Alexa asked as liquid reinforcements arrived. Madeline evaded the question by lifting her glass to the others.

"Cheers!" they all responded, with glasses held high.

"Hey, congratulations on the ball. It was fabulous," Natalie said. The others echoed this sentiment.

"Thanks. I appreciate all your support." While the replies of her four friends collided in an undecipherable cacophony, Madeline felt the desperation of not being able to remember a single moment of the auction. She drank a hearty sip of her wine and instantly regretted it as it hit her empty stomach. She snagged a piece of bread from the basket and devoured it as the conversation galloped along.

"I'm still pissed that Larry let Roger Dickens beat him out of the Venetian holiday," Natalie said.

"Oh, I bet! Mark wouldn't even let me raise my paddle on that one," Jane groused.

"Yeah, but you got him to spring for the Post Ranch—that was pretty sporting of him," Alexa said.

"I know, where did that charitable urge come from?" Natalie asked.

"I don't know, but whatever made him do it wore off by the time we drove home," Jane replied.

"Buyer's remorse?" Amanda joked. Jane nodded.

"All he kept saying was '$8,000 for one weekend!'" Everyone laughed. Even Madeline, who was attaching two fragments of knowledge to the void in her memory of that night, gave a good impersonation of someone having fun at her friend's expense.

"I think he was so gaga over the way Maddie looked, he just kept raising his paddle to get her to smile at him again."

"Well, it worked," Madeline said, grateful that she could contribute something to the conversation, though it was purely ad lib.

"How's Steven?" Alexa asked after the laughter died down. The question caused a coughing fit, as Madeline literally choked on it.

"Give her some water," Natalie suggested as Madeline grew red in the face. Jane pounded her on the back.

"I'm fine," Madeline croaked, waving away all the well-intentioned interference.

"You're not getting what Steven had, I hope," Alexa said, eyeing her suspiciously.

"Steven had food poisoning—that's what he told John," Amanda added for the record. This got Madeline's attention: John was one of Steven's partners.

Seemed like Steven had a different set of lies for everyone. She wondered how he could keep them all straight.

"Hope it wasn't from something he ate at the benefit," Jane said. It took Madeline a few seconds to realize everyone was looking to her for the answer.

"Oh, no—he was fine in the morning. I think it must've been something he had at lunch." Their entrees arrived, effectively taking Madeline out of the hot seat for the moment. The chatter died down as they took their first bites, only to rev back up as other gossip of the latest social event demanded to be aired.

"I thought I would *die* when Monica Strand walked in with that rent-a-stud," Natalie pronounced gleefully. Madeline racked her brain: had she seen this guy with Monica? Was he her mystery man?

"I think I missed that," she said innocently.

"You've got to be kidding? The super-tan blonde with the killer bod? He would've had to gone into Chippendale-mode to have been any more noticeable," Jane mocked. Madeline felt relieved and disappointed at the same time.

"I was so focused, I really didn't even notice half the people there," she said, hoping her friends would offer further enlightenment. She hated to come out and ask if anyone knew who she danced with, but she had to find out somehow.

"There were a lot of people I've never seen before," Alexa admitted, though by her tone, it didn't sound as though she approved of them all.

"It was a big turnout. I think our patrons brought a lot of guests," Madeline offered.

"It's a good time of the year to have a fundraiser—after the holidays and before tax season," Natalie reasoned. Madeline took a long sip of wine while she thought of ways to steer the conversation back to the guests.

"Who was that tall, dark, handsome guy you kept dancing with?" Amanda's question nearly got Madeline choking again.

"Yeah, talk about a stud muffin!" Natalie's remark had everyone cackling like hens.

"I honestly don't know," Madeline admitted. Everyone tittered except Jane.

"Oh, come on! You danced half the night with him," she challenged.

"No I didn't," Madeline protested.

"Uh huh, yes you did," Alexa said. Madeline was aghast. She felt as if all the once friendly faces around her had suddenly grown sinister.

"I danced with several men after Steven went home," she insisted. "I don't even know what that guy's name was."

"At least she remembered who we're talking about," Amanda mock-whispered to Natalie.

"Well, do any of you know who he was?" Madeline asked defensively. Her tone seemed to take the sting out of their mocking. They all shook their heads in unison.

"But then again, we weren't dancing with him half the night," Alexa said, raising a few naughty snickers.

"All I can say is the evening must've been a bore if you all didn't have anything better to do than keep track of my dance partners." The rebuke hung in the air as Madeline gazed at the four faces seated around her.

"The evening was a blast. Don't get your knickers in a knot," Jane admonished her. "I think somebody's been working too hard lately," she added, regarding her friend out of the corner of her eye.

"Now that the ball's behind you, we should go out and just let our hair down," Alexa suggested, squashing the note of animosity that had crept into the conversation.

"That's a good idea," Jane seconded, looking at her friend in a conciliatory manner.

"Yeah, that would be fun," Madeline agreed. But there was no way she was going to waste her limited time with this gang. If they couldn't tell her who her rapist was, she was going to have to look elsewhere.

TWELVE

Madeline waved goodbye to her friends as she pulled out of the parking garage. She headed toward home out of reflex, but her stomach knotted at the thought of wandering her house like an unwelcome guest who was about to be shown the door. Yet, she couldn't wear the same outfit indefinitely. She felt somewhat better when she remembered she did have the beach house to hole up in; at least she wouldn't have uncomfortable encounters with the staff there.

With a temporary escape plan forming in her head, the pluses of a change of venue started piling up. She could take a run on the beach and clear her head, maybe make sense of what was happening to her life. *Ha,* she thought bitterly, *that would be too tall an order for one day.*

As soon as she pulled up, Hughes appeared to ask if she needed any assistance. She thanked him, told him no, and told him she was going out again. While she was thinking of it, she went in search of Erma and told her she'd be having dinner out with friends. As she walked to her bedroom, she debated whether she should tell her she'd probably stay at the beach house that night. She retraced her steps to the foyer, then changed her mind. Any knowledge of her comings and goings would surely be passed on to Steven.

This thought stopped her in her tracks. She hadn't given her shadow a thought after lunch. Was she followed? Wasn't she supposed to report back to Burt Latham if she lost sight of Russell Barnett? This worry sent her into high gear. She stripped and pulled on running clothes, then packed a carry-on bag with assorted wardrobe essentials, plus her toiletries bag, her laptop and chargers. She was out the door and down the driveway without any more contact with Erma and Hughes.

❖ ❖ ❖

Madeline reached Loon Point and looked back toward Miramar Beach. She had run without stopping, her mind churning as fast as the sand beneath her feet. She panted as she rested, hands on her knees, bent over until she caught her breath. She had run hard, her muscles pumping like pistons, in hopes of outrunning her nightmare. As her chest heaved and heart thumped, she had to admit she was no closer to understanding what the hell had happened to her perfect life.

She headed back in the direction she had come. She could see well beyond Miramar Beach to the harbor and the Mesa. She pushed her aching muscles and tried to get back into the rhythm that had brought her to Summerland so swiftly. But after thirty seconds, she became too dispirited by the coastal beauty, a sight that normally filled her with joy.

It's no use, she thought as she walked, hands on hips, head down, ostensibly studying the tracks left by shore birds. As she confronted the here and now, she began to cry, much to her embarrassment. There was no one around to witness her shame, but crying with abandon wasn't going to help matters. She had to focus her mind and figure out what she was going to do.

Just the thought of having to sift through the rubble of her failed marriage made her cry all the harder. She gave up and sat on a rock, letting it all out.

After sobbing like she'd hadn't done since her mother died, she felt surprisingly lighter inside. She dabbed at her wet face, using the backs of her hands as squeegees, and got to her feet. She fell into a comfortable jog as she sniffled her way past Summerland. When she rounded Shark's Cove at Fernald Point, her mind was as steady as her breathing.

Now that she could think clearly, she reviewed her list of known facts:

> *I was drugged and raped*
> *I have the photos to prove it*
> *Someone set me up*
> *Steven wants a divorce*
> *Steven hired a private detective.*

As this last known fact registered, Madeline saw it in a completely different light than before. She ground to a halt as she seized on it and turned it around in her mind. Steven *did* hire a detective after slamming her with the photos, but *maybe* it was because he had his own doubts about them. Maybe Steven hired Barnett to keep tabs on her to see if she had contact with her supposed lover while he was out of town. Or maybe Steven was secretly trying to vindicate her...

Madeline stood there drinking in this fragile hope. It filled her to the point that she twittered with happiness. She started to run, her optimism spurring her on. Maybe Steven was secretly trying to prove her innocence. Twelve years of marriage was hard for anyone to just throw away on circumstantial evidence. Well, it was pretty damning evidence, circumstantial or not. But it was *possible* that Barnett had been hired to clear her. Maybe Steven was having the P.I. search for whoever was responsible for the disgusting photographs...

Madeline climbed the steps to the beach house, her mind now completely focused on building this hopeful theory into a plausible truth. She ran every element of the last five days through her mind while she showered and washed her hair. She had maintained her innocence from the beginning and had never wavered. That was definitely a point in her favor. Plus, she swore to Steven the night before that she'd never stop loving him, in spite of the fact that he was kicking her out. That was all good. She hadn't confessed, she hadn't turned nasty on him...

By the time she had dried her hair, she had more or less established this rosy scenario as irrefutable reality. Steven wouldn't just instantly toss her aside, not even if he had strong physical evidence that she had cheated on him. He'd want to know for sure. She had never once given him a reason to doubt her fidelity. That had to count for something.

She was putting on her makeup when she heard the unfamiliar ring of her loaner cell phone. She ran to the bedroom, scrambling to find the right phone.

"Hello?"

"Glad I caught you. Where are you right now?" Burt asked, his voice low.

"I'm at the beach house," Madeline whispered back.

"Inside?"

"Yes."

"Can you walk outside, right now?" Burt's urgency was starting to frighten her.

"Yes."

"Good. Walk as far from the house as you can. I'll call you in a couple minutes." Madeline struggled into a sweater and headed for the side door, grabbing her tote on the way out. The way Burt was talking, she was half afraid the place was about to blow up. She was past the old, defunct Miramar Hotel by the time the phone rang again.

"Sorry to be so cloak and dagger," Burt said as soon as she answered, "but it occurred to me that we didn't have enough time to go over precautions."

"Oh," Madeline replied, looking back over her shoulder at the house she'd just vacated. It was still intact. She took a deep breath and tried to calm herself.

She was glad Burt had called because she wanted him to confirm for her that it was plausible her suspicions about Steven might be unfounded after all. He had intimated as much at his office. But she wanted to see if he really felt it was a possibility, or if he was covering all bases out of habit. As she stood there in the sand, the cool breeze and the alarming call making her extra alert, she realized how quickly she'd become invested in that hope.

"I'm sorry I had to cut our meeting short, but I had to finish up another case. So…"

"So…," Madeline echoed.

"What concerns me is the fact that your husband has not only hired Barnett to trail you, but that he also has his own in-house security detail. You mentioned that Steven wants you out of the main house by the time he returns from Dallas."

"That's right. He told me I could live at the beach house until the divorce is final. But there's something I wanted…"

"This is what I'm thinking… Is Barnett still shadowing you?"

"No, I didn't see him after I came here earlier today."

"What time was that?"

"Um…1:30, quarter till two."

"Here's my gut take on what's going on—Steven tells you to be out of the Park Lane house by Saturday. He arranges for your things to be taken to the Miramar house by the time he gets back. He leaves town, which gives you the impression he's away and unaware of your activities. He knows you stayed at the main house last night. This gives his security team time at the beach house to install surveillance devices. Barnett waits for you to leave Park Lane this morning, informs Steven's security that you're out, then follows you around town until he gets the all-clear."

Madeline had listened to this long-winded theory impatiently. She was anxious to tell him her own theory, to get his concurring opinion, to put her mind to rest. But as Burt's hypothesis unfolded, Madeline's body went rigid. It had the unmistakable ring of probability shaped by a professional investigator's instincts. Only minutes ago she was certain Steven was secretly on her side. Now listening to Burt's logical, unbiased appraisal of the situation, it hit her how desperate and pathetic it was to hope her problems could be so easily solved.

"Are you still there?" Burt asked.

"Yes, sorry…I'm here. I hadn't thought about that," Madeline muttered, a fresh wave of panic and distrust quickly eroding her pleasant fantasy.

"If I could be sure your place wasn't being watched, I'd find a way to clear the beach house myself. But for all we know, Barnett could be driving around in a rental car, which would be a common enough move in a surveillance case. Or Steven's own guys could be watching it remotely. My guess is you're not going to feel comfortable unless you know for certain the place isn't bugged."

Madeline bit her lower lip to keep from crying. Problem was, she really wanted to cry. There was so much injustice in what had happened to her in less than a week, she couldn't get her arms around it. She needed a friend she could confide in, someone she could tell the whole awful story to. But this was too much of a bomb to lay on anyone, even if she could bring herself to admit the facts and suspicions surrounding the demise of her marriage.

"I'm sorry, what were you saying?" Madeline asked, her voice thick with emotion.

"I was just suggesting that you might rest easier tonight if you took a room in a hotel. At least you'd be assured the place wasn't bugged."

"Okay. That sounds like the best idea." Madeline hung her head, feeling pushed into a corner once again.

"There's a small inn downtown that I like to use to keep tabs on my clients. It's very discreet and they know me there. If you're comfortable with that, I can book you a room and set up my own surveillance on the street. That way, if you're still being watched, we'll know. By the way, where's your car parked?"

"In the garage. The door's down."

"Good. I don't mean to scare you here, but you know better than anyone the ruthlessness of whoever set you up." Madeline glanced across to Santa Cruz Island as she braced herself.

"Burt...can I just run one stupid thought passed you?"

"Shoot."

"Could it be remotely possible that Steven hired Russell Barnett to find out if I was telling the truth? Maybe he's hired Barnett to find out who took these pictures and why," Madeline suggested, trying to keep her enthusiasm in check. The silence on the phone told her she was about to have her hopes dashed for good.

"I would say that was as good a theory as any, if I didn't have a piece of information I haven't told you yet. I'm just starting to work on your case, but the first thing I did was have the airline manifests checked to confirm Steven's travel plans." Madeline stood stock still. Could the situation possibly get worse?

"Steven boarded the 6:05 flight to LAX out of SBA on American Airlines. But he didn't continue on to Dallas. He boarded an 8:10 flight to Boston.

I've got my feelers out, but haven't gotten any confirmation back on his final destination."

Madeline barely heard this last sentence. Her mind was filled with images of Steven ranting at her, calling her a whore, slamming the door in her face. It was all true, what she had suspected since she saw the payoff: Steven was a scheming, conniving bastard. God only knew what he was really up to.

But if it involved framing her to stiff her on a divorce settlement and alimony, it had to mean he was one of the cheapest, cruelest men alive, or that he was in deep financial trouble. Whatever his reason for sabotaging the beautiful life she had made for herself, she wasn't going to play the patsy.

"Madeline?"

"I'm still here. What's the name of that hotel?"

"Eastside Inn. On Garden, just up from Canon Perdido. And there's one more thing—do you belong to a gym?"

"No. We have a gym at home."

"I want you to sign up for a membership at the Santa Barbara Fitness Club tomorrow. They have a 30-day refundable policy, which should take us through this investigation. We can meet there discreetly without attracting attention. You know where it is?"

"Yes."

"Great. Go in as early as possible tomorrow to sign up, then we can arrange to meet later on."

"Okay."

"If you try to contact me on this number and I don't answer, don't leave a message. I'll see I have a missed call from your phone and I'll call you back. Any questions? I know this is a lot of skulking around and I'm sure you're not used to it."

Madeline laughed half-heartedly.

"You could say that. I never thought I'd be hiding from my husband's goon squad and fleeing my own homes out of fear of being spied on."

"We'll get the facts sorted out and you'll be in charge of your life again," Burt assured her. Madeline shook her head mournfully; it was hard to imagine she could outsmart her evil husband, let alone have a life to be in charge of again.

THIRTEEN

Madeline caught a glimpse of Burt Latham relaxing casually next to his car as she drove into the motor court of the Eastside Inn. He signaled to her with a nod of his head as she handed her keys over to the attendant. She carried her tote and a deli bag while the attendant fetched her other things. Once she was checked in and had been escorted to her room, the hotel phone rang.

"Is the room satisfactory?" Burt asked.

"Very," Madeline replied as she glanced around at her temporary digs.

"You need anything before I leave?" She looked skeptically at the salad she had picked up on the way over.

"No, I think I'm good."

"Okay. I'm going to head home and get back to work. Call me if anything unusual happens or if something spooks you."

"I will," she promised.

"Alright. Rest well and I'll call you tomorrow."

Madeline replaced the receiver. She felt vaguely uneasy knowing that her protection was now off-duty. She took stock of the amenities her small but well-appointed suite had to offer.

The minibar was the first thing she checked out. It had the customary array of booze in miniature, including half-bottles of local wines. She reached for the chardonnay, then changed her mind. She opted instead for two scotches, which she opened and poured into a glass with a few cubes of ice.

She took her highball into the bathroom, where she discovered an oversize tub perfect for soaking in. *Maybe later*, she thought as she shed her sweater. As she reentered the sitting room, she realized the drapes were still open. She approached them from the side, keeping her silhouette out of view as she tugged the draperies closed.

"Oh God," she moaned, dropping into an overstuffed chair. She took a slug of her drink and enjoyed the burning sensation as it went down. The burning was soon replaced with a pleasant numbness. She drained the glass and sat there debating what her next move should be: make another drink, eat her unappetizing salad, take a soak, have another crying fit. In the end, she opted for sitting in the semi-darkness, as it required the least amount of energy and no effort.

Downing her meager cocktail had the hoped-for calming effect. The details of the last two days' events continued to bump around the fringes of her mind, but it was as if the sound had been turned off. She had become momentarily deaf to her fears and doubts.

It wasn't until her stomach registered a loud complaint that she realized how hungry she was. She reached over and removed the compostable container out of the deli bag and used the plastic fork to attack the wilting lettuce and limp vegetables. Unfortunately, she had a raging hunger but no appetite. A few bites were all it took to lose interest in eating altogether.

She hoisted herself out of the chair and started to unpack her things. She plugged in her laptop and charged both phones—her iPhone and Burt's loaner—and stashed the Saks shopping bags in the closet. She stripped out of her jogging clothes and into a pair of grey cashmere sweatpants and tunic. She grabbed a bottle of water out of the fridge and seated herself on the sofa cross-legged, placing her laptop in the cradle between her knees.

After prioritizing her needs, she began searching the Internet. The most pressing matter at this juncture was to find a good divorce attorney outside the area. She made a search of L.A. lawyers, taking down names as she scrutinized the copious offerings. She narrowed it down to one, with two backups. She hoped and prayed she could wangle an appointment the next day. She sighed heavily at the thought. This was a whole new arena for her, one that made her feel like a loser just for having to enter it.

Now that her primary concern had been sorted with a mental note to call for an appointment first thing in the a.m., Madeline staggered to the bed, where she keeled over like a felled tree. She lay there on her back with arms flung out to the sides, her body aching from too much of everything, her mind a rotating barrage of anxieties. She drifted off into a brief, terror-filled sleep. When she jerked awake, she was so disoriented, it took her several petrified seconds to figure out where she was.

With her heart pounding, she headed for the bathroom, where she sat on the toilet in a daze. She managed to get herself up by realizing she would be paralyzed by this whole situation if she didn't fight it with every ounce of strength she could summon. At this point, her weapons were limited, but she did have a private investigator and her God-given smarts. It was time she put the latter to use in earnest.

Time for another list, she thought as she seated herself at the desk. She took the hotel notepad and pen from the desk drawer and proceeded to put an order to her most pressing concerns. Next to the number 1, she wrote down the name Barry Houstein, Esq. and his contact information. After jotting down the number 2, she sat back, stumped.

*Okay…*she prompted herself…*I've got legal worries, financial worries, safety worries and housing worries.* As she had addressed the legal issue, she put down *find a place to live* next to #2. This got her mind into gear. It was already Thursday night; she had less than two full days to remove her belongings from the Park Lane house. Knowing the new Steven Ridley, he might have all her things hauled to the dump just out of spite. There was no telling how deep his cruel streak ran.

Though her current residence was fine for a night or two, she had to have something bigger and less expensive—not that she cared about the price as long as Steven was ultimately paying the bill. But she rationalized it'd be better for her in the long run if she used those funds on tangible items that could be resold on eBay, if and when she got really hard up for money.

She grabbed her laptop and tapped on the keys absentmindedly as she ran through her requirements. She needed a place she could move into quickly without having to commit to a long-term lease. That was one set of issues. It also had to be a decent size—a studio apartment in some dark complex wasn't going to cut it. She'd need at least a two-bedroom to house all her clothing. And she needed something furnished. She typed in "furnished short term rentals Santa Barbara."

Her search came back with a broad assortment of offerings. But as she clicked through the listings, she became discouraged. The rentals she liked were either unavailable for weeks or too pricey. If she got into a rental situation, she wouldn't be able to pay with a credit card, so price was a consideration.

As she scanned further down on her search, she came across several ads for vacation rentals. That was the perfect solution, once she thought about it. She clicked on site after site until she found one that didn't overwhelm or aggravate her. Right away she spotted a cute Spanish-style cottage in West Beach, just two blocks from the ocean.

After viewing the photos of the 2-bedroom, 1 bath with charming private backyard and off-street parking, she clicked on the calendar. It was available for the rest of February and all of March. She filled out the inquiry form and emailed it to the owner.

While she was searching for backups, she received a reply. *The property is available for the period you requested and can be shown tomorrow. The monthly rate for off-season is $2,750.* Madeline quickly replied that she'd take it—sight unseen—and asked that the rental agreement be emailed to her as soon as possible.

With all the mental anguish she'd been through the last few days, the prospect of settling herself somewhere outside of Steven's domain made her feel almost lighthearted. Living in that part of town would be fun. It was only a temporary arrangement, until she could get her life sorted out.

But even if she could prove Steven had her set up to be raped and photographed, it would take time to get what she was legally owed. She was hanging all her hope on what Burt had told her, that a prenuptial agreement could be broken under certain circumstances. At this point, she couldn't consider the alternative.

To reassure her fragile psyche, she located her tote bag and the envelope with the "proof." It gave her a fresh pang of anxiety to imagine what her situation would be like if she lost those photos. Once a disgusting and horrifying reflection on her, they now represented the silver bullet that would release her from Steven's treachery—if, that is, Burt Latham could dig up evidence that would provide her with the gun.

By now it was 8:15. Madeline felt like she'd been awake for two days, which basically she had been. Dead tired as she was, she was still too keyed up to even imagine trying to go to bed. She knew she'd never fall asleep with her mind running in twenty different directions. She stripped off her clothes and got in the shower.

She forced herself to stay under the hot spray until she couldn't stand it any longer. It helped. By the time she dried off, she was so relaxed she could barely keep her eyes open. She gathered her phones and turned down the bed. She lay down, enjoying the sensation of release as her muscles gave up the fight and went limp. She switched off the light and closed her eyes.

Just as she was about to drift into a deep sleep, the process reversed itself, making her instantly wide awake. She rolled over, trying to push thought from her mind. Now no position felt comfortable; her body had become as restless as her mind. After thirty minutes of flipping back and forth, she gave up and switched on the light. She looked at the clock. Only 9:25.

It's too early to go to bed, she rationalized, as she threw back the covers. But what could she do at this hour? Her brain was fried by the constant bombardment of the last day and a half. She marveled at the way time had become so elastic, leaving her in one long, never-ending day.

She reached for the remote control and started flipping through the channels as she propped herself against the headboard. This diversion lasted five minutes before the mindless blathering became harder to endure than her own improbable drama. She switched the TV off and got out of bed. She grabbed another bottle of water and sat back down at the desk.

Her list wasn't very impressive; she knew she had a lot more to deal with than just finding an attorney and a place to live. She started a new list—a random list—where she could record the miscellaneous tasks that had to be dealt with by Saturday night.

> *Get new DL with maiden name*
> *Withdraw more $$*
> *Arrange for movers*
> *Sign up at SB Fitness Center*
> *Get a P.O. Box*
> *Remove jewelry from safety deposit @ MB&T*
> *Get safety deposit box @ my bank*
> *Put photos in new box*
> *Committee meeting @ 7pm*

Realizing that she was about to careen into a new day—possibly without sleep—kicked her anxiety into high gear. She got up and paced, fighting the urge to cry out of utter frustration.

"I'm going to go insane!" she said out loud. Just hearing her own voice was reassuring. She needed to talk to someone. This solitary confinement was going to drive her out of her mind. She grabbed her phone and scrolled through her contacts, landing on Mack Dawkins. She clicked to open his info and stared at his photo.

"Oh, Daddy," she moaned, sinking to the sofa. Her finger hovered over his phone number, but she backed out before the call was placed.

It would make all the difference in the world to get her father's input, to hear the comforting sound of his voice telling her that everything would be all right, that Steven would pay for what he'd done to her. But there was no way to edit out the seamy details; they were essential to the sudden collapse of her bright, beautiful life. And there was no way she could bear to burden her father with the truth. He would take it even harder than she did. Plus, he'd want to dismantle Steven with his bare hands.

As she traced her finger back up the screen of her phone, rejecting the long list of contacts, she came across a name she hadn't thought of in years. She tapped lightly to display the details. Before she could talk herself out of it, she could hear the ringing as her phone connected to his.

"Hello," the voice said, slightly groggy, obviously unaware of who was calling him.

"Mike, it's Madeline." In the quiet, she could imagine him squirming to a more upright position.

"Madeline," Mike said, drawing out each syllable. "Madeline Dawkins. Excuse me…Madeline *Ridley*," he said, his tone a little playful, a little sarcastic.

"Michael Delaney," Madeline said in the same mocking tone.

"My, my, my…what could I have possibly done to rate a phone call from you? It's not my birthday, I don't think…"

"I won't insult you by pretending I've called to see how you're doing," Madeline said, hoping to preempt any more condescending remarks.

"That's what I've always liked about you, Mad Dawg—you just tell like it is," Mike said with a cynical snort. *This was a mistake*, Madeline thought, tempted to end the call. "Hey, indulge me a little—I haven't heard from you for five years—"

"It hasn't been that long," Madeline protested. "I saw you at Monica's wedding. That wasn't that long ago," she argued, but she couldn't say for sure when that memorable occasion had been. Just mentioning it got a laugh out of Mike.

"Oh God, you're right! How could I forget *that?* Anyway, it's been *years* since you favored me with a phone call. Are you that hard up for entertainment?" Mike asked snidely as he went to the refrigerator for something cold to drink. Madeline let the sting of his remark subside before answering.

"I need someone to talk to," she said.

Mike held the phone to his ear with his shoulder as he twisted the cap off a soda bottle. The somberness of her tone got his attention.

"What's up, Maddie?" He took a swig from the liter bottle as he returned to the sofa. He switched off the TV to give Madeline his undivided attention.

Now that she had someone she could confide in, she didn't know where to start. The longer she hesitated, the more apprehensive Mike became.

"Are you okay?" Madeline cradled her head in the heel of her hand. "What's going on?" he prompted again.

"I'm in a very bad situation," she said, her voice hollow.

"How bad? Are you in jail?" he asked after a brief pause. This made Madeline laugh weakly.

"Not yet. I could be though, if I kill Steven."

Mike let out an appreciative *ahhh*.

"Okay…guess you better give me a little background info."

FOURTEEN

Madeline gave Mike what he asked for in a succinct outline, beginning at the ball. When she was finished, the line was so quiet, she had to ask if he was still there.

"Yep. I got every word of it. I'm just trying to digest it all. Jesus, what a nightmare. What a bastard!" Madeline kept quiet while he absorbed everything. "Oh my God, this is like one of those psychological thrillers. Holy Christ. What are you going to do?"

"I…I'm going to fight him. I don't know how, exactly. It really all depends on what my P.I. can unearth. Oh, I forgot to tell you… According to Burt, Steven didn't actually go to Dallas. He took a flight from Santa Barbara to L.A., but he got on a flight to Boston instead."

"So, you think maybe *he's* two-timing *you?*"

"Why else would he make a big point of saying he's got a business meeting in Dallas if he's really going to Boston? Burt's got his 'feelers out' to confirm his final destination."

"Well, that was a good move on your part, hiring your own spook." Mike became reflective again. "Maddie, Maddie, Maddie. You poor baby. *You* do not deserve to be treated like this. That son-of-a-bitch is very damn lucky he's not within driving distance. I'd risk prison time to give him just a taste of what he deserves."

Though she could tell Mike was almost as infuriated as she was, hearing his reaction was a balm for her raw nerves. She relaxed against the sofa, effectively letting some of her load transfer to her old friend and former lover.

"So, you've got a couple days left before Steven gets back to town. What's the agenda?"

"I hope I can get in to see an attorney, or at least set something up. I'm worried about money. I don't know if he's going to want anything up front. I really don't have access to much, and who knows how long that's going to last me—even without exorbitant legal fees. I'm thinking about selling my car…"

"What's it worth?"

"I don't know. It's less than a year old. I think I've only put about 6,000 miles on it."

"What's the make, model and year? I'll check it out on Kelley Blue Book," Mike said as he logged onto his computer.

"It's a 2011 Porsche Carrera S," Madeline said, knowing she was going to get some ribbing for this. Mike let out a low whistle.

"Well, at least you've got some chips to play with. I take it the car's in your name…?"

"Yes, it was a fortieth birthday present."

"At least you got that out of him," Mike said. His pragmatism struck her as being a little crass until she remembered who they were talking about. "I'll assume it's got everything but the butler… Okay…retail price, $91,300. Private party sale, $87,700. Does that make you feel any better?"

"A little. Now how do I go about selling it? I don't have the time to be placing ads and dealing with inquiries," Madeline said.

"I think you'd have better luck selling it down here—bigger market and bigger egos. What color is it?"

"Ruby red."

"*Nice.* Sure you don't want to just give it to me? After all we've meant to each other?" Madeline let out a soft snort. "Okay, just checking…"

"I don't see how I can sell it down there while I'm up here—unless I take it to a dealer, but I wouldn't get as much for it."

"When will you know if you're coming down?"

"I don't know. It depends on if I can get in to see an attorney down there. I've got a list of things I need to take care of up here… I don't know—I'll just have to wing it."

"Alright, when you know what your agenda's going to be, call me. I'm not sure what help I can offer, but I'll do anything for you, Maddie. You know that."

These were the words she'd been craving to hear. She let all the air escape from her lungs. It made her feel like she was ridding her body of toxic gases. At least she had one more person on her side.

❖ ❖ ❖

When Madeline awoke from a deep slumber, she yawned and stretched, a peaceful expression on her face. But reality soon sabotaged her naturally sunny disposition. She sat up abruptly and took stock of her surroundings and registered their implications. She sighed heavily, her spirits taking a tumble as she came to grips with all the chores and errands on her list, none of them qualifying as habitudes.

She allowed herself five more minutes to get adjusted to her new status and review the objectives of the day on her mental list. After plotting a path that would take her through Santa Barbara and Los Angeles—hopefully—she got up and availed herself of the complimentary coffee. Once she got that brewing, she took a quick shower and got herself physically and mentally ready for the long day ahead of her.

Had she been thinking more clearly, she would've grabbed more impressive clothing from the main house, outfits that would subtly announce her station in life. But she had brought more serviceable pieces—black slacks, boots, cashmere sweaters for layering. She put on the pants and a cream-colored sleeveless sweater and a long, open-front cashmere cardigan with bell sleeves. It was all elegant, expensive attire, but it made her feel drab. And forty. And almost divorced.

As she was putting on her diamond studs, it hit her she had bags of new finery perfect for transforming her look. Hurriedly, she grabbed the shopping bags from the closet and rummaged through them until she found what she was looking for. She pulled off her boots and slipped her feet into the zebra-striped pony hair Manolo slingbacks.

"Now we're talking," she said, as she admired her enhanced ensemble. "The necklace!" she remembered as she contemplated her reflection from the waist up. She rooted around the piles of tissue paper until she found the small box with the silver chain and pendant. "Perfect," she declared, admiring the way it pulled everything together. She grabbed her Prada tote bag, gave herself one more look for courage and left the room.

As she strode through the lobby to the front door, the day manager hastened to catch up with her.

"Mrs. Ridley? Hi, I'm Jeff Bowen," he said, extending his hand. Madeline, puzzled and a little annoyed by the interruption, was slow to shake it. "If I might have a word with you, in my office," Mr. Bowen said, his voice just above a whisper. His cautiously discreet manner was like a blow to Madeline's solar plexus, but she covered it with an air of pragmatic efficiency. She nodded for him to lead the way.

"We tried to process the card number we got from you yesterday, and we received a message to call the issuer of credit immediately. They told us the card was reported stolen last night," Jeff Bowen said from his side of the desk.

"That's not possible. I've had it in my possession the whole time, and I certainly didn't report it stolen," Madeline said, as she removed it from her wallet to prove this was all some sort of mistake. The way Mr. Bowen's eyes were glued to the card caused Madeline to retract it from his reach.

"Since Burt Latham made the reservation for you, we contacted him first thing this morning. He explained that you are going through a divorce and that it's becoming rather acrimonious.

"Because of our relationship with him, and our regard for our clientele, I have to tell you we were ordered by the creditor to seize your card. If you can pay the balance of your bill in full by another means, I'll tell them we were unable to retrieve the card. But if you try to use that card again, it will be confiscated. Just a word of warning," Mr. Bowen said.

He was trying to walk the tightrope of bearer of bad news and welcoming host, not an easy thing to do. Madeline almost felt sorry for him. She put the now useless card back in her wallet and took out her new debit card, which she handed to him without a word.

"Thank you. I'll be just a minute," he said as he excused himself, leaving Madeline to fume in private.

This humiliation had chased away the last bit of doubt and naiveté. Steven was going to systematically beat her down; that was obvious now. But he had already blown her out of the water by demanding a divorce; why was he wasting his time with stunts like this? Just to prove he's in the driver's seat? Maybe it was to make himself so odious to her that she'd back off her claim that she'd never stop loving him.

"I'm sorry for all the unpleasantness, Mrs. Ridley," Mr. Bowen said as he came back into his office. Madeline stood and took the proffered debit card, placing it back in her wallet while the manager fumbled over himself trying to smooth over the incident.

"It's no problem, Mr. Bowen," she said as she moved toward the door. "It's all forgotten. Could you please have my car brought around? I'm running behind now."

It was all Madeline could do to keep her impulses in check and keep her Porsche somewhere within ten miles of the speed limits. Her embarrassment had given way to pure, black hatred and a hankering for revenge. She took the surface roads to the fitness club, and was surprised by the number of cars on the road so early. She parked in the almost full lot and went inside.

The club was like a city within a city. Members and staff were everywhere: the squash courts were thrumming with the constant *thwak* and *thump* of balls and the occasional muffled curse. Madeline waited her turn at the reception counter, as members received towels and locker keys.

"Good morning," a college-aged employee greeted her. Madeline returned the salutation and told the girl she wanted to become a member. This caused the girl's face to cloud over. "I'm sorry, the sales staff doesn't arrive until ten." Madeline grimaced and let out a weary sigh. This day was not starting well.

"Isn't there anyone who can help me?" The girl shook her head apologetically. Madeline looked at her watch, not bothering to hide her irritation. It was quarter to eight.

"Let me just get this man his key. Hi Eric! How's it going? Good! Have a nice day. Sorry about that," the girl said, feeling the ire exuding from Madeline and heading her way.

"Can I just have a form to fill out and then bring it back later—save a little time...?" The girl wobbled her head sadly.

"I'm sorry, but we don't have access to those forms. But if you come back between ten and four, there will be someone here who can help you." Madeline's gaze had wandered while she listened to this unwelcome news. She was searching for some way to salvage the time spent on the trip over.

"Is there someone who can show me the facilities, so I can make sure I really want to join?"

"Oh sure—one of us can do that," the girl replied happily. She looked at her coworkers who had become subliminally aware of the situation.

"I can do it," another twenty-something said, abandoning the report she was running. "Give me one sec," she said before disappearing to the back. She returned a moment later with brochures and motioned for Madeline to follow her.

"Hi, my name's Stacy," she said as she walked briskly down the hallway. Madeline smiled politely and told Stacy her first name.

After a cursory run-through of the facilities—which were much larger than they appeared from the exterior—Stacy showed Madeline the women's locker room and showers. Madeline thanked her for the tour and said she'd be back later to sign up.

At least it wasn't a complete waste of time, Madeline thought as she got back into her car. Now she'd be able to skip all that later. But the real question would be if she could be back before four o'clock. She glanced at her watch: 8:01. She searched for Barry Houstien's number and hoped her luck would start to improve.

"Houstien Marcus & Winthorpe," a curt, professional voice announced. "How may I direct your call?"

"I'd like to make an appointment with Mr. Houstien."

"And your name, please?"

"Madeline Ridley."

"I'll connect you to Mr. Houstien's assistant. One moment, please." Madeline thanked the abrupt silence and waited to find out what the next hurdle would be. After four minutes filled with anxious ponderings, a woman's soft voice came on the line.

"This is Ms. Wendt. I'm Mr. Houstien's personal assistant. Am I speaking to Ms. Ridley?"

"Mrs. Ridley. Madeline Ridley. Soon to be the ex-Mrs. Steven Ridley."

"How can I help you, Mrs. Ridley?" Madeline could hear the soft clack-clack of a keyboard as Ms. Wendt logged the conversation. Madeline took a deep breath, hoping she could get her point across before being put on hold again or simply dismissed.

"My husband is trying to use a clause in our prenuptial agreement to divorce me without a settlement or alimony. I have reason to believe he has manufactured evidence which supposedly proves I violated the infidelity clause. He has pictures of me in a compromising position, which I believe were taken after I had been drugged at a social event, of which I was the co-chair." Madeline paused and waited for the clacking to end and Ms. Wendt's response.

"So, you believe your husband is fraudulently trying to accuse you of adultery in order to enforce the infidelity clause of your prenup. Have I got that right?"

"Yes. And I have copies of the photos of the alleged affair."

"How did you obtain these photos?"

"My husband presented them to me before he demanded I move out of the house."

"You are both California residents, I presume?"

"Yes."

"With a California marriage certificate?"

"Yes." Madeline heard more clacking while she waited for the verdict.

"Mr. Houstien has a very full case load right now," Ms. Wendt informed her. There was a message within this statement; it took Madeline a couple beats to understand what was being asked of her. She didn't hesitate.

"I was referred to you by Michelle Lambert, the wife of Herb Lambert, the film producer. They're neighbors of mine."

"If I could have you hold for just one more moment, Mrs. Ridley..." Madeline let go of the air she had been holding and sat back listening to the Musak playing softly on the line.

"Mrs. Ridley, I was able to speak to Mr. Houstien regarding your situation. He can see potentially being able to help you with your matter. As I said, he *is* rather swamped right now, but if you could be at our offices on Wilshire Boulevard at 11:20, we'll fit you in. Will that work for you?"

"I'll be there. Can you confirm the address for me?" Finally, something had fallen into place.

FIFTEEN

Buoyed by the hope of arming herself with a powerful attorney, Madeline's brain began to crackle with productive thought. She hadn't chaired or co-chaired several major fundraisers without coming away with the shrewd ability to dissect a block of time and squeeze every second out of it.

Next stop, the UPS store on Anapamu Street. She knew she couldn't order checks or get a new driver's license until she had a new mailing address. She filled out the form and was given the key to her new box.

That accomplished, she retraced her path to the DMV, which was across the street from the fitness center. Her timing was good; only two people ahead of her. She had done her research online and had her birth certificate and Social Security card with her; all she needed to do was fill out another form and have her photo taken.

Her Porsche growled out of the DMV parking lot and breezed through two yellow lights and onto the 101 South. Next stop: home, or what used to be home. She placed a call to the bank while in route and gave the assistant manager her new mailing address so her checks could be ordered. She paid for express processing, which would get the checks to her in three business days. Things were definitely falling in place now.

She made it to the Park Lane house before nine o'clock. Hughes, surprised by the hour of her return, didn't reach the driveway until Madeline was walking up the front steps. She asked him to keep the car out front—she'd be leaving in less than an hour.

She swept into the house and headed to the storage closet in the master suite. She chose another carry-on, a Louis Vuitton with wheels—a particular favorite of Steven's—and took it into her dressing room. She found her jewelry travel case and began to methodically secure her favorite and most expensive pieces in the folds and zipper pockets. What didn't fit inside that case, she shoved haphazardly into a jewelry roll up. She placed both of these next to the LV bag; they would go on top, where she could get to them easily.

Next, she headed into Steven's study and went straight to the center drawer, where she found the ashtray filled with keys. She wasn't surprised when none of them worked on the locked drawer.

She stepped back from the desk, hands on hips as she pondered the situation. She needed that pink slip because she needed the money it would fetch. She tried to reassure herself that she'd replace her beloved sports car when this hellish nightmare was over, but she didn't have much faith in anything at the moment.

She spied a letter opener on top of the desk. *Why not?* she thought, picking it up. She'd seen it done in movies, and she had no better ideas. Besides, this may be her last chance to get access. She tried to stick it in the keyhole, but it was too large for that. She needed something smaller, like a paperclip. She got one out of the center drawer and unkinked it. After jamming it in and jingling it this way and that, she tossed it in the waste basket.

It hit her as she stood there that the room was probably bugged. *Who cares?* she thought angrily. With renewed determination, she seized the letter opener and jammed it into the lock with such force that it stuck. She tried wriggling it free, but it wouldn't budge. She sat on top of the desk, and with the bottom of her expensive new shoe, she stomped on it. All this did was hurt her foot and slightly bend the opener.

She got down and jerked the bent lever as hard as she could in every direction. She was scanning the room for another tool, when she spied a heavy onyx dish, a souvenir from a trip to Yosemite. She held the dish aloft with both hands, then thrust it down with all her might.

The combination of stone on metal produced a tinny, cracking sound, the final result being a severed letter opener. But on closer inspection, Madeline saw that the lock had been slightly dislodged. She pulled up on what was left of the opener and yanked it back and forth, loosening it further with each jerk. When it worked free of the hole, Madeline staggered backward, the metal remnant and the severed lock held aloft like a freshly-picked posy.

This triumph left her feeling elated, until a prudent sense of urgency spurred her on. She got the drawer open and rifled through the folders, coming at last to one marked "DMV Records." She found the pink slip for the Porsche, which *was* solely in her name. After the stunts Steven had pulled lately, she hadn't been sure of anything. She stuck the proof of ownership in the waistband of her pants and continued her search.

Might as well, she thought, flipping through the rest of the files in the drawer. Nothing struck her as being helpful, but she decided to start from the front again, just to be sure. In her rush, she almost missed the folder marked "Madeline/1998."

She opened it and found a stapled document that looked vaguely familiar. It was a copy of the prenuptial agreement she had signed just prior to her wedding twelve years earlier. Her signature dated August 13, 1998 was a harsh reminder of her gullibility and blissful ignorance. She folded it in half and stuck it in the top of her pants along with the pink slip. She pushed the drawer back and stuck the broken lock and letter opener in the center drawer.

As she headed back to her sanctuary, she ran a search for moving companies on her phone. She had the feeling she might have better luck with such short notice going with Starving Students Movers. She glanced at her watch: 9:15. Time was running out. She placed the call. She explained what she needed and when, and they promised to have a truck at her place by 9 a.m. the next day.

Now things were really starting to go her way. The angst she had been feeling about leaving her perfect home had been replaced by a sense of purpose and urgency. This was all about saving herself now.

She went to the desk in her sitting room and flipped through folders trying to locate anything of importance. She grabbed her passport and the statements pertaining to her personal savings account. She also discovered the annual statements for her almost forgotten IRA. She put all this in a manila envelope, grabbing a couple extras, just in case.

She glanced around the room, taking stock of her favorite personal possessions and keepsakes. What could she take and what would she have to leave behind? This reminded her that she needed to contact the owner of the vacation rental to set up a time to meet her and get the keys. She had already paid for the month in advance with her credit card...

Madeline's mouth dropped open as she realized what she had inadvertently done. Her mind became so muddled, she couldn't remember what she was looking for on her phone.

"Oh!" she swore, shaking with rage and anxiety. She sat down and willed herself to concentrate. She closed out of her contacts and searched her email until she found what she was after. She rang the woman's number, desperately hoping she would answer and believe her explanation.

"Is this Elaine? Hi, this is Madeline Ridley...I booked your Yanonali Street rental...?

"Oh, yes… Your card was declined. I was told it had been stolen. I've actually reported the incident to the police." Madeline began to sweat all over. She tugged off her cardigan, one arm at a time, while pleading with the woman to hear her explanation. After breathlessly informing her that she was in the middle of a nasty divorce, she discovered the line had disconnected.

"Oh my God, oh my God," Madeline cried out. She felt like she was about to be sick. She stared at her cell phone while the reverberations of what Steven had set into motion registered in her brain. She put the iPhone down, realizing with a start that the woman now had her phone number. There could be a warrant out for her arrest soon, despite the fact that she hadn't stolen her own card. This was becoming more of a nightmare than she could fully comprehend.

She grabbed Burt's phone and called him as she walked through the bedroom to lock the door. She listened impatiently to his message, panicking as the fear of not being able to talk to him became a reality. She was just about to leave an urgent message when she remembered his directive to never do that. She ended the call and sank onto the ottoman as tears fairly leapt from her eyes. She was on the verge of letting go and giving in to self-pity and despair when her loaner phone rang.

"Where are you now?" Burt asked before she could get a word out.

"The Park Lane house."

"Inside?"

"Yes."

"Go outside, away from the house and any prying ears. But take your time—act naturally. Call me back in five." Burt hung up.

"Okay. I will. See you then," she said, playing along for any unseen cameras or microphones.

Madeline took advantage of the time by relieving her bladder and grabbing a bottle of water from her mini fridge. She packed a few more things in the carry-on and then casually went through her bedroom, past the foyer to the guest wing, letting herself out through a door in one of the guest rooms. When she had walked beyond the koi pond, she took Burt's phone out of her pants pocket.

"What's going on, Mrs. Ridley?" Burt asked, skipping the formalities.

"Please don't call me that. My name's Madeline. Madeline Dawkins. I'm going back to my maiden name as of this minute."

"Okay, Madeline—take a deep breath and tell me what's going on."

It didn't take long to summarize Steven's latest act of sabotage, as Burt already knew that her credit card had been reported stolen. She then told him how she'd wangled an appointment with an L.A. divorce attorney that she was very anxious to keep.

"I came here to grab a few things and figure out what it's going to take to remove my stuff before Steven returns tomorrow. I've got movers coming at 10 a.m., and I don't have any place to send them," she said, her voice tinged with hysteria.

"They can put your things in storage for the time being, so don't stress yourself over that. I'm more concerned about the authorities finding you through your phone. You can't be guilty of stealing your own credit card, but it might take a chunk out of your day to prove it." Madeline snapped to attention when he said this. "The best thing to do is leave your phone there." Madeline balked.

"I can't leave my phone—it's got my whole life on it," she said, trying to keep her voice down.

"You can be tracked through GPS. Chances are, you've got apps loaded on your too-smart phone that can lead someone right to you. As far as your credit card company is concerned, someone—but not you—is fraudulently trying to use your card. The landlady you spoke to has that number now. She says she's already filed a report with the local police. That phone is hot now. Stash it somewhere in your house—somewhere Steven wouldn't think to look for it, like in his own closet. Make sure it's turned off. Got it?"

"Yes, but I've got so much data on there that I need—all my contacts…"

"Take down any numbers you need in the meantime. Tomorrow you can retrieve it along with the rest of your things. Keep the credit card on you in the unlikely event that you get pulled over."

Madeline was feeling the impotency of knowing Steven was holding all the cards. He was using strategies against her that she had only heard of in spy thrillers. She wasn't cut out for evasion tactics; she was a fundraiser, a trophy wife, a Good Samaritan. But already she could feel a shift; she was going to have to become an adept street fighter. Her whole future now depended on it.

SIXTEEN

After checking the contents of her carry-on to make sure she had everything she had come for, she zipped it closed. She put the tote on her left shoulder and pulled the LV bag behind her, its rhythmic clacking announcing her departure. As she opened the front door, she caught sight of Hughes as he buffed out the shine on her now clean car. The gesture touched her, and at the same time reminded her of what she was being forced to relinquish.

"That was so nice of you, Hughes," Madeline said, as she came to a halt behind her car.

"It was my pleasure, Mrs. Ridley," Hughes replied modestly. Madeline wished there was something she could say, some way of explaining that she was not the villain in this drama. But she could tell by his actions and his demeanor that regardless of what his employers were going through, he still had a great deal of respect for her because of the kindness she had shown him over the years.

Hughes relieved her of the carry-on and stowed it in the trunk. Madeline placed the tote on the floor of the passenger's side and crossed in front of her car to the driver's side. She was just about to get in when she remembered the movers.

"Oh, Hughes—to make things simpler, I've arranged for movers to come at 9:00 tomorrow. They'll take care of boxing up everything, so you don't need to worry about it."

"Are you sure, Mrs. Ridley?" Hughes asked doubtfully. "Erma was going to supervise me with the packing of all your clothing. I took the liberty of ordering twenty wardrobe boxes, on Erma's advice. She said that way there wouldn't be crowding. We were going to start on it this afternoon, unless you prefer we didn't." Again Madeline was touched by his thoughtfulness.

"Of course, that would be very much appreciated. I would feel a lot better having you and Erma take care of my things than strangers." Madeline could feel her throat close up, in spite of her desire to remain calm. "Thank you, Hughes. I'll see you in the morning," she said, ducking into the refuge of her low-slung car.

Madeline drove down Olive Mill Road in a daze. When she came to the stop sign, she had to force herself to remember where she was going. She fished the list out of her bag and scanned over it with eyes that flitted unseeingly until someone behind her honked.

"The bank," she said, trying to focus her mind. "Both banks." She turned right onto Coast Village Road and drove to the Bank of Santa Barbara parking lot, giving herself a minute to collect her thoughts. The objective here was to remove her most valuable pieces of jewelry from the safety deposit box. She wanted to withdraw more money to secrete away in her own bank account, while she had a chance.

As she was getting out of her car, someone called her name. She swiveled around and caught sight of Lucy Montenegro heading her way. Madeline groaned but covered it with a bright smile.

"Lucy, how are you?"

"I'm just fabulous! How about you—your picture's everywhere these days," she said, holding up the latest edition of the Montecito Gazette. There she was again, in that damnable dress with her damnable almost ex-husband. Madeline turned up the wattage on her smile, hoping nothing more would be required of her.

"I just picked this up, so I haven't had a chance to read the article—but how about the headline? *Madeline Ridley and Carla Dickens: Montecito's power fundraising team.* Nice job!" Lucy said, somehow turning all of Madeline and Carla's hard work into something only valuable for its social implications.

"Listen, I was talking with Becky Morrissey about recruiting your talents for the Cheetah Rescue Project. We've got some powerful connections, *but*… not everyone has the same gift for shaking the change loose, if you know what I mean."

Madeline opened her mouth to beg off, but Lucy steamrolled right over her. "You don't have to give me an answer right now—just think about it, okay?" Madeline nodded as she shifted her body in the direction of the bank.

"I will think about it, Lucy—I promise. But right now I've got to get some banking out of the way, or I'll be late for an appointment."

"Oh, sure. I was just going in myself..." They fell in step, Lucy gushing gratuitously over the cover photo. "I loved that dress on you, by the way. It was *perfect* for the event. Almost like Valentino designed it with that in mind," she said with a giggle as Madeline held the door open for her.

"Okay, I'll talk to you later," Madeline said, stopping pointedly at the assistant manager's desk. Lucy waggled her goodbye and left Madeline to conduct her business.

"Good morning, Mrs. Ridley," Lois said, standing to greet her.

"Good morning, Lois. I need to put something in my safe deposit box and get a cashier's check for ten-thousand dollars," she said. Lois's throat constricted as she swallowed hard. "Is there a problem?" Madeline asked, her tone at once solicitous and challenging.

"Umm...Excuse me one moment, please," Lois said, leaving Madeline standing at her desk. She returned shortly and told Madeline the branch manager would like to speak to her privately. Madeline made no attempt to hide her displeasure from Lois, but she donned a neutral mask as she walked across the lobby, head held high.

"Madeline," Ben Larreman greeted her, while dismissing Lois with a half nod.

"I don't know what all the secrecy's about—I just want to put some of my jewelry back in our safe deposit box and get a cashier's check," Madeline said. Ben was already shaking his head apologetically. "What is it?" Madeline demanded as politely as her irritation would allow her.

"Steven telephoned me last night—at home." Right away, Madeline knew where this was headed. She was glad they were away from prying eyes and ears because she was one word away from throwing a major tantrum.

"I can't believe Steven would drag you into this," she said, her voice a notch below shrill. "Look, Ben—you've always been our go-to guy, always been there whenever we needed something done. But I really don't think it's a bank manager's job to put himself in between two warring spouses." It was a flat-out affront to his integrity, one designed to make him resent Steven's imposition. Madeline stared at him with eyebrows raised, challenging him to play by the book.

Ben cleared his throat, swallowing the insult with effort. "Steven asked me to freeze all your joint accounts because someone had hacked into his computer."

Madeline let out a petulant huff. Knocked out once again. Steven sure knew how to land his punches.

"I'm sorry, Ben," she offered humbly, "I didn't know about that. You see…" Madeline gave him a doleful look, which Ben was gentleman enough to accept without further apology.

"Let me get someone to bring you your box," he said, walking her toward the door. "Once I get the all-clear from Steven, I'll unfreeze your accounts."

"Thank you, Ben. Please forgive my outburst." Ben waved it away with a benign smile.

"Don't give it another thought."

Madeline stared at the contents of the box in disbelief. Aside from some insurance papers, there was nothing else in it. Never in her life had she ever felt such outrage; she now completely understood the concept behind the phrase "crime of passion." If Steven had been in the room with her, she would've had no remorse bashing his skull in with the virtually empty deposit box.

At the same time, she had never felt such fatigue—not physical fatigue, but fatigue of the spirit. She couldn't mesh the two currents of emotion, nor imagine how it was possible to feel both at the same time. She listlessly dropped the useless documents back in the box and closed the lid. She locked it—a farce if ever there was one—but denial made her unlock it and look inside again.

What upset her most was that she was actually heartbroken to find the things given to her as tokens of love and devotion had been taken away out of pure evil spite. It would be one thing if she really *had* cheated on Steven. But the reality was much, much worse. And taking back the diamond necklace with the dramatic teardrop emerald and matching earrings he had given her on their fifth anniversary was cruel, insulting and demeaning. It made her wish with all her heart she had never met Steven Ambrose Ridley.

She left the bank in a state of numbness. She exited the parking lot and headed down Coast Village Road to the freeway entrance. But at the stop sign, she broke down. She turned right and drove toward the beach.

She parked on Butterfly Lane where there were no other cars and cried herself out. She was drained, angry—make that livid—but mostly terribly sad. She couldn't understand what she had done to deserve this kind of treatment, especially from the man who had promised to love and cherish her for the rest of his life.

Again, crying helped. It relieved the pressure that had built up inside her head making it almost impossible to think. But she was thinking now. With dry-eyed determination, she picked up the remnants of her well thought-out agenda for the day and realized she had forgotten to stop at her own bank. She touched up her makeup and turned the car toward the cemetery and back around to Coast Village Road.

It took longer than she had hoped to obtain a deposit box from her bank, but at this point it was essential she have one. When the guard left the room, she stowed her most expensive jewelry in the box. As a safety precaution, she removed all but one of the seven photos, which she slipped into a new envelope, and rolled the one with the other six to fit inside the box. That was her insurance policy. With the way things had been happening, she couldn't afford to take any chances.

Feeling somewhat in control again, she stopped for coffee and a muffin to go at Starbucks. When she got on the freeway, she called Mike and updated him on her schedule. They arranged to meet after her appointment with the attorney.

"Wish me luck," Madeline said as she signed off.

"Hey, you've got something better than luck going for you—you've got me in your corner," Mike said with his usual bravado. Madeline laughed weakly. *Oh great,* she thought ending the call on that doubtful note. *Now I'm really in trouble.*

SEVENTEEN

B arry Houstien listened to Madeline recount the events of the last six days. She paused at one point to hand him the envelope containing the single photo of her *inflagranti delicto*. The attorney made no reaction except to ask if he could make a copy of it for his file. Madeline agreed as long as he assured her no one else would see it.

"Also, I found a copy of our prenuptial agreement," she said, pulling it out of her tote.

"Excellent. I'll make a copy of that too. And while I'm doing that, I'd like you to make a list of your community property assets—real estate, retirement accounts, etc., with addresses and approximate values." He handed Madeline a legal pad and a pen and excused himself.

While she was at her task, she struggled not to think of him entertaining his associates with the sordid picture of her at the worst moment of her life. But he returned so quickly, she was relieved of that humiliating visual. He handed the photo and the prenuptial agreement back to her and resumed his seat, his mind already focused on the document.

"Well, it's pretty straightforward," he said, flipping back to the page with the infidelity clause. "The photos are his proof that you've been unfaithful and broken that agreement, which then relieves him of the obligation of providing a divorce settlement and alimony."

"But I wasn't unfaithful to him, Mr. Houstien," Madeline said, her voice becoming strained with agitation. The attorney held up his hand to reassure her.

"I'm on your side, Mrs. Ridley. And call me Barry," he said smiling in an effort to make her relax. Madeline's features softened and she returned a cautious smile.

"Please call me Madeline," she said. "And I'm going to start using my maiden name, which is Dawkins."

"Alright, Madeline. But don't get me wrong when I say the document is straightforward. If we can prove your version of what this photo represents, then our job is also pretty much by the book—we move to have the prenup dissolved on the grounds that evidence was manufactured in order to claim you violated the infidelity clause. So, that leaves you with the burden of coming up with the proof that he somehow orchestrated all this in order to leave you without a cent."

"I've hired my own investigator, and he's working on it as we speak," she replied hopefully.

"Good." Barry swiveled in his chair as his lawyerly mind connected the inevitable dots. "You know, if you can prove your claim, you're looking at a lot more than just getting what by law is owed to you," he said, leaning forward, visions of protracted legal battles stretching across his mind's eye.

"For starters, you'll be a very sympathetic party to this divorce. We can make a rock-solid case for mental cruelty, bodily and psychological harm. Plus, you can press a number of charges against him, including conspiracy to commit assault and battery, accomplice to the assault and battery, as well as soliciting for prostitution, if he did indeed hire someone to commit the sexual assault.

"Honestly, after what you've been put through, this guy would be extremely likely to spend time in jail. I don't know about you, but if anyone did to me what it appears your husband did to you, I would find that outcome *very* satisfying.

"And while we're at it, we can also file a civil lawsuit against your husband on the grounds of fraud, intentional infliction of emotional distress, civil assault and personal injury stemming from an intentional tort. We'll have him buried in suits and countersuits," Barry said, a grin of professional glee spreading across his face. Madeline's shell-shocked expression made the unseemly smile fade away.

"Can we really get him?" she asked, her voice sounding small and far away.

"Mrs.—Madeline, if your investigator can get concrete proof that he's behind these photos, the answer is yes." Madeline sat back, allowing herself to breathe as she took it all in. As if reading her mind, Barry added, "How confident are you with your P.I.?"

"I think he's good. He has excellent qualifications. He was with Special Forces in the military, and a detective with LAPD for ten years before going solo. So far, he seems sharp and competent."

"If you have any doubts, we have our own stable of investigators who are crackerjacks." Madeline realized she still had the legal pad in her lap. She handed it over for Barry's perusal. His head nodded slightly as he glanced over the figures.

"Am afraid I don't really know what kind of bank accounts we have except our checking account. I'm sure there are others. I don't know anything about his business aside from the fact that it's very profitable."

"Why don't you write down the name of the business and the address and I'll put my team to work on that. And then I guess we need to discuss my fee…"

Madeline looked up from the menu just in time to see Mike alight from an early model Mercedes convertible parked across the street from the restaurant. She had to smile in spite of her mood. She watched the breeze ruffle his shoulder-length, blond hair and Hawaiian shirt as he limberly dodged traffic. As he approached, his eyes scanned the windows, though she couldn't tell if he was looking for her or merely admiring his reflection. When he waved heartily, she figured it was the former, or possibly a combination of both.

"Even with all the hell you've been through, seeing your face still makes my heart stop," he said, bending to kiss the top of her head. The smell of ozone wafted off him as he brushed past and flopped down opposite her.

"Hello, Mike," she said, closing her menu to regard him. Though the years showed on his face, he still had the same irresistible, rakish good looks. His smile was contagious, and soon she was fighting to retain her composure. There was something about him that radiated disdain for morality and a perverse delight in all things forbidden. He reached across the table with his long arms and took her hands in his. She held his gaze for a moment, then gave his hands a squeeze and released them.

"I haven't ordered yet, but I need to. I'm starving and I don't have much time," she said, browsing the menu solely as a diversionary tactic.

"I was surprised you wanted to come here," Mike said, laying his menu aside. "I thought The Ivy or Fig & Olive were more your style these days."

"I'm in need of some comfort food. Besides, Montecito isn't exactly swimming in true delicatessens," Madeline said, smiling up at the waitress who was poised to take their order.

"What can I get you folks?"

"I'll have the Reuben with horseradish instead of the Russian dressing."

"Corned beef, pastrami, or turkey?"

"Corned beef."

"Potato salad, coleslaw, French fries or onion rings?"

"French fries."

"And you, sir?"

"I'll have exactly the same as her, and a side of onion rings," Mike said, handing the menus to her.

"Anything else to drink?" Madeline shook her head.

"I'll have a Coke," Mike said. The waitress nodded and was off. "So…how did it go with the attorney?"

Madeline took a sip of icy water, the glass slippery with condensation.

"Good, I think," she said, as she ineffectually wiped at the water drops on her pants.

"Yeah…? Can you stop Steven from divorcing you without a settlement?"

"If we can find proof he set me up."

"How hard is that going to be?" Madeline gazed out the window at the passing traffic.

"I don't know. That reminds me—I've got to call Burt before I head back."

"I wish you'd stay down here for a while. I've got plenty of room," Mike said, appraising her from his relaxed position. Madeline huffed curtly. "Hey, I'm not trying to put the moves on you," he said, leaning over the table, attempting to persuade her his motives were purely compassionate. "Giving you a safe place to lay low is the least I can do for you."

Madeline ran her hands through her hair as she leaned back and tried to pop her spine back into alignment. Mike's compliment aside, she felt much worse for wear. She felt as though she were in a strange movie where odd characters kept popping out of the shadows, saying things that made absolutely no sense.

On one hand, she kept thinking this was all a charade and that Steven would snap back to his old self and everything would be picture perfect, like it was before. Equally ludicrous was the haunting feeling she was guilty of cheating after all. She certainly felt guilty of something—guilty of being hopelessly stupid, guilty of looking past Steven's obvious personality defects, seeing only his glamorous lifestyle and all the luxury and security he could provide her.

Madeline smiled wanly at Mike as she linked her fingers in his. They sat there for a moment, not saying anything, just sending and receiving the comfort that came from having been through a lot with each other. Without warning, Madeline burst into tears. Alarmed by the sudden breakdown, Mike slipped in beside her, wrapping his arms around her as she shook, great sobs racking her whole body.

"What can I do to help?" Mike asked as Madeline sat back and dried her tears on her napkin. She laughed helplessly as she tried to blot the wet patches on Mike's shirt. Mike pulled her hand away and kissed it. A current passed through them, one that threw her further off kilter. She let go of his hand and began searching through her purse. She pulled out her compact and groaned at her reflection.

"Stop—you look ravishing." She laughed out loud at this.

"If you're buttering me up for a loan, I can't help you right now," she cracked, discreetly dabbing powder on her face.

"Ha, ha," Mike said, stung by the wisecrack. "I'll have you know I'm quite financially secure now, but thanks for your concern." Madeline gave him a sideways glance.

"Yeah?" Her eyes traveled out the window to the brown, two-door Mercedes with the top down, circa 1960, as if putting it and Mike together for the first time.

"It was my dad's. He left it to me, along with an apartment complex in West Hollywood. You should see it—old-time '40s glamor. It's priceless." Madeline stowed her compact, her eyes never leaving Mike's.

"I'm sorry. I didn't know he passed away," she said, laying her hand on his arm. Mike's features became pensive, but the mood passed quickly.

"Yeah, it's been a couple years now," he said, sitting up straighter as their food arrived. Madeline ate a fry while she waited for further disclosure.

"You got everything you need for now?" the waitress asked, her mind already on her next task.

"Yeah, we're good," Mike said, avoiding Madeline's inquiring gaze for as long as he could. "We came to terms with each other about a year after I sobered up. We were good together at the end. He had emphysema for five years, but I didn't even know about it until I finally got over myself and went to see him. There'd been a lot of bad blood between us, as you probably remember. But we both had been through enough bad times to know what mattered and what didn't. Anyway…"

"I'm glad you were able to get past your differences," Madeline said before she worked her teeth around the impossibly full sandwich.

"Yeah, it all worked out in the end. I took care of him for eighteen months, and now he's taken care of me. That man saved almost every nickel he ever made. Kind of made up for all my frivolousness. So, if *you're* in need of a loan, look no further." Madeline had to laugh. This was certainly a unique situation for them; it had always been the other way around, as far back as their college days.

"Thanks, but I'm not there yet. I do have to sell my car, though. That's something I'm not looking forward to. I need the money, but I just don't have the time to deal with it."

"I bet you're going to miss a ride like that. Where is it?" Mike asked, craning his neck to look out the window.

"It's parked two cars in front of yours." Mike leaned over the table to look up the street.

"*Sweet!* Hey, I've got an idea—let's trade."

"That's not really going to help me," Madeline said.

"What I meant is, you take my car back to Santa Barbara, and I'll get yours sold for you." Madeline stole one of his onion rings while she tried to figure out if he was joking. "It makes sense, if you think about it. I've got nothing but time on my hands, and this is a much better market for selling a vehicle like that." Madeline still wasn't convinced, nor was she sure she could really trust him with something as important as this.

"You can trust me," Mike said, reading her thoughts. "I'm a solid, sober dude now—no booze, no drugs, no money worries, no monkey business." Madeline took another bite as she weighed the pros and cons of his offer.

"Do you think you can get a good price for it?"

"I'll put it out there and see what kind of responses I get. We already know what the Kelley Blue Book is on it."

"How does it run?" Madeline asked of the Mercedes. She said this out of due diligence, but judging from the exterior, it had probably been babied the past fifty years.

"Like an elegant racehorse with nothing to prove." Madeline smirked at the analogy. If there was anyone who knew racehorses, it was him. "Hey, if it makes you feel any better, I checked out what the Benz would fetch—just out of curiosity—and it was significantly more than you could get for yours."

"Really?"

"About thirty-five grand more." Madeline took another look at Mike's eye-catching car.

"Are you sure you want to loan it to me?"

"Sure. I know where you live...actually, that's not true anymore. Where are you going to be living, now that Steven's given you the boot?" Madeline groaned and dropped what was left of her sandwich.

"Oh," she murmured, shaking her head in disbelief. She filled Mike in on Steven's rotten stunt that cost her the vacation rental.

"Unbelievable. That guy's a psycho. Forget the car trade—I'm going back with you."

"What? Why? No," Madeline said adamantly.

"Then you're not going back," Mike said, snagging the last onion ring as Madeline made a move for it.

"I have to go back, Mike. I've got to join the gym so I have an anonymous place to meet the private investigator. Plus, I've got a committee meeting at seven. Oh, God—I'm dreading that. And I've got to meet the movers at nine tomorrow morning to get all my stuff out of the house before Steven returns."

"I can't believe that monster is forcing you to move out."

"There's no way I could stay in the same house with him, not after all the crap he's pulled on me. He told me I could stay at the beach house until the divorce is final."

"That was big of him."

"But I'm not going to. My P.I. thinks it's probably bugged." Mike huffed. Madeline could feel his body tense beside her. She looked up at him and saw the muscles in his jaw quiver. In the old days, this was the only warning before he threw a fit of rage. She put her hand on his arm.

"It's okay, Mike," she said, trying to calm him.

"Bullshit!" he snapped. "Nothing about this situation is okay," he said. He wiped his mouth with the paper napkin and tossed it on his empty plate.

"I don't want you to get upset," she said.

"Too late for that," Mike replied. "Look, I'm not going to rip the table from the wall or anything like that," he said, modulating his tone for her sake. "But you can't expect me not to harbor thoughts of tearing that tight-assed sadist into little pieces."

"That makes two of us." Mike grunted and shook his head.

"Maddie, God knows I was no angel when we were together, but the number Steven's doing on you is beyond sadistic. It's criminal, probably on many levels."

"I know, I know…"

"Did your attorney talk about pressing charges against him?"

"Yes, but we have to prove he's behind the photos—and the drugging, and the…" Madeline let out a long, sad sigh. Mike gave her hand a squeeze. When she smiled to reassure him, she saw his eyes were blurry with tears. She held his hand tighter and turned toward the window. Seeing a meter maid pass in front of the restaurant made her aware that time was ticking away.

"I should get going," she said, reaching for her wallet. Mike gave her a stony look as he took a money clip from his pants pocket. Madeline had to laugh.

"Another part of your inheritance?" Mike proudly displayed the 14 karat gold dollar sign that held a fat wad of cash.

"Classic Milton Delaney," he said, taking a twenty and a ten out for the bill. "I'm telling you, the guy was stylin' all the way." They both laughed. The waitress laid a ticket on the table and cleared their plates. Mike took a quick look at it and laid the cash on top of it.

"So, what's the plan? Do you want me to try to sell your bitchin' wheels for you?" Madeline looked out the window as she followed Mike out of the booth.

"I guess that makes the most sense. Thanks for offering." He put his arm around her and led her out into the harsh afternoon glare.

EIGHTEEN

Madeline made it back to the fitness club ten minutes to four. Luckily for her, the traffic through L.A. hadn't been at a standstill yet. She grabbed the bag with her workout clothes and raced up the steps. She breathlessly told the young man at the counter she wanted to become a member. He looked up at the clock, excused himself and bounded down the hallway to a door marked Employees Only.

A couple of anxious minutes later, he emerged with a woman in her mid-thirties. Though she wasn't snarling, Madeline could tell she wasn't happy with the prospect of staying beyond her shift.

"Hi," Madeline said as the woman walked around to the back of the counter. "I know you leave at four, so I'll make this as easy as possible. I've already had the tour and I know what kind of membership I want."

"Fantastic," the woman said, her mood brightening as she slid an application across the counter. "All I need is for you to fill this out, and then I'll need to photocopy a picture I.D. and a credit card to keep on file. You can pay your monthly dues by check or credit card, but we need to open a house account for incidentals."

"That's fine," Madeline replied as she filled out the form. She went ahead and used the Park Lane address so there wouldn't be any discrepancy with the driver's license. The last thing she wanted to do was explain her twisted state of affairs. Because no charges would be put through, she gave her the "hot" Visa card to match her other ID. She'd give them a new card number and address later. It hit her how dubious her once upstanding life had now become.

As Madeline was waiting for the woman to return from the back room, she glanced around the club. It was much quieter than it had been in the morning, as Burt said it would be. She was putting her cards back in her wallet when the front door opened, letting in a gust of cool air.

At first Madeline couldn't tell that the man entering—backlit as he was by the low-slung sun—was the man she had arranged to meet. For one thing, his hair was dark brown, as opposed to Burt's black turned mostly grey. Dark sunglasses obscured his eyes. But when he took them off and winked at her, she realized it was him, incognito. She clamped her lips together to keep from laughing as the wig-topped P.I. passed behind her and down the ramp toward the locker rooms.

When Madeline entered the gym, there was only one other person using the equipment besides Burt. By the layout and the direction the woman was moving, she figured they'd be alone in the room before too long. Burt looked at Madeline casually as she walked to the first machine in the rotation and went about adjusting the weights down from where Burt—who appeared much more fit in tank top and shorts—had them.

As soon as the woman left the room, Burt got up from the weightlifting bench and sauntered over to Madeline with the pretense of showing her the proper technique for doing the lat pulldown bar.

"How's it going?" he asked.

"Okay, I guess. I think I found the right attorney."

"That's good."

"How are things going with you?" Out of habit, Burt surveyed the room before replying.

"Good. I now know where your husband is staying in Boston." Madeline eased the weights down and let go of the bar. "My source was able to trace him to the limousine service he used from the airport. He was dropped off at a house in Beacon Hill, 141 Chestnut Street. A title search of the property shows it's owned by Elizabeth Collins-Wainwright. Ring any bells?"

"No," Madeline said, a sudden weak and dizzy sensation coming over her.

"I did a search online and found quite a bit of info. Her name and picture came up in connection with many social events, as well as the gossip columns. It seems her real claim to fame came with her marriage to husband number two—Logan Wainwright III. The Wainwrights are an old Boston family going way back. They were married just shy of three years. She received an undisclosed settlement, but everyone my contact spoke to said it had to be in the eight figures. Just before I left the office, my source emailed me photos of Mrs. Collins-Wainwright and your husband leaving the Chestnut Street house."

Madeline listened to this report with a look of astonishment on her face. Inside, her mind was suffering a series of mild shockwaves, making her feel as though she was bouncing through space. After all she had been put through in the last week, she would've thought it impossible to be surprised by anything Steven did. His latest act of treachery hurt her in a way she didn't think was possible at this stage. But the thought of Steven with another woman made her feel completely wretched—unloved, discarded and replaced.

How bloody convenient for him, she thought bitterly, tears stinging her eyes. But she was too angry to cry. What she wanted to do was scream at the top of her lungs and slug something or someone very hard.

Two men entered the gym, forcing Madeline and Burt to relocate separately. Madeline found a new machine and was taking her aggressions out on it in the most punishing way. As the newcomers struck up a conversation, Burt decided it was safe enough to talk to Madeline without being overheard.

"I'm sorry about dropping that bomb on you. It's never easy to tell someone they've got a cheating spouse, even in a situation like this." Madeline acknowledged his apology with a slight nod. She executed a few more leg lifts, then gave up, letting the weights clank loudly as they hit the stack. She slid off the machine on wobbly legs and cracked open a bottle of water. She observed Burt out of the corner of her eye while she drank.

"Even though finding out he deceived you doesn't constitute proof that he set you up at The Edgecliff, it does give us some clues to work with," Burt continued, undeterred by his client's reaction to his report.

"What kind of clues?" she asked. The only clue she'd gotten was how deaf, dumb and blind she'd been where her husband was concerned.

"I don't think it's a coincidence that he 'received' incriminating pictures of you the same week he lies about having a business meeting in Dallas. I think he orchestrated every detail of this scenario. The only question in my mind is why did he decide he no longer wanted to be married to you?"

As the two men had advanced their way through the various exercise machines and were now within hearing range, Burt led Madeline over to the far side of the room, where there were padded mats for floor exercises.

"I'll show you a good exercise for your abs," Burt said, motioning for Madeline to lie down on the mat next to him. "Now, if a man has a beautiful, charming wife who is not only a good companion but a business asset as well, what reason would he have for suddenly wanting to be rid of her?" Burt posed hypothetically. "It really comes down to three things—sex, money and children." Madeline stopped mimicking his movements and sat up.

"I think I hit a nerve," Burt surmised between crunches. Madeline glanced around the room, the muscles along her jaw and neck tightening as she wrestled with some unseen demon.

"We've been 'officially' trying to get pregnant for three years," she finally admitted. Burt sat up, giving her his full attention. "We tried in-vitro four times. I actually carried a pregnancy halfway through the second trimester, but lost it." Burt let his head drop. Madeline could tell, despite his line of work, that Burt didn't relish learning all the gritty details of a failed marriage.

"Did you officially stop trying?" he asked after a respectful pause. Madeline shook her head.

"No. I've been chasing one weird treatment after another. So far, nothing has worked."

"Who was more anxious to have children, you or Steven?" Madeline arched her brows as she considered this.

"I always thought of it as a mutual quest," she said, looking inward. "But thinking back, having an heir has always been something Steven thought a great deal about. When I failed to become pregnant by the time I was thirty-seven, we started seeing fertility specialists."

"So, would you say that not having children with you would be reason enough for Steven to start looking elsewhere?"

Madeline let out a heavy sigh—part contemptuous, part bemused. "You might be asking the wrong person. Apparently I don't really know much about the man I married." Madeline took stock of the growing crowd. Burt was on the same wavelength. He helped her to her feet.

"Time for a change of venue," he said, looking at his watch. "I think this would be a perfect time to take a stroll on the Douglas Preserve. You know how to get there?" Madeline nodded. "Let's meet there in fifteen minutes. Park by the main entrance. I'll meet you as you come into the park."

NINETEEN

The sun was just setting as Madeline pulled into the Douglas Family Preserve parking lot. She was grateful Mike had put the top up on the Mercedes, as the late afternoon air had lost all its warmth. The park was mostly in shade, except for the slanted rays emanating from the horizon. Madeline pulled her sweater tightly around her as she walked straight into the breeze coming off the ocean.

Burt came out of the shadows as she hit the walking path. They walked without speaking for a couple of minutes, as walkers and dogs found their way out of the park. Closing time was near and soon they were the only ones heading the wrong direction.

"It's going to be a spectacular sunset," Burt said, as he canvassed the area. Madeline shivered as the wind blew her hair in several directions at once. Burt walked her to the cliff's edge to watch the evening's vibrant display of color against the darkening sky, then took pity on her and led her back in the direction of the exit. They found a bench shielded by a stand of trees and took a seat.

"I spent some time at The Edgecliff today," he said. "I showed the front desk staff photos of Steven and Russell Barnett, and gave a description of the mystery man, but nobody remembered any of them checking in last week. I don't suppose you can remember the room number you were in?"

Madeline thought back to the horrible morning when she had awoken completely disoriented. She remembered looking at the phone—that's how she figured out where she was. The number would've been on the front of it. *If only I'd thought to look…*

"No," she said. "I left through the French doors."

"Do you think you'd remember what area you were in? If we went back there, do you think you could recall which path you took?"

"Possibly." Madeline shivered harder at the thought of reenacting her getaway from the scene of the crime. *If only I'd known it was a crime scene then...*

"We'll try that then. We'll go back this evening when it's dark." Madeline nodded woodenly.

"Anyway, I got them to check the reservation log and neither Steven's nor Barnett's name showed up. No big surprise there. I imagine Steven's managed to keep several degrees of separation between himself and everyone he's used to frame you. I'll go back there later when the shifts change and see if I have any better luck. I wish I could have access to the entire reservation log. If we can get *something* we can take to the police, their detectives will have complete access to that and the surveillance cameras. Those things would give us what we're looking for."

Madeline took this news in only superficially. Her mind was still preoccupied with thoughts of Steven and the woman in Boston. It was like another character had joined the macabre performance that waltzed through her head on a continuous loop. She felt as though she was suffering a mental breakdown. This was lasting way too long to be a nightmare. Perhaps her mind had slipped a cog and she was now drifting into insanity.

"I'm sorry... What were you saying?" Burt looked at her features in the fading light.

"I said, maybe it's time to turn this matter over to the police."

"What? *Why?*" she asked, alarmed.

"Because a crime was committed against you, Madeline—several, in fact." Her eyes welled up again, an occurrence that was becoming all too common. Burt put his arm around her tentatively. That simple act, coupled with his last words, caused the dam to burst again.

"I'm sorry," she said, pulling away from him, ashamed of her breakdown. *I really am ready for the rubber room,* she thought, disgusted with herself. "Are you quitting?" she asked, her voice raspy with fear and embarrassment. Burt coughed lightly.

"No, I'm not quitting. But I do think you should get some counseling." Madeline looked at him aghast. She was losing her mind, and everyone could see it. Burt almost laughed at her distress.

"Madeline," he said, taking her hand in his, "don't get me wrong. I don't think you're crazy. And I'm not going to abandon you. I feel a personal need to get satisfaction in this case. But you've been dealt more crap in the last week than most people see in a year. You need to talk to someone—an experienced grief counselor." Madeline sniffed and looked him in the eye.

"It's not that I don't think you're handling things. You're holding up amazingly well. But you've been severely traumatized, over and over." He held his tongue for moment while Madeline absorbed what he was saying. "You need to talk to someone who can take you through the process of acceptance and healing."

"I've got my friend, Mike—and I've got you," she said. "At least I have two people who know the truth and believe me."

"There's no question of that—not anymore." This remark struck Madeline as odd.

"You didn't believe me when I came to see you...what day was that... yesterday? God, I can't believe that was less than 36 hours ago..." she removed her hand from his.

"It's not that I didn't believe you then," Burt said. "I don't make judgments about my clients. In my line of work, I have to stay open to every fact that comes my way. *You* probably never considered this, but not only innocent people employ private investigators. Take your husband, for instance."

"So, you were going through the motions, regardless of whether I was telling the truth or not?" she asked, her tone hard and aggrieved.

"Yes. I'm doing my job, the job you hired me to do. But in your case, I know on whose side the truth lies." Madeline regarded him, trying to gauge his sincerity.

"How do you know?" she asked. Burt stood and held out his hand to help her up.

"The park's about to close," he said. They walked in silence a short distance before Burt spoke again. "I've become pretty good at assessing people, regardless of what I told you earlier. But like I said, I postpone judgment until it's all said and done. There have been several cases where—if I hadn't held to my credo of not mentally assigning guilt or innocence—I would've been completely duped.

"But I don't believe that anyone who erroneously claims to have been forcibly raped while drugged—and has photos to prove it—would shed a tear upon learning her husband was cheating on her. If you were trying to frame your husband, and not the other way around, that news would not come as a surprise to you. You would've been looking for a way to get even with him for hurting you, and this would all be more ammo to use against him in court. Then it would be up to the judge to sort out who was the bigger louse. But I think you've been completely broadsided by what's happened to you."

"So, you know I'm telling the truth," Madeline said, testing the words out loud.

"Yes. And I'm breaking my personal code by telling you that," Burt said, shepherding her out of the park.

"I really appreciate hearing that, Burt," she said as he walked her to the only other car in the parking lot besides his. "It means more to me than you can imagine."

"Where'd you get the car?" Burt asked, admiring Mike's babe magnet.

"How did you know it wasn't mine?" she asked.

"I checked for all the vehicles registered to you, Steven and his company. This one didn't show up on any of my searches." Madeline was slightly taken aback by this news. When she went seeking a private investigator, it didn't occur to her *she'd* be investigated. Burt read her discomfort.

"When I take on an assignment, the first thing I do is run searches on all the public databases I have access to. Like I said earlier, I have had clients who've hired me for less than honorable reasons. Compiling every verifiable fact I can get my hands on is standard operating procedure for me. Think of it as wanting to have all the jigsaw pieces before trying to put the puzzle together." Madeline had to admit that a proactive detective had to be a plus as far as she was concerned.

"Everything I unearth will remain strictly confidential, unless I'm subpoenaed to give evidence in court," he added. "By the way, have you gotten a copy of the guest and donor lists yet?"

"I should be getting them at the meeting tonight."

"Sorry, I don't mean to push."

"Well, I'd rather have a too-thorough P.I. than a lazy one. You and the attorney are the only weapons I've got right now," Madeline replied as she held out her hand. Burt took it solemnly.

"We will nail this bastard. It might take a little longer than we'd like, but we will get him. Call me later and we'll set up a time to meet at The Edgecliff."

TWENTY

"So…even though it feels like we just finished the annual fundraising, it's already time to start planning next year's event," Arielle Liscombe said, eliciting resigned groans from some of the board members. "What's that saying about resting on our laurels?" Arielle asked, her picture-perfect smile belying the fact that hard work never bothered her, as long as someone else was doing it.

"Don't worry, Arielle—I'm still fired up from last weekend!" Carla Dickens said with a high cackle of enthusiasm. Madeline rubbed the sore spot between her eyes, wishing she were anywhere but there.

"Fabulous. That's just what I want to hear," Arielle said.

"My mind's been in overdrive since the event," Carla continued. "I thought everything came off splendidly, and of course, the amount we raised was frankly beyond our expectations. But as I said, I've been coming up with all these other ideas that would just add to the sizzle—"

"I'd love to hear your ideas, Carla, as I'm sure all of us would, but right now we need to focus on the agenda," Arielle said, clearly wresting control of the meeting out of Carla's all too eager hands. Carla's face froze, leaving her with an expression that was startled, euphoric and baffled all at once. "We must first discuss the benefactors' thank-you dinner, which I think should be held at the San Ysidro Ranch. All in favor of this, raise your hands…"

Madeline sat through the interminable meeting comprehending little of what was said. Other than the occasional kicks and aggrieved looks from Carla, Madeline was only cognizant of her own personal drama. Several times she had to restrain herself from getting up and walking out the door, away from the veiled bickering and the tedious urgency of issues that didn't mean a thing to her anymore.

Every now and then she was hit with the fact that her days in this rarified environment were surely numbered. The glowing looks of admiration she received whenever she dared to raise her eyes from the printed agenda nauseated her. She was tortured with glimpses into the near future when news of her upcoming divorce from Steven would be wagging every tongue in town.

The way everyone praised her tireless efforts and the roaring success of the benefit made her feel that much worse. She doubted anyone in the room would be caught in her company once Steven's version of their breakup hit the airwaves. Though she couldn't bear to think of it, Steven's new propensity for meanness almost assured that those disgusting photos of her with the stranger would make their way around town, if not the entire world.

"Are you alright?" Carla whispered, snapping Madeline out of her dismal reverie.

"Yeah," Madeline replied, straightening up in the chair, trying to look cheerful and alert, but not pulling it off very well.

"It's probably exhaustion," Carla said, hand to her mouth in an attempt at discretion.

"Was there something you wanted to add, Carla?" Arielle asked, interrupting herself with feigned solicitude.

"Oh, no," Carla said, tight smile on her face. As soon as Arielle had the floor to herself again, Carla murmured "bitch" out the side of her mouth. For some reason—probably because it was the most lighthearted moment of her day—Madeline burst into a fit of giggles which she covered with a coughing attack. Grateful for the excuse, Madeline left the room in search of water.

"I don't care if her husband is our biggest benefactor—I think this organization needs a good shuffling," Carla said as she sidled up next to Madeline at the refreshment table. If Carla thought this sentiment was a news flash, she was only kidding herself. Madeline was sure Carla dreamed of the day when her name came up first on the local NHDF board of directors' masthead. "Are you sure you're okay? You don't really seem yourself." Madeline took a deep breath and let it wheeze out of her.

"I don't know—maybe I'm coming down with something," she replied, hoping that would scare Carla away. "I really miss Lauren," she added, with such weariness Carla laughed sympathetically.

"I told you you'd regret giving her a whole week off," she bragged. Madeline huffed. "You know, you're just feeling the anticlimax of the benefit. I'm sure that's it."

"You think so?" Madeline asked, though she wasn't the least bit interested in Carla's theories. In fact, she had absolutely no interest in a thing anyone in the building had to say. She was only there on Burt's insistence that she mingle with her peers while she still could. This might be the last chance she had to find out about her behavior Saturday night. But all she could think about was drowning her sorrows—and maybe herself—in a hot bubble bath.

"Honey, think about it…you put a *year* into the planning of Saturday's ball, and *pouf!* it's over in a flash, and now we're starting over at square one like it never happened." *I wish it never happened,* Madeline thought morosely. "Really, it's no different than a wedding—except there was no honeymoon!" Carla brayed at her witticism.

"But if it's any consolation, you couldn't have been more radiant if it were your wedding." Carla stopped her prattle long enough to regard Madeline fondly. "You really were something that night," she said with a chuckle, shaking her head.

"What are you talking about?" Madeline asked, mortified by her tone and the suggestive leer on her face.

"I'm talking about your Las Vegas nightclub persona." Madeline's ears started to buzz and her face turned red. Carla took this as a sign of Madeline's normally self-effacing manner being forced to reconcile with her more outlandish, usually dormant self.

"Why do you think the bidding became so frenzied? It was all you, girl. I wish I could take credit for it. Had I known what a ham you could be, I would've never gotten up there with you. What are you looking for?" Carla asked as she watched her co-chair dig through her handbag.

"Did I seem drunk?" Madeline asked, pretending not to care. Carla waffled her hand non-committedly.

"No, I wouldn't say *drunk*. Just relaxed…you know, self-assured. I'd say you had a light buzz on. But nothing like Natalie! *She* was in a world of hurt the next day, let me tell you. *Were* you drunk?" she asked belatedly.

"I don't know. No, not drunk…just a little intimidated at being up there." Carla laughed loudly, a jarring sound to Madeline's ears.

"If that's the case, you sure hid it well. Did you lose your keys?" she asked. The way Madeline continued to scrounge through her tote was starting to get on her nerves.

"I'm trying to find some ibuprofen." Madeline's search was made all the more difficult due to the large manila envelope she was too paranoid to leave unattended.

"Got a headache? Here, let me hold that envelope for you." Madeline grabbed it just as Carla tried to snatch it out of her way.

"I just remembered I'm out of them," she said as she hastily stuffed the pornographic bombshell back in her bag and zipped it closed.

"I've got some. Let me get my bag. Oh, that reminds me—did you get those lists I sent you?" Madeline stared at her uncomprehendingly. "The guest list and the donor list," Carla prompted her.

"Oh…ah…I'm sure I did. Sorry, with Lauren being gone and losing my cell phone, I just feel completely discombobulated."

"How'd you lose your phone?" Carla cried out in sympathy. Madeline shrugged. "I'm sure it'll turn up," Carla said, patting Madeline affectionately on the arm as she went back into the conference room to get her purse.

Madeline had to smile at the image of her iPhone resting at the bottom of the toilet tank in her bathroom. She wondered idly if Steven's goons could still track it from its watery grave as she seized the opportunity and disappeared through the front door before anyone else could waylay her.

TWENTY-ONE

Madeline stood on the curb across the street from The Edgecliff, waiting for her rendezvous with Burt Latham. Merely being so close to where her life began its unraveling made her feel tense and vulnerable.

"Where the hell are you, Burt?" she muttered under her breath while debating whether she should get back in the car or stand out there feeling conspicuous. *I'll give him two more minutes,* she vowed as she tried to read her watch in the dim light radiating from a street lamp.

"I'm right behind you," Burt said.

Madeline turned and saw his silver hair glimmering in the light. The tank top, shorts and wig he'd been wearing earlier had been replaced with a dark suit, open-collar dress shirt and his attractively greying hair. The transformation took Madeline by surprise. He motioned for her to follow him. She hesitated only slightly before falling into step with him.

"You think you were in one of the cottages," he said, seeking confirmation as he led her down the pathway that wound through the high foliage into the maze of cottages, each containing four separate rooms. Madeline nodded. She was trying to remain calm, but the physical memory of her early morning departure made her pulse race. She stopped suddenly, grabbing onto Burt's arm for support.

"What is it?" he asked.

"I don't think I can do this," she said, trembling.

"Okay, that's fine. We'll turn around and get you out of here," Burt said soothingly. Madeline held onto his arm until they were back on the sidewalk by her borrowed car.

"Are you okay?" he asked. Madeline nodded hesitantly.

"I'm sorry," she said.

"Don't be. I'll have another crack at the front desk staff. I'll see if I can find out who booked rooms in this section that night and take it from there." Burt looked back in the direction they had just come from. "Did you get the sense we were close to where you exited Sunday morning?"

Madeline turned slowly to face the path, her mind retracing their steps. It seemed a shorter distance this time than it did the first, but she didn't feel confident in her recollection. Fear had warped both escapes.

"I think it was further in," she said. *Had there been another turn in the walkway?* She shook her head apologetically.

"It's no problem. Would it help to refresh your memory if we went inside the public rooms, retrace some of your steps that evening?" The suggestion sent her into a panic.

"No, no—I can't do that!" she said under her breath as a couple passed them on the sidewalk. "Everyone in there knows who I am."

"Alright. Time to get you back to your hotel," Burt said, gently escorting her to the driver's side of the Mercedes. "Are you okay to drive? Do you want me to follow you back?"

"I'm fine," she said, breathing hard with relief. "Would you mind sitting with me for a minute, let me get my bearings back?"

"Not at all." Burt took the key from her hand and unlocked her side, holding the door open while she seated herself. He went around the front of the car where she could see him and unlocked the passenger's door. He ducked in and placed the key in the ignition

"How are you feeling?"

"Better. Sorry I couldn't be more useful." Burt held up his hand to stop her. "It's been a really long day," she said, becoming more fatigued as she recalled just how long and emotionally charged it had been.

"It's been a really long week," Burt corrected her. She laughed half-heartedly. They sat in silence for a few more minutes. The only sounds they could hear were the crashing of the waves and the occasional passing car. Burt recognized her fragile state of mind and didn't want to leave until she had time to recover.

"You must have a very strong stomach," Madeline said, breaking the soothing silence.

"What do you mean?"

"I don't think I could stand to dredge through the sordid details of other people's lives. I'm having trouble just dealing with my own." Burt chuckled.

"To me, it's a matter of sifting through the garbage to find the truth."

"Is there such a thing as the truth in situations like this?"

"Yeah. It's not always easy to find. There are usually several variations of the truth, but there's always at least one solid fact at the center of every conflict. I guess I've always thrived on getting to the core of the matter, righting a wrong, helping people get out of jams." Burt shrugged. "Just my calling to be nosey, I guess." Madeline thought this over for a moment.

"What about the 'ick' factor? Don't you ever get sick of humanity?" Burt favored her with a lopsided smirk.

"I make sure I take a long, hot shower at the end of every day," he said. This made Madeline smile.

"Speaking of which," she said, pushing the key into the ignition, "I think I'm going to need to bathe twice tonight."

"I better get back to work. I'll check in with you tomorrow, let you know what I've found out."

"Thanks, Burt," Madeline said.

"Get some sleep," he said, then stepped out and closed the door. He waited until the Mercedes receded from view, then headed for the lobby, taking the long way through the grounds, retracing their steps. He played back the conversation they had at the Douglas Preserve in his head, wondering if he'd jinxed his luck by confiding in a client. *I better not be slipping*, he thought. There was no room in his line of work for mistakes.

Madeline lay on the bed, staring at the ceiling, trying to assimilate everything that had happened since morning. She was dead tired and having difficulty remembering all the encounters she'd had. Hopscotching around wasn't helping matters. She forced herself to start at the beginning of the day—a day so long and disturbing, she felt like she'd aged two years.

"Okay, disaster number one—the credit card debacle. Disaster number two—Steven freezing our bank accounts. Disaster number three—the missing jewelry." This last offence got Madeline off the bed and pacing. There were too many injustices to take lying down.

"Number four—Elizabeth Collins-Wainwright. Oh that miserable, lying, ruthless bastard!" She fairly bristled with anger as she raided the freshly stocked minibar. This time she couldn't be bothered with ice. She drank the double in straight gulps and braced herself for the one-two punch of the burning gullet and the onset of pleasant numbness.

Every bit of this nightmare was perfectly calculated. God knows how long he's been romancing Elizabeth Whatever-the-hell. He's probably got it worked out that he'll move her in right after he's got me moved out. This last thought ignited a flame of defiance. "Maybe I just won't move out. Maybe I'll continue to play the repentant, confused dope, hanging onto hope and my undying love for that scum-sucking monster."

Madeline flopped onto the sofa. No, the mere thought of actually having to look at him again was enough to veto that plan. She had her attorney now; they'd wait for the first volley and respond in kind, plus start hitting him up for financial support while they haggled over the details of the divorce. But hopefully that wouldn't last long; hopefully Burt would have something concrete to tie Steven to the frame-up. Then the tables would be turned. She had a pleasing visual of Steven being hauled away in handcuffs as she slammed the front door of *her* house.

That gleeful apparition disappeared as soon as reality reared its ugly head. She was so far from untangling the ropes Steven had hogtied her in, she had no time to indulge in fantasies. She had to keep her guard up and stay proactive. She sighed and scraped at the cold, hardened cheese left over from the enchiladas she'd picked up on the way back to solitary confinement.

As she ticked off tomorrow's must-do's, she absentmindedly polished off the leftover tortilla chips and salsa. She grabbed a beer out of the minibar, enjoying the whooshing sound as she pulled the tab back. She tilted her head and drank straight from the can, something she hadn't done since her college days.

The beer and the carb-overload definitely buoyed her spirits. She found the notepad and began to diagram her strategy for the following day. It was going to be relatively easy compared to the previous day. But just thinking about saying goodbye to her house and Erma and Hughes made her anxious. She got off the sofa and perused the hotel snacks.

She gave into her sudden craving for sweets and ripped off the wrapper of a dark chocolate bar. It tasted impossibly good. She hadn't allowed herself to eat anything like that in years—none of it. She pulled up her sweater and eyed her full belly with defiant detachment. *Good thing I joined a gym,* she thought as she dropped the wrapper in the pile with all the other trash.

Feeling satiated, she ran the bath water, stripped out of her clothes and brushed her teeth. While she washed her face, a fresh wave of depression broke against her false sense of serenity. She sank to the edge of the tub and gave herself over to tears of self-pity.

"This can't be happening," she lamented. "This simply can't be happening." She turned off the water and lowered herself into the bathtub, all effort to stem the tide of tears abandoned. She cried until she could barely see out of her swollen eyes, then cried some more. Every time she thought there was nothing left to mourn, she'd find a fresh wound to pick at.

"What did I do wrong?" she wailed. She beat her hands against the now tepid water, sending sprays all over the floor. "What in the hell did I do wrong?"

As she wallowed in all her grievances, she realized she was finally cried out. There was no use railing against fate; her enemy was her husband, for whatever reason. Now that she had calmed herself, she reviewed what Burt said to her at the fitness center. It gave her a sharp pang to think all this evilness stemmed from not providing Steven with an heir.

If only I hadn't lost the baby, she thought. But it chilled her more to imagine having given Steven a child and then suffering the same kind of rejection. And what sort of father would he have been? She splashed cold water on her face and climbed out of the tub, mortified by the thought of his demonic need for control. *Why didn't I notice it before?*

As she wrapped the bathrobe around herself, she had to acknowledge that she was not blameless; she had been looking for a man of wealth and privilege to sweep her off her feet, and she hadn't once scratched his immaculate facade in search of his soul. She tossed the evidence of her despair-induced gluttony in the wastebasket, turned out the lights and crawled under the sheets. She was safe for the time being, but she needed to be on top of her game if she was going to make it out of this marriage with her sanity intact.

TWENTY-TWO

It was still dark out when Madeline pulled on a sweatshirt and primed herself for an early morning run. There was no sign of life in the lobby as she pushed out the front door. She could see the first rays of light coloring the clouds over the ocean as she turned left and headed for the Mission.

The number of cars and service vehicles on the road increased as the sun established itself over the horizon. She turned in front of the Mission and ran past the rose garden and up the incline of Alameda Padre Serra. When she reached Jimeno Road, she headed back down into the city. Her descent rewarded her with a spectacular view of Santa Barbara, the harbor and the Channel Islands.

The day was officially underway by the time she got back to her hotel. Even though it was Saturday, people were out—many of them carrying empty bags as they flocked to the Farmers Market. Madeline quickly showered and dressed. She grabbed a blueberry muffin and an apple in the lounge off the lobby before heading to the car. Her mind was focused, as if this day were no different than any other day in her busy life. She had a schedule to keep; it was all about getting the job done. Emotions were not going to get in her way anymore. She was through with self-pity, at least for the time being.

The first stop was Verizon to report her phone stolen and purchase a new one under her maiden name and her own SSN. She beat the rush and was out of the store in thirty minutes, new iPhone in hand, with all her data restored and a new phone number.

She was exhilarated at having possession of her favorite tool again with the added bonus of anonymity. Her old phone number had disappeared and not a soul had her new one. She felt sly and in charge, like her old, efficient, no-nonsense self. So far, this day was off to a good start.

Despite her early start, the movers were already there, lounging against their truck, Hughes standing a wary vigil over them. They jumped to attention when she pulled up the driveway and quickly got to work. True to their word, Erma and Hughes had all the contents of her dressing room packed in wardrobe boxes. They were loaded in forty minutes.

There was a minor snag when the driver wanted to confirm the destination. Madeline had forgotten to arrange for them to store her things until she had a place to live. Their orders were to deliver everything to the Yanonali Street address. After a few anxious minutes, everything was straightened out. Madeline had them wait while she made one more walk-through.

She took stock of her sitting room, picking up odds and ends to be boxed and stored along with the rest. But the task made the reality of what she was doing all too final. She looked around, taking in all the cherished, familiar sights. She looked at the objects in her hands—a hand-blown Murano glass vase from a trip to Italy and a photo of her and her girlfriends in Paris—and laid them back down on the desk.

There was no way that siphoning off a few mementos was going to keep her tethered to the life she was being forced to give up. If her clothing and accessories hadn't been packed and carted off for her, she doubted she'd have the heart to do it herself. What was the point, anyway? She had no place to take them yet. The beach house wasn't an option; if Burt was right, then she'd be monitored like a zoo exhibit. Without looking at anything else, she walked straight through her bedroom and foyer and out into the bright February sunlight.

Now that she had dealt with all the imperatives of the morning, she had time to chart her next course of action. Sitting outside a coffee house on State Street with a latte in front of her, she started a new list.

Topping the list was *Housing,* followed by *Money* and *Assistant.* The assistant she had, but because of lack of money and a place for her to work, her assistant, Lauren, would have to go. This fact niggled at her almost as much as her own dire situation. But the truth was, she didn't have anything for her to do, except for answering emails from people who were destined to snub her once word of the Ridley divorce got out. So, where did that leave her?

Madeline watched the parade of Saturday morning foot traffic, in all its dubious splendor. Downtown wasn't what it was when she moved to Santa Barbara, but neither was the rest of the world. *If I had any sense, I'd be checking out other cities,* she thought as she finished the dregs of her coffee.

But she didn't want to leave Santa Barbara. She loved it. She didn't have to be married to Steven Ridley to enjoy the city. She could create another identity for herself and disappear into the woodwork. Once she was out of the Montecito social scene, she could do anything she liked; no one would care anymore. The titillation over the circumstances of their breakup would be forgotten when a fresh scandal took its place.

Having been so busy dodging Steven's land mines, there was another possibility she hadn't really considered: if she had any luck at all, she could be holding the winning hand. There was the distinct possibility—from what Burt and the attorney had told her—that Steven could end up being the one out on the street.

It was nice to fantasize about counter-suing him and having his unscrupulous ass thrown in prison, but the likelihood of Steven having overlooked any possible obstacle to the furtherance of his master plan seemed pretty doubtful. It was better to stay focused on her immediate needs and let the professionals go after Steven Ridley with everything they had.

Though the last thing she should be doing was shopping, it was the only thing that appealed to her at the moment. She left the coffee house and walked up State Street to Saks where she could bask in the glow of recognition while she still had her good name. As soon as she entered the store, she let everything slip from her mind. She was going to shop—browse, at any rate—and only buy anything that she absolutely couldn't live without.

After a pleasant stroll around the handbag and shoe departments, she stopped at one of the cosmetic counters as she toyed with the idea of picking up some ultra-expensive eye cream to undo the damage from all the tears she had shed. As she waited patiently for the sales associate to finish up with another customer, an attractive young woman caught her eye.

"Madeline?" the young woman asked with a bright, hesitant smile. Madeline turned toward the woman, racking her brain for a name to go with the face. "You are Madeline Ridley, aren't you?" the twenty-something asked awkwardly.

"Yes," Madeline said, smiling cordially, hoping the woman would save her the embarrassment and divulge her own name. Instead, she reached into her satchel and produced a fat envelope.

"You've just been served. Have a nice day."

"I can't believe this," Madeline cried into the phone. "He must have someone following me again." She had called Burt as soon as she was safely back in Mike's car. She had taken a circuitous route, doubling back and meandering all through Nordstrom and hiding out in the ladies' room a couple times to make things more difficult for whoever was trailing her.

"I take it you haven't made your tail yet." Madeline looked in all three mirrors before answering.

"No. I don't know who it is." She was almost too mad to talk. She had a fury building inside her and she was afraid she might bite someone's head off.

"Steven's obviously planning his punches for full effect," Burt said. "If you can keep your objective clear in your head, then his pranks won't be as effective."

"*Pranks?*" Madeline replied acidly. She clamped her hand to her forehead to steady herself. "I didn't mean to snap at you."

"It's alright. I usually waive the verbal abuse charge for the first two offenses." This made Madeline laugh. "That's better. Just remember you've got a team behind you. And right now, I think you need to make contact with your attorney."

"You're right. I know." She sighed deeply as she searched for Barry Houstein's business card. "And of course he does this on a Saturday. I'm sure I won't get a call back until Monday, if I'm lucky."

"Try emailing him, too. Everybody's glued to their smartphones these days. Who knows? Maybe he'll feel like racking up some billable hours on the weekend. All you can do is try. Unfortunately, I didn't have any better luck last night after you left. But I am pursuing other avenues that might be just as effective in thwarting Steven's plans." Now Burt had Madeline's full attention.

"Such as?"

"I don't want to go into it over the phone, but I'm working every angle. The more ammo we have, the less power he'll have to torment you and strip you of your rights. If my hunch pans out, he could be taken out of the equation altogether." These words struck her as being rather sinister, though she couldn't understand why she should care.

"How do you mean?" she asked.

"Let's just say that when a person goes on a rampage for no apparent reason, it usually means they've lost control somewhere along the line." Madeline was still mystified but intrigued. "I think I've found his weak link, or more specifically, his motivating factor."

"Great! I can't wait to hear more," she said, already feeling much steadier. "When can we meet?"

"Give me a call after you've made contact with your attorney. I'd like to hear what his tactics are going to be. If you don't hear back from me, give me a ring around three and we'll make a plan."

"Okay, I'll let you know what happens."

"Are you okay with staying at the hotel?"

"I guess so. I don't really have any other options."

"Keep your eyes peeled. And drive around the block a couple times before you go back to your room. Just to be safe. Call me if anything else happens." Madeline stared at her cell phone as the call ended. What else could possibly go wrong?

TWENTY-THREE

Feeling defeated and lacking anything better to do with her time, Madeline began the arduous task of going through several days' worth of emails. The main purpose of this exercise was to find the email from Carla containing the attendees and donors lists. Sifting through dozens of emails was drudgery enough, and she didn't relish scanning hundreds of names in hopes of finding an unfamiliar, possibly Italian-sounding name.

After deleting and scanning through a plethora of emails, she finally unearthed the one she was looking for. As soon as she opened the first file, she knew she'd go blind or mad if she didn't have both files printed out. She saved them to a thumb drive and went down to the front desk.

While her request was being carried out, she stood near the window by the entrance, which gave her an oblique view of the street. She was starting to feel like a caged animal, the small, skittish sort that is anxious in its cage yet too fearful to venture far from the safety of confinement. It was a gorgeous day; every passerby made her ache with a longing to be out in it.

"Here you go, Mrs. Ridley." Madeline flinched at the sound of her name. She covered her repulsion with a reflexive smile and took the thumb drive and a sheaf of paper from the receptionist. "Beautiful day, isn't it?" the young woman said, taking a moment to look outside before heading back to her post. "Hope it's this nice tomorrow. I'm supposed to go sailing with some friends," she said gaily.

Madeline was overcome with a sense of loss as she headed back up the stairs to her room. She still couldn't fathom how her life had been hijacked and stripped of all its former privileges. She felt almost dead inside. Just a few hours earlier she'd felt so in charge and so fired up, believing she was going to best Steven at his own game. Now, she'd almost rather flee Santa Barbara, cave in to Steven's demands, try to scratch out a new life somewhere else.

She laughed harshly at the notion that she could simply drive out of there, with a few bags worth of possessions, and recreate herself. Goodbye Madeline Ridley, hello Madeline "Mad Dawg" Dawkins. Just like that. As if the last dozen years had been nothing more than an indulgent fantasy.

She supposed that in some regards it had been a fantasy. How else could it disintegrate so quickly? Besides a storage space full of clothing, what did she have to show for all the years she had given to the illusion of being the perfect wife, hostess, volunteer? Had she really developed any skills, other than how to schmooze and delegate?

As soon as she opened the door to her room, she wanted to scream. It was all she could do to keep her curses to a low growl. "I hate you, you son-of-a-bitch!" she swore, flinging the stack of papers across the room. The act was unsatisfying, both in its impotency and the mess it left for her to sort out. She continued to rail at her soon-to-be-ex as she bent and snatched the pages off the floor, barely resisting the urge to rip them to shreds.

She was on the verge of furious tears as she tried to smooth and order the rumpled lists. It was not a task to be performed while highly agitated. She didn't care about all these names, familiar or not, nor did she believe the perpetrator's name would be conveniently listed there. She took a few deep breaths as she paced back and forth, trying to calm herself and refocus.

She needed something constructive to occupy her mind, but reading through several hundred names wasn't going to do the job. It occurred to her she had something else she was supposed to do that wasn't quite as tedious. She went back to her laptop and searched for the files from the photographer and the videographer. She got lucky: an email from the videographer had just come through a few minutes earlier. She got a bottle of sparkling water from the minibar and perched herself on the sofa.

It didn't take long for her to wonder why she thought this task would be less mind-numbing than staring at a couple dozen pages of names. After twenty minutes of watching the constant crawl of what the videographer had captured, she got impatient and began to fast forward to more eventful scenes.

She finally decided to skip ahead to the dinner scenes, hoping to get to the part where the diners took to the dance floor. She went a little too fast and had to go back. She enlarged the image and carefully watched as the camera lens panned around the room, occasionally focusing on individuals or groups for a moment or two.

Her adrenaline was pumping as she sensed how close the camera was to capturing the proof she desperately hoped to find. There was a flash of a long red dress and dark blond hair that caused her heart to thump.

It disappeared, then appeared again. She was dancing, dancing with the unknown man. There she was, smiling as though she didn't know the camera was pointed her direction. Her face was then obscured by the close-up of the back of her dance partner's head and tuxedo jacket. The camera panned away for a second, then came up on the other side of them, closer. Another couple danced in front of the camera and spun away. There was one more split second of her in profile, but her partner was not in the frame.

She watched attentively for another fifteen minutes. She paused it and backed up. She knew she had only been out on the floor with him for ten minutes, at the most, prior to going back to her table. There was no footage of the row with Steven or her chasing after him as he stormed off. She reviewed the few seconds of the dancing and found nothing new. She went back to where she left off and studiously examined each frame.

There she was again. Coming back into the ballroom, on the steps. She paused it and stared at herself. It gave her chills to see the momentary flash of hurt and bewilderment on her face. She started it again. Dark hair, dark suit. Was it the guy? Impossible to tell in a crowd of similarly attired men.

She continued to watch the video, utterly absorbed now. Maddeningly, there wasn't any sight of the mystery man. But there were plenty shots of her. She was astonished and embarrassed as she watched footage of herself presiding over the auction. It was so eerie, watching herself act like she had completely shed all her inhibitions. Carla was right; she sounded like a Las Vegas MC. No wonder her friends were acting a little differently around her. None of them had ever seen her alter-ego before. Neither had she.

After two hours of dissecting the video without gaining any new information, other than seeing she could be quite the extrovert when under the influence, she connected her computer to the charger and put it to sleep. It was 3:15; she felt as though she had lost a good part of the day without accomplishing anything that would help her cause. So far, the day had been spent playing defense. She picked up Burt's phone and called him.

"I emailed you a copy of the video. I couldn't find any good images of the guy, unfortunately. I still have to go through the photos, but I'll have to do that later. If I don't get out of this room soon, I'll go crazy."

"Feel like a trip to the gym?" Burt asked. "Not much action around there at this time on a sunny Saturday. I can fill you in on my progress so far."

"Sounds good. I hope you've had better success than I have. I'll be there in ten," Madeline said, bag in hand as she headed for the door.

TWENTY-FOUR

"I had an interesting talk with your predecessor today—your husband's second wife," Burt said, as he pretended to coach Madeline through a series of stomach crunches. Madeline froze mid-crunch.

"My predecessor was Steven's *second wife?*" she asked incredulously. Burt nodded and Madeline flopped back against the mat. *When would the deceit end?* she wondered. *Do I even know the first thing about my husband?*

"But probably not the wife you know about. Something told me you were unaware of Steven's complete marital history," Burt said, as Madeline worked herself into a sitting position.

"I feel like a fool in a nightmare," she said, flabbergasted by her compounding ignorance. Burt regarded her sympathetically. "Well, at least there's only *one* wife who wasn't accounted for," she said, struggling to her feet. She sat down on the workout bench and Burt joined her. The only other diehard fitness fiend had called it quits. They now had the room to themselves.

"That we're aware of," Burt cautioned. Madeline couldn't help but laugh. The bad dream had become too farcical not to. "But he could've used another name that I haven't uncovered yet." It took Madeleine two beats to comprehend his meaning.

"Don't tell me…"

"Steven Hartford, like the insurance company. That's the way the former Mrs. Hartford put it." Madeline stared at him aghast.

"How do you know her ex-husband is the same man I'm married to? What proof do you have that Ridley isn't Steven's real name?" Madeline asked defensively. It was bad enough to think her husband had framed her in a sexually explicit manner. But using an alias, flying to Boston instead of Dallas? Madeline was starting to have doubts about the man she'd hired to get the goods on the man she'd married.

"Actually, Ridley is Steven's real last name. For some reason, he chose an alias during the time he met Margery Gulbranson. Hartford came up when I pulled a credit header with his social security number. I thought that was pretty interesting, so I ordered a full factual credit report and did some research around the previous addresses. I cross-checked all the addresses and did title searches and found the name Margery Hartford." Madeline was too stunned to speak.

"They were divorced in 1996. Mrs. Hartford is still very bitter about it. They were married for three years, and according to her, he took her to the cleaners."

"*He* took *her* to the cleaners?" Burt nodded.

"Margery's first husband was quite well off. When he died of stomach cancer in '92, he left her with close to six million dollars."

"How did Steven take her to the cleaners? They weren't married very long, if what you're saying is true. If she's bitter about the break up, she might be trying to get back at him," Madeline suggested.

"It's easy enough to verify. I can get a copy of their divorce agreement."

"How?"

"We detectives have our sources," Burt replied. "You'd be astonished what info is out there just for the asking."

"So…if she's telling the truth, which I'm not convinced of yet, how does this help me?" Madeline was on her feet, facing Burt, her body language telegraphing her sudden distrust of her private eye.

"Because she was more than happy to help me out when I explained that he was working over another unsuspecting woman." This revelation did not make Madeline happy.

"You told her about my case?" she asked indignantly. "You assured me you would keep everything I told you confidential." With all that had transpired in the last week, she had plenty of pent-up anger to vent. She could feel her body gearing up to unload on the nearest person, which meant Burt. This wasn't the first time he'd taken grief from frustrated clients.

"I told the ex-Mrs. Hartford nothing about your situation," Burt said calmly.

"But you just said…"

"I originally told her I was an old friend from high school, looking to reconnect with Steven Hartford. She said she had no idea where he was and wouldn't help him under any circumstances. That's when I knew I had an ally."

"You lied to her?" Madeline made no attempt to hide her disapproval.

"In our business, it's called 'pretexting'—fabricating a scenario designed to elicit facts from a source close to the suspect. In this case, I started with one pretext, pretty certain she'd give me a piece of her mind. Once I knew how she felt about Steven Hartford, aka Steven Ridley, I dropped the charade and explained that I had been hired by a woman who was going through a situation similar to hers."

"Which is what, exactly?" Madeline asked, warming to the results of Burt's work if not his methods. He shifted on the bench as he chose his words carefully.

"Blackmail. The same basic tool he's using on you, with a twist." Burt could tell by Madeline's expression he'd struck a nerve. "He was twelve years younger than Margery when they got married. She was just getting over the death of her husband, feeling insecure about being single at the age of forty-seven. Steven 'enveloped her in a dream,' as she put it. She was overcome when he proposed, but nervous. Steven worked on her, assuring her the age difference meant nothing to him. They were married five months after they met." Madeline stared at Burt in awe. *So, this is why people hire private investigators,* she thought.

"But Steven isn't blackmailing me," she said, trying to fit the pieces together.

"He's holding those photos over your head to get you to comply with his demands."

Madeline realized this was true. Steven had gotten her so off-balance with his incessant surprise attacks, she'd lost track of the initial motivating mechanism. In reality, Steven had never actually threatened to broadcast those photos; he'd only lamented how they would damage *his* reputation if they were ever made public. She was dancing to his tune just because he claimed to be the injured party. She sank back onto the bench next to Burt while she absorbed the whole rotten setup.

"You following me now?" Burt asked.

"Yeah, I think I've got it—finally.

"In Margery's case, Steven had home videos of them in rather passionate and unbridled moments."

"She told you that?" Madeline asked, incredulous that she'd disclose such a thing to a stranger over the phone.

"She put it more delicately, but I got the gist of it."

"Oh my God. Okay…so, how does knowing Steven blackmailed his second wife help me?"

"Every piece of information we dig up helps us understand his true motives and where he's going. So far we already know he's been staying with a recently divorced woman worth millions, and that he received a settlement of three million dollars from his second wife. This tells me he might have actually married you for love."

Madeline looked at Burt, trying to figure out if he was putting her on. When he held her gaze, she turned away. She couldn't understand why she found that possibility so disturbing, but it hit her like a punch to the gut.

"But unfortunately, for whatever reason—either the need for more money or lack of an heir—I think it's safe to assume Steven is back in the market for a new wife. My hunch here is it has more to do with financial need than the lack of offspring. Now I will start focusing on his business assets and see if I can find any irregularities."

"How are you going to do that?" Madeline felt sure Steven would be as crafty at hiding any wrong doings as he had been at disposing of unwanted wives.

"The old-fashioned way—poring over any and all public records I can get access to. That will require time, but I think it will be a good way for you to get leverage against him, in the event we can't prove he was behind the incident at The Edgecliff. In any case, I've got a lot of ground to cover still. How are you holding up?" he asked, thinking of the bomb Steven had dropped on her earlier.

"I'm okay, I guess. I honestly feel like I'm in limbo land—like I'm here, but not here. Like I'm watching a distorted version of my life that I have no control over. In the course of one week, I feel as though Madeline Ridley has been deconstructed, leaving me to figure out just who the heck I am now." She gave Burt a sad, ironic smile.

"Even if we get proof Steven was behind all this, I'm never going to have my life back. Either he wins or I win, but in both cases I won't be married to him anymore. I won't have the same role to play, and from where I'm standing now, I wouldn't want any part of it again, anyway. I'll have to reinvent myself somehow. But I'd really like to settle the score before I slink out of Steven's life. There's just no way in hell I'm going to let him get away with what he's done to me." Burt regarded her silently for a moment.

"I can already see a change in you. I see the fighter emerging. I don't think Steven knows who he's toying with." This observation made Madeline smile. "Okay, I think that's enough iron pumping for one day," Burt said, standing. "Got to stick my face back in the computer. We've got a skunk to skin."

TWENTY-FIVE

Madeline sat in the Mercedes, enjoying the sun-warmed air inside the car after the brief walk in the cool afternoon breeze. Aside from warming herself, she occupied her time by trying to assimilate all of Burt's recent discoveries. There was so much to process, and she was still harboring a fair amount of denial. Never in her life had events buffeted her so fast and furiously. It was all she could do to stay on top of the barrage of new developments.

But the real reason she sat with the engine off was because she lacked any kind of practical plan. The thought of going back to the hotel room filled her with despair. She had no home anymore; most of her possessions were in storage, she was sitting in a borrowed car, and her husband was already romancing a rich divorcée. If the downward spiral continued, she could find herself homeless soon. She slumped against the seat, wondering if this speculation was merely self-pity or a dose of reality.

She was aware of a gnawing in her stomach, a reminder she hadn't eaten anything since morning. She needed to eat, but she couldn't stand the thought of food. Or eating take-out, or sitting by herself in a restaurant. She needed to find a place to live so she could at least feel somewhat grounded. She needed to sell her car. She needed to call Mike and see how that was progressing. She needed to do many things, but all she really wanted to do was kill Steven.

A strong desire to drive to her former home and confront her future ex with everything she knew—the payoff to Barnett, the surreptitious trip to Boston, and the missing necklace and earrings—was powerful enough to set her in motion. She started the car and headed out the parking lot, a heady steam of anger making her drive Mike's stately old car like her road-hungry Porsche.

As she tore down the open road, a string of avenging curses made her adrenalin pump. *Oh, it would be so satisfying to expose his heinous deeds in front of the staff,* she thought gleefully. *They deserve to know the truth about their employer. But it might be more satisfying to sneak onto the property, take a shovel from the gardener's shed and bash his rotten brains out.*

A thought occurred to her that almost made her choke: what if Steven had already ensconced his new love interest in the house? What if she got there and broke up some revolting scene of domestic bliss? After she recovered from the shock of that possibility, her fury returned, fanned by the outrage she had been too off-kilter to acknowledge. *But wouldn't that make the confrontation that much more fulfilling?* A malicious smile worked at the corners of her mouth as she envisioned giving the next Mrs. Steven Ridley a rundown on her suitor's marital history.

But as she exited the freeway and drove up San Ysidro Road, passing all the familiar streets, home to many friends and acquaintances, her anger deflated, leaving her feeling empty and anguished. She wanted vengeance; she wanted to make Steven answer for all the wrongs he had committed against her. But she couldn't confront him, not yet. She would only be giving him the satisfaction of unhinging her and giving away any hope of nailing him properly, in a way that would stick.

She turned left onto East Valley Road, away from the direction of their house. Now she moved at a crawl, in a manner more fitting the vehicle and her vanquished frame of mind. She wiped at the slow leak of tears, admonishing herself to stay strong. *We'll get him. With Burt's help, he will see his day of reckoning,* she promised herself.

"I've had five calls on the car so far," Mike said. "One guy offered me $65,000—sight unseen." Madeline huffed wearily.

"What'd you tell him?" she asked as she picked at the potato salad that came with her club sandwich.

"I told him to piss off. He was probably a dealer, looking to make a quick flip."

"Five calls—that's not very many," Madeline worried.

"The ad's only been up a few hours. I think we'll get some good nibbles. What would be the lowest offer you'd take?" Mike asked. Madeline could hear him chewing on the other end of the line. It struck her as mildly comforting that they were having a long-distance meal together. At least it was better than eating alone.

"I don't know. I've had that figure of eighty-seven thou' in my head, but I'm sure that's not realistic."

"No, not in this market. My personal feeling is you'd be lucky to get anything over seventy-five."

"Yeah, you're probably right," Madeline said, getting up to get herself a Coke. She marveled at the way her eating habits had gone the way of everything else in her life, namely south. "If you get an offer that high, jump on it. I'm going to need the money."

"Just remember, I'm a man of means now, so I can help you."

"I appreciate that," Madeline said, suppressing a laugh. Who would've guessed that Mike Delaney would've ended up more financially secure than her?

"Hey, I've got an idea—why don't you come stay with me? I've got a really bitchin' pad—you'd love it. It's got a separate guest suite, totally styled-out—"

"I'm too whipped to drive down there right now," Madeline protested.

"I'll come get you," Mike offered enthusiastically.

"That won't work. I've got your car, remember?"

"Oh. Well, after we get the Porsche sold, we can fly up and get it. Or better yet, take the train. I've always wanted to take the train out of Union Station. Wouldn't that be fun?" He was so giddy at the prospect, Madeline almost regretted bursting his bubble.

"I don't think that would be a good idea," she said.

"Why not?"

"I'm all strung out here. Most of my stuff is in storage, I need to find a place to live—which I can't do if I'm down there—"

"Maybe you should look for a place down here. Maybe I can raise the rent on one of my tenants and make them leave. I'm telling you, this place is a gem."

"Mike, thanks, but I don't want to live in L.A. I love Santa Barbara." They sat in frustrated silence for a moment.

"Are you going to be okay, Maddie?"

"Yeah. Eventually. I have a feeling the worst of it isn't over yet." Mike huffed angrily.

"What else could that bastard possibly do to top himself?"

"I can't even let myself go there," Madeline said, dropping her fork in disgust. "Anyway, I should go…" She felt Mike's empathy through the phone. And maybe something more, maybe a longing to be with her like in the old days. But those days were in the distant past, never to be repeated.

"Call me, anytime. I mean it, Mad Dawg. I'll always be here for you. And I'm available to kick some ass—anytime, anyplace."

Madeline laughed, blew a kiss into the phone and disconnected. She sat there, phone dangling from a limp wrist. Inertia was setting in and she didn't see a way to prevent it. She could think of things to do, but the will to do them was absent.

Her phone vibrated for the umpteenth time, signaling another message. She hit the button and saw the depressing news that she had 113 new emails. She tapped the icon and brought up the list. More poured in as she scanned through the older communiqués. In streamed four red flagged messages from a frantic Jane. She cut to the chase and read the last one first.

Maddie—where the hell are you??? I just left your house. Erma told me you moved out this morning—what the hell??? I ran into Carla—she said you lost your phone, which explains why your number is disconnected. CALL ME!!!!!

Madeline groaned and scanned similar entreaties from Jane. She deleted all the promotional emails as she went along. Not only was she not interested in shopping the latest trends, she no longer had an unlimited credit line at her disposal. She was so relentless with the delete button, she almost deleted a message from Lauren.

Hey, I'm back! Had too much fun!! I called your cell. # out of service. What did I miss? Hope you get this ms. Call me. Lauren

Another wrinkle: what to do about Lauren. Even if she could afford to pay an assistant $2,500 a month, she didn't need one anymore. But she couldn't stand the thought of firing her without notice; she'd have to give her a month's severance pay and try to place her with one of her friends, if anyone would still speak to her once word got around.

She opened her laptop and got online, picking up her search for a place to live. The vacation rental idea was still her best option; it would be her best chance of finding something immediately. It would also give her some flexibility on the departure date, which was important. She had to keep reminding herself that she had an attorney who was being paid to void the prenup. If that happened, she would be entitled to half their assets. That thought made her smile. Then she'd be able to hold her head up high. People would forget all about the breakup of Montecito's darlings and it would be business as usual. It all came down to finding Steven's fingerprints, literally or figuratively. She just hoped Burt was the right guy for the job.

TWENTY-SIX

Madeline awoke to a spectacular sunrise as the sun lit the banks of clouds from underneath, coloring them vibrant hues of rose madder and vermillion. It was a thrilling sight, and for a moment she forgot about her current circumstances. The temporary memory loss was soon filled by a crowd of concerns, all clamoring to be addressed.

In an effort to elude them, she dressed for a run and did an abbreviated stretching routine. The cloud cover made it cooler than the previous day, a reminder that winter wasn't officially over yet. She zipped up her hoodie and headed for the hills.

Being in motion always made her feel better, as though it were physically possible to outrun her problems. To stretch out the time away from the hotel room, she detoured to one of the downtown coffee houses and had a breakfast of berries and yogurt, a latte and a scone. Afterwards, she meandered down State Street, enjoying the mostly deserted streets. As distant church bells chimed nine o'clock, she turned up Garden Street, heading for the inn. It wasn't until she was fifty feet from the entrance that she spotted Burt leaning against his car.

"How long have you been waiting for me?" she asked as she got closer.

"About forty minutes. I take it you didn't have either phone on you." Madeline came to a stop in front of him. "For safety's sake, you shouldn't go out without one."

"You're right, I'm sorry. I guess I needed that feeling of complete freedom."

"Understandable," Burt allowed. "No skin off my nose. I bill by the hour." Madeline smirked at this.

"What brings you out so early?"

"I've been up for hours, working on your case." Burt checked his watch. 9:35. "How long will it take for you to change and get ready?" he asked.

"Depends. Where are we going?"

"Back to The Edgecliff. I've got another theory I want to check out."

"In that case, I'm going to need a shower, so give me fifteen," she said, as she headed toward the lobby.

Madeline parked just up the street from Burt's car. They had both found spots on the back side of The Edgecliff Hotel.

"So, tell me about this theory of yours," she said, as she met Burt on the pathway into the hotel grounds.

"First let's try to retrace your steps again," he said. When Madeline made no move to follow him, he stopped and regarded her. "It's okay, Madeline. It's daylight, I'm by your side. We're going to approach from a different direction, then retrace our steps, if we need to. But this has to be done. I've got to know for sure which room you were in. It's the only way I'm going to find out who the room was registered to."

Madeline gave herself two seconds to pull her courage together. *It's like jumping off the high dive,* she told herself; *the scariest part is the anticipation.* She nodded to Burt and fell in behind him. When the path widened, he slowed up until they were in step together.

"Let's just take this slow. Try to put yourself back in the moment when you made your exit."

Madeline's eyes roved from side to side as she searched for anything that might trigger a memory, or a sense of recognition. Burt had been right about one thing: the setting seemed much more benign in the full light of day. The path curved, leading them to the left. If they had continued going straight, they would've come to the main building's garden entrance.

They had walked only a few steps when Madeline grabbed Burt by the arm. They stopped as a feeling came over her, like a body memory. She could barely breathe as she cautiously approached a set of French doors. She turned, pretending to be stepping through them. She scrutinized everything in her path, trying to visualize that morning one week ago. She gasped as she stared down at the pathway, transfixed by a vague recollection.

"What is it?" Burt asked, coming up beside her as she scanned the sidewalk for confirmation of her discovery.

"See the wet mark right here?" she asked, pointing at the arc of damp on the sidewalk. A quick check confirmed that the sprinklers in the other beds nearby did not overshoot their mark. Burt bent down and examined the head. By looking at it he could see that someone had placed a full spray head on the stem instead of a half, probably installed temporarily until they got the right part.

"I remember getting hit with the spray on my bare legs," Madeline said, staring at the mark on the walkway. "I had my gown hiked up because I was carrying my shoes. The water hit my calves."

"Good work. Now let's see if there are any other spots like this on the grounds."

Like a pair of bloodhounds, they continued on until they reached the sidewalk that ran along the beach road. Finding no other evidence of over-spraying, they reversed direction and walked all the way back to where they had entered the grounds. Other than that one spot, the walkways were dry. To further test Madeline's story, Burt examined each head in the dry areas to make sure the sun or breeze hadn't dried up other wet marks.

"Excellent," Burt said, pulling a grounds map from his pocket as he walked to the wet pavement. "Okay. So, are you sure about which side you came out on?"

"I'm positive."

"And can you recall for certain how far you had walked before getting sprayed?" Madeline reenacted her departure once again, slowly, as she let the memory guide her.

"Yes, it was right as I rounded this bed, before I passed this other room. I remember because I kind of skittered out of the way and landed in the mud on this side..." They both bent and examined the site. Even after a week and regular waterings, it was still possible to see a distinct print of Madeline's toes and the ball of her foot. Burt handed the map to her and took out a small camera, making a record of their findings.

"It's a good piece of evidence, but it doesn't do anything to link Steven to the setup. But it does give us a specific room number to work with, which helps immensely. With any luck, we'll get a name to go with the room and date."

"That's incredible," Madeline said. She was tingling with excitement and almost giddy with relief.

"You'd make a pretty good P.I." Burt kidded her. "You've got a good eye for detail." Madeline laughed.

"I guess that comes from years of planning big events," she said.

"Don't knock it. All sorts of people make good investigators. It's how you apply your own special knowledge of life that matters." Madeline took this as a compliment.

"So, now what do we do?"

"I'm going back to chat with the front desk. You can go do whatever you want—have brunch, go shopping, or just enjoy the gorgeous day."

"What I want to do and need to do are two different things. But the first thing I *have* to do is find a place to live, before my money runs out."

Madeline had just rounded the front of the Benz when she heard someone call out her name. Her instinct was to pretend she hadn't heard it and get away from there as soon as possible. But unlocking a car door the old-fashioned way without benefit of remote keyless entry slowed her progress. She kept her head down as the female voice beckoned her again. She had half-convinced herself the unfamiliar car would give her pursuer doubts. She was almost in the driver's seat when Lauren appeared on her beach cruiser.

"Hey, I thought that was you!" Lauren sang out happily, oblivious to Madeline's less than welcoming body language.

"Oh, hi there!" Madeline said, managing a fairly convincing look of surprise.

"I wasn't sure it was you," Lauren said, all smiles. "I didn't recognize the car and you didn't seem to hear me."

"Sorry, I'm a little distracted right now."

"I bet! The whole time I was in Cabo I kept thinking how much you must've regretted letting me off for a week."

"Looks like you had a good time…"

"It was *amazing!* But I'm back and ready to get to work." Madeline's smile froze on her face. She had to tell her assistant the sad reality sometime. Might as well be now.

"Umm…feel like a coffee?"

"Sure."

"How about The Coffee Bean?"

"I'll be right behind you," Lauren said, guiding her bicycle back into the street. "Cool car—is it new?"

"No, it belongs to a friend of mine."

"Oh, nice," Lauren replied, not knowing what to make of that answer. The Ridleys had plenty of cars at their disposal. But her curiosity died quickly and was replaced by her old eager-to-please, competent self. "Do you want me to order you a latte, if I beat you there?" she challenged her employer.

"That'd be great. But don't be so sure you'll get there before me."

"Maybe not, but I don't have to park," Lauren cried out as she set the clunky bike into motion.

A sinking feeling came over Madeline as she conceded this point with a tentative smile. She had two minutes to figure out how to spin her story and how much to disclose. And figure out how to fire a perfectly good assistant without actually firing her.

TWENTY-SEVEN

Lauren took the news of the Ridley breakup harder than Madeline had expected. To look at her, one would assume she'd just learned that her own parents were getting divorced. She was tearing up, and Madeline regretted telling her the bad news in such a public place. She took a tissue out of her tote and handed it to her. Lauren snuffled into it for a moment before letting loose.

"Lauren, honey, please don't cry," Madeline said under her breath. "It's going to be alright," she lied. She had expected maybe a quivering bottom lip when she told her that she couldn't employ her anymore. Now Madeline wasn't sure she could bring herself to tell her. But she had to; one month's severance pay was more than she felt comfortable spending at this point as it was.

"The worst part of all this is that I'm not going to be able to keep you on as my assistant." The words hung over the table as Lauren's force field rejected the notion. "I can pay you for one more month, but you really should spend that time lining up a new job." This point hit home, eliciting another jagged sob from Lauren. Madeline gave her a weary smile as she held her hand, conveying the full scope of her own loss. Lauren sniffed and grasped her hand tightly.

"If there's anything I can do…" Lauren offered. Though she had no right to feel sorry for herself, given what her employer was going through, she couldn't help but see this as a complete upheaval of her once promising life. Even though Madeline was facing a divorce, she was going to be a rich divorcée, which was a lot better than being an unemployed poor person.

"If Steven wasn't trying to cut me off without a cent, I'd keep you on. I'm going to find it very difficult to function without you," Madeline confessed, earning a moody chirp from Lauren. "But I will put the word out, and I'm sure you'll be snatched up right away. I know several people who've coveted you for themselves. Now's their chance. I'll make a few calls and you'll probably have a bidding war going in no time."

Her words worked liked a bouquet of hundred-dollar bills. Lauren tried to remain somber, for Madeline's sake, but it was obviously sinking in that she had just earned $2,500 for doing nothing and would be able to hold out for an even better salary.

"Especially after the success of the ball…" Madeline added. Though she had been trying to put a good spin on the situation, thinking of that fateful night made her own spirits plummet.

"The ball was awesome!" Lauren gushed. "You were amazing. You looked so beautiful and you held it together perfectly after Steven stormed out on you." Madeline looked up from her empty latte cup.

"What did you see? What do you remember of that night?" she asked, startling Lauren with her urgency.

"Uh…I…well, you did a *great* job with the auction—"

"But what about before that…after Steven left…how did I seem to you?"

"Uh, fine…I mean, I could tell at first you were upset, but once you started dancing again—"

"You saw me dancing?"

"Yeah…"

"Who was I dancing with?" Madeline's grilling her put her on edge. "Lauren, do you remember me dancing with a guy with dark, slicked-back hair? He was about my height with my heels on…" Madeline looked as though she were trying to bore a hole through Lauren's vapid expression.

"Yeah, yeah…I remember the guy…"

"What do we know about him? Was he on the guest list or was he a guest of someone else? Do you know where he was sitting?" Lauren shook her head, a vacant look on her face.

"I don't know who he was…I just figured it was someone you knew. I mean, you were dancing with him a lot…" Madeline couldn't hide her exasperation. She ran her hands through her hair as she took a deep breath. "Is there something wrong?" Lauren asked anxiously. An odd, quizzical look came over her features. Madeline could almost see the gears turning.

"It's nothing like that," she said, rushing to erase the notion she had a personal interest in the man. "He was acting strangely when I was dancing with him, and I heard some other women saying the same thing. You know how it is at these big, high-dollar events—you sometimes get crashers looking for easy pickings."

"Oh…I see. You think he might have been a pick-pocket or a jewel thief…?" Madeline shrugged equivocally. "Oh, I didn't know…"

"It's okay. I just wondered if you happened to know how he got in, just in case we had reports of anything missing."

"Right…"

"So, anyway…that's the sad story about our breakup," Madeline said, eager to finish their conversation. "And I hope you know how sad I am to have to let you go."

"I know. You're the best boss anyone could ever hope for," Lauren said, laying it on thick.

"Well, I don't know about that, but thanks. I'll put the word out that you're available."

"Thank you." They smiled forlornly at each other.

"I better get going," Madeline said as she stood up. Without warning, Lauren threw her arms around her.

"Keep in touch, and good luck!" Lauren said, waving goodbye as she bounded out of the café.

Madeline was walking back to the car when Burt appeared beside her, making her jump.

"How did you know I was here?" she asked. There had been no parking on Coast Village Road and she had to park behind one of the business complexes, hidden from the street.

"GPS. It's in the phone I gave you. I like being able to keep tabs on my clients. I never know when one might go missing." This ominous admission startled her. "You've probably had your fill of caffeine," Burt surmised. "Let's find somewhere less public where we can talk."

They met back at the Douglas Preserve. Madeline found Burt sitting on a bench just off the trail. She sat down beside him and took in the view while she waited for him to speak.

"Your discovery was a good one," he said.

"What did you find out?" Burt looked at her askance. He could tell the suspense was getting to her.

"The room you were taken to was not registered to any hotel guests that night. And neither were the three others facing it." Madeline was dumbstruck. "One of the four had guests who checked out Saturday morning. Another had guests checking in on Sunday. And that was all the activity in that group.

"How could that be? I'm positive that was the place. We looked everywhere else…" Burt shifted his body so that he was facing her, left arm propped up on the back of the bench in a pose of nonchalance.

"My guess is the perpetrators had inside help. It wouldn't be impossible for them to break in, but they had to have known which rooms were going to be vacant that night." Madeline felt her body sag, as if something essential to her being had just evaporated. "I think it's time you took this to the police."

The look on Madeline's face made him quickly amend his opinion. "I'll keep working on this, but we're going to need access to surveillance videos and employee time cards and background checks and other things that the hotel is not going to grant a P.I. I'll share with them everything I've uncovered pertinent to the assault, and I'll work with them any way I can. But I also have hunches I want to pursue outside of their purview, at least for now." Madeline was shaking her head as he spoke.

"I can't go to the police. I can't give them those photos. They'll go to Steven and he'll tell them a load of B.S. He is *so* convincing—Mr. Upstanding Citizen, friend to all the big wigs in town. No one will take my word over his." Burt held up his hands to stop Madeline's justifiably paranoid ramble.

"You can't jump to conclusions. At this point, there's no reason not to get the police involved. The longer you wait, the harder it'll be to find evidence. Security tapes are often erased or taped over after a certain period of time." Burt faced forward, looking down at the ground as he chose his words. "I think focusing on catching your husband has been a way to avoid dealing with the reality of what happened that night." Madeline made no move, but Burt could feel the tension emanating from her body.

"You need the law to find out who did this to you, and you need to get counseling. I don't mean this to sound harsh, but look how your husband has kept you off balance since that night. He hasn't given you a single day without dropping a bomb on you. You've been so busy reacting to his systematic destruction of your life, you haven't had a moment to grieve or take care of yourself."

A tear trickled down Madeline's cheek. She wiped it away before daring to look Burt in the eye. She knew if she opened her mouth, she'd lose it. Burt sat back, giving her time and space to absorb what he'd said.

"Will you come with me?" she asked. Burt nodded. Madeline let out a deep sigh. It surprised her that now the unthinkable had been faced, she actually felt calmer inside. Burt was right; she had been allowing Steven to whip her in private, convincing her she would be worse off if she didn't suffer in silence. The more she thought it over, the more it made sense to hand the burden to the police.

Maybe nothing would come of their investigation; maybe Steven would flood the Internet with the horrid photos. She couldn't be sure he wouldn't do that anyway. If he did, his precious reputation might suffer too as a result. Either way, she couldn't control what he did with them, so it was better to strike where she had the best chance of exposing his role in her molestation.

"Do you think they'll believe me?" Madeline asked, a new tide of trepidation washing over her.

"I think they'll treat it as a legitimate complaint." Madeline snorted at Burt's delicate phrasing. "You've got the photos, your version of the events—the blackout and waking alone in the room—and we've got photos of your footprint in the flower bed and the sprinkler spray, which corroborates your story. It's not a lot, but victims of rape often have less to go on than that."

"Should I tell them I think Steven is behind it?"

"No. They'll interview Steven about receiving the photos, but let's keep our theories to ourselves for the time being. It'll be much better for them to come to their own conclusions about him rather than us trying to lead them that direction."

"Should I tell them Steven has filed for divorce?" Burt thought this over.

"That's better coming from you than Steven. They might figure you've concocted this story to save your marriage if they found out through him."

"Then they might think that anyway," Madeline said, getting to her feet. She stood staring out at the ocean as she moved the chess pieces around in her head.

"When should we do it?" she asked at length.

"Tomorrow. There's no reason to wait any longer. But take some time to think it all over. The more confident you are with the facts as you know them, the more convincing you'll be."

"What are the 'hunches' you want to pursue?" she asked, sitting back down beside him. Burt leaned back against the bench.

"I still feel money is the motivation behind Steven's actions. If progeny were all he was after, he could've taken a mistress here in town, waited until she got pregnant, and then pulled this number on you. But as soon as this plan was in place, he went hunting big game. There's no shortage of beautiful young women in this town, and I don't think it's any coincidence he's gone to court a wealthy divorcée. I think he's in deep financial trouble. I started looking into a certain area of his business dealings that have been goldmines for crooks in the past."

"What area would that be?"

"Real estate loans." Madeline mulled this over.

"I'd love for you to find some major dirt on Steven, but all his business dealings are in group partnerships. I don't see how he could slip anything past his investors."

"This type of thing has been done before, and with much larger firms than your husband's. It has to do with loan payoffs and reconveying the deed, or more to the point, *not* reconveying the deed."

"You lost me," Madeline said.

"There was a pretty famous case years ago that had to do with a title company, whose owner—unbeknownst to his employees—was handling loan payoffs through escrow, but not recording those final payments. The people who thought they now owned their properties free and clear, found out some time down the road that the money was never given to the lien holders."

"Seriously?"

"Twenty years in prison seriously."

"But how was that possible?"

"The guy was very bright, but also a little naïve to think someone wouldn't catch on sooner or later. All it takes in a scam like that is for one borrower to start a new refinance, then bingo, they find their property is as encumbered as it was before the payoff and all their money is gone." Madeline scratched her head.

"I just don't see how something like that would be possible in Steven's partnership. There are too many people involved. Surely someone would notice…" Burt shook his head.

"Not necessarily. And again, this is just speculation on my part. But my instincts tell me Steven Ridley has to put on a pretty good show in order to attract new investors. The money's got to look like it's raining from heaven. Chances are he started postponing the actual repayment of certain loans by a week or two in order to make his balance sheet look more impressive. Once he figured out this delay went unnoticed, he got bolder. Next thing he knows, he's habitually treating other people's money like it's his own. Before long, he's got a lot of empty cupboards to replenish, and maybe he didn't hook as many big investors as he needed to, or maybe he simply got greedy."

"That sounds like a Ponzi scheme," Madeline said.

"Yeah, just like this one." Madeline sat back against the bench, utterly flummoxed. She found it difficult to believe Steven could be that corrupt—squeaky clean, ultra-conservative Steven. But she quickly reminded herself of all the plotting that had gone into her frame-up. No doubt, there was a side to her spouse she had been completely blind to.

"So, when he comes up short, he has to get money from somewhere..." she said. Burt smiled, nodding his head.

"My guess is you are unaware that Steven had been trying to pull money out of your real estate holdings."

"What do you mean, like a loan?"

"Yep."

"How do you know that?"

"I saw several inquiries by banks on your credit report, all within the last five months."

"Steven never mentioned that to me."

"Why am I not surprised?"

"Okay, it sounds like you've got a reason for suspecting him of stealing. But how do you go about proving it?"

"First I searched for trust deeds held by Steven's company. I was surprised how many came up. Now I have to sift through them to find out if any of these borrowers are under the false impression that their payoffs have been recorded."

"How will you do that?"

"Pretexting. I'll pose as a rep from a lending institution offering to lower the rate on their mortgage with RAM L.P. I'll call each one of these property owners until I find any who've been duped."

"And if you're right...?"

"If I hit pay dirt, then Steven's screwed." A happy wheeze escaped Madeline as she saw how close they were to turning Steven's plot upside down.

"I don't want you to get too excited yet. It may take me a few days to find what I'm looking for, if I'm not totally off-base. And even if I'm right, there's a significant downside where you're concerned."

"What, you mean I'll have a jailbird for an ex-husband?" Madeline joked.

"I mean it might be a rather hollow victory for you, if you've been counting on breaking your prenup and cashing in on half of the Ridley assets." Madeline's expression became suitably sober. "If Steven goes to prison for misappropriating funds that he had a fiduciary responsibility to safeguard, your joint estate will be sued left, right and center. And any ill-gotten gains will probably be confiscated."

"Oh," Madeline sighed. "I win, but I also lose." Burt nodded. "Well, isn't that just the way my luck is running these days—I can't seem to win for losing." They were silent for a moment, both running alternate scenarios in their heads.

"If there was a way to get Steven for the rape, we could keep the embezzlement for later, after the prenup was voided. But so far we can't find a way to connect Steven to the photos or the man from the ball, who is starting to seem like a ghost, so there are no grounds for voiding the prenup," Madeline concluded glumly.

"There might be another way around the prenup."

"Which is what?"

"If I can find proof of Steven's larceny, that could be used as leverage against him," Burt said. He usually wasn't one for Machiavellian scheming on his clients' behalf, but this case was not his standard fare. He hated unfair fights and Steven Ridley was wiping the floor with an innocent woman, his own faithful wife of twelve years. Any man capable of his misdeeds deserved everything he had coming to him, with interest. And as long as Mrs. Ridley was his employer, he was going to make sure this misogynist didn't skate free.

TWENTY-EIGHT

Madeline was so preoccupied by the time she returned to the hotel, she couldn't have said with certainty what streets she had taken to get there. She was fumbling around in her tote for the room key when Steven's voice made her jump.

"What are you doing here?" she demanded, hand to her heart.

"Nice car," Steven said. The tone of his voice made her wish she had something very heavy to hit him with. Her instinct to bolt for safety kicked in a second too late; Steven blocked her as she tried to slip past him. He grabbed her by the arm as she pivoted away from him.

"Let go of me," she said defiantly, keeping her voice steady and loud enough to be heard if anyone was in the vicinity. Steven held his hands up as he took a step back. "What are you doing here?" she repeated.

"We need to talk," Steven said.

"Anything you want to say to me will have to go through our attorneys."

"Madeline, I've had time to think things over." Madeline's heart stopped, then started pounding, making her feel faint. "I have a proposal for you, one I think you'll be quite open to." She let out an exasperated huff. For one crazy second she thought he was talking of reconciliation. She backed away, into the line of sight of the front desk.

"Look, twelve years is a long time. I don't want to you to walk away penniless, despite what happened." Madeline stared at him, trying to deduce what his real motivation was.

"Have your attorney tell it to my attorney," she said, standing defiantly with her arms wrapped closely around herself.

"Can we go somewhere, talk about this like adults?"

"No." Her heart skipped a beat when she remembered Burt saying he had "secured" the hotel. It comforted her some to imagine him watching this scene from his monitor. Maybe he was on his way over already. She fixed Steven with her stare, letting him know any talking he wanted to do would have to take place in the motor court.

"Would you like me to park your car, Mrs. Ridley?"

"Could you keep it out for a moment? I might be leaving again soon."

"Sure no problem," the valet said, backing away cautiously. It was clear to him a confrontation was taking place. He positioned himself where he couldn't overhear their conversation, but could keep a discreet watch on them.

"Can we at least get in the car?" Steven asked, his rancor seeping through his mask of deference.

"No. Anything you want to say to me, you're going to have to say right here. And you better make it fast." Steven licked his lip as he surveyed their surroundings. If he figured out there was a security camera fixed on them, he didn't let on.

"Alright, we'll do it your way," he said. Madeline almost laughed at his feigned magnanimity. "I believe I was rash in throwing you out of your home. I could've handled the situation better, but I was so devastated by your infidelity." Madeline's features hardened as she weighed the benefits of listening to this utter bullshit. "Just let me finish," Steven said, sensing her urge to flee.

"Get to the point," she said, running out of patience.

"I'm willing to offer you a cash settlement, even though our prenup frees me from that obligation."

"That's really big of you Steven, especially after you cut off my use of our credit cards and froze our bank accounts." A smirk threatened to undermine Steven's sincerity. Madeline continued to glare at him, warning him to speak up or take a hike.

"Here's the deal," Steven said, removing an envelope from the inside pocket of his jacket. "I have a cashier's check made out to you for $250,000." Madeline couldn't hide her shock. "In exchange, you'll agree to a quick divorce."

"No sale," she said. She tried to get past him, but he grabbed her by the arm again.

"Get your Goddamn hands off me!" The valet looked up from his book. His posture was rigid, as if he were ready to intervene in a moment's notice.

"Sorry, sorry…" Steven said, his hands raised in the air to show the valet he meant no harm. "Look, Madeline, I'm trying to be fair here."

"Oh, please—give me a break! You think you can bully and bribe me and I'm going to jump when you say jump? No, that's over, Steven. The prenup will be broken and I will be getting quite a bit more than 250 grand. Now if you'll just get out of my way." Steven moved to block her but was smart enough to keep his hands to himself.

"I know you're going to find this hard to believe, but I'm actually doing you a favor." Madeline didn't even try to hide her incredulousness. "Right now, you've got a limited amount of money that will last only a few months, even if you get the Porsche sold. A long, contested divorce will only diminish both our resources. If we can agree to a settlement that is fair, then you can be completely finished with me in ninety days. Think about it—you can start a new life and not suffer the embarrassment and financial hardship of a protracted, public divorce."

"You mean, you can have me out of your life faster without giving me what I deserve. I'm not listening to this anymore. If you have any *real* settlement offers, have your attorney talk to my attorney. Now, get out of my way. And stay away from me."

Though she was proud of the way she stood up to Steven, her hands were shaking so badly by the time she got to her room, she could barely get the key card in the slot. Burt's phone rang as she was bolting the door.

"Are you alright?"

"Yeah, I suppose so. I wasn't expecting him to show up here. It was all I could do to keep from beating him with my fists. I guess I'm not as well hidden as I thought."

"The hotel name probably showed up when you used your credit card. He reported the card stolen right after the hotel tried to process the charge. We weren't going for complete secrecy, just a place I could monitor. If you want to be moved, I can arrange a more private location."

"No, that's alright. He already knows where I am. I guess that's why no one bothered to follow me here. Where are you now?"

"I'm going back to my place. I headed over to the hotel as soon as I got an alert from the front desk." Madeline took a little comfort in knowing she had backup. "So, what did he want?"

"He was trying to buy me off with $250,000, provided I give him a quickie divorce. I told him to forget it."

"Interesting. Especially considering all the trouble he went through to make sure a divorce didn't cost him anything."

"I know. Maybe hiring my own attorney prompted the offer."

"That, or he's trying to clear the decks for the new Mrs. Ridley. Either way, I think we can assume by the offer that he's getting nervous. Okay, I better get back to work. Call me if anything comes up. What time do you want to go to the police station tomorrow?"

"Oh, I don't know…around ten?"

"Fine. I'll call and set something up. If you have a change of heart, let me know."

"No, I think I need to do it and get it behind me."

"Good. We'll talk in the morning. Get some rest."

Madeline laid Burt's phone next to hers on the coffee table. She knew she had to start looking in earnest for a place to live, but inertia had set in, making it hard for her to care about anything.

TWENTY-NINE

Madeline scoured the Internet for suitable housing until midnight. She sent out a few emails to landlords and management companies, but she was less than enthusiastic about anything she'd seen. As the night wore on, she started imagining what her prospects would be like if she had a quarter of a million dollars at her disposal. That line of thinking spawned the idea of relocating someplace with more affordable real estate. But as nice as it was to imagine having the security of owning her own home, she couldn't bear the thought of leaving Santa Barbara.

Though she only slept for six hours, she awoke with some of her former vigor. She had things to take care of and nothing motivated her more than having tasks to check off a list.

She had just gotten out of the shower when her cell phone rang. The call was coming from her attorney. It was only 7:45.

"Hope I'm not calling too early," Barry Houstein said. "I didn't wake you, did I?"

"No, not at all. I take it you got my rather hysterical message."

"Yes, I did. I'm sorry I wasn't able to get back to you sooner."

"I understand."

"Listen, I just got off the phone with Richard Laird of Pillman, Guillaume & Laird. Says he's representing your husband in your divorce. I guess they've had a little reality check and decided to offer you a settlement, with caveats—500,000 and a seven-day stay in Guam."

"That's very interesting. It was only 250,000 yesterday."

"So, you already know about this? When we met on Friday, I got the impression he was trying to cut you off without a cent. Half a mil is not what we'd be looking for if we had proof he framed you. But the nice thing is if you were in the mood to make a quick settlement, you could still go after him on assault charges, etcetera, later."

Madeline thought this over. If Burt's hunches were right, then Steven would be in serious legal trouble. This new overture was more evidence that he needed her out of the way in a hurry in order to replenish the coffers. She would be helping him avoid prison if she took the deal, allowing him to clear the field and usher in Mrs. Moneybags. The whole notion turned her stomach, but what choice did she have?

"Why the trip to Guam?" she asked belatedly.

"A seven-day stay to establish residency. Guam divorce is the new Haitian divorce—it's legal in all fifty states, which the Haitian divorce isn't anymore. It takes up to ninety days to be final, but only one party has to make the trip there, as long as both parties agree to the terms. What do you think? Should we go long, hold out for your fair share, or do you share your husband's desire to put this behind you?"

"Hmm…I don't know. What do you think?"

"Breaking the prenup requires proof of coercion, duress, fraud, or bad intent. How confident are you that you can get that proof?" Barry asked.

"At this stage, we haven't got anything. He seems to have wiped his prints away. My investigator has run into a dead end, which is why he wants me to go to the police today. He says important evidence could be erased if I don't get them involved." Now Barry's side of the line became quiet.

"Does your husband know you're turning this over to the authorities?"

"No. As far as he's concerned, I still think I got drunk and slept with some stranger who just happened to be photographing the whole thing."

"So, if you hold out for the big payoff and reject this settlement, you could end up with no proof that you were set up. No disrespect to you or Santa Barbara's finest, but your story is not exactly kosher, if you know what I mean. You can go in there, spill your guts and then when they find out you're embroiled in a nasty divorce, they start thinking they're pissing up a rope to help one disgruntled spouse gut the other. You see what I'm saying?"

"Yeah, I do."

"I'm not saying they won't find you or your version of events credible, but finding evidence that implicates him might be a long shot. On the other hand, if you take your husband's offer, there's nothing in the agreement that says you must hold him harmless in your attack. So far, anyway. And really they couldn't put something like that in writing without tipping his hand. But as I was saying, you get the money, collect as much proof as you can while the divorce is pending, *then* you go to the cops. At least that way you've got some walking around money. Make sense?"

"Yes, it does. Especially since my private investigator has reason to believe Steven's been commingling investor funds with his own to the detriment of both the investors and the borrowers."

"TAKE THE OFFER!" Barry said. The forceful way he said this made Madeline laugh.

"Can you send the agreement to me so I can read the exact terms?"

"Coming your way right now. But let me just go over the fine points of it while I've got you on the line. Okay, you'll be paid $250,000 before you board the plane and the other $250,000 once the divorce is final, which is essentially ninety days later."

"Do I have a say in this?"

"Absolutely! At this moment, you're in the driver's seat. How do you want me to respond?"

"I want the $500,000 upfront."

"Understandable. Anything else?"

"I want my diamond and emerald necklace and earrings returned before I leave for *Guam*," she said, the name sticking to her tongue as she tried to expel it. Never did she imagine she'd be traveling to that remote island, and certainly not for a quickie divorce.

"Okay, anything else?"

Madeline thought about this. She was very tempted to demand the beach house, but thought better of it. He'd never agree to that. If she got greedy, she might blow the whole thing. And from the cards she was now holding, this was probably going to be the best deal she could ever get out of her ruined marriage.

"No, that's it. No, wait—what about your fees?"

"You want me to include those, too?"

"Yes."

"You got it. Stay by the phone, in case I need you. This might not take too long."

"I think that was a wise move," Burt said. Madeline called him as soon as she hung up with the attorney. "It takes you out of the hot seat, puts some cash in your pocket, and gives me time to continue my investigation. If you're sure you're okay not going after him for the rape—for the time being, anyway—then I think you've set yourself up pretty well. At least you shouldn't have any more bombs dropped on you."

"That would be a refreshing change," Madeline agreed. "But I've still got the photos to worry about. He could send them out to everyone I know." Burt was silent for a moment.

"The only hope you've got is that doing so might have a negative impact on him. He claims he's fearful of his reputation being hurt if they got out. Plus, if everyone's snickering behind their hands, how's that going to affect the woman he's courting?"

"I guess I've got that in my favor."

"The photos were taken to cheat you out of your fair share of the community property. They're what made you so amenable to settling for half a million."

"Do you think I should've held out for more?"

"That's your call. As for my personal opinion, for what it's worth, I doubt you'd get any more than that, not if he's short on funds. For all we know, he might've borrowed that from Mrs. Collins-Wainwright, or from an unsuspecting borrower." Madeline let out a disdainful wheeze.

"You're probably right," she admitted.

"I'll call Detective Slovitch and tell him we need to postpone our appointment."

"Thanks."

"Don't mention it. Now that's off the calendar, what's on your agenda today?"

"I was going to look for a place to live. But I can do that while I'm sitting on my hands in Guam. I guess I'll wait for my attorney to tell me what my next move's going to be, and figure out what to do from there. I suppose I should find out where the heck Guam is and what to wear this time of year." Burt laughed, a pleasant sound she didn't remember hearing before.

"Call me when you hear back from your attorney. I'll be heading over to the courthouse soon, but you can reach me on my cell."

Madeline set Burt's phone down. The physical sense of pressure she'd felt for over a week had lifted. She could actually breathe freely again. After the whirlwind of being tarred and feathered, the prospect of walking away from a deceitful marriage with half a million dollars made her feel like a net winner.

THIRTY

"Okay, here's the new deal—they caved to the full amount upfront. But in exchange, they want you to leave for Guam tomorrow morning. They've got you booked on an 8:26 departure out of LAX. You'll be gone a total of nine days—"

"I thought it was only supposed to be seven."

"You lose a day going. Guam is eighteen hours ahead of Pacific Time. Plus, it'll take you almost seventeen hours to get there." Her attorney ignored her moan. "It's almost 6,100 miles from here, and there aren't any non-stops. But once you get there it won't be so bad. I've heard it's actually a nice little island. Give you time to rest and regroup. But getting back to the settlement…I'm afraid the jewelry is a lost cause."

"Those pieces were gifts to me. I want them back."

"I understand. But according to Mr. Laird, they are no longer in your husband's possession."

"What does that mean?" Madeline asked irritably, though as the words left her mouth, she got the picture. Either Steven hocked them or they were used to romance his latest conquest. Barry let the question slide. Now that his fee had been set, there was no reason to drag this case out any longer than necessary.

"The other good news is they agreed to pay my fees, so you can put that in the plus column with the 500 grand." Madeline swallowed her rancor with effort and tried to focus on what this settlement meant for her.

"So, how does all this work—the money and the plane tickets and all that?"

"You'll need to sign the agreement, either here or in Laird's office. It's probably easier for you if you sign there, but if you feel more comfortable with me being present, then we can arrange for that to be done down here. As it stands, a cashier's check will be ready by noon, along with the tickets. Just give his office a call and they'll arrange a time for you to sign the paperwork. You'll be given the check and the tickets then."

"Does Steven have to be there when I sign?"

"No, unless you want him to be."

"No. Definitely not."

"I'll make sure Laird knows that."

"Thank you. Is that it?"

"That's it. Laird will be shepherding the divorce through the Guam courts with a local attorney. You are to contact Laird's office once you arrive and the representative will walk you through the process. You can call me anytime if you have questions. I advise you to spend the night down in L.A. in order to make your flight."

"Well, sounds like it's all final, then," Madeline said. She felt dazed and hollow, but she didn't really feel like everything was actually over. It had all happened too fast to feel real. Something was missing, like a goodbye or "I'm sorry it had to end this way."

"Am I doing the right thing?" she asked.

"That's a question you have to ask yourself," Barry said. "As your advocate, I can say that you are positioning yourself well, regardless of what happens with the criminal case, should you choose to pursue it. The beauty of this settlement is that it takes your life out of limbo, gives you a financial cushion and allows you to step back and decide what legal action you want to take. In other words, I don't see this settlement as being anything but beneficial for you. If we had evidence against your husband in hand, that would be a different story."

Though he had told her nothing new, she felt a little reassured hearing it again. She felt like she was about to step off a cliff; she had to at least be sure no one on her side was against her doing so.

Now that it was almost official, Madeline had to think pragmatically. She only had a few hours to prepare herself for the undoing of her marriage and the pilgrimage to Guam. She was grateful now that she only had a few bags of possessions to worry about. But she could hardly board an international flight with a couple carry-ons and assorted shopping bags. She grabbed the notepad and began another list:

Call Laird's office
Buy suitcase
Call Mike
Arrange for a late check out

She became aware of acute hunger pains, but she was too keyed up to eat anything just yet. She had to dress and make herself presentable, then organize her things before she could think of venturing out of the room.

While piling the odd assortment of belongings she had in her possession on the bed for assessment, she called Mike. The grogginess in his voice made her check the time. Only 9 a.m. and she felt like she'd been awake for days.

"Did I wake you up?" she asked as she took the extravagant, unworn shoes out of their boxes and stuffed them in their protective bags.

"Uh…no…I'm awake, I think."

"I hate to spring this on you, but can you put me up for the night?"

"Tonight?"

"Yeah."

"Sure," Mike said, sounding more alert and chipper at the prospect of seeing her so soon. "Hey, I was going to call you. I got a decent offer on your car. The guy's very interested."

"Great. You can tell me all about it when I get down there. Oh, do you think you could take me to LAX tomorrow morning? I've got an early flight. I probably need to be there by 6:30."

"Now you're pushing the friendship limits," Mike said. She could tell he was delighted to be put out. "Where you headed?"

"Guam. I'll explain everything when I get down there."

Madeline sat in Mike's Mercedes, staring at the cashier's check for half a million dollars. She knew she was lucky to have gotten anything at all, considering the devious monster she had married. But the victory felt empty, and not because the settlement was far less than she should've gotten. She had been ejected from her beautiful life with a fat check as a consolation prize. She had failed to stay married to the only man she truly loved. But her biggest failure came from misjudging his character.

She dabbed at her weepy eyes, dismayed to find herself crying again. Over the last six days, she had vacillated between sobbing wretchedness and an insatiable desire for vengeance. She'd hoped the check would've put a finality to all that, but now she realized money had only given her comfort when she had no worries and no scars in need of healing. She had no idea where she'd find a cure for what ailed her now—a violated psyche and a broken heart.

As she left her bank, Burt's phone rang.

"How did it go?" he asked.

"Fine. I signed the divorce agreement and walked out with a cashier's check and a roundtrip ticket to the middle of nowhere."

"When do you leave for Guam?"

"Early tomorrow morning."

"I didn't realize you'd be leaving so soon," Burt said. Madeline felt the first pangs of separation anxiety; her private investigator had become her protector and key ally. The 18-hour time difference was going to make it hard for them to stay in touch.

"It was part of the deal. Apparently, Steven can't get rid of me fast enough."

"I wouldn't take it personally. Sociopaths never let anything or anyone stand in the way of what they want." Madeline let out a sad sigh.

"For years I thought all he wanted was me." She was sounding pathetic, even to her own ears. "You'll have to forgive me for being so maudlin. It's not like me. I'm usually all sunshine and laughter," she said, her flippancy falling short of convincing.

"Don't be so hard on yourself. You've weathered this like a champ. Most people would be out of their minds with terror and grief by this point. You're a lot sturdier than you look." Madeline had to laugh at that.

"Thanks. You really cheered me up."

"All in a day's work," Burt said. "Speaking of which, I better get back on the case. I'll send you text messages to keep you updated on my progress while you're away. You might want to turn off the sound when you go to bed so I don't wake you up."

"That's a good point. Well…"

"Call me anytime—I mean it."

"Thanks, Burt. Hopefully you won't hear from me at all."

THIRTY-ONE

"Jeeze, you'd think you were planning on staying there a year," Mike chided her as he lugged her baggage over the threshold.

"This is all the stuff I had at the hotel. I had to take it with me—everything else is in storage."

"You can leave some of it here," Mike suggested, as they passed into his living room.

"Thanks. I'll take you up on that. I've got a carry-on with nothing in it that I certainly don't need to lug all the way to Guam. Wow, what a gorgeous place," she said, stopping to take it all in. "You weren't kidding—this is like a time capsule. I bet you have to beat the women off with a stick having a pad like this."

Mike beamed at her praise. He was quite proud of his refined digs. They hinted at a more dignified side to his persona than his physical appearance suggested.

"Are all the units this nice?"

"They're all sweet, but this is the manager's unit. It's 1,500 square feet of '40s Hollywood glamor."

"You're a lucky bastard," Madeline said as she took in the view of the courtyard fountain.

"Yeah, I know. Credit goes to my dad—he was smart enough to know value when he saw it. There are fifteen other units here—who knows when I might have an opening…" Madeline caught his meaning and smirked at the insinuation. "Rents are a little steep, but you can afford them now."

"Thanks, but I can't see myself living in L.A."

"This is a great spot. Sometimes I forget I'm in the middle of tinsel town." Madeline was clearly unmoved by his sales pitch. "Your room is over this way." Mike stood aside and let her check out the guest suite. Now he knew she was impressed.

"If the manager's unit ever becomes available, let me know," she said.

"Ha, ha. There's plenty of room for two here…" Madeline ignored him and fell backwards on the bed.

"Ugh," she moaned, kicking off her shoes. "I can't believe how long this day has been!"

"It's not over yet. I'm going to take you out for the best high-end Mexican food you've ever had," Mike said, as he flopped onto a chair in the corner of the room.

"Do they deliver?"

"You're exhausted, aren't you?" Madeline nodded weakly. Mike got up and slid onto the bed beside her. "I'll take you there when you get back. I'll run out and get us some Chinese or something in a bit." Madeline closed her eyes. It felt so good to lie down, it hurt.

"Do you have any eggs?" she asked.

"Yeah. You want me to make one of my famous omelets? That sound good?" Madeline smiled at the thought of Mike's spinach, cream cheese and green onion omelet. She'd forgotten how good simple food could be.

"What really sounds good is a stiff drink," she said. Her eyes popped open at her faux pas. "Sorry," she said, rolling on her side to face him.

"It's okay. I don't start frothing at the mouth when someone talks about booze. Why, I can even walk down the liquor aisle of the grocery store without breaking into a sweat."

"I forgot for a second," she said.

"I do too, occasionally. Don't worry—I haven't slipped up in four years."

"Is it hard being sober?" Mike laughed.

"No harder than constantly apologizing to people. It's my new normal. I have no problem hanging with it. And you shouldn't feel like having an open container around is going to expose me to toxic fumes and drive me right back into the bottle. It's not going to happen."

"Well, I'm glad to hear that. What's so funny?"

"You'll never believe what I do on Tuesday nights."

"What?" Madeline asked, propping herself up on her elbow.

"I tend bar at a little hole in the wall around the corner."

"No way!"

"It's true."

"How can you do that?"

"You mean, does it violate the principles of sobriety, or how do I keep from drinking straight out of the bottle? Really, it's like therapy for me. Every week

I get reminded of how pathetic I used to be when I drank." Madeline grinned and scooted closer to him. He slipped his arm under her neck and they lay there in companionable silence.

"You were the only person I could count on to help me," she said. Mike kissed the side of her head.

"I'm glad I was here for you. Makes being sober worth it." After a couple minutes passed, he asked, "Do you think we would've stayed together if I hadn't been such a raging jerk?" Madeline rolled over to face him.

"That's like asking me if I'd have married Steven knowing what a psychopath he is." Realizing how harsh this sounded, she qualified her statement. "In other words, pointless." Mike looked at her thoughtfully for a minute.

"Given what you know about both of us now, do you ever see yourself giving me a second try?" Madeline sat up and scooted away.

"I'm barely out of my first marital wipeout and you're asking me a question like that? I'm not even divorced yet."

"Yeah, but you will be soon," Mike argued.

"Look, maybe it was a mistake to impose on you like this..." she said, swinging her legs off the bed.

"Hold on a sec...don't be like that," Mike said, reaching out to grab her arm, but she was too quick for him. "Come on, now—you're starting to hurt my feelings."

"Oh, please. You expect me to believe after all this time you're ready to mix things up again?" Madeline barked, though she could hardly keep from laughing at the sight of Mike Delaney, lady killer, humbly submitting his heart to her. "And don't expect me to believe you're not already involved with someone, or several someones. I'm sure you had to do quite the tap dance to clear the decks for my arrival." Mike's sly smile betrayed him.

"Not true. I live a monk-like existence. I'm a changed man. Spend some time with me—you'll see."

"Ha! I bet if I opened your closet I'd find all sorts of evidence to the contrary."

"Oh...did I tell you I perform in a transvestite bar every Wednesday?" Madeline laughed.

"Just as I figured. What did you tell them all, that you had a maiden aunt coming for a visit?"

"You know, this isn't a very nice way to treat your host," Mike said, almost managing to pull off a hurt look. "Is it really so farfetched for me to still have feelings for you?" After all the spoofing, this appeal caught Madeline off-guard.

"Okay, okay," Mike relented. "I shouldn't be hounding you in your vulnerable state. But I just have to know one thing…" Madeline braced herself. "Did you stop to fill up the Mercedes?" Madeline laughed, in spite of herself.

"See, I made you smile…" he teased her. "It's a good thing I didn't ask if you feel like getting lucky."

"I've got to pee," Madeline said, completely ignoring her host's remarks. "Oh, this is so darling!" she said of the adjoining bathroom. "Did you do all this yourself—the decorating and everything?"

"Of course. What do you think I am—a tasteless slob?" he asked, rocking himself off the bed to stand vigil beside the bathroom door. "You never answered my question."

"About getting lucky?" Mike heard the toilet flush and the sink water run.

"No, about the gas."

"Oh, no—I didn't even think of it," she said as she came out of the bathroom. "Sorry."

"New plan—I'm going to call in a pizza order, fill the car up with gas, and stop to get you a bottle of anything your heart desires. How does that sound? How about a nice Chianti to go with the sausage and meatball pizza, just like the old days…?"

"You're my hero," Madeline said, folding into his arms for a hug. The proximity had more of an effect on them than either was expecting. Madeline kissed him on the cheek, breaking the spell.

"I'll be back in a jiffy. Just make yourself at home."

"Thanks, Mike. You're too good to me."

"Don't I know it," he said, treating her to one of his wicked smiles before disappearing out the door.

THIRTY-TWO

"I'm sorry, this line is for first class travelers only," the woman at the check-in counter said, handing her ticket back. "You'll need to get in line behind those folks," she said, already motioning for the next person. Being a little slow on the uptake, Madeline started to protest. But as she checked her ticket, she discovered Steven's latest slap in the face. She flipped to the second page of the ticket and found more bad news: the second leg of the trip would also be spent in the back cabin. She should've known.

She lowered her sunglasses and dragged her bags to the end of the general check-in line. Her head throbbed dully, thanks to having drunk three-quarters of a bottle of Chianti. She shuddered at the thought of drinking with such abandon. It felt good going down, but now she felt like one of the sorry patrons Mike ministered to on Tuesday nights.

She felt even worse as she remembered blubbering like an idiot as Mike undressed her and got her into bed. What a pathetic mess she was. She hardly recognized herself anymore. But that was the rub: Madeline Ridley had ceased to exist. In a mere three months it would be legal and final. She had to consciously define who she would become next. As it stood now, she was an almost unmarried, unemployed forty-year-old, homeless and without prospects. *How did I get here?* she asked herself again. As usual, there was no answer.

As she inched her way toward the front of the line, her wine-soaked brain started sending her alerts, which registered like unwanted emails in her mental inbox. Chief among her worries was the fact that she still hadn't called her father. She couldn't figure out how to break the news to him about her sudden divorce without giving him any of the sordid details. She toyed with taking the cowardly way out by emailing him her new phone number, but she was afraid that would prompt a call from him.

Yet, if she waited any longer, he might call the house—or worse, Steven—and find out the truth the hard way. She'd have to work up the courage soon before she got to Guam or the time difference would make it impossible to reach him. She glanced at her watch: the plane would board in forty-five minutes.

As she maneuvered her bags another two feet, she regretted not taking Mike's advice. If she didn't have a bag to check, she could've headed through security and gone straight to the gate. Instead, she was stuck with a second bag with almost nothing useful in it. She nearly laughed out loud as she thought of what all she had chosen to drag to Guam—a weird collection of high-end footwear, sweat pants, t-shirts and cashmere sweaters. Not exactly the right apparel for the tropics.

As she cast her mind back, she recalled that she was also carrying a fair amount of her good jewelry—not a smart move—plus a few impractical articles of clothing still wrapped in tissue paper that she had purchased at Saks during her final shopping spree. She should've returned it all and pocketed the cash. At least then she wouldn't be burdened by the cumbersome load.

Once her bag was checked, she moved with the flow of bodies and filtered through security. By the time she reached the gate, her flight was already boarding. She took her seat in the rear of the plane, right across from the restrooms and a new mother with a squalling infant. She stuffed foam plugs in her ears and fell into a troubled and disorienting sleep. She awoke when the flight attendant told her to bring her seatback forward.

The double latte from the nearest concession in the Honolulu airport soon brought her back to semi-alertness. The second cup pushed her into hyper-drive. She had two and a half hours before her flight left for Guam. She used the back of her ticket to make a list:

Call Dad
Search hotels in Guam
Call Burt
Look into first class seats for return flights
Buy swimsuit, tunic, shorts, sandals
Kill Steven

She hazarded a glance at her surroundings and scratched the last item off her list. It felt surprisingly good to write those words, but the way her luck was running, they might come back to haunt her.

To keep the caffeine from eating a hole in her stomach, she bought a turkey sandwich and relocated to an empty gate. She rehearsed several dialogs with her father as she ate, but every opener led to the same conclusion. No matter which tack she took, her father was going to hit the roof. She put her sandwich aside and picked up her phone. She had to get this over before she drove herself crazy.

"Hello?"

"Dad, it's me, Madeline."

"Madeline! Jesus Christ, where are you? I have been frantic trying to figure out what's going on." Madeline cringed.

"Dad, I'm sorry you've been worried—"

"Worried? I've been out of my mind. I tried your cell phone, but the number's no longer in service. I was just about to book a flight to Santa Barbara when you called." Madeline covered eyes, as if that could dispel the visual of her father on the verge of a stroke because of her.

"Dad, I'm alright. Please calm down. I'll explain everything, but please relax. I don't want you to have another heart attack." Mack Dawkins heaved an emotional sigh, making Madeline feel even worse.

"Just tell me what the hell's going on, would you please?" Madeline took a deep breath and gave it to him straight.

"Steven and I are getting divorced."

"Oh, for Chrissakes," Mack said. Madeline could hear the devastation in his voice.

"Daddy, I don't want you to be upset. Please, don't be upset. It's all going to work out for the better. I'll have to go into it some other time. But for right now you just have to believe that I'm okay and things will work out in the long run."

"Where are you calling from?" he asked, as an announcement went out over the P.A. system.

"I'm in Honolulu—"

"Honolulu?"

"I'm about to board a plane for Guam—"

"Guam? Why in God's name are you going to *Guam?"* he demanded, making Madeline feel like she was back in the sixth grade.

"It's the most expedient way to get a divorce these days."

"Oh God," Mack muttered. Madeline could imagine him casting around the room for something to steady himself.

"In light of the way things ended with Steven and me, it's really for the best to get this behind us."

"Why I am only hearing about this now? You never told me there was trouble between you and Steven."

"I know, Daddy, I know. Like I said, I can't really go into all the details now, but—"

"Did he cheat on you?" Mack asked angrily. "Is that what the son-of-a-bitch did to cause this?" Madeline hung her head. She knew she wasn't prepared for this conversation.

"It wasn't any one thing…"

"Then what's the big rush to get divorced? Have you gone to counseling? You and Steven have been good together. Not all marriages are a cakewalk, you know. Sometimes you have to step back and take a fresh look at the situation. You've invested a lot of years in your marriage…" Madeline held the phone away from her ear. She waited for her father's ranting to die down before trying to speak.

"Dad, they're boarding my flight now," she lied. "I probably won't be able to reach you until I get back from Guam. But after I get back to Santa Barbara and get settled—"

"Why were you the one who moved out? Why didn't Steven move out?" Mack snapped.

"Okay, Dad—I really have to go now. I'm sorry for all the anxiety I caused you. I'll contact you as soon as I get back." To add believability to her lie for her own sake, Madeline gathered her stuff and started walking in the general direction of her gate. "I love you, Dad. Bye." She pressed the end button, not giving her father a chance to reply. Now she really hated herself.

She could feel the onset of bitter tears and headed for the restroom. After she ran cold water over her wrists and got her breathing under control, she scoped out another secluded waiting area. In an effort to refocus herself, she reviewed her list and revised it. This time she underlined the words *Kill Steven* so forcefully, she ripped the paper.

THIRTY-THREE

Madeline dragged her carry-on down the gateway behind her slow-moving fellow passengers. Fortunately for her, the plane was only sixty-percent full and she was able to stretch out over three seats on the flight from Honolulu to A. B. Won Pat International Airport. It was some consolation for being stuck in coach, something she hadn't experienced since her pre-Steven days.

She could already feel the heat and humidity coming through the cracks between the plane and the ramp, and it was almost 9:00 at night. She felt wilted and jetlagged beyond anything she could remember. It seemed like days since she took off from LAX. She followed the signs through the terminal out to the street where she looked for a shuttle bus to the Westin Hotel.

She had used her spare time in Honolulu to do some research on her destination and figure out where to stay. It showed how ill-prepared she was for this new phase in her life that she had been assuming a room had already been booked for her. It proved she hadn't fully accepted her fate. In the back of her mind, she had been relying on Steven to handle things like hotel accommodations. For the first time she was glad she'd have a week of isolation so she could retool her mind and start thinking like a single woman again.

It was almost ten o'clock at night by the time Madeline was checked in and taken to her room. Though she couldn't tell at this hour, she had been given a corner room with full ocean and coastline views. The room itself was clean, spacious and elegantly spare. She stepped out onto the balcony and listened to the crash of the incoming waves. A few voices could be heard, but other than those two sounds, it was starkly quiet.

Her inner clock was at odds with the time zone; she was starving and not ready for sleep. After flipping through the hotel directory, she discovered there was only one place still serving food, a bar called On The Rocks. She could've ordered room service, but she'd had enough of being confined to small spaces.

She unpacked her bags, washed her face and sorted through her clothing for something semi-appropriate for dining in a hotel bar.

She wasn't surprised to find the place almost empty on what was now Wednesday night. There were three men sitting at the bar, far enough apart from each other to not be together, but close enough to still converse. Madeline took a seat at a banquette table in a corner. She was deleting emails on her iPhone when the waiter appeared. She ordered a fancy rum cocktail and a couple appetizers and munched on the bar snacks as she continued to search for a message from Burt.

It finally occurred to her to check Burt's phone for messages. There she found a text he had sent several hours earlier while she was still airborne. *Very good day. Clld 24 of 67 borrowers w/ liens held by RAM L.P. Offered to lower rate as pretext. 4 said they'd paid off loans.*

She reread the message, her hand trembling as she reached for her drink. Did this mean what she thought it meant? A surge of adrenalin hit her heart, making it thump erratically.

In her excitement, she had overlooked his second text, which made the message clearer: *Got him. How do u want to proceed? Use as leverage, turn over to law, enlighten borrowers and let them handle it? Advise. B.*

She was too stunned to think. Did they finally have the upper hand? From this remote locale, she couldn't tell if it was just wishful thinking or reality. As the possibility of ending her nightmare started to sink in, she felt like letting loose a victory yell. The waiter appeared with the spring rolls and chicken skewers. She looked at the appetizers as though she didn't know why he'd brought them to her.

"Would you like another cocktail, Miss?" Madeline stared at her empty glass with amazement.

"Sure," she replied tentatively. She attempted to pry the chicken from a bamboo stick and soon tired of the effort. She bit into a spring roll, burning her tongue in the process. The waiter brought her second drink, providing her a good remedy for the scorched taste buds.

"Is it possible to get a green salad?" She asked between sips.

"I'll see what I can do, Miss."

"And can you please have the kitchen remove the skewers?"

"Yes, Miss."

She ate the now-cool spring rolls voraciously as she tried to string together the ramifications of what Burt had uncovered. His instincts about Steven's behavior had been dead-on from the day she hired him. Finding him was her best stroke of luck so far, aside from catching Steven's payoff to Russell Barnett.

Whether due to relief, booze or jetlag, Madeline suddenly felt utterly exhausted, weary with fatigue down to the soles of her feet. She hardly noticed when the waiter placed a nice green salad and the de-skewered chicken strips in front of her. She forced herself to eat in hopes of synchronizing her inner rhythms to local time.

Using her last bit of cognitive ability, she determined it to be just after 5 a.m. in Santa Barbara. She was eighteen hours ahead of Burt; Wednesday, February 24th was about to end for her and begin for him. She'd give him another twenty-five minutes before sending him a text. Hopefully by then she'd know what to tell him.

After wandering the public areas of the hotel for as long as she could manage, Madeline took a seat in the deserted lobby and composed her message to Burt.

Great news! I'm overwhelmed. What do u think is the best plan? Call me.

She sat for another couple minutes willing Burt's response to show up on his phone. Figuring he had the sense to turn off his sounds, she headed to the elevator and rode up to the seventh floor, his phone in her hand.

Once in her room, she undressed quickly and placed the phone on the bathroom counter while she brushed the endless day off her teeth. She wanted to shower, but lack of strength and fear of missing Burt's call made her postpone it till the morning. She managed a few sloppy stretches before giving in to her dire need for sleep. Her eyes closed the second she laid her head on the pillow.

Five minutes later, Burt's phone rang, startling her out of her travel-weary senses. In her confusion, she almost knocked the lamp off the table while grabbing the wrong phone. By the time she realized her mistake, the call had gone to voicemail. She frantically called him back.

"Hello?" she croaked as Burt answered. "Sorry. I guess I fell asleep."

"I'm not surprised. This time difference is going to be a challenge, isn't it?" Burt said. He sounded surprisingly jovial given the earliness of the hour.

"Yes, it is," Madeline said, forcing herself into a sitting position, hoping it would stimulate brain activity.

"Since you sound like you just swam all the way to Guam, I'll try to do most of the talking." Madeline let out a snort that was meant to be a laugh. "I'm assuming you understood my messages...?"

"Yes," she said, blinking hard as she turned on the lamp.

"Good. Well, my instincts were right. But to be honest, I didn't think finding the proof would be so easy. I guess it goes to Steven's perceived credibility that so many people would take him at his word. Now we know for a fact Steven is in it up to his neck. And I'm not even halfway through the list yet. For all we know, he's been doing this for years, the only difference being he was able to replace the funds and reconvey the notes before anyone got wise. But unless he can move heaven and earth simultaneously, I don't think he's going to be so lucky this time."

"What do you think we should do now that we have proof of what's going on?"

"Well, first we need to develop this 'proof,' which means I'll have to confirm their claims. I can approach it a couple of different ways. I can either call them back and continue the pretext, saying the most current data still shows the lien on their property, or I can say I'm investigating fraud charges against the company that made the loan. I can advise them to contact the district attorney immediately, or I can meet with them, get their statements for the D.A. myself. Or send them to Steven's investors.

"So you see, there are a number of ways to finesse this situation. But since our assumption has been that you were quickly disposed of in order to secure bailout money, I think we need to move fast on this, before Steven can reconvey those notes and put the monies back into his investors' coffers. Are you following me?"

"Yes," Madeline said, wide awake now.

"One thing I forgot to mention—my Boston contact informed me that Mrs. Collins-Wainwright left from Logan Airport yesterday morning on a private jet. I was able to confirm the jet landed in Santa Barbara at 2 p.m. yesterday."

"She's already there?" A horrible feeling came over Madeline as she imagined Steven's new victim presiding over her home. Even though she had suspected as much a few days ago, Steven's capacity for subterfuge was truly shocking. It was as though he had no conscience at all. He had to be a true sociopath. How had she missed that side of him? She was afraid it didn't speak very well of her.

"That's correct. My source at SBA confirmed the jet's arrival," Burt said. "I'll keep my eyes and ears open for any news of her whereabouts. But in the meantime, I need you to tell me which course of action to take. I realize you're dead tired—why don't you sleep on it. I'll continue to plow through my list, then we'll have all our ammo ready."

Madeline tried to imagine actually sleeping with her mind so full of quandaries. "What's the cleanest, most reliable way to make all this stick?" she asked. Burt thought this over.

"I'm not sure that hybrid exists. The cleanest way to drop the dime on Steven is to set the borrowers after him. That way there's nothing to link you or me to his exposure. But the most reliable way to make sure he doesn't wiggle out of it somehow would be turning the evidence over to the D.A.'s office. The downside to that scenario is getting our fingerprints all over it. You see what I'm saying?"

"I think so. If you subtly tip off the victims, they may go straight to Steven, who would then come up with some cock 'n bull story and make it all right. Then the evidence goes away and we'd have nothing to pin on him."

"Exactly."

"So, it's better if we gather the statements and turn them over to the D.A."

"It's the best way to make sure Steven doesn't sidestep the charges." Madeline let out a deep sigh, her eyes wandering heavenward, as if the answer were written on the ceiling.

"And you want me to make that call."

"It's got to be your decision," Burt said.

"But doesn't that potentially put you in a dangerous position?"

"And possibly you. I've been in worse, so don't worry about me," Burt replied with a sanguine laugh. "You hired me to get the goods on Steven. That's what I'm prepared to do."

"I hired you to find out who was behind the photos," she corrected him.

"Yeah, but that's how these investigations go sometimes. If we've got a criminal and we can't get him on one crime, then we get him on anything we can."

"If you're okay with the risk, so am I."

"Okay, that's the plan then. I'll call the four I contacted today, let them know I'm investigating fraud and embezzlement charges and take their statements. I'm anxious to get through the remaining borrowers. I find it hard to believe I lucked out and found all the victims already. I'll keep you posted."

"Thanks, Burt. I'm so glad to have you for an ally. I can't imagine what this last week would've been like without you."

"Fortunately, you don't even need to think about it. Now get some sleep. You've got to go see the attorney tomorrow, right?"

"Oh God, yes—thanks for reminding me! Oh, I'm so thrashed, I forgot about that," Madeline said with a groan.

"Hey, from what I saw online, it looks like you've landed in paradise. Get your divorce business settled and then work on your tan. You'll be the envy of all your friends when you get back."

"Ha! What friends?" Madeline rasped. "After the multiple scandals hit the airwaves, I'll have to go into permanent hiding. I might have to stay on Guam indefinitely."

THIRTY-FOUR

"Mrs. Ridley? How do you do? I'm Alfonso Winogo. This way please."
Madeline followed the attorney into his office, noting with distaste how cramped and disorderly it was. She had a hard time making the association between this lawyer and Pillman, Guillaume & Laird. She took a seat in front of the file-laden desk as Mr. Winogo cleared a place for her to sign the documents.

"I hope you're enjoying your stay here so far," he said, beaming pleasantly at her, as if he were a hotel concierge and not an accessory to her shotgun divorce.

"Yes," Madeline replied curtly, ready to get this task behind her.

"It is a good time of the year to visit, after the rainy season." Madeline smiled tightly. "Okay then, let us get down to business. First, may I see your identification and your travel itinerary, if you have it?

Madeline removed her driver's license and handed it over. She was glad she had kept her flight information, until she remembered the notes she had written to herself—or more specifically, the heavily underlined reminder to *Kill Steven.*

"It looks like all I have is the return flight info," she said, carefully separating it from the incriminating epitaph.

"That will be fine, as I can attest to your presence in my office here today," Mr. Winogo said, placing a legal document in front of her. "I am working in the capacity as an affiliate to the law firm of Pillman, Guillaume & Laird of Santa Barbara, California, United States of America. As their representative, I will establish the fact that you will have been a resident of the territory of Guam for a minimum of seven days. Once you have fulfilled that requirement, I will take this uncontested divorce agreement to the court and proceed to file for your divorce. Do you understand the terms of your divorce as stated in writing on the pages in front of you?" Mr. Winogo asked, reciting a speech he had undoubtedly delivered hundreds of times.

"Yes."

"Very good. You should read the entire document and sign where indicated. If you do not understand any part of the divorce agreement, you are advised to contact your legal counsel and postpone signing said document until you are satisfied and confident that your position as stated is in accordance with your best interest. Do you understand what I've told you?"

"Yes."

"Good. Any questions at this time?"

"No," Madeline said, already well into the document. She found it to be the same as the one she signed in Santa Barbara, with no oblique or misleading language or terms added. She accepted the pen Mr. Winogo had at the ready. When she had finished, she handed both back to the attorney.

"May I have a copy of that?"

"Of course. I will make copies of your ID and itinerary also and be right back."

Mr. Winogo left Madeline alone with the artifacts of his professional and personal life. If the photos were up to date, Mr. Winogo was a married man with four little Winogos to his credit.

"Nice family," Madeline said, having been caught examining his brood.

"Thank you," he said, taking a moment to pay homage to the compact woman, the three wiry sons and petite daughter, all dark haired and smiling for all they were worth. A wave of unexpected longing rushed over Madeline, making her feel acutely unloved and unwanted. She coughed to drive away the threat of another emotional breakdown.

"Well, if that's everything, I guess I should be going," she said, holding out her hand to Mr. Winogo. "Thank you for handling this…"

"My pleasure, dear lady. And best wishes to you in the future." Mr. Winogo's benediction rang in her ears as she exited the two-story stucco building and collided with the intense mid-morning sun. She hurriedly donned her sunglasses and walked purposefully to the waiting town car.

On the way back to the hotel, Madeline realized she had some shopping to do before she could take advantage of the tropical paradise she now found herself in. The driver took her to the Tumon Galleria, which was a short walk back to the Westin. Though she was aware Guam boasted duty-free shopping, she had no idea how high-end the shops were, or how plentiful. Gucci, Chanel, Louis Vuitton, Armani and Rolex proudly displayed their wares, along with many of her other favorite designer labels. After the hell of the past week, Madeline felt as though she had died and gone to heaven.

Now that she had dismissed the driver, she was able to really indulge herself. She could spend all day shopping and it was nobody's business but her own. She needed to shop for beachwear first, but as soon as that was taken care of, she would deny herself nothing. It would be retail therapy of the highest order, and duty-free to top it off. She had to pinch herself. She couldn't wait to enlighten all her friends about the best-kept divorce secret.

Her improved outlook and light mood were dampened by this last thought. Her friends; would she have any left by the time she got back to Santa Barbara? Suddenly, nine days out of the country felt akin to hard-time on Devil's Island.

Oh, stop being so dramatic, she chided herself as she slowed down to admire the window displays at the Chanel Boutique. *After all the titillation dies down, everyone will go on as if nothing ever happened.*

Though Madeline wanted to be reassured by her own pep talk, part of her knew nothing would ever be the same. Would she, Madeline Dawkins, be so sought after to sit on charity boards? Of course not. Besides, $500,000—though it sounded like a lot of money—would have to be parceled out very carefully to make it last. And that would have to be her nest egg; she would have to find some sort of employment to pay her monthly bills.

Now that reality had successfully squashed her cheery attitude, Madeline lost the desire to spend thousands of dollars on handbags and couture when she had more than enough of those treasures to last her a lifetime. *Besides, the way things are now, I doubt I'll have any place to wear all that finery,* she thought glumly.

She was so dispirited, she turned around and headed for the Westin. Surely she'd be able to find a bikini, a cover-up and some flip flops in one of the hotel boutiques. If she couldn't, she'd just stay in her room and sulk. Even paradise had its limitations when one's life was as screwed up as hers was.

Although she felt like wallowing in self-pity, there was simply too much to like about being stuck where she was. Guam, despite her fears, was a beautiful island. It was quite small, but it had just about everything a sun-loving vacationer could want. Shopping, even for beach necessities, brought a smile back to her face.

She left the boutique amid a chorus of well-wishes, loaded down with two shopping bags. All she needed was to see the vibrant colored tunics and swimsuits to get her enthusiasm for shopping back. The boutique had better merchandise than she had expected, and she soon found herself spoiled for choice. In the end, she walked away with two bikinis, two tunics, two pairs of strappy sandals, a pair of flip flops, shorts and a wide-brimmed hat for hiding under.

After ten minutes back in her room, she was ready for sunshine and white sand beaches. But, as she strolled through the hotel lobby, she realized she was also ravenously hungry. She knew the hotel had several dining options, but as nice as they sounded, she was primed for being out in the beautiful day. Luckily, she discovered a poolside bar that served a variety of fare. She took a seat facing the beach and ordered an exotic-sounding salad, something to offset her recent diet lapses.

As she sipped a Campari and soda with a splash of mango, she felt her whole body shift into vacation mode. If she could keep her mind off Steven, she should be able to use this downtime to her advantage. She needed to recuperate from his relentless acts of sabotage and come to grips with her new station in life. She probably needed a month's worth of appointments with a good shrink, but she was hoping a few massages, facials and something called "ocean wraps" would work just as well.

As the waitress placed a huge, beautiful salad in front of her, she thought of Jane. How many times had they split a salad like this? Countless. Her heart tightened, this time for the absence of her closest girlfriend. Madeline checked her phone and tried to figure the time difference as she wrangled with the dauntingly large salad. Every bite made her long for the chance to confide in a friend.

She'd been able to do that with Mike, to a certain extent, but that was different. Mike was like a brother to her at this point. She had known Mike for twenty years, and they'd weathered many hard times together. Now it was his turn to rescue her, and thank God he'd been there. But as much history as they had, she didn't feel like she could really open up to him the way she could with someone of her own sex.

She wanted to talk to Jane so badly, but she couldn't imagine what to tell her. She couldn't just call up and say, *Hey, I'm in Guam getting a quickie divorce so my conniving, criminal husband can marry someone with a lot of money to keep him from going to jail. Oh, and did I tell you I hired a private detective to find out who raped me while having the whole thing photographed?*

After only a few bites, she lost her appetite. What good was paradise if she didn't have someone to share it with? She left a big tip to absolve her from wasting so much food and went out to the sand.

A flutter of the joy she felt earlier returned as the squeals of happy children punctuated the crash of the surf. She felt herself smiling as her feet treaded on the soft, warm sand. She walked a short distance to find a spot to lay her things, then pulled off her hat, tunic and sunglasses and went running into the water. The sensation was magical. She laughed out loud as a wave crashed against her back. She rode the current out and ducked under as a wall of water came toward her.

The water was so refreshing—clear and buoyant—and she floated on her back, rising and falling with the undulating tide. She felt like she could float out there forever, let herself be carried into the middle of the Pacific Ocean, be lost and rid of all her problems for good.

But as she bobbed along the surface, a new hope began to grow inside her. All things considered, this was not a bad way to begin a new life. That she hadn't wanted to give up her old life no longer mattered. From this day forward she would need to think of her life as a convict saw his on the day the prison gates opened. Whatever transpired before was erased in favor of a new, hopeful start in life. This was the day the old Madeline Dawkins was re-baptized. All she had to do was decide what she wanted her life to consist of now and figure out how to achieve it.

THIRTY-FIVE

After she had showered away the sand and sea, Madeline turned on her computer. She found a time zone converter and downloaded it to her phone. It was now 3:30 p.m. in Guam and 9:30 p.m. the previous day in Santa Barbara. By the time she got used to the difference, it'd be time to reenter reality.

It hit her that this was a perfect window of opportunity to contact the mainland. Her first inclination was to contact Burt, but her eye wandered to the instant messaging icon in her tray. Nine-thirty on a school night was an ideal time to reach Jane; the girls would be in bed and she would likely be updating her blog. Madeline opened the Instant Messenger window and took herself off "away."

Hey, are you there? she typed and waited. After about thirty seconds, a message appeared telling her Jane was responding.

it's about time! where the hell r u?? Madeline braced herself.

Guam. It took less than five seconds to receive a reply.

Guam?? Madeline watched as Jane composed another reply. Now that she started this, she didn't know where she was going to end it.

what's going on? i finally went to your house. Erma said u moved out. what happened?

Steven sent me here to get a quickie divorce...

what? why? what'd i miss?

It's a very long, awful story...i'll tell you everything when i get back.

i don't understand how this could happen so fast. your cell was disconnected. what's your new #? Jane replied.

Madeline stared at the computer screen. She knew she couldn't give out her number; it was just too risky. With Jane's limited knowledge of the situation, she couldn't expect her to understand how evil Steven had become. For all she knew, he could be planning something even more foul now that she was 6,000 miles away.

I can't give it to you right now.

y the hell not??

u need to trust me – it's not safe.

now you're scaring me.

don't be scared. i think things might settle down now that Steven's gotten what he wants.

which is what?

a speedy divorce so he can marry someone else.

u gotta be joking

i'm not. my P.I. says she's already arrived in SB – from Boston.

your P.I.?

Oh boy, Madeline thought. Now she'd really screwed up.

you must swear to not tell ANYONE! Madeline watched anxiously for the caption to show that Jane was responding.

r u still there?? she typed after a minute had passed.

i'm here. i swear not to breathe a word. i just wish i knew what was going on. when will u b back?

In a week.

Where is guam, exactly?

Middle of the pacific – 6,100 miles from sb, to be exact. it's 18 hours ahead of the west coast. their motto is Guam—where America's day begins.

that's cute. I've only seen pics of military base there – looks awful.

it's not – the beaches are gorgeous. And u wouldn't believe the shopping – Rodeo drive meets duty free! You'd love it. we'll have to come here together sometime.

no thanks – i don't want to get divorced. Madeline laughed.

lol. u won't have to – i promise! I guess I should let you get back to your blog.

no – don't go! I miss u!

I miss u 2. I'll check in w/ u soon. xxoo

back at u!

Madeline closed out of Instant Messenger. She felt empty inside. This was only a short exile; she knew that. But she also knew she would be going back to Santa Barbara as a changed woman. The lifestyle and friends she had relied on would recede from her. As much as she willed herself to be strong and embrace the opportunity to redefine herself, she couldn't help feeling sad, and alone.

When she came out of her soulful reverie, she realized she hadn't had contact with Burt all day. It was now a little after ten his time. She called him from his phone, hoping she wasn't calling too late. But from what she had seen so far, Burt seemed to never sleep.

"Hello," he answered, no hint of fatigue.

"Hi. How was your day?"

"Very fruitful."

"That's good to hear. What happened?"

"I was able to make contact with two of the four individuals I spoke to yesterday. Both agreed to meet with me tomorrow."

"That's fantastic! I assume you told them why you wanted to meet them…?"

"Yes. I told them I'd been hired by a party who suspected there were some 'irregularities' concerning the paybacks on certain loans made by RAM, L.P." Madeline felt her chest constrict as she listened to this indictment.

"Wow, it's happening," she said breathlessly.

"Yep, it's on. No turning back now. I hope you're still okay with this," Burt said.

"Yeah, I am, absolutely. It's just…scary and exhilarating at the same time."

"I know. I'm used to this kind of thing—it's how I make my living. But I seriously doubt there's anything in your background that prepared you for the situation you're now faced with."

"You can say that for sure," Madeline agreed. "Okay, walk me through it—how will tomorrow go?"

"I'm meeting one fellow at one o'clock at his home. The other guy wants to meet me in my office at five-thirty."

"I see…"

"I've told them both I will show them an up-to-date title report for their respective properties as proof the loan made by Steven's company is still showing as an lien. And that I'll need to get a statement attesting to the fact that they have paid back their loans. I asked them to bring a copy of the canceled check showing the loan had been repaid."

"Okay…"

"Then, I'll tell them my client will be taking the statements to the district attorney—"

"*I* will be?" Madeline asked, alarmed by this detail.

"Yes. I have no reason to be snooping into the affairs and practices of RAM, L.P. I'm acting solely as your agent. My license doesn't provide me the ability to investigate persons or entities on a whim. I have the authority to act on behalf of my clients. You understand the distinction, don't you?"

Madeline was too shocked to speak. It never occurred to her that she would have to pit herself against Steven in the public arena. The thought of such a thing put her in a panic.

"I didn't realize…I thought that you would…"

"When we spoke last evening, we went over the ways we could handle this. We both agreed the safest way was to drop the hint to the swindled borrowers and hope they went to the D.A. with their fears. The downside to that was the possibility they would go to Steven instead...remember?" Madeline nodded weakly at the recollection.

"Yes, I do remember." She let out a deep sigh. "I guess I didn't totally understand that I'd have a role in this."

"Don't spook yourself too much here—you will be delivering the goods as an estranged spouse of the perpetrator. Once the D.A. looks into the allegations, it will be a matter between their office, the victims and RAM, L.P. Plus, these people might decide they want to hire their own attorneys and sue for damages. It won't be you against Steven. It will be the people he swindled against him and his company." Madeline exhaled the breath she'd be holding.

"Okay. That sounds better. I just have to take the...statements to the D.A. and ask that they don't reveal my involvement...?"

"Yes. It would be more convenient if you were able to take them in immediately, but seeing as you're stuck in Guam for several more days, I'll put their statements in safe place. I'll keep trying to contact the others I spoke to yesterday—a man and an elderly woman—and see if I can get them to cooperate like the others. The good thing in a situation like this is the more people you have with the same problem, the easier it is to get them to join in. And I still have thirty-some borrowers I haven't tried to contact yet. So you see, this is coming together very well."

"You're right—I see that now. I just got nervous at the thought of running up against Steven again. I haven't recovered from the all the crap he's already pulled on me."

"I know, believe me. You're a brave, strong woman with a lot more guts than most people. What your soon-to-be-ex has done to you would send frailer psyches to the loony bin." Madeline had to laugh.

"I don't know, I think I've landed in the world's most luxurious loony bin."

"I think your sense of humor might be your saving grace," Burt said.

"I think *you've* been my saving grace," Madeline amended.

"Glad to be of service. On another front, I've been back to The Edgecliff a couple times, still trying to find out who might be the inside connection. It's slow work, trying to infiltrate without tipping anyone off. I'll keep at it, though."

"Thanks, Burt. I really appreciate all you've done for me."

"I'm just doing what you paid me to do," he replied modestly.

THIRTY-SIX

Madeline sat bolt upright, the wisps of a particularly vivid nightmare dissipating as she switched on the lamp. She panted as she tried to convince herself it was only a dream. When she had calmed down, she turned out the light in hopes of getting back to sleep. But her mind held stubbornly to the half-remembered images of Steven cavorting with her replacement, in Santa Barbara, in front of her friends, in her own home.

Finally, at quarter to two, she gave up and got out of bed. By this time she had the beginnings of an obsession brewing, and the only way to satisfy her curiosity was to find out everything she could about Elizabeth Collins-Wainwright.

After half an hour of scouring the Internet, she could at least put a face to the name. Ms. C-W was attractive, at least in the way that time and money could compensate for rather average features. In all the photos Madeline had been able to unearth, it was clear this woman had used hairstylists, makeup and clothing to the fullest advantage.

It was mean-spirited to accuse this woman of relying on the stealthy artifice of modern beauty when she was just as guilty. But what other weapons did she have in this situation? Gloating over her genetic superiority was the only way Madeline could whittle her down to a more manageable entity. By the end of her unkind examination, she had convinced herself that Steven was only using the newcomer for her money. At least she felt confident she hadn't been thrown over for a younger, prettier model.

Other than having a reasonable idea of what her rival looked like in any given setting, from any given angle, Madeline's knowledge of this woman was still frustratingly scant. She hadn't served on any charitable boards or launched any businesses. She seemed to gain all her press coverage by being connected to rich and powerful men, and divorcing them.

Madeline sat back and contemplated this match up. How was it this woman—who now had a reported $60 million from two lucrative divorces—would suddenly develop a fancy for Steven? He was successful, but hardly of the caliber of her last husband. But he was very handsome and *oh so* charming when he wanted to be.

But still, a woman like Elizabeth Collins-Wainwright would hardly be wooed by Steven's attributes in the space of one weekend. No, of course she wouldn't. And she wouldn't have him staying at her home after a casual introduction.

Madeline began to pace as the implications registered. This whole mess—from discrediting and displacing her, to the sudden appearance of her successor—had to have been planned well in advance.

Madeline's pacing halted abruptly as the horrible truth hit home. This thing between Steven and the rich divorcée didn't just happen out of thin air. Madeline's hand flew to her mouth as the veil fell, exposing Steven's outrageous betrayal. The whole elaborate plot to frame her as an adulteress was a ruse to cover *his* broken wedding vows.

Madeline felt like she was going to be sick. All his cruel acts against her were a mechanism to push her out of the way to make room for the woman he must've been courting for months, maybe longer.

Her head spun as she imagined how Steven had gone in pursuit of this woman, claiming he was in a loveless marriage, wanting to be free of his heartless wife. He probably strung E C-W along, giving her hope, dragging it out, making her desperate to have Steven's cold, unloving wife out of the way. Madeline sank into a chair, her face as pale as the moon.

It all had to have started with a need. That need had been money. Burt had pretty much proved that. So, the question was, when did the shortfall begin. Madeline would bet every penny she had that the need coincided with the pursuit.

Perhaps Burt could recreate a timeline, starting with the first deed that was not reconveyed at the time the mortgage was paid off. But that wouldn't be conclusive proof, for Steven could've been running this scam without a hitch for some time, replacing funds in a more timely matter.

She grabbed her notepad. *Ask Burt when the loans were paid off,* she wrote. So far, Burt had uncovered four instances of embezzlement. How many more would he turn up? Was there any way to unearth the other tardy reconveyances that had eventually been paid? Sure, there had to be. The district attorney would put a forensic accountant on the case. Burt was right wanting to handle it this way. It was too bad they had to wait for her to return to the mainland before they could sic the law on her reprehensible soon-to-be-ex.

Okay, she thought, *we're on the right track. But what if Steven is able to siphon money out of Elizabeth and repay his investors before the borrowers act?*

Madeline got up and began pacing again. *It's okay; Burt's made at least two people aware of the time lag. That's probably enough to launch an investigation.*

She walked out onto the balcony and listened to the sound of the waves as they broke on the shore. She tried to make her breathing match the cadence of the tide, calming her mind in the process. But it was no use; as long as she was stuck on Guam and Steven was using all his wiles to win Elizabeth's trust, there was a chance he would get away with everything.

She went back inside and used the time conversion site on her phone. It was 10 a.m. PST, the previous day, which was Friday. *Perfect.* She grabbed Burt's phone and called him. It went to voicemail. She hung up and held the phone thoughtfully against her chin. Either he would call back right away, or he was in the middle of an interview. She gave him a couple of minutes to reply before figuring it was the latter.

There was no hope of going back to sleep now. Fortunately for her, the hotel had 24-hour room service. She perused the menu, settling on tropical pancakes with macadamia nuts and papaya, sausage and fresh guava juice. Naturally, Burt called the moment her breakfast arrived.

"You're up early," he said, as Madeline let the waiter in.

"I couldn't sleep," she replied, motioning for the waiter to set the tray on the coffee table.

"Sorry to hear that."

"I've used the time for thinking," Madeline said as she signed the check. She mouthed the words "thank you," and turned her attention back to Burt.

"Thinking is a good use of time," he said.

"Well, actually, I've been mostly worrying."

"Ah, not such a good use of time. What's on your mind?"

"I guess I'm feeling nervous. I'm afraid Steven will manage to come up with the money needed to cover the notes before we have enough evidence of what he's done. If we don't catch him on this, then we're not going to catch him on anything. He'll walk away as the Golden Boy hero he's always been, with a garnish of wronged husband to further endear him to the faithful."

"You get quite eloquent in the middle of the night."

"Please tell me I'm worrying for nothing."

"I can't blame you for worrying after what your husband's put you through—"

"Ex—*ex-husband,*" Madeline reminded him.

"Almost ex," Burt reminded her.

"Okay, almost ex. Wait a second—should I be waiting until we're legally divorced before we go after him?" she asked, her voice high with new concern.

"No. We definitely don't want to wait. Time is crucial right now."

"But I'm just thinking that I—"

"I know what you're thinking, but as you're not a partner in the L.P., you won't have any liabilities as far as criminal or civil litigation goes. So don't be looking for problems that don't exist. You've got enough on your plate as it is."

"Okay, I just needed to hear that from you. Any updates?" she asked hopefully.

"Yes, as a matter of fact. I've found another duped borrower."

"That's fantastic," Madeline said, suddenly jubilant. "Well, I guess that's not so fantastic for the borrower. Have you set up any more meetings?" she asked before she stuck a forkful of pancake and sausage in her mouth. She made a mental note to start visiting the hotel gym.

"One confirmed. Still waiting to hear back from the fourth victim. We have a tentative appointment when he gets off work. Either way, we'll have plenty of ammo to hand over to the D.A."

"Thanks. I feel so useless stuck out here in the middle of the Pacific. I feel like my world is imploding and all I can do is watch it from afar. Hey, would there be any benefit to putting Steven under surveillance? It might be a good idea to keep tabs on his moves."

"Two problems with that—I'm a one-man operation, and Steven's got his own in-house security. Even if I partnered with another P.I., chances are very high we'd be detected before we got anything."

"Oh, I guess you're right." Another scary thought occurred to her. "Do you feel like you've popped up on their radar? Are you worried they know you're investigating Steven's company?"

"I wouldn't say 'worried,' but it is always a concern in a situation like this—especially in light of Steven's shady dealings and his posse of hired thugs."

"Hired thugs?" Madeline was taken aback by this characterization of men she had always assumed were the "good guys." She never knew much about them, but had always taken comfort in their presence. How silly to not realize they were Steven's stooges all along. Still, it gave her a creepy feeling to think of them as thugs. "Did you do a background check on them, too?" she asked.

"Let's just say I got a snapshot of their operation and an outline of their work-slash-military history. I guess I shouldn't have referred to them as thugs, though I do think as a group they could be pretty dangerous if called upon."

Chills ran down Madeline's arms. She found herself grateful for being on Guam, away from all the possible dangers. Hopefully, now that Steven was getting his expedited divorce, all the scare tactics would be dropped. But what if he got wind of Burt's investigation?

"Burt...are you sure you're okay with snooping around Steven's business dealings?"

"What do you mean?"

"You called Steven's security team hired thugs. Maybe we should let sleeping dogs lie." There was a long silence on Burt's end. "Burt?"

"Are you saying you want to drop this? I thought you wanted to nail Steven for embezzlement since you couldn't get him on the rape." Madeline let out an exasperated sigh.

"It's not that I don't want to nail the bastard—believe me, that desire is still as strong as ever, if for no other reason than to show him he can't ruin people's lives and walk away unscathed."

"But...?"

"But I don't want you to be in any danger."

"Don't worry. I know my way around scum like your husband. I've been chasing after his kind in one capacity or another for many years." Madeline wasn't reassured by this. Now that she had the specter of the goon squad in her head, she couldn't think of them in less malignant terms. "Let me put it this way, I've been up against worse. And I'm not worried. Okay? Feel better now?"

"I guess so."

"Do you want me to stop the investigation into RAM, L.P.?" Madeline didn't answer. "Do you want me to just confine the scope of my duties to finding out who set you up? Madeline, I need to know if you're still behind this. If you're not, then we drop it—plain and simple. By law, I can only investigate in accordance to your wishes." More silence on Madeline's end.

"I've got a couple appointments to cancel if you've got cold feet about this," Burt said. "I guess there's really no harm in letting it go—we've already put the bug in the borrowers' ears. They can look into it on their own and pursue Steven if they want. I mean, really, it's no skin off your nose if they've been burned by your ex. You had nothing to do with any of that."

"I don't know what to say," Madeline replied, getting up to pace again.

"I need a decision from you one way or the other, and honestly, it doesn't matter to me which way we go. I do have to tell you that I'm feeling the trail go cold on the rape case. You can always take your story and the photos to the cops and maybe they can shake something loose. But the truth is, we really don't have a lot to go on. I mean, you could scour the fundraiser photos and video footage some more, see if you can find a clear image to work off of…"

"Oh, God—I really don't know what to do here," Madeline moaned as she looked out at the predawn glow from the east. Something about the lighting brought her back to that horrible morning at The Edgecliff.

"I guess there's really less harm in you taking their statements than in letting the worry fester in them. Just because you take their written statements, doesn't necessarily mean that I have to act on them…?"

"I don't know about that," Burt said. "I think you need to fish or cut bait. I don't think you can compromise here. You can't leave the borrowers with the false impression that someone's taking action on their behalf."

Madeline sighed, looking up, as if she were appealing to a higher authority. She was afraid of Steven now. But she was even more afraid of living with herself if she didn't hold him accountable in some way. If she didn't, she would always have the feeling he still had control over her.

"Continue as planned," she said. "A man like that can't be allowed to go free and seek other victims."

THIRTY-SEVEN

After she hung up with Burt, Madeline tried to think of anything but Steven and her replacement. It was hard, given the circumstances. Being stuck in a hotel room didn't help. She felt boxed in, mentally and physically. But she needed to focus on her future, one that would begin the moment she landed back in California.

In an effort to concentrate, she got down on the floor and began stretching exercises. The old habit had the desired effect, and soon her mind became more or less a blank slate. On that clear surface, she started prioritizing her needs.

Housing was still the most urgent requirement. The dilemma was what kind should she look for: the very temporary hotel/vacation rental type, or the type that required a commitment, i.e., a lease? This brought her to her second most pressing matter: how best to spend and protect the proceeds of her divorce?

Thinking of money led her to thinking about her car. The sale of it would mean more money and a more secure future. She gave one final stretch and got off the floor. Seizing the window of compatible time, she picked up her phone and called Mike.

"Hey, I was wondering when I'd ever hear from you," he said. "I guess you forgot about your old pal once you hit the duty-free boutiques."

"How did you know about those?"

"I can go *virtually* anywhere you go," he reminded her. "Now you'll be able to put a sizeable dent in their inventory…"

"Did you sell the Porsche?"

"Sure did."

"For how much?" she prodded him.

"More than I thought we'd get…"

"How much?" Figures he'd want to drag this out for theatrical purposes.

"Hey, I think you need to show your dealer some respect."

"Okay—the suspense is killing me. Just tell me so I can praise you inordinately," Madeline said.

"Eighty grand," Mike said dreamily, managing to evoke the image of stacks of 800 C-notes.

"No way! That's amazing!"

"Now, that's more like it," he said. Madeline shook her head. Some things never change, like Mike's constant need for stroking.

"You are magnificent, Mike Delaney," she said. "Truly, truly incredible—"

"You don't have to be snide."

"No, really—I'm over the moon with gratitude. Seriously."

"Now you're being condescending," Mike pouted.

"Oh, stop. Tell me how you got so much for it. I thought we'd be lucky to get close to seventy."

"Well, there's luck, and then there's skill. You were *lucky* to entrust the task with such a *skillful* negotiator." Madeline groaned. If the preamble was going to take this long, the story would be never-ending.

"Okay, you told me a guy was interested before I left…"

"Yeah, he was very hot to trot. But while I was showing it to him, I got two other responses. So…I worked them a bit, let 'em know there were several other parties interested—"

"And you got the first guy to come up to eighty grand," Madeline deduced, thoroughly spoiling Mike's big wind-up.

"You are a real killjoy, you know that?"

"Hey, don't be sore. You're still my number one hero."

"Oh really? Who died?"

"Okay, so I'm a killjoy—"

"And a sore winner," Mike added testily.

"I'm just bored out of my gourd, stuck on this speck in the ocean. I'm holed up like a fugitive, my life's been yanked out from under me, I've got no future—should I go on?"

"If you're apologizing, I accept," Mike said magnanimously.

"Apologizing for what?" Madeline barked before giving into the silliness of the conversation. She could never really stay mad at Mike, though there'd been times she'd wished he'd get out of her life for good. Thank God he didn't.

"So, are you happy about the sale?"

"Ecstatic. Thank you, thank you, thank you."

"Have you given any more thought to moving down here?"

"No, Mike—L.A.'s really not the place for me. I'd feel more lost and insignificant than I already do. I'm sure I'll feel like a pariah in Santa Barbara, though I can't understand why. I didn't do anything wrong. But scandals like this one are hot one minute, and forgotten the next. I'll have to hide my face for a while until it all calms down. But I plan to stay up there, see if I can find a way to support myself."

"Got any prospects?"

"No, not really. I'm sure I'm good at something, I just can't remember what it is."

"You'd make some lucky guy one hell of a wife," Mike hinted.

"Oh please! Don't even pretend that's an option. Just because I'm single again doesn't mean we have to torture ourselves with another bad relationship."

"We didn't have a bad relationship," Mike protested.

"No, you're right—we had three or four," Madeline reminded him.

"They weren't all bad," Mike insisted meekly. Madeline had to laugh.

"Right. And they say hindsight's 20/20."

"Okay, now that I've gotten your car sold and let you trash my fond memories of our time together, I suppose you're ready to move on. No, no—it's alright. I'll pull through somehow. But if you ever need me again, I'll come running."

"I know. That goes for me, too. We're better friends than lovers…"

"Well, I wouldn't say *that*…"

"Okay, crazy man, I've got to go. I've got a week to sort my life out, and so far it's not looking very promising."

"If I may make an innocent suggestion…"

"What is it?" Madeline asked guardedly.

"I think you should stay over in L.A. at least a day. You really can't do anything until you find a replacement car, and you might as well take advantage of the competition down here."

In the excitement of becoming $80,000 richer, Madeline had overlooked the fact that she was now car-less. She was no longer privileged to have a stable of high-end automobiles at her disposal. She saw her monetary triumph suddenly dwindle.

"You're right. What was I thinking? I don't even know what kind of car I should be shopping for. I don't even know what cars cost these days."

"You can always lease something."

"Yeah, but what?"

"Guess that's one more thing for your 'to do' list," Mike said. Madeline sighed. She was even less equipped for the single life than she realized.

From her cozy, spherical beach cabana on the hotel's plot of white sand, Madeline took a hard look at her prospects. As she would be solely responsible for her success from this point forward, she started with an assessment of her physical attributes.

At forty, she was still in good shape. Thanks to a rigorous workout regimen and a mostly stringent diet, her figure was basically the same as when she left the singles arena. Her body had not betrayed her with the inevitable sagging of skin and muscle yet. The amount of time, effort and money that had gone into skincare had paid off, so she counted that as a check in the plus column.

Her wardrobe and jewelry would get her through many years—maybe not on the cutting edge of fashion, but she would still be considered well-dressed by most standards. So, on the exterior, she was on solid ground. On those two fronts, she gave herself a B+.

Where she had allowed herself to fall behind was in the professional domain. She hadn't held a real job for almost thirteen years. Fortunately, keeping up with technology was not only hip but essential for a woman of her means in this day and age. As far as skill sets went, she felt comfortable enough that she could learn to work any software program put in front of her.

But what field would she best be suited for? That was the big question. From straight work experience, she was not qualified for much. With the fierce job market, this would make it especially hard. She tried to envision herself interviewing for job placement, imagining the kinds of questions she'd have to answer. It was not a comforting prospect. Nor was the thought of resorting to her last occupation, which was hotel concierge.

Besides, where could she do that? She didn't want to go back to Denver; she hadn't kept pace with the changes there and would not find it easy to land a job. Santa Barbara was the place she knew best, but where would she feel comfortable sitting in full view of everyone, including her former friends. How humiliating would that be? Besides, the pay wasn't great. No, another avenue had to be found. But what else was she qualified to do?

In an attempt to pump up her attributes, she made a mental list of her talents. She had a gift for shopping, no one could deny that. But she had a hard time picturing herself rounding up outfits for the fashion-challenged in a department store.

What else did she know how to do? She was stumped. She had considered herself a good wife, but applying for that position again was not an option, not after what she'd just been through, not for the foreseeable future, at any rate.

Other than that, all she had done for the last twelve years was issue orders, plan events or serve on nonprofit boards.

Of course! she thought, realizing belatedly that she *had* learned some marketable skills. She had become quite adept at organizing functions of all sizes and budgets. She could do what she'd been doing for years *and* get paid. And it would be an easy transition; instead of just shelling out the cash, she could be pocketing some of it too. *What a perfect idea!*

With that end in mind, she began to examine the logistics of setting up her own company. She started making a list on her iPhone of what it would take to put her in business. All she really needed was a website, some business cards and some referrals. This last thought gave her pause; could she really switch from the front entrance to the back so seamlessly? Would her friends be so accepting and supportive now that she wasn't married to Steven Ridley, man of many charms and accomplishments?

If I approached it with the right attitude… she mused. *Many women have reinvented themselves after divorce,* she reasoned. *Events by Madeline,* she tried on for size. She frowned; not exciting enough. *Life of the Party.* That had potential.

Yes, yes—she could see herself in the business of planning events for others. It would still be noble work, even if she wasn't giving of her time and experience for free. She would do it. She would have a career.

Feeling as though she had made sizable headway, she became restless. She needed movement. But frolicking in the water didn't qualify. She needed a change of scenery. She needed to meander. She packed up her bag and headed for a neighboring hotel.

THIRTY-EIGHT

Madeline awoke with a start. Sleep had a disorienting effect on her these days. The room was bright with afternoon sun. A trail of dried saliva ran from the corner of her mouth to her chin. She wiped it away, wondering how long she'd been out.

The impromptu nap left her feeling drugged; every movement required thought and effort. She sat up on the bed, right leg dangling off the side. Being several time zones ahead of normal was confusing enough without the loss of her customary existence. She consulted the time converter app on her iPhone.

It was 4:10 Saturday afternoon, which made it 10:10 p.m. on Friday, PST. Her mental clock was so out of kilter, she felt as though it were only morning. She had to fall into some sort of groove, or she'd be doubly confused by the time she got home. *Home.* Where was home? She had to figure that out soon and get something lined up before Thursday, or she'd find herself living in a hotel room again.

She grabbed Burt's phone and rang his number as she went to the minibar for something to rehydrate her parched throat. She chugged down a bottle of water as she absently listened to Burt's message. When she heard the tone, she belatedly hung up. She carried the phone out to the balcony and took a seat while she waited for a return call.

She was so absorbed with myriad thoughts, twenty minutes passed before she realized Burt had not called back yet. 10:35 wasn't too late she decided, redialing his number. She hung up this time when she heard the recorded message. She stared at the phone, willing it to ring. After another five minutes, she tried again. Still no answer.

She didn't like being out of touch with her P.I. Without his updates, it would be easy to languish in this idyllic setting. She needed his reality checks to tether her to what was left of her life. She also needed his daily reports to fuel her hopes of getting concrete proof of Steven's crimes. Or at least some of them.

As she showered, she weighed the pros and cons of vacation rentals versus long-term leases. It seemed like all she thought of these days was finding a place to live. It made her feel so ungrounded, like she had slipped the ties that bound her to earth and was floating aimlessly. At this point, it was hard to imagine she'd ever have a normal life again.

She wrapped herself in a towel and took a seat at the desk. Once again she trawled through the various sites. She sent off three emails for properties that would suit her well for the time being. She had her fingers crossed on one in particular, but she'd take anything that would get her out of limbo.

Having done all she could on that front for the time being, her mind wandered back to Burt. She was anxious to know how the interviews went. She had this niggling fear in the back of her mind that Steven had been able to throw up a wall, getting to the borrowers before they could make their statements. If that was the case, they'd be out of luck again.

Unless…unless Steven wasn't able to pay his investors back on every loan yet. They needed one small fissure to turn into an irreparable chasm. They'd found it; all they had to do was hand it over to the authorities and stand back. When Steven went down, it wasn't going to be pretty.

As the sky darkened, she gave up hope of hearing from Burt until morning. Once again, she found herself starving. She realized with alarm that she hadn't eaten anything in almost fourteen hours. *No wonder I feel so out of it,* she thought as she stood in front of the closet eyeing the weird concoction of clothing.

She checked her tunics for signs of wear and odor, bagged one for the laundry pick up and slipped the other one on. She discovered a pair of Manolo Blahnik slides she had purchased at Saks during her revenge shopping spree went rather nicely with the cotton batiste. And so did the beautiful tanzanite pendant.

She laughed as she looked at herself in the mirror. *Designer wear meets beachcomber,* she decided, a look that gave her spirits a much needed boost. She made a clutch out of her jewelry bag; it was just big enough to hold her two phones, lipstick, debit card and room key. She piled her hair into a messy up-do and went in search of a proper meal.

The Westin had several bars and restaurants, offering something for all tastes. She'd had a hankering for pasta at the Italian ristorante, but even with the A/C going it still seemed too muggy for heavy fare. The sushi and teppanyaki bars at the Japanese restaurant were cool and inviting, and on closer inspection, very crowded. There was one chair available at the sushi bar and she took it.

After she got herself seated and had been greeted by the sushi chef, she casually scoped out her fellow diners. To her right was a young Asian couple, who smiled and nodded politely. *Perfect,* Madeline thought, taking a relaxing sip of her sake. There was a man to her left, but he seemed to be with another man and woman. She let out a happy sigh as she looked over the menu.

As soon as she had placed her order, the man to her left turned his attention toward her. He smiled and nodded, lifting his beer glass to her as she raised the sake cup to her lips. She smiled tightly and busied herself with her iPhone. This bought her a little time, but the man had obviously seen something he couldn't get his fill of.

"Where you from?" he asked, a jovial, non-threatening smile on his face.

"California," Madeline replied, looking quickly back to her phone.

"That's what I would've guessed," he said, unperturbed by her apparent disinterest. "What part?"

"Excuse me?" Madeline said with a distracted air. *Some people just can't take a hint.*

"Where in California do you live?"

"The Central Coast." The man nodded appreciatively.

"I live in La Jolla," he offered.

"Nice."

"Paul Jahnke," he said, reaching out a hand to her. Madeline was seconds away from asking for her order to go. But the thought of sitting in that lonely room again made her shake his hand, grudgingly. "Nice to know you...?"

"Madeline."

"Madeline," Paul repeated. "Pretty name. You don't hear it very often, do you?"

"Actually...I do." To Madeline's amazement, Paul found her reply inordinately funny.

"So, pretty Ms. Madeline," Paul said, shifting his body to face her, "what do you do in 'the Central Coast'?"

"I'm a homemaker," Madeline said with no trace of a smile.

"Ah," Paul said, his eye going directly to her left hand. "I didn't see a ring," he said, half apology, half accusation.

"I left it in the safe."

"On purpose?" Paul asked after a couple of beats. Before Madeline could assess her next move, the sushi chef placed a tray of yellowtail sashimi in front of her. A waitress appeared on her right with a bowl of steaming edamame. This was all Madeline needed as an excuse to pretend that Paul Jahnke didn't exist.

"So, what brings you to Guam?" Paul asked, all smiles and good will. Madeline made a face as she chewed a piece of sashimi. Paul waited patiently.

"It's just a stopover," she said, hoping that would satisfy his curiosity.

"I see. From where?"

Madeline chased the raw fish with a large swallow of sake while fabricating an alter ego.

"Singapore," she said, popping three soy beans into her mouth with one squeeze of the pod. Paul murmured vaguely.

"What took you to Singapore?" he asked nonchalantly, as if quizzing a perfect stranger was his birthright. Madeline barely restrained herself from telling him to get lost. She glanced around, hoping to find a vacant seat somewhere else. The place was packed and a long line had formed.

"I'm a freelance travel writer," she said, liking the sound of it. She nodded, happy with her choice of fictitious career. Paul was apparently convinced, for he was nodding along with her.

The sushi chef came to her rescue again, trading her empty plate for an exotic-looking sushi roll. He also checked in with Paul, giving her a moment's peace. This had not turned into the relaxing dining experience she'd been hoping for. She had been craving human contact as much as she'd been craving food, but she had bargained on the more anonymous, less interactive type. It was just her luck to have found Mr. SoCal in a restaurant otherwise packed with foreigners.

"So…you're a writer and a homemaker," Paul surmised. Madeline couldn't be sure if he was challenging her or not, nor did she care. She nodded almost imperceptibly and went about devouring the sushi roll. The waitress placed a plate of freshwater eel next to her. Madeline was getting full just smelling it.

"You've got a pretty good appetite for such a slender girl," Paul said, looking hopeful, condescending and skeptical all at once. Madeline swallowed the mouthful of food and turned to face Paul.

"I'm sorry to be rude, but I'm not really in the mood for small talk right now," she said, not bothering to sugarcoat it. "I came down to eat some dinner so I could get some rest before my flight out. I'd really like to be alone with my own thoughts, if you don't mind."

She couldn't have gotten a chillier response if she had thrown a glass of sake in his face. He wore the startled expression of someone who'd never had his feelings hurt before. Without a word, he knocked back the remainder of his beer and motioned for the check.

"Nice talking to you," he said coldly, as he squirmed out of the chair. Madeline swung her knees out of the way and gave him as much room to maneuver as she could. She engrossed herself in the business of grabbing the slivers of eel with her chopsticks. Thinking she was out of harm's way once Paul shoved his chair against the counter, she relaxed and brought the eel to her lips.

"FYI, don't think you're going to fool anyone with that bullshit story. You're no more the homemaker type than the guy behind the counter," Paul said in a voice just above a whisper. She looked up at him reflexively. Their eyes met for one long, unnerving second. It felt like all the blood in her body had turned to ice. She looked away, feigning obliviousness to this passing stranger's departure.

Although her appetite had been snuffed out, Madeline lingered for another fifteen minutes. She felt exposed and vulnerable and didn't want to walk out into the lobby to find him waiting for her. But the longer she sat there, the more anxious she became. She paid her check and left the restaurant as fast as her Manolos would carry her.

THIRTY-NINE

Madeline's eyes sprang open, triggering a wave of nausea. She got her physical and mental bearings and checked the time. 3:45. She had fallen into a regular schedule, but it was not compatible to either of the time zones that mattered.

She got up and went to the bathroom. She was tired and strung-out, yet she knew that if she got back in bed she'd only toss and turn. She switched on a few lights, squinting at the glare. She ordered coffee and yogurt with fresh fruit and dry whole wheat toast and slipped into her tunic.

By that time, it was almost 10 a.m. in Santa Barbara; a good time to reach Burt, but it was also a Saturday. She had to concede that the man needed to sleep sometime. He had been working on her case for nine days straight. She had to give the guy a break and trust he would contact her as soon as he was able. She knew this was the right thing to do, yet she was about ready to start crawling the walls.

In the end, she laid Burt's phone down. More than likely, his was turned off, so calling would be useless, anyway. She picked up her iPhone and dialed Mike. Maddeningly, her call went straight to voicemail. She took it personally, as if the two men she counted on the most had consciously decided to avoid her.

She knew she was being oversensitive and irrational; being remanded to the island of Guam made her feel utterly isolated and forgotten. It made her seethe to think of how Steven had completely overturned her life, stripping her of any rights or choice. He framed her and disposed of her as easily as if she'd been an insubordinate employee. Maybe that's all she'd ever been to him, a necessary associate, the essential "wife"—his assured entry into Montecito society.

A sense of frustration settled on her, making her want to scream at the top of her lungs. She fairly shook with rage as it hit her once again how she was paying for Steven's greed and maniacal need to control. She was filled with an intense desire for revenge. She almost didn't care what happened to her if it meant getting even with him.

As riled up as she was, it was still hard to imagine what she could possibly do to him that would settle the score. She had a vision of getting on the next plane back to L.A. and driving up to her former home. She could see the startled faces of Hughes, Erma, Steven and whatshername as she stormed through the front door, screaming accusations of rape and blackmail, embezzlement and fraud. What she would give to tear down the sterling image of Steven Ridley: suave, cultured man with the golden touch. Few people knew how calculating, heartless and cruel he was underneath the perfect exterior.

A knock at the door startled her out of her resentful reverie. She let the waiter in, suddenly mindful of the inconvenience she was putting him through. Just because they offered 24-hour room service didn't mean a staff stood like soldiers at the ready around the clock. She added a tip that exceeded the bill and thanked him as she led him to the door.

She poured a cup of coffee with a splash of cream and drank it down. The instant jolt she received told her this was not the smartest move. Now she was hyper-aware, as if she hadn't been keyed up enough already. She took a bite of the toast, but chewing it nearly made her gag. She wasn't ready for food; what she needed was to work off her anger before it became poisonous to her. She traded her tunic for a pair of shorts and a T-shirt and went to the hotel's 24-hour gym.

Madeline sat on her balcony, staring out at the ocean. She had both phones on the table next to her, willing one of them to ring. She picked up her iPhone and checked the time converter, though by now she had it pretty well figured out. 7:45 a.m. Sunday, February 28th was 1:45 p.m. Saturday, the 27th in Santa Barbara. Even if Burt needed to sleep sixteen hours straight, she had given him ample time. She picked up his phone and called him.

"Your call cannot be completed as dialed. Please check the number and try again." Irritated, Madeline checked the number she had been redialing for over a week. She knew there couldn't be anything wrong with the number, because it was Burt's phone and only one number had been dialed on it since he gave it to her.

The call log showed no deviation, so chalking it up to a satellite glitch, she tried again. Same message. She tried a third time. When that didn't work, she manually pressed the numbers. Same result.

A quiver of worry started in a remote part of her brain and quickly turned to real panic. *Oh my God—what if there's been an earthquake?* She jumped up and retrieved her laptop. Within a minute, she had the local Santa Barbara television station online.

It was obvious from a glance that no seismic trembler had interrupted telephone service. Everything looked to be business as usual. It struck her as odd that she had jumped to that conclusion in the first place.

She sat back as she tried to come up with the most logical answer. It took five seconds to start fearing the worst: if Burt's phone was out of commission and he had not made contact with her in… She counted the hours since their last phone call. It had been Friday morning, his time. Almost two full days had passed. Madeline felt her throat and heart constrict simultaneously.

For one confused second, she thought *she* was experiencing an earthquake. But the only thing shaking was her laptop, balanced on two legs that were jiggling uncontrollably. She was about to close her computer and get up when a headline under "Breaking News" stopped her cold:

Body Found on Beach ID'd as Local P.I. She stared at the headline, unable to breathe. The cursor shook erratically as she tried to move it to the link. As soon as she clicked on it, a photo of Burt Latham materialized. Madeline felt all the blood drain from her head. She sat the computer down on the table just before losing consciousness.

When she opened her eyes several minutes later, her mind was blank. Other than the pain in her left shoulder and hip, nothing alarming registered, except for the fact that she was lying on the balcony instead of sitting in a chair.

But as she pulled herself up, the reason for her collapse hit home again. Panting, with tears obscuring her vision, she jiggled her mouse pad, bringing the shocking news of Burt's death back crystal clear. She staggered to the bathroom where she threw up what little was in her stomach. She slid away from the comforting coolness of the porcelain toilet bowl and wailed.

FORTY

The persistent ringing of a cell phone woke Madeline. She looked around as she raised herself off the bathroom floor. Shaken and disoriented, she came to life in short bursts as she pieced together the memory of what had leveled her.

She lurched out of the bathroom and staggered to the balcony, a wild hope spurring her forward. She grabbed Burt's phone, her heart sinking again as she discovered it was not the one ringing. By the time she realized this, her iPhone had gone silent.

She clutched both phones to her chest as she stumbled back inside. She bumped against the bed and sank onto it, the expression on her face that of disbelieving fear.

Slowly, she lay down on the bed and inched her way toward the head, where she traded the useless phones for a pillow. She buried her face in the thick loft and began sobbing.

She had almost fallen into a merciful sleep again when her phone rang, jolting her to alertness. She hesitated a moment before answering.

"Hello."

"Hey there," Mike said in his oddly jocular and languid tone. "Sorry I missed your call earlier…" It crossed Madeline's mind what had prevented him from answering her call, but only as an observation. She found that she cared about nothing. It was as though she had passed the point of feeling and entered a state of permanent apathy.

"Are you okay?" Mike asked after the lengthy pause.

"Burt's dead," she said flatly.

"Burt? Your P.I.? What? Dead? How do you know?" he asked incredulously.

"I found out online," she said, as she forced herself into a semi-upright position against a clump of pillows.

"Where?" She gave him the URL and listened as he tapped on his computer keys.

"It's the first story on the right, under 'Breaking News.'" Mike mumbled as he read the report to himself. "Read it to me," she said hoarsely. She hadn't gotten past the headline and the photo of her now-deceased private eye.

"'The body found on Hendry's Beach has been identified as Burt Latham, a local private investigator. His body was discovered by a parks department maintenance crew. Detective Michael Driscoll of the Santa Barbara Police Department says the death is being treated as 'an accidental death by drowning' pending an autopsy. "From the injuries to the body, it would appear Mr. Latham fell to his death from a height of approximately forty feet, which is consistent with the height of the bluffs at the Douglas Family Preserve. That scenario fits with the direction of the current and the timeframe in which the victim was last seen," Det. Driscoll commented. He added that they do not suspect foul play at this time.'"

Mike waited for Madeline to say something. He could hear the rustle of tissue and faint whimpering. He didn't know how to comfort her from a distance. He was also still absorbing the implications of what had happened. It slowly occurred to him that Madeline was feeling more than a sense of loss; the fact that her P.I. was now dead boded badly for her personally.

"I'm flying to Guam," he announced, eliciting a wheezy, fatigued laugh out of her.

"No you are not," she said, drying her swollen eyes. She took a deep breath and expelled a cloud of sorrow. She went limp with exhaustion and fell back against the pillows.

"I'm not going to let you stay there all by yourself," Mike said assertively. His attempts at chivalry were as ludicrous as they were comforting.

"Don't be silly. By the time you got here, it'd be time to turn around and go back."

"There's a flight leaving tomorrow morning—looks like the same flight you were on. Gets into Tamuning at 8:45 p.m. Tuesday night. What…?"

"See what I mean? You'd get two days of 18-hour travel for barely a day here on Guam. That's not happening, so forget about it. I'll be fine. Nothing's going to happen to me. Steven can't get to me here." Even as the words left her mouth, she began to wonder if that wasn't just wishful thinking.

"I'm coming. I don't care about jetlag—I can't stand the thought of you dealing with this all by yourself." Madeline let out a long, weary sigh.

"I appreciate the offer, Mike—"

"It's not an offer, it's an announcement," he said. Madeline recognized that implacable tone in his voice. She hung her head as she listened to him drone on.

"No, Mike—listen to me!" she said more forcibly than she had intended. "Think about it…the last guy who stuck his neck out for me is now dead. I can't be worrying about your safety as well as my own."

"But that's my point. You need someone to protect you—"

"And who's going to protect *you*?"

"I can handle myself," Mike said defensively. Madeline laughed harshly.

"Right. You've got more experience with the criminal element than a recently deceased ex-Marine, ex-cop, private investigator. Sure, I believe that."

"Maddie, this is not okay. I'm going to be worried sick until you get back here. And by the way, you are *not* going back to S.B. now that your P.I. is dead. That's non-negotiable. You're staying with me until you get the goods on that monster—"

"But Mike, how can I do that if I'm down in L.A.? I have to go back…I have to find another detective to take over…" Madeline's voice trailed off as the synapses in her brain started firing again. She didn't have Burt anymore, but she had to have someone pick up the trail he'd been on.

She got up on unsteady legs as Mike continued to assert himself as her protector. She opened her laptop and began searching for private investigators. It occurred to her that she did not exactly fit the bill of an ideal client, having a P.I. die during the course of an investigation on her behalf.

"Okay?" Mike asked.

"I'm sorry, I was thinking about something." She heard a long, frustrated wheeze on Mike's end.

"I was saying the best thing for you to do under the circumstances is stay the hell away from Dodge. Comprende? When you lay it all out, you've got to realize you're ahead at this point. You're alive and well and you've got half a mil, plus the eighty I've got for you. This is good. It's enough to start a new life with. I know you're not interested in picking up where we left off—I totally get that. But that doesn't mean I can't be here for you emotionally, or financially, for that matter."

"Mike…" Madeline sat back from the computer and tried to put everything in perspective. "Look, I need your emotional support—I'm not trying to reject that. Believe me, you're all I've got now, and I'm so grateful that you're here for me, figuratively speaking. I'm not going to commit to any plan right now. I've got way too much to sort out. And really, even though I'm completely devastated by Burt's death, I know I have to get my head together."

"I just wish I could help you," Mike said, his voice low and raspy.

"You can. You can help me brainstorm. We can do this over the phone. We'll just go through it piece by piece until we have a timeline of all the events that have happened since the night of the fundraiser. I'll take notes and once we have it all laid out in front of us, maybe some clues will surface. Can you help me with that?"

"Sure, absolutely. You want to do it now?"

"Yeah. The sooner the better. I won't be able to rest until I can make some sense of what's happened, and what I should do next."

FORTY-ONE

Ninety minutes into their conversation, Madeline had a comprehensive outline of events that occurred over the last two weeks—by any measure, the worst fourteen days of her life. She had four pages of notes on her computer and had sent a copy to Mike's email so he could analyze it, hopefully finding hints to what Steven's next move might be.

"You know, there are a couple things here that are still unknowns," Mike said as he read over the summary. "The big one is that we don't know for sure if Burt was killed or if he did accidentally fall to his death. If the latter is true, then we might be able to assume Steven is satisfied with the quick, uncontested divorce and that you won't get any more trouble from him."

"I'd really like to believe that, especially since it would be my fault if he was murdered."

"Not necessarily," Mike said. "You don't have any idea what kind of vendettas Burt might have racked up against him over the years. It could just be a terrible coincidence that someone offed him in the middle of your case... It could happen," Mike argued as Madeline rejected the idea.

"Too coincidental."

"It's good to look at this set of facts from all angles. It was your idea and it's a good one. So, you can't go dismissing a theory out of hand without some fact to back it up."

"You're right, you're totally right. Whew. I think we need a break. I'm exhausted and half-deranged from hunger and grief. Let's knock off for now and talk it over again later. What time is it there?"

"Quarter to seven."

"Saturday night, right?

"Right."

"And it's quarter to one Sunday afternoon here. Okay, finally I'm on a reasonable schedule. I'll get some lunch and…well, maybe we should just wait until tomorrow to talk," she suggested.

"We don't have to talk about this, but I definitely want you to check in with me later, before I go to bed."

"Are you sure I won't be interrupting anything?" she asked mischievously.

"Are you sure you don't care if you were?" Mike asked, eliciting a groan of protest from Madeline.

"Don't be silly…"

"I think you care more than you want to admit…" Mike teased her. Madeline laughed. There would always be a murky, grey area between them, romantically speaking. But Mike could always be counted on to lift her spirits.

By the time Madeline undid the damage of her emotional breakdown, she barely made it to Prego before the lunch service was over. The wait staff didn't seem to mind, so she gratefully luxuriated in the peacefulness of the nearly empty restaurant.

She ordered a glass of red wine, a mixed greens salad with a caprese salad on top, and a prosciutto and goat cheese pizza. It struck her as unseemly to have such a ravenous appetite after just learning of Burt's death, but she knew grief could manifest itself in strange ways. She was also glad she wasn't repulsed by the thought of food; she could already tell her bizarre hours and lack of regular meals had knocked a few pounds off her already lean figure.

The wine came, and not a moment too soon. She took several sips and felt the alcohol do its job. She was almost feeling the return of her equilibrium when snippets of the last conversation with Burt flooded her thoughts.

Why didn't I tell him to drop it? Why did I tell him to get those statements? He so much as admitted it was a dangerous move. Why the hell did I let him walk into that danger?

She reached for her wine glass with a shaky hand. Her aim was off and the glass toppled, spewing red wine all over the white tablecloth. The waiter was at her side in seconds, quickly swapping out the soiled linen with a fresh one.

"I'm so sorry," Madeline said, mortified by her clumsiness. But the waiter wouldn't hear of it. The hostess appeared with another glass of wine as another waiter brought her double-decker salad. They were overly solicitous before making themselves scarce so she could enjoy her lunch in private. Madeline figured she probably wasn't the first unhinged customer they'd encountered on a tiny island that specialized in divorces.

The food and wine were such treats, she almost forgot her dire predicament. But she was still in trouble up to her neck. She had to come to grips with the truth or she would never make it to safety.

As she sipped her second glass of wine—or third, depending on how you were counting—she made a silent pact with her former private eye, promising him she'd find out the truth about his death in exchange for some otherworldly guidance. She sealed the deal with a prayer for his soul and an entreaty for the strength it would require to continue her battle without Burt Latham, may he rest in peace.

When the waiter offered her coffee and dessert and assured Madeline she was not keeping the staff overtime, she ordered a cappuccino. She appreciated the quiet buzz of the restaurant in transition mode; it was a good environment for marshaling her thoughts and determining what her priorities were. A calm settled over her that she felt certain was heaven sent.

Despite the alcohol, or maybe because of it, her thoughts were now clear and orderly. She would retire to her room and do some research on other private investigators in her area. She would have to be careful how she approached prospective replacements for Burt; it was hardly a glowing endorsement that the last guy who attempted to help her was now undergoing an autopsy.

But as Burt had said, Santa Barbara was a small community, especially in his line of business. That, and his apparent cooperation with other P.I.'s in different cities, led her to believe one of his peers might be inclined to find out the truth about his demise.

As it was a Saturday night in California, it would be a lot to hope for that she'd get a return phone call. Chances were high she wouldn't hear back from anyone until Monday morning, PST. She'd scope out her options, make some calls, send some emails and wait as patiently as possible. Other than that, she didn't know what else she could do but think. If she could concentrate hard enough, surely she could grasp the situation from all sides and determine the best course.

This led her back to the beginning: identifying her objective. *What is it I want to accomplish?* she asked herself. Well, killing Steven was still at the top of her list of fantasies. But realistically, she knew that would either be impossible or lead to an even more miserable existence.

So, pragmatically speaking, what did she want? She wanted to find out the truth about Burt's death and she wanted to nail Steven for setting up her rape. She knew an autopsy would be the starting point for the former. She also knew that if Burt couldn't get anywhere on the rape, it was unlikely another P.I. could at this point.

That left her with going to the police with her photos and her story. How likely were they to believe her without Burt's credibility to back her up? At least he had made an appointment with a detective prior to her leaving for Guam. That was one bit of luck. Now if she could only remember the detective's name…

There was still one other avenue of possible recourse, and that was proving Steven had misappropriated borrower and investor funds. This was the money shot, as far as she could determine. Burt had found proof of his embezzlement; all she had to do was find what he had uncovered and take it to the D.A.'s office.

She let her mind drift back to their conversations. How exactly had Burt traced the breach of fiduciary responsibility? He said he had done a search of properties that listed RAM, L.P. as a lien holder. How did he do that? Madeline drummed her fingertips on the table, coaxing the missing pieces from the fringes of her memory.

He said that information was available at the County Recorder's Office, she recalled. *But he also said there was a website where he could search for that kind of information.* She took another sip from her almost empty cup, pleased she was able to conjure up these valuable timesaving insights. So, the question now was how to find that website.

As she figured she had many hours of computer work ahead of her, she paid her bill, tipping generously for having been so lavishly accommodated. Her mind was moving into its characteristic tunnel-vision mode. She was on her game and ready to start work.

She was so focused on her thoughts, she was blindsided by the sudden appearance of her annoying fellow diner from the sushi restaurant.

"Hey, slow down…" he said affably. "It's island policy to take it *slow,*" he said, smiling like he was one of God's most irresistible creations. Madeline's face was a stony mask of disinterest. "I sat next to you at the sushi place last night, remember? Paul Jahnke…?"

"I'm sorry, I'm in a hurry," Madeline said, waiting impatiently for one of the elevator doors to open.

"You're not going back to your room, are you? The fun's out there," Paul said, motioning in the general direction of the pools and the beach.

"I'm not feeling well," she said, her eyes riveted to the numbers above the elevator doors.

"Sorry to hear that. Hey, maybe you'd like to give me a jingle later, when you're feeling better…"

A ding sounded and a door opened. Madeline scooted down and waited as the passengers left the car. She got in, pressing the "close door" button as fast as she could. She held it down, hoping her new nemesis wouldn't be able to call the car back by pressing the "up" button. The elevator hesitated. She kept her finger jammed on the button. She heard the sound of another car announcing it was going up. She felt the shifting of pulleys as she began to ascend.

Once she was on her floor, she walked briskly to her room, slipped inside and deadbolted the door. Fortunately, her room was only three doors down from the elevators. She listened for the ding and the sound of the elevator doors opening, while keeping her eye trained on the peephole. After a few minutes, she relaxed her guard.

Now that she was safe in her room, she found her paranoia a little silly. But then again, it wasn't like serious trouble hadn't been hovering over her for weeks. She had to start going with her gut feelings, now that her hired protector was permanently out of commission, probably because of her.

She found Paul Jahnke unsettling; maybe he wasn't just trying to get lucky. Madeline's adrenaline started pumping as a new fear presented itself. Was it really farfetched to think Steven would go to extreme lengths to frame her, possibly having her P.I. killed, without making sure she kept up her part of the bargain?

The way she and Burt had reckoned it, clearing a path for the future Mrs. Ridley was of utmost importance. Until Madeline was out of the way, she was a stumbling block to saving Steven's hide. Maybe it was worth it to him to have an informal babysitter, someone who could keep tabs on her and make sure she fulfilled the residency requirement.

Madeline sank into a chair as she contemplated this hypothesis. It would certainly be in keeping with his M.O., but Mr. SoCal didn't really fit the picture. For one thing, she had sat down next to him at the sushi restaurant, not the other way around. She hadn't made any dinner reservations and even she didn't know where she was going to eat.

So, that put Paul Jahnke out of the running as far as spooks went. But she'd been oblivious to her surroundings ever since she arrived. That was not prudent of her. She had to keep her wits about her at all times. And she wasn't going to sleep until she figured out if someone was watching her every move.

She looked around the hotel room. How would she know if it had been bugged? She didn't know the first thing about surveillance devices, except that they could be very tiny and hidden almost anywhere.

This unnerving thought got her off the sofa. She couldn't just sit there and be spied on. But what could she do? *Oh, Burt—what should I do?* She had worked herself into a mild panic now. She had to take some kind of action or she would go mad.

As casually as she could manage, she went to the closet and assessed her belongings. While ostensibly deciding what to wear, she was calculating what she felt comfortable leaving behind. She had a beach tote that she emptied of beach paraphernalia, replacing it with the pricey shoes still wrapped in their bags, plus all her cashmere sweaters and a pair of jeans.

She left her boots and the casual stuff—along with everything she had purchased since she got there—in the closet. She took her jewelry roll out of the safe and dropped it in her handbag. She relocked the safe, left enough clothing and personal items lying around—including all of her toiletries and her travel bags—slipped the laptop into the beach tote and grabbed her purse.

When she emerged from the elevator, she headed straight for the car rental agency at the Nikko Hotel. She rented a Ford Mustang convertible for the remainder of her stay and arranged to drop it off at the airport.

Once she had everything securely stowed in the trunk, she headed for the duty-free shopping mall. There she purchased replacements for her carry-on bag and cosmetics. She drove down the main road to the larger retail chains and bought toiletries and new tunics, shorts, a bikini, T's and flip flops.

Using the map she was given at the car rental agency, she got her bearings and headed for the southern part of the island for a day of sightseeing, which would give her an excellent opportunity to find out if she was being followed.

FORTY-TWO

Madeline spent the rest of the day driving around the island, taking in the landmark sights and watching out for any possible tails. She imagined what Burt might do and tried to think proactively, executing sudden turns and doubling back, watching her rearview mirror for any copycats. It was easy to play lost and dumb in an area she'd never been before. But with all her efforts to trip up potential bad guys, she came to the conclusion none of her fellow travelers cared where she went. This was some comfort, and as she headed back toward Tumon Bay, she relaxed and enjoyed the scenery.

Though she felt confident she hadn't been followed, she couldn't shake the thought of Steven having her hotel room under surveillance. She remembered all too clearly Burt's concern that both her homes had been bugged in her absence. How difficult could it really be for Steven to hire local talent? She'd already been framed as the cheating spouse and sent to Guam for an expedited dumping. What was to stop him from keeping her under a microscope until she'd completed her part of the bargain? She made a mental note to check online for private investigators on the island, see if she could find one who could at least prove her fears were unfounded.

The sun had just set as she cruised along Route 14A toward the ocean. When she came to the intersection at San Vitores Road, she turned left instead of right, which would've taken her to the Westin. She drove south to the last of the large hotels on the beachside of Tumon Bay, the Guam Hilton.

When she checked into the Westin, she had used the driver's license bearing the name Madeline Ridley, the same name that appeared on her airline tickets. Before she went to the car rental agency, she switched that license out for the new one showing her name as Madeline Dawkins. It had been easier than she thought to get a new license in her maiden name, though she had to lie about losing her old one in order to keep it. Getting the new one before her trip was just a stroke of luck. Now, she effectively had two last names, and she was hoping the difference would be enough to keep her off Steven's radar screen.

She let the valet take her car and the bellman handle her bags. Instead of checking in, she asked to speak to the hotel manager. As it was a Sunday evening, only the assistant manager was available. *So much the better,* Madeline thought, as a young, eager-to-please Chamorran woman came out to greet her.

She had changed her clothing after her shopping binge at the designer duty-free shops, and had added the appropriate amount of tasteful jewelry. She had to strike just the right chord: sympathetic on one hand, sophisticated and moneyed on the other.

She explained to the assistant manager her desire to check in unregistered, as she was eluding the unwanted attentions of a man who had developed something of an obsession with her. She was only on the island to establish residency for a divorce, and wished to remain as anonymous as possible.

The AM seemed enthralled by Madeline's story and was quite eager to accommodate her needs. Madeline further ingratiated herself by requesting the best suite available for three nights, and swore to herself this would be the last of the splurges.

Once she was escorted to her new temporary lodgings, she was grateful she had opted for the extravagance. This was more her idea of vacationing in a tropical paradise. As nice as the Westin had been, she much preferred the spaciousness of the suite; it made her feel less claustrophobic and less like an exile. The suite was the size of a small apartment, with white shutters framing the views of palm trees and the beach beyond, large comfortable furnishings and an elegantly simple décor.

She had determined from her research that the Hilton, being older and the furthest away from the shopping and nightlife, was not as popular as the newer hotels closer to the action. It was also six hotels removed from where she was registered. If anyone had been watching her at the Westin, she felt confident they wouldn't be able to trace her to this location. All she had to do was lie low, which wouldn't be hard with all the investigation she needed to do.

Before she tackled the Internet, she treated herself to a long soak in the huge granite tub. She then ordered room service. She made another list, this one of her most immediate tasks, while she waited for her dinner to be delivered.

First on the list: assessing the local P.I. offerings. If Steven did have someone keeping tabs on her, that would be significant. It would confirm that he didn't take her compliance for granted, and that freeing himself up to remarry was an urgent priority.

It would also indicate he was more paranoid than she had expected. If her room at the Westin had been bugged, then Steven or his goons would've been aware of her reaction to Burt's untimely death. If anyone in Steven's employ had been connected to his demise, then it was a pretty sure bet they were aware Burt had been hired to get the dirt on Steven. If they hadn't put one and one together before, it was likely they had by now.

If Steven or his associates were responsible for Burt's death, then they were sure to have searched his office and home for any evidence he might've had. There was a tangled web of intrigue waiting for her back in Santa Barbara, and she had to glean as many facts as possible before waltzing back there.

She ate the delicious dinner of fresh Opah, steamed lemongrass rice and assorted vegetables, but hardly tasted it. Her mind was too preoccupied. She had the worst urge to call Mike, but it was the middle of the night for him. Even if he forgave her, he wouldn't be sufficiently coherent to be of any use.

Damn, Madeline thought; she'd have to wait another day and a half until that part of the world was open for business. Fortunately, she'd be able to scope out the local detectives and hopefully retain someone who could check out her room at the Westin for bugging devices. That would be a relief, one way or the other. Either way, she'd learn something about her enemy's mindset.

After an hour's worth of online research, Madeline was finding it harder to suppress the urge to speak to a confederate. It was now two in the morning, Los Angeles time. The old Mike would consider that still early, but she wasn't sure if the more mature Mike would appreciate a call at that hour. *More mature Mike?* She placed the call. He answered after four rings.

"Sorry," Madeline said in response to his groggy hello. "I forgot to call you earlier," she said, trying to gauge his mood.

"Yeah, I noticed," he said. He treated her to a strenuous yawn. "2 a.m.?"

"I didn't know if you'd be madder if I called too late or didn't call at all," she said.

"It's okay. I would've freaked out if I'd woken up at a civilized hour and realized I hadn't heard from you."

"That's what I was betting on. So, I just wanted to let you know I'm alright."

"Good. Thanks," he said, yawning again. One more yawn and he'd be wide awake.

"I'll let you get back to sleep."

"Wait—are you feeling better?"

"Yeah, I'm doing okay. Definitely better than earlier. Thanks for being there for me."

"My pleasure. You know that."

"If we keep talking, you'll never go back to sleep," Madeline said, secretly hoping he wouldn't care. "I didn't interrupt anything, did I?" Mike chuckled.

"Why don't you just come out and ask if I'm sleeping with someone?"

"It's none of my business."

"You sure act like it is."

"I did something kind of crazy today," Madeline said, ignoring his last remark. It was rather selfish of her, but she knew Mike couldn't resist confessions.

"You, something crazy? I don't believe it."

"I rented a car and took a drive around the island."

"Yeah?" Mike said, clearly disappointed.

"I left the hotel I was staying at, leaving most of my stuff behind. Then, after I was sure no one was following me, I checked into another hotel, away from the crowds, and far enough away from the other hotel to throw someone off the scent." She could hear rustling on Mike's end as he got out of bed.

"Did anything trigger this wacky bit of subterfuge?"

"I guess I just got spooked. There was a guy who kept popping up…I think he was probably just a guy on the make, but it got me to thinking about how vulnerable I am…was…"

"That settles it. I'm getting on a plane and I'm coming to get you," Mike said.

"No, you're not. I shouldn't have called you. I should've let you sleep."

"Why did you call?" Madeline was caught off guard by the tone in his voice. "You called me knowing I was probably cutting Z's. You're scared, and it sounds like you have every reason to be. I'm coming to get you and I won't take no for an answer." Madeline held her forehead with the palm of her hand. She'd really done it this time.

"You're right about one thing—I was scared. But I'm not anymore. I was able to check into this hotel on the sly, and as far as the rest of the world knows, I'm still staying at the Westin. I'm going to hire a local gumshoe tomorrow and have him check out that room, just to put my mind at rest. If he doesn't find any bugs, then I've let my imagination get the best of me. So, see—there's nothing to worry about. I'm fine."

"Looks like I can still catch the 8:26 flight, which is only a few hours from now."

"Mike, didn't you hear me? I said I'm fine. I should've never called you so late. You're in a susceptible state of mind right now and you think you need to come and rescue me. It's my fault. I'm sorry. But please, Mike—do not do anything stupid like getting on a plane to Guam. Really. I mean it—I don't want you to come. I need to do some heavy-duty thinking and I can't do that if I'm worrying about you worrying about me."

"Sorry, faulty logic. I'm not buying it."

"What can I say to make you change your mind?" Madeline asked.

"You sound like a hostage negotiator."

"C'mon, Mikey—"

"Don't "Mikey" me," Mike said testily.

"I should've never gotten you involved in this," Madeline lamented.

"That's not true. I'm glad you did. You know I'd do anything for you."

"Really?"

"Of course, you already know that."

"Then please drop the coming to rescue me idea," she said.

"No."

"You just said you'd do anything for me."

"That's not what I meant," Mike protested.

"So, you'd rather give me one more thing to worry about than do as I ask."

"No, of course not. I just want to protect you."

"And exactly how are you going do to that? Right now, we don't even know for sure if I have any reason to be afraid. You could spend thousands of dollars and the equivalent of a day and a half traveling for nothing. And honestly, I do feel safer now that I've changed hotels. Let me find a P.I. and then I'll know for sure if I'm being hysterical or not. Okay…?" The line was quiet. "Mike?"

"Okay, I see your point. But you can't blame me for being worried. Look at all that's happened to you. I mean, this kind of stuff doesn't happen to the average person. You'd think you were some CIA operative, not a charity fundraiser, for Chrissakes."

"Believe me, I know. The last two weeks have been completely surreal. But I just don't think there's any reason for you to come rushing to save me yet. I may need your help when I get back to Santa Barbara, but it seems highly unlikely anything is going to happen to me while I'm here. So, sorry I woke you up and got you all worried. I'll call you tomorrow at a more reasonable time once I've got something newsworthy to report. Okay?"

"Alright," Mike relented. "Call me tomorrow, and don't forget." Madeline assured him she would and hung up. She sat with phone in hand, hoping she hadn't been too glib. For all she knew, her sense of security could merely be an illusion.

FORTY-THREE

After Madeline hung up with Mike, she resumed her research. Unfortunately, the listings for private investigators on Guam were fairly scant. The same agency held the first seven of the eight listings on her search. She would've felt more comfortable with a larger selection, but she checked out the Hobart Detective Agency anyway. It was a respectable enough site, but it was a fairly large operation. That had put her off when choosing a P.I. in Santa Barbara.

Thinking of the lone P.I. brought her mind back around to Burt. She bit the inside of her lip as she fought back the tears. She felt in her bones that she'd been the catalyst to his death. That would haunt her for the rest of her life.

The only way she could assuage her guilt was to avenge his death. The only way she could do that was to find out who was responsible. That would hinge on being able to find another private detective in S.B. And she probably couldn't even begin the interview process for another 36 hours. Her stomach churned at the thought of all the daunting tasks ahead of her.

She backed out of the Hobart site and scanned the search results again. The only other listing shown was PIs.com. She gave it a try, finding what she had expected: a countrywide map, including Guam, for clicking on. But as she moved her cursor to the tiny dot on the map, the left-hand panel caught her eye. She then realized this site was meant for industry use as well as public use.

She became more intrigued as she read down the available options. She was able to search by specific need: infidelity specialist, background investigations, missing persons, etc. As she scrolled down the side bar, she came across something that really piqued her interest. She stared at the "Espionage Store" link for a couple of seconds before its potential registered. She clicked on it and a page of electronic equipment appeared showing items she'd only been marginally aware of through watching spy capers.

But as she read over the descriptions of this bounty of spyware, her pulse started to race. Here, for purchase, was the answer to her most pressing concerns: a multi-functional portable sweep device, roughly the size of a walkie-talkie. And it could be hers for a mere $500.

As she read through the description of the instrument's capabilities, she was awakened to the complexities of the P.I. game. This one gadget could detect wired and wireless cameras, mics, phone taps, and computer bugging devices.

She sat back, suddenly wary of her computer. She had felt smart ditching her old iPhone and replacing it with one under her maiden name and social; her old phone had been on Steven's account under his SSN. He wouldn't have access to her new account, and that gave her a sense of security. But she had been oblivious to the danger of having her movements tracked through her computer.

She regarded her laptop as she digested all this new—possibly invaluable—information. If she could arm herself with her own equipment, like this sweeping device, she wouldn't need to hunt around for two different private detectives. That would resolve so many issues for her. But she felt uncomfortable making a purchase like that on her computer, just in case it had been bugged, or worse yet, hacked. The thought had never occurred to her before.

She consulted the hotel's directory of services and amenities. As she suspected, there was a business center that was open all hours to accommodate their international clientele. *Perfect,* Madeline thought, as she slipped into a T-shirt and jeans, and went in search of an anonymous computer.

Because of the hour, she had the place to herself. She typed in the URL and went right to the "Tools of the Trade" section. She already knew what she wanted, but she became fascinated by all the handy devices that made modern-day sleuthing a whole lot easier.

As she read one product description after another, she had to wonder if Burt had an arsenal of this kind of gadgetry stashed in his home or office. As with every time she thought of him, a horrible mixture of anxiety and guilt resurfaced. She couldn't get past their last conversation, when she thought she was being resolute instead of fainthearted; in reality she had been cavalier with Burt's life.

Her sense of anxiety and loss made her feel morose. She stared at the computer with unseeing eyes. What was she playing at? Did she really think she was any match for Steven and his gang? Even with all the new evidence to the contrary, it was hard for her to replace the image of the man she'd loved for thirteen years with his calculating, heartless alter ego.

Subconsciously, she kept reverting to the hope that this was just a bizarre aberration in Steven's character and would soon pass. But as she tried to take the fantasy to the next level—a tearful reconciliation and the simultaneous departure of the divorcée from Boston—she knew she was clinging to a life that had simply ceased to exist.

She berated herself as the sting of tears warned of another breakdown. But it was no use. There was so much hurt, loss, anger and resentment burbling up inside her. The only way to expel it was through a torrent of tears. Even as she succumbed, she felt the tandem urge for physical violence; crying her eyes out repeatedly wasn't going to give vent to all her feelings of frustration and rage. She thought of the gym, but that fell short of her desire to inflict pain on her persecutor.

Oh, Steven—if I had you in front of me right now, I would rip your eyes out, she swore to herself. But instead of making her calmer, the curse only made her feel more frustrated. Steven wasn't there, and the likelihood of ever having the opportunity to get even with him was remote. She turned back to the computer screen and tried to focus on her reason for being there.

The image of Burt rose up in her mind's eye, this time bringing her strength and determination. *Think like Burt,* she prodded herself. She closed her eyes and took deep breaths, willing her body to relax and her mind to sharpen. After a couple of minutes, she opened her eyes, alert and eager to proceed.

What Burt would do was use every bit of his intelligence and every tiny clue to figure out Steven's game plan. He had laid out all the pieces she had given him and saw right away that Steven's actions were linked to financial dealings gone awry. She had the benefit of Burt's insight and she had access to this website, which would give her the tools she needed to catch Steven at his own game…if her mind didn't cave in to her emotions.

Mentally refreshed and stimulated, Madeline resumed her perusal of all the nifty electronic gear she could arm herself with. Each item she clicked on gave her an education in the world of spy vs. spy. As she added items to her cart, she could feel the wheels of her mind turning, incorporating each new fact into the lacy network of knowledge her brief association with Burt Latham had given her.

After nearly an hour in the business center, Madeline had five indispensable items in her shopping cart: the portable sweep, a 128-hour digital voice recorder pen, a GPS tracker that fit in the palm of your hand, a 16 GB high-resolution mini camcorder, and a pair of small, powerful binoculars.

She could've kept going, but a new concern occurred to her: how fast could she get the bug scanner? The fastest shipping option offered was second-day air. That wasn't going to be soon enough. She saw an 800 number at the top of the screen and called it. Her brain was too overwhelmed to figure the time difference; either someone answered or they didn't.

On the third ring, a live voice greeted her and asked how he might be of assistance. Madeline explained her desire to purchase the handheld Multifunctional Portable Sweep and asked if they offered a next-day shipping option. She told the customer service rep there were other items she wanted shipped to her mailbox in Santa Barbara, their arrival to coincide with her return from Guam. He placed her on hold for a moment while he conferred with his supervisor.

"We can get the portable sweep to your hotel in Guam within 24 hours, at an additional cost of $150. Will that work for you?"

"Yes, that'll work perfectly," Madeline said, goose bumps running up her arms as she realized what she had just accomplished.

Her next task was to arrange for the front desk to sign for the delivery. She sent an email to the Assistant Manager asking her to inform all the front desk personnel of a very important package that would be arriving within a day, and requested that she be sent a text upon its arrival. That taken care of, she shut down the computer and made her way back to her room, thoroughly exhausted but calmer than she'd felt in weeks.

FORTY-FOUR

Madeline rolled over and looked at the clock: 4:26. She had only gotten four hours sleep, but she was wide awake and not at all tired. She lay in bed as she reviewed her actions of the last 24 hours. She laughed at the lengths she had gone to evade detection without any evidence that anyone was in fact interested in her movements.

Better safe than sorry, she thought, though when she recalled her extravagant late night purchases she couldn't help feeling a little foolish. The portable sweep seemed like such a brilliant idea at the time, but what would she do if she actually found something on her computer or in her other hotel room? It probably came with operating instructions, though she doubted it came with a manual on how to be a private detective.

This last thought propelled her out of bed. *Why didn't I think of this sooner?* she admonished herself as she pulled on her jeans and T-shirt.

She headed back down to the lobby level and walked along the ghostly-quiet corridors to the business center. Again, she had the place to herself. She wasted no time, typing amazon.com in the search bar. Once in, she selected Books from the dropdown menu and typed in *how to become a private investigator* and hit Go.

Instantly, her request brought up 57 results. She waded through the titles, many of which weren't what she was looking for. But there were a few that looked like they could teach her more than she currently knew about counter-espionage. She put five in her cart, all of them in eBook format, which she could read on her Kindle. She checked out and they were all instantly uploaded to her device.

She had plenty of reading material to occupy her remaining time on Guam and on the arduous trip home. The downside of this plan was not knowing for certain if she'd be able to put her finger on the specific knowledge she'd need once her scanner arrived. What she really wanted was some sort of private tutoring, though that would be too much to hope for. She'd be lucky if any of the detectives she had contacted would even return her calls or emails.

As she sat pondering the likelihood of finding a private investigator willing to take on her case, a fragment of memory floated to the surface. "This is what I really need," she mumbled to herself as her fingers typed in a new search. She received an unwelcomed jolt as Burt Latham's name appeared along with the other listings for Santa Barbara P.I.'s. It was eerie to see his name among all the others knowing he was no longer on the receiving end of any potential callers.

But it wasn't a private investigator she was searching for. She had already exhausted that avenue. What she was interested in this time were the sponsor ads at the top and on the right side of the screen. Her memory hadn't failed her. There, competing for possible enrollees, were listings for several online courses in the field of private investigation.

Madeline's pulse quickened as she chose a site. She browsed through the offerings and the curriculum, then backed out and checked another site for comparison.

For the sake of thoroughness, she did another search, which included only training courses specific to California laws and requirements, not that she had any intention of pursuing a career. The mere thought of trying to pull off an act like that made her laugh. She could just imagine Burt rolling his eyes at the idea.

Well, she didn't need to become a bona fide P.I., but there was no harm in educating herself. At the very least, she would become a better client, more able to assist in her case. And if she couldn't find anyone to stick his neck out for her again, she would at a minimum be able to recognize—or maybe even anticipate—any traps Steven might lay in her path.

She browsed through four more sites before opting for the one that seemed the most credible. It was also the only one to offer the price without first having to speak to a "course advisor." She studied everything about the site before committing to the $785 "full payment" option. She held the cursor over the button, giving herself a chance to back out. She'd been throwing money around like it had no value, which had certainly been her M.O. for the last dozen years. But now she had to get a grip on her spending habits or she'd burn through her half-million severance pay in no time.

This is the wrong time to worry about finances, she decided as she clicked on the button and began filling out her billing information. She felt slightly giddy and a tad dubious, and she hoped she wouldn't regret this in the morning.

Once she was through the process, she was at liberty to start studying. Though she felt shaky from the adrenalin rush, fatigue was starting to catch up with her. But she couldn't go back to her room until she took a peek at the course materials, just to make sure she had gotten what she was looking for. After skimming through the table of contents, she found exactly what she needed: How to Recognize and Disarm Surveillance Devices.

"Yes!" she cried out, her hands clenched in victory. She could do this; she could arm herself with spyware and know-how and defend herself. She wouldn't have to explain her predicament to wary P.I.'s or put anyone else in harm's way. Steven would never suspect she had the faintest idea of his behind-the-scenes machinations, so she'd have that going in her favor. She could play the ignorant, broken-hearted fool and he wouldn't give her a second thought. And why should he? As far as he was concerned, she was in the past. Once she signed the divorce settlement agreement, she had sealed her fate.

She smiled to herself as she closed out of the Internet. The game wasn't over yet. It was her turn to serve.

FORTY-FIVE

Wakefulness came on slowly as Madeline fought her way out of a deep, almost paralyzing sleep. Twice she decided against getting up and fell back into a chaotic dream world. She awoke for the third time drenched in sweat, her heart pounding as she tried to snatch the fragments of her disturbing dream before they evaporated like ether. She pulled herself up and looked at the clock. It was already 9:35.

She struggled off the bed and went in search of water to erase the stale, cotton-like dryness in her mouth and throat. She guzzled a warm bottle of Perrier as she hunted for the room service button. She ordered yogurt, fruit, coffee and dry toast and jumped into the shower.

She ate her breakfast looking out at the bay. She tried to savor this moment of peace and tranquility, but her mind was too jumpy for relaxation. By now it was 10:15, only seven hours since she purchased her bug scanner and expedited shipping. She couldn't realistically expect to see delivery for several more hours.

She had plenty of studying she could do until then, but she had a craving to be outdoors. It was too beautiful a day to waste inside. Like it or not, this was the last "vacation" she'd have for the foreseeable future.

She drank the rest of her coffee, brushed her teeth and slathered herself in sunscreen before getting into her swimsuit. She threw together a bag of essentials, including her Kindle and her cell phone, and headed to one of the hotel's five pools.

Madeline sampled each of the eBooks on private investigating, honing in specifically on anything to do with finding, identifying and disabling audio/visual recording devices. It was fascinating and enthralling reading. Before she knew it, two hours had passed. Her brain was in such a blur, all she could think of was getting the scanner and putting it to use.

She checked her text messages, but nothing new had appeared. She called the front desk to make sure a package had not arrived.

"No, Ms. Dawkins, nothing yet. But everyone has been alerted to send you a text message as soon as it comes." Madeline thanked the woman and hung up.

She sat on the chaise longue, a foot planted on each side, as if she were in the middle of standing up. There was so much going on in her head, her body was left in limbo. She forced herself to focus on the here and now and hoisted herself to a standing position. From there, her body took over, guiding her past the pool, out onto the pathway to the sand.

Without realizing what her intentions were, she waded into the water, a smile of delight and surprise breaking out across her face as a wave hit her in the waist. She waded out farther than she thought was possible, then the sand fell away from her feet as the deeper, cooler water enveloped her.

She swam out far enough that she could see all of the hotels along Tumon Bay. The hulking resorts looked so small from that distance. She executed an underwater turn and floated flat on her back, her head pointed in the general direction of the shore.

It was so soothing being out in the pristine water, with only the bright blue sky and amorphous white clouds overhead. Out there, away from everything and everyone, she could think—really think—her thoughts coming in an organized fashion, without the background noise of sundry worries.

In her mind, a chain of actions fell into place, as orderly as name cards being placed on a dinner table. The first card: the arrival of the scanner, followed naturally by the scanning of her computer. This left her to consider the next card: either it would be an uninvited guest, or it would be relief at finding the computer free of any bugging device.

If she found something on her laptop, she would have to determine if it was an audio or visual device, or a GPS tracker. If it were a tracking bug, then all her efforts of evasion were worthless. She could take the computer back to her room at the Westin and attach the bug to something else. That would work. The other option would be to abandon that room and the suite at the Hilton and check in somewhere else, which was unappealing on all levels.

Either way, she had a plan in place for the unwanted guest. Next card: finding out if her room at the Westin had been tampered with. That had to be done to ascertain how threatened Steven felt by her mere existence. The divorce was the only piece not securely in place, and it wouldn't be until she'd completed her residency requirement and the attorney took the case through the court system, which she now knew could take as little as 30 days. Then he'd have nothing to worry about…unless she could somehow pin him to her rape… There would be room at the table for that, but it would be further down the line.

Next place card: a Santa Barbara P.I. There was probably a 50-percent chance that spot would be a no-show. She did the math in her head; she had at least thirteen hours until she could reasonably expect a callback or an email response. Then it was a matter of selling her case, which at this point was rangy and unpalatable. Right now, her chief reason for engaging a detective would be to find out if Burt Latham tragically fell to his death or was pushed.

Now it was time to invite law enforcement to the table. If she could remember the name of the detective Burt had lined up, that would help her immensely in the credibility department. If she could successfully persuade him that she was set up to be raped while being photographed, then perhaps Detective…Blank might take an interest in Burt's lethal plunge.

So, accompanying this guest would be the autopsy results. She had doubts she'd be satisfied with a conclusion of accidental death by drowning. Burt was obviously very familiar with the Douglas Preserve; she had met him there twice. He would know to stay away from the steep drop-offs.

Her gut told her that Burt had arranged to meet the fourth or fifth duped borrower he had uncovered at the park—or maybe that was the set up. He had gotten too close to getting the dirt on Steven. That would never do, not after all the trouble Steven had taken to secure a solution in the form of a rich new wife.

She abandoned the guest list and started thinking about necessities, like a place to live and transportation. In just three days she'd be headed back to Los Angeles, where she'd probably be waylaid by Mike for a few days. That thought caused her some anxiety, but trying to envision arriving at the Santa Barbara airport with no final destination in mind was equally troublesome.

Maybe it was okay to hang out with Mike for a few days. She'd be starved for companionship by then and being around him would be a comfort. She wouldn't have to put on a front for him; she could unburden herself of all the pent up rage and remorse. He'd been through months of counseling, so he'd know how to drag it all out of her. It would be cathartic. Plus, he could help her shop for a new car…

Madeline's eyes sprang open. She raised her head and listened. She heard the faint sound of splashing. She rolled over, her face in the water, her eyes open. She saw something—a pair of legs bobbing just below the surface. She popped up, gasped enough air to fill her lungs and went back under, swimming at a right angle from the intruder. Fear gripped her so hard, she had to use every bit of willpower to get her arms and legs working in unison.

She came up for air again, taking the opportunity to scout out her pursuer. He had turned in her direction. *Please God, no,* she prayed silently, as she envisioned a watery death at the hands of a stranger.

She plowed her arms through the water as fast as she could, but a second glance confirmed he was gaining on her. He had the advantage of coming from the shore, which meant she had to travel in an arc to get around him. She came up for air again and her heart stopped. There was no possible way to out-swim him. She changed to the breast stroke, but she started swallowing water as great sobs of panic broke from her chest.

"Hang on!" she heard the man say. She turned her head to face him and for the first time saw the red rescue tube sticking up in front of his chest. "Stay there—I'll come to you." Madeline treaded water as she cleared her nose and tried to calm herself. The lifeguard reached her in seconds, thrusting the rescue tube toward her. She grabbed it and held on.

"Are you alright?" he asked. Madeline nodded her head as she panted. Her heart felt like it was on the verge of exploding.

"From the shore, I couldn't tell if you were in trouble or not," the lifeguard said. "I started worrying I might have a dead body on my hands," he said with a chuckle. Madeline chortled weakly.

"Not yet, though when I saw you coming after me, I thought I was going to have a heart attack."

"I'm not that scary, am I?" he joked. Even soaking wet, Madeline could see the Chamorro native was quite the looker, with his dark skin and dazzling smile. "C'mon, I'll give you a lift back," he said as he braced Madeline's hands on the rescue tube. He stroked away from her until the line on the tube became taut and she felt him tugging her toward the beach.

"What hotel are you at?"

"The Hilton," Madeline said.

"I can take you as far as the Holiday Inn—that's where my post is."

"Once I get to the shallow part, I'll be fine," Madeline assured him.

She swam along with him, not letting him shoulder the extra burden by himself. When they started to rise and fall with the incoming tide, she knew she was getting close to being on her feet again. They rode a wave in partway and she stood up, shaky and nauseated, but okay. She thanked her rescuer and waved goodbye as she trudged through the water, heading at a diagonal toward the Hilton.

When she finally reached the beach in front of her hotel, she felt as though she'd just swam the English Channel. She staggered back to the chaise she had abandoned an hour earlier and was relieved to find her bag and its contents still there. She rinsed off at the shower stall and lay down to dry off. She checked her iPhone; still no text from the front desk. She closed her eyes and fell into a deep but brief sleep.

When she awoke, she was disoriented and famished. She ordered a mineral water and a hamburger from the cocktail waitress. While she downed the water she got a look at her neglected nails. It had been over two weeks since she had a manicure and pedicure, and her toenails were especially battered from tromping through the sand.

That's an easy fix, she thought as she devoured her burger. When she was satiated and had recovered her senses, she gathered her things and headed for the salon, where she could treat herself to the works. And hopefully when she was finished, her package would be there and she could finally get down to the serious business of amateur sleuthing.

FORTY-SIX

The text came through as the manicurist was finishing her toenails. She had spent almost three hours in the salon, starting with a massage, then a shampoo, a facial and the mani/pedi combo. She had splurged again, but it was worth it. She felt like the semi-Bionic Woman—no new parts, but a full rehab.

She hastened back to her suite, where she set about unwrapping her package. The main problem was finding something sharp to cut through the packing tape. She couldn't travel with her Swiss Army knife anymore, and she didn't have any keys because she no longer owned anything that required one. She ended up poking the parcel open with a pen, which took an inordinate amount of time and made her edgy.

When she finally pulled the contraption from its box, she was breathless with anticipation. She messed with the controls for a minute before resorting to the "quick start" guide and instructions. She became frazzled when she discovered the unit had to be charged, but once it was plugged in she was able to use it. Immediately it started beeping, startling her half to death.

She read through the info impatiently and figured out how to stop the beeping. She changed the setting to "flash only." That solved, she read on, gleaning just enough to understand how the device operated. It could detect bugs at 30 feet. That could be anywhere in the suite.

She picked up her computer and brought it closer. The scanner flashed faster the closer she got. With shaky hands, she opened the laptop. The flashing continued, but she wasn't sure what she should be looking for. She consulted the brochure again.

She laid the scanner down and flipped her computer over. She carried it over to a window and examined it in the light. Everything was black and there weren't that many raised surfaces, just the rounded feet that elevated it. On closer inspection, she detected that there were five raised bumps, four on the corners and one placed rather oddly that didn't really look like the others. It was larger and wasn't the same depth. And there appeared to be a hole in the center…

She turned off the scanner and switched on the desk lamp. She placed the laptop upside down on the desk in preparation of debugging it. Again she was vexed at the lack of proper tools. She looked at her freshly manicured fingernails and sighed. *They could always be touched up,* she decided as she ran her thumbnail around the edge, looking for a loose spot. Finding none, she took a sharp jab at it and off it flew, breaking her nail in the process. It landed on the rug and rolled under the coffee table.

Madeline suppressed a whoop of triumph, mindful of what she had uncovered. She picked up the black disc and scrutinized it. There was no way she could be sure when it had been attached; it could have been put on while she was still at the Park Lane house or while she was staying at the Westin.

Assuming the former, what conversations could it have picked up? Madeline racked her brain trying to recall everything she had said in the presence of her computer. She watched the events of the last two weeks as they raced through her mind.

She stopped the playback as bits and pieces of her phone conversations with Mike came back to her. What had she said? Had she tipped her hand in any way? She froze as she remembered telling Mike she hired her own private investigator. Had she ever mentioned him by name? She thought hard. It seemed like she had. Damn! And she definitely recalled breaking the news to Mike that "Burt" was dead.

She had also told Mike that she had moved to the Hilton. *Damn, damn, damn!* she cursed herself. But then she realized she had called him from the bedroom, while her computer was on the desk at the other end of the suite. That was a small relief.

She sank to the sofa, hands clasped to her face as she remembered her last conversation with Burt. Whoever had been listening would've only heard her speaking, but what had she said? She knocked the sides of her head, trying to shake pieces of their last exchange loose. She rose up like a zombie as snippets came back to her. *"I'm afraid Steven will manage to come up with the money needed to pay off the notes before we have enough evidence of what he's done."*

A strangled cry escaped her as she staggered toward the French doors. *"If we don't catch him on this, then we're not going to catch him on anything…"*

She covered her ears in a vain attempt to block out what she had tried so hard to remember. But now that the last conversation came flooding back, she couldn't stop it. She had tipped off whoever had planted the listening device on her computer. They could've easily pieced together everything she and Burt had been up to from her dialog alone.

"Are you worried they know you're investigating Steven's company?" she remembered asking. She wanted to end it right there...but she hadn't. No, she wanted to get Steven for *some* of the crimes he had committed. She turned ghostly pale as her inner voice replayed the final *coup de gras*: *"Continue as planned. A man like that can't be allowed to go free and seek other victims."*

She gingerly picked up the tiny microphone, wondering what she should do with it. Could the brief beeping of the scanner and the fall from the back of the computer alerted anyone listening in? The beeping could've come from a variety of electronic devices, and the mic had landed on the carpet. She was probably in the clear, but she couldn't decide if it were better to pitch the bug outside or play dumb.

She set it down on the coffee table and changed out of her swimsuit and tunic. She thought for a moment while she dressed in clean shorts and a T-shirt. She decided to leave the listening device alone and go check out her other hotel room. She wouldn't have any concrete answers until she knew if Steven had local surveillance on her too.

FORTY-SEVEN

Madeline parked her rental car at the Nikko Hotel and walked through the Aurora grounds to the Westin, her mind churning. There were so many possible scenarios at play here, she could barely keep them all straight. What she really needed was a professional to put the pieces together. But she would have to rely on her new gadget and her own intelligence to determine how far Steven had gone to assure her cooperation.

She spent a few minutes dallying in the lobby of the Westin to make sure no one was following her. There was quite a crowd waiting in front of the bank of elevators, as a new influx of vacationers was shown to their rooms. Fortunately, no one else got off on her floor.

In her absence, the maid had cleaned and tidied her room. Madeline set her bag down on the desk as she made a visual assessment of all the places one might hide a bugging device. In the process, she kicked off her sandals and turned on the television. She used her flashlight app on her iPhone to discreetly look behind the dresser and armoire.

She felt completely out of her depth as she ran her hand under the desk and turned the telephone upside down. She could spend an hour going over the room and never find what she fervently hoped didn't exist. Someone could've placed a video camera or a microphone almost anywhere. Or this could just be an exercise in paranoid futility.

She sat on the edge of the bed and considered the most probable locations to plant a bug. She looked up at the sconces above each bedside table. Both would be an ideal place to hide a voice recorder. But what she wanted to rule out before searching for them was any possible video cameras.

She checked all around the mirror above the dresser and the two framed prints. She shone the flashlight over the A/C vent, but it would be impossible to eliminate it unless she got up there and took the grill off. On second thought, the rushing of air when the A/C was running would hamper the sound quality. She also wrote it off as a poor vantage point for a camera.

She turned on the bathroom light and did a visual inspection. All her toiletries had been lined up in an orderly fashion that showed the care the maid had taken with her things. She checked all sides of the makeup mirror and every other fixture in the room, including the blinds that covered the ocean view window over the bathtub. Nothing out of the ordinary.

She turned up the volume on the TV as she headed for her tote bag. It was time to break out the spyware. If the room was bugged at all, it would probably be with a wireless microphone. What she had to say to someone would be more relevant to Steven's concerns than images of her walking around in her underwear. She switched the scanner on and it immediately began to flash.

As she walked toward the bed, the flashing increased. She stood on the mattress and peered inside the up-turned glass shade. She couldn't see anything. She walked across the bed to the other sconce, the tracker flashing faster with each step. She tested the sturdiness of the side table with her foot, then shifted her weight to give her another couple inches in viewing height. She dropped the scanner to the bed and used both hands to probe inside the sconce.

Down toward the base, stuck to the wall, her fingers ran across the uneven texture of the mesh covering a mic about the size of a quarter. She hopped back to the bed, retrieved the scanner and held it up to the sconce. The flashing light became a solid beam of red. She'd found her bug. She turned the scanner off and lowered herself to the bed.

Now that she knew what she was dealing with, it was easier to surmise Steven's intentions. It wasn't good enough to know that she was in Guam proceeding with the divorce as agreed. For whatever reason, he felt it necessary to make sure she didn't have a counter attack in the making. She couldn't fault him for being stupid, only evil. His goons had used her expectation of privacy to their advantage, which in turn led them straight to Burt.

What troubled her now were the conversations she'd had with Mike. She sat rigidly as the possible consequences of those phone calls filled her with dread. She sprang off the bed and grabbed her phone, her impulse being to warn him of possible danger. She stopped just short of repeating the same mistake that had put both him and Burt in jeopardy.

A murderous rage was building inside her, one that made her want to tear the room apart and throw the furnishings off the balcony. But what she really wanted to do was beat Steven to a bloody, unrecognizable pulp.

She fought back the powerful urge to flee the room with her newfound determination to retaliate. She had awakened one horrible day to a never-ending nightmare. If she ever wanted to be free of it, she'd have to concentrate like she'd never had to do before. She'd have to turn herself into a one-woman defense team and turn the tables on Steven. She prayed she'd have the guts and perseverance to go the distance.

While she had Mike on her mind, she sent him a text: *Just checking in. Nothing new to report. All's well. Call u tomorrow.* That done, she went through the motions of feigning a conversation with him. It was important to make Steven's crew think everything was under control now that Burt Latham was out of the picture.

"Hi Mike, it's me. I just wanted to let you know I've moved back to my room at the Westin," she said to her iPhone. "I guess I over-reacted to the news of Burt's death. I just got paranoid. Plus, the other place wasn't nearly as nice as this one. I've got a gorgeous view of the ocean from my bed and the bathtub… Oh yeah, it's amazing. I could definitely get used to it… I know. I was so freaked out. But I got to thinking about what you said, about how Burt probably had any number of vendettas against him. I suppose it comes with the job. But I'm still shaken up by it… Oh, I know, but it seemed too coincidental at the time. I was his last client, so I just assumed I was somehow responsible."

Madeline paused as she pretended to listen to Mike's reply. She lay back on the bed and twiddled a strand of hair with her free hand.

"I'm just glad you didn't hop on a plane to come rescue me," she said with a laugh. "No, I'm totally okay now. The way I look at it is I've got two and a half more days in paradise before I head back to L.A." She paused, imaging what Mike would say.

"Well, actually, I have given it some thought. Yeah… I'm thinking I should take you up on your offer, if you still want me hanging around," she said coyly. "Well, I really appreciate it. But you know this is a 'no-strings' deal…we'll take it as it comes, alright?

"Okay, I should let you go," she said, yawning. "Same here. Bye." She went through the motions of ending the call and pulled herself off the bed with effort. She ran a bubble bath and stripped out of her clothes. After soaking for about fifteen minutes, she rinsed and dried off. She put on a little makeup, rearranging everything so it would be obvious she'd been there.

She put on a different outfit, pulled back the sheets and rumpled the pillows, then collected her scanner and a few odds and ends she decided not to leave behind. She closed the blinds, turned out the lights and made her way back to the Nikko Hotel along the shore. She easily blended in with the clusters of people trying to draw out the day before submitting to cocktails and dinner.

To make sure no one was on her trail, she lingered in the lobby as though waiting for someone to join her. Once she was convinced she wasn't being watched, she returned the rental car, then took a cab to the anonymity and obscurity of the Hilton.

FORTY-EIGHT

As soon as she was back in her suite, the tension of the last few days fell away. The panic and devastation she had felt upon learning of Burt's death had given way to a solid kernel of self-confidence. She had pulled herself together and come up with several strategies for dealing with Steven. She had ordered electronic gizmos and a detective course and several enlightening books. She had done her own sweeping and put a counter-offensive in play. Not bad for a day's work.

She stared at the listening device she had pried off her computer. Until she had time to read the course material that dealt specifically with this kind of dilemma, she had no plans to destroy it, for fear that would tip her hand in some way. Instead, she wrapped it in a hand towel and slipped it into a shopping bag, which she then stowed in the back of the closet.

She checked the time: ten to seven. Now that the excitement of her mission was behind her, she felt fatigue fill its place. But that was the beauty of having a suite: she could stay in and not feel claustrophobic. She studied her dinner options and dialed room service. Believing she had cause for a mild celebration, she ordered a half bottle of champagne to go with her lobster bisque and diver scallops.

In anticipation of her feast, she slipped into a silk sheath dress she'd picked up at one of the duty-free shops and turned on her computer. She finally felt up to dealing with the hundreds of emails she'd received since her life imploded. Before she got Outlook opened, the Instant Messenger icon flashed on the screen. Jane. The message had been posted several hours earlier. Madeline sat down at the desk as she scrolled up to the beginning of the message thread.

r u there?? OMG! u r not going to believe what's been circulating via email. I'm assuming u don't know about this... Madeline read the next message. *I just forwarded the link to u. brace yourself. Oh, girlfriend —i'm so sorry for u. CALL ME!!*

Madeline waited impatiently for her email to populate. During the long process of loading the program, dozens upon dozens of emails appeared in her inbox, starting with a few days ago. She hurriedly scrolled through the messages until she came across the one from Jane. On her preview pane, she could see the link and nothing else. The subject line read simply OMG!

She clicked on the link and was taken to a website. Before she activated the arrow, a sinking feeling came over her. It only took a couple of seconds to confirm the video was the parent of the still photographs Steven had used as his excuse to divorce her with impunity.

A strangled cry escaped her throat as she stared in disbelief at the footage of her having sex with whom she assumed was the mystery man from the ball. Tears of shame and disgust streamed down her face, leaving wet trails on her new silk dress. She fumbled with the mouse until she was able to stop the video. She stood up, knocking the chair backwards, as great, painful sobs rackedher entire body.

"NO!" she yelled at the top of her voice. "NO!" Her knees buckled and she sank to the floor. Her cries became incoherent babble that eventually ceased altogether.

She sat in stunned silence as she assimilated this latest affront. As the minutes ticked by, the look of anguish in her eyes gave way to steely resolve. She got herself and the chair off the floor and sat back down at her computer.

She stared at the freeze-frame shot of herself, her head lolling awkwardly as her assailant had his way with her. As much as it wounded her, she knew that Steven had gone too far this time. He might have several layers between him and this videotaped rape, but those layers could be peeled back, one by one, until the mastermind of her ultimate humiliation would be revealed.

Putting this out for public consumption was the cruel move that would become his undoing. No matter what she had to do, she wouldn't stop until Steven Ambrose Ridley paid for his crimes, in spades.

Madeline lifted the silver dome covering the seared scallops and nearly gagged. She quickly recovered the dish and called room service to come and get the tray. She was so distraught, she could barely function. She wandered out to the patio and perched on one of the chairs. She was a physical and emotional wreck, but she didn't care anymore.

She snorted contemptuously as she thought of what she used to hold so dear: money, prestige, connections. What did those things really matter in the larger scheme of things? She had lost something a lot more valuable—her dignity—and she could see no way to redeem it.

What galled her most was the way Steven had disposed of her. It wasn't like she had been a shrew; they had always more or less been on the same page. She believed they actually had quite a successful marriage. *Hah! What a joke that is,* she thought bitterly, using her fingers to wipe away the tears.

"What did I do wrong?" she asked out loud. The sound of her voice startled her; it was the raspy, brittle voice of a much older woman, one who felt herself victimized by life. Madeline cleared her throat and tested it again. "I won't let him do this to me," she said adamantly, her inner strength and fire returning. "Whatever it takes, I'm going to set the record straight," she pledged, her mind already conjuring up a viable game plan.

FORTY-NINE

While Madeline was hard at work on her computer, Jane logged on. Madeline pounced on the chance to get a damage assessment. Jane replied immediately.

how are u??

ok. they finally agreed to take the video down, Madeline replied.

thank God! what was that??

I can't get into it now, but i can tell u Steven was behind it.

what? r u kidding me?!

no, unfortunately.

what's going on?

i'll tell u when i get back to sb.

when is that?

thursday or friday. I need to know who sent u the link. I need u to forward the original message with the full address of who sent it.

ok – why?

i need to trace it back to the original source, if possible. How many people do you think got it? Madeline asked, though she was afraid of the answer. Jane's balloon remained motionless for a few seconds, increasing Madeline's dread.

everyone.

Madeline bit her lip, willing herself not to cry. She knew when she saw the video the whole purpose of releasing it had been to cause her as much shame as possible. That's when it occurred to her Steven was trying to force her out of Santa Barbara. He probably figured she'd never be able face anyone she knew after her character had been so thoroughly trashed.

what have u heard? Again, Jane hesitated.

everyone thinks Steven kicked u out because he found out u were having an affair. Natalie said u were being blackmailed and Steven refused to pay anymore.

Madeline clenched her teeth, the muscles in her face twitching as she read this outrageous lie.

where did she hear that?

Amanda told her.

Madeline barked a harsh laugh as she sat back and connected the dots. Amanda was married to John; John was one of Steven's partners. So cozy. All Steven had to do was confide in his partner and share the video link and it was *un fait accompli*. Destroying her reputation had been so simple, it hardly seemed sporting.

is it true? Jane asked.

of course not! it's all a pack of lies. but u can't let anyone know that you've been in contact with me. just go along with it for now and feed me the latest developments. ok?

absolutely! what else can i do to help? Madeline sighed as she replied.

if I think of anything, i'll let you know. gotta run.

hey – i'm on your side 100% - i want u to remember that.

thanks. XO. delete these messages.

Madeline closed out of Messenger and stood up. She stretched her arms toward the ceiling and twisted, eliciting a series of pops and cracks down her spine. She took a swig of the now warm beer and regretted it. She nibbled on a leftover crust from her club sandwich to get rid of the unpleasant taste as she went to inspect the minibar.

She had sent back the unopened champagne in favor of a draft beer, seeing as her call for celebration had been premature. Beer was definitely more fitting for her downtrodden frame of mind, as some sort of sedative was in order after the shock of finding herself starring in an X-rated Internet video.

Now that she had let her natural calm dictate her counter-measures, she felt somewhat vindicated and worthy of a stiff drink. She opened two mini Jack Daniels bottles and poured them into a highball glass with two cubes of ice. She grabbed a notepad and pen and took her drink to the sofa, where she set about doing some serious strategizing.

After two sips of the heady booze, her whole body relaxed. It was late and she'd had another long, stressful day. But the good news at 2:37 a.m. was the video had been pulled off the Internet.

Once she recovered from the shock, she took the necessary steps to inform the site of the video's content and its link to a sexual assault. It hadn't been as easy as she'd hoped to get her issue addressed, but once she made it clear the video documented an unsolved crime, she finally got the response she was looking for.

She would have to track down its origins and pursue legal action at a later date. From what she had already learned through her detective course, tracing the user back would probably lead to an account with bogus registration information. If RAM L.P.'s security team was mixed up in this—and she'd bet her life they were—they'd be too clever not to cover their tracks. For the time being, she'd have to focus her attentions on the plan of attack that would afford the best results.

Now she assessed what her next moves should be. She thought of labeling this list "Getting Even with Steven," but the mere thought of his name made her tense up all over. She decided instead on "Operation Justice."

The order of her objectives wasn't as important as trying to get her head around all the different avenues she needed to pursue. She'd made up her mind to take her suspicions to the SBPD. She needed to remember the name of the detective Burt had spoken to about her rape. It would come to her, she hoped. She wrote "Call SBPD" on the list.

Something told her not to expect much from the detective agencies she had contacted in Santa Barbara. In one respect, she was okay with that; she didn't relish having to explain the twisted circumstances behind her desire to find out the truth about Burt's death. Trying to get anyone on board with the rest of her baggage seemed impossible at this stage. Who would believe her?

At least she wasn't completely unschooled in the steps it would take to unearth Steven's felonious financial dealings. Item number two on the list was "Hall of Records." That was where Burt had found the thread that led him to the unrecorded loan payoffs. The way he had explained his steps seemed straightforward enough.

The secret to finding the pertinent information lay in searching for deeds of trust listing RAM, L.P. as the lien holder. The website Burt used allowed him to search for...*private party loans*. Madeline circled this; she'd have to investigate that in the morning.

So, if she was able to pull up a list of all the real estate loans made by Steven's company, then she could go to the courthouse and ask to see those records. She took a healthy slug of her drink, hoping that would somehow meld these facts into a plan of action she could imagine carrying out. She didn't know anything about public records and trust deeds. How would she know what to look for?

I'll just have to go through it one trust deed at a time, use a pretext, like Burt did, offering to lower their interest rate... Then, if I contact any borrowers who've already paid their loan off—or think they have—they'll tell me. Then I've got him. Piece of cake. She let out a groan and took another swig of the now watery bourbon.

"Okay, back to the list." She drained the remainder of her drink and sat back down on the sofa, her hands forming a pyramid as she pieced the steps together.

She would contact the borrowers under a "pretext" the way Burt had. If any told her they had already paid off their loan to RAM, L.P., she could either get statements from them, or play it safe and turn the names over to the district attorney's office. She winced at her choices; she didn't like either one. She didn't relish the idea of putting herself in danger on the one hand, or having the file collect dust at the D.A.'s office on the other.

She'd have to leave that quandary for later. The question now was what to do next. What, if anything, could she do from her exile in Guam? Not much.

The solution seemed so simple, she gasped at not having thought of it sooner. The one thing she had going for her right now was her seeming cooperation. So far, she hadn't given anyone who might be listening reason to doubt she would fulfill her obligation of staying on Guam long enough to establish the required residency. She had given herself an extra buffer by pretending she would stay in L.A. for a few days before going back to Santa Barbara. Assuming someone had been listening, she had bought herself some breathing room.

She logged on to her computer and checked flight schedules. Tamuning, Guam to Los Angeles, March 2nd, one-way. She sat back and waited impatiently for the search to return the flight information. Now that it had occurred to her she could get off this island earlier—the main advantage being two days undercover in Santa Barbara—she couldn't stomach the thought of lingering on Guam any longer.

After five minutes of staring and swearing at the rotating dots, she gave up and tried a different approach. Instead of a broad search, she tried a specific airline. Much easier; her search came back in seconds. But there was a problem: all of Delta's flights had a stop in Tokyo, which meant she'd have to travel with a passport. That wouldn't work. She needed to purchase the fare under the name Madeline Dawkins and show that driver's license at check in. She was already booked on a flight leaving two days later under the name Ridley. She had to let that reservation stand and fly under the radar with her maiden name.

She backed out and tried a different airline. Same problem. Now that she had her heart set on getting back to Santa Barbara early, it depressed her to think she wouldn't be able to. She tried a third airline. Success: Guam to LAX via Honolulu. There was a flight leaving at 7:15 a.m.—in just four hours. Could she possibly get herself together by then? She'd have to. Getting back to Santa Barbara only one day early wouldn't give her enough of a leg up on Steven.

On top of boarding a trans-Pacific flight after a night of zero sleep, she'd have a five-hour-forty-minute layover in Honolulu. She massaged her neck as she tried to envision pulling this off. She went back a screen and tried a different approach. A business-class one-way ticket would cost her $2,905. It would be well worth it. At least she'd be able to sleep somewhat comfortably.

Out of curiosity, she checked first-class. She balked at the price tag of $9,329 and gratefully settled for business-class. She thought through the steps carefully before booking the flight. She clicked the button, setting her plan into motion.

Now that she had set this crazy new plot into action, she had to go over the next steps very carefully. She was aggravated at herself for getting rid of the rental car, for now she wanted to make one last stop at the Westin to clear out the rest of her things. She had to figure this out.

She rang the front desk and asked that her bill be prepared; something had come up and she needed to leave early. She also asked for a cab to pick her up in 30 minutes.

That done, Madeline selected her travel attire and laid it out on the bed. She charged her laptop, cell phone and Kindle. She then hopped in the shower. While still in her underwear, she rounded up all her personal items and packed them for the long journey back to Santa Barbara. She managed to get it all packed into her LV carry-on and her tote, though both were bulging.

Now it was time to get dressed, something she had not been looking forward to. While it was still in the high 70s at 4:30 a.m., she pulled on the black slacks she had worn on the trip over, along with a black T and black cashmere trapeze cardigan. She then selected a pair of unworn shoes from the bunch she'd picked up at Saks. They elevated the outfit to a whole new level.

For the embellishments, she put on the diamond stud earrings, Rolex watch, the tanzanite pendant, and her four-karat diamond wedding ring—all carefully selected to give her the look of understated wealth, which she knew could come in handy at check in. If she was really lucky and the plane wasn't full, she might get bumped up to first class. It wouldn't be the first time that had happened, which supported her lifelong belief that dressing mattered.

According to her watch, she had five minutes left before the cab arrived. It was Monday, mid-morning in California. She took a deep breath and placed a call to Mike. He answered on the fifth ring.

"Am I catching you at a bad time?" she asked.

"No, I'm up. Already had my run, shower and shave." Madeline had trouble with the image of Mike Delaney running.

"Oh, good," she said, resisting the impulse to mock him. "I'm glad I caught you."

"What's up?" Mike asked, his demeanor turning serious.

"Nothing…"

"Isn't it the middle of the night there?" he asked suspiciously.

"Yeah. I'm still having trouble syncing to this crazy time difference. By the time I get used to it, I'll be back home." *Home.* She had to stop using that word. "Anyway, I finally broke down and bought something to help me sleep, so I was afraid I'd oversleep and miss calling you."

"Well, that was thoughtful of you. I'm sorry you can't sleep. That sucks. After all you've been through, you really need to have good sleep. Maybe when you're back here you'll be more relaxed."

"Yeah, hopefully," Madeline said, her eye on the clock. She let out a yawn that didn't require much faking.

"Better let you get some shut eye. I miss you," Mike said, catching her off-guard.

"I miss you, too," she said, a guilty feeling niggling at her. She almost confessed her true intentions, then stopped herself in time. "Look, if I don't call tomorrow, don't get panicky, okay? It just means I've finally broken the sleep drought."

"Alright. You'll be back here when? Wednesday? Thursday?"

"Thursday. But I'll definitely call you before then."

"You better!"

"I will."

"Okay. Sweet dreams."

"Thanks."

"Maddie?"

"Yeah?"

"I love you." Madeline held her breath for a second.

"I know you do." She held the phone to her ear for a few seconds longer, then saw that the call had been ended. The phone in her room shattered the silence with its harsh jangling tone. She seized it before it rang again.

"Your taxi's here, Ms. Dawkins."

"Thank you. I'll be right there."

FIFTY

Madeline told the cab driver she'd be gone as long as half an hour, but to keep the meter running. She took the room key from her pants pocket as she entered the Westin, holding it out so that any late-night security would know she had a right to be there.

She slid the key card into the slot and opened the door as quietly as possible. She crept to the bathroom and flushed the toilet, using the noise as a cover while she bundled up her cosmetics and toiletries in a towel and laid them on the bed. She retrieved Steven's Louis Vuitton carry-on and quietly set about packing it with all the things she had left in the closet, then added the toiletries.

One thing she hadn't counted on was the disposal of the cheap suitcase she'd picked up in Santa Barbara. She pulled the tags off and carried it over to the bed. She flattened it out and gently slid it underneath the bed frame. She put the tags in her tote, along with the other miscellaneous items lying around.

Whatever was in the dresser drawers was going to be left behind, for she couldn't risk the noise a squeaky drawer might make. So far, all the sounds that could trigger the wireless mic had been consistent with getting up in the middle of the night to use the bathroom.

She lifted the LV carry-on off the bed and held it aloft as she took it to the door. She gave herself a few seconds to go over everything in her head before placing the key card on the dresser. She breathed deeply and crept to the door, easing the handle down. She removed the "Do not disturb" card from the inside of the door. She positioned herself and the bag, then opened the door and slipped out.

She let the door come almost to a close, then caught the heft of it on her hip and let it slide noiselessly over the strike plate while she held the handle down. She raised the handle and the door securely closed without making a sound. She placed the "Do not disturb" card in the key slot.

That ought to take care of that, she thought, as she exhaled deeply and walked down the hallway to the elevators. At 5:15, she walked through the lobby as the hotel showed the first signs of preparing for another day of service.

Madeline smiled gratefully as the flight attendant placed a cup of chamomile tea on her tray. She enjoyed this small triumph of finagling her way into a first class seat. All she had to do was make polite conversation and ask for an application for their frequent flyer program. The rest came as a spontaneous gesture on the part of the representative.

When she'd finished the tea, she rang for the attendant and asked that she not be awakened for meal service; she was dead tired and needed to get some sleep. The attendant gave her an extra pillow and wished her sweet dreams.

Madeline made herself as comfortable as possible, closing the window shade to darken her space. As exhausted as she was—mentally, physically and emotionally—sleep was not as easy to coax as she'd hoped. There were still too many doubts and fears that hadn't been laid to rest yet.

In an effort to clear the slate, she started a mental list of all the loose ends that were niggling at her subconscious. She had received two calls from the 805 area code as she was walking to her gate. She let both go to voicemail. The calls could only be from people returning her calls, as no one else with that prefix had her new cell number.

Madeline couldn't decide what to hope for the most: a call back from a detective agency or from one of her rental inquiries. She'd check them out during her layover in Honolulu. She smiled to herself. She was definitely enjoying the fact she had set this ambush in motion, and had finessed it so she'd have access to the executive lounge where she could conduct a few hours of business before the flight to Los Angeles.

There were of course two huge concerns that she refused to let intimidate her: fear for her safety and the small matter of having broken the agreement to produce a super-quick divorce. From her soft leather perch, she shrugged off those concerns. Everything depended on her ability to get enough evidence against Steven to send him to prison for years, hopefully decades.

What else? she wondered, drumming her fingers on the armrest. She'd have to arrange for a rental car pick up in Los Angeles. She thought about getting her list out, but sleep was peeking coquettishly around the corners of her eyes. She needed to set alarms so she could call Mike at intervals to keep him securely in the dark. She hated lying to him, but she couldn't risk his safety.

She shook her head as thoughts of Burt's death jostled her budding confidence. The only thing she had going for her was the fact that she'd already hit rock bottom. Sure, there could be more pain ahead, especially if Steven managed to cover his tracks on the embezzlement and fraud. He already had the solution at hand. He had the advantage over her of being a duplicitous double-crosser from way back. She really didn't stand a chance...

But as she reflected on being so grossly out-matched, a technicality occurred to her that actually did put his plans in jeopardy. Unless he had the influence to sway the laws governing Guam divorces, Madeline had just thwarted his quick divorce/rapid marriage plan by leaving Guam before meeting the seven-day-stay requirement. Of course, once Steven learned of this, she'd have a target on her back.

Oh, what a treacherous course this has become, Madeline thought as her lids closed and blissful sleep took the rudder from her hand.

FIFTY-ONE

The plane landed in Los Angeles at precisely 7:15, fourteen minutes ahead of schedule. Madeline experienced a strange sensation as she looked at her watch and discovered she had traveled for eighteen hours, only to arrive at the exact same time on the same day she had departed from Guam. It was a surreal feeling to discover that she had already lived a day that had yet to begin.

By the time she took her checked bag off the carousel, LAX was already in high gear. Madeline moved with the throng that billowed from the exit doors out into the morning rush, as travelers competed for viewing space along the curb. She caught sight of an Alamo shuttle as it whooshed past her. She sighed and stepped out of a taxicab's way and waited for the next shuttle. Another popped up on the horizon within two minutes. She waved it down.

Twenty minutes later, she was walking the lot, looking for the best car in her price category. Spoiled as she'd been for the last twelve years, she had little awareness of the makes and models in the "intermediate" range. She regretted her decision to compromise, and almost went back inside to upgrade. But an influx of savvy travelers changed her mind. She selected a silver Hyundai Elantra, loaded her bags in the trunk and pulled through the gate. Five minutes later, she was on the 405, headed north.

Now that she was back on familiar turf, Madeline began to relax. It felt good to be back in civilization, good to be out of the false summer and back in the brisk late-winter chill. She was also buoyed by her travel back in time, now seeing the advantages of having cheated another day out of life. She would be in Santa Barbara two and a half days earlier than Steven realized, giving her roughly three workdays to unearth enough proof to turn the tables on him.

Once she made it out of the L.A. sprawl, she decided it was time to eat. As far as food and sleep went, neither had appeared in regular intervals since the night of the ball. *Was that really only two and a half weeks ago?* she wondered, as she pulled off the freeway and headed in the direction of one of the chain restaurants in the Oaks Mall.

While she waited for her hearty American-style breakfast, she decided it was time to check in with Mike. But she still had to deal with calculating the time difference between California and Guam in keeping with her charade. Realizing it was only 3 a.m. ChST, she set an alarm for 5:00, PST. Her mind reeled as she tried to keep her previous schedule straight. There had been too much action topped off with a double dose of jet lag.

As Madeline drove through the parking lot trying to find an exit that would put her in the right lane for reentering the Northbound 101, she passed several shops lined up in the last leg of the shopping complex. She digested the existence of the various stores subconsciously, not giving them a thought as she waited in line to exit the lot.

She was edging along with the traffic when something of significance registered in her brain. At the first opportunity, she executed a quick left and worked her way back to the shop that had belatedly caught her attention. She found a space near the front and parked, her mind mulling over a whole new approach to what she was about to embark on.

"Perfect," she said, as she grabbed her bag and started thinking about what color would be best: bleached blond, brunette or red.

"Good morning!" the saleslady greeted her as she entered Imelda's House of Wigs. "How may I help you today?" the woman asked, smiling eagerly.

"Well…I'm not sure," Madeline said. She deposited her heavy tote on one of the stools lined up in front of the counter, which was topped with featureless heads displaying hairpieces in a variety of styles and colors.

"Are you looking for a wig for yourself?" the woman inquired politely. It occurred to Madeline that purchasing wigs could be a touchy subject. She imagined there was a certain amount of embarrassment attached to *needing* a wig. Madeline smiled broadly to assure the woman she was looking for recreational use only.

"I was driving by and thought it might be fun to wear a wig to a party I'm going to on Saturday," Madeline lied.

"Oh, yes—so many of our clients like to 'test-drive' a new look. A party is a great place to see what kind of reaction your choice will get. Did you have anything specific in mind?" she asked, fluffing a couple of the wigs on display. "A specific color or length, perhaps?"

Madeline examined the row of potential candidates, her eyes shifting to the shelves behind the counter.

"And we have even more on the other side of the store. My name's Maureen, by the way." Madeline turned to take in the thirty or so hairpieces behind her. "And if you don't see what you're looking for out here, I've got many more styles and colors in the back."

Since this idea was so spur of the moment, Madeline had to ask herself what it was she was after. The obvious objective was to make herself unrecognizable while she skulked around Santa Barbara, AWOL from Guam. She was drawn to the fun wigs—bright shades with lots of length and curls—but what she really needed was something so ordinary, no one would give her a second look. She wanted to deflect attention, not draw it.

As she selected a few to try on, she could sense Maureen's disappointment at her rather humdrum choices. She sat down and let Maureen help her get the first wig on.

"Your hair is so pretty," Maureen said as she gathered Madeline's hair and twisted it into a tight bun, which she secured with bobby pins. "We don't get many people with hair as nice as yours in here," she confessed as she scrutinized her handiwork in the mirror.

Madeline laughed at her reflection. With different accessories and makeup, no one would know her. She tried on four different wigs. They all produced the desired effect, and she had trouble making up her mind. The old Madeline would've solved the problem by purchasing all of them. The new Madeline limited herself to just two: a blunt cut dark brunette with eye-skimming bangs that gave her a sexy, mysterious air, and a short, light blond wig that made her look like she'd just stepped off a yacht, not as a passenger, but as part of the crew.

Madeline left the shop with two wig boxes. Inspired by the idea of going incognito, she headed for a nearby drugstore and picked up a few items that would further alter her appearance.

The first stop was at a rack of sunglasses. Her designer frames were too eye-catching and envy-producing, and therefore memorable. She found a pair of oversize black-rimmed glasses that went well with her dark brunette wig. She decided white rims with rhinestones were just the right touch for her sun-bleached blonde.

She then picked out shades of lipstick she would never wear, and eye shadow and liner, which she didn't wear at all. She was certain she wouldn't even recognize herself once she had completed her transformation. But as she caught her reflection in the window of her rental car, she realized she had overlooked something. What she needed to solidify the look was clothing that cost a fraction of what she was accustomed to spending, and accessories to match.

The smug satisfaction of her latest tactical maneuver started to seep away as she rounded Mussel Shoals. Taking its place was an odd fluttering in her stomach and an increase in her breathing, which came now in short, shallow bursts. Once she hit Carpinteria, her anxiety had given her sweaty palms and a tension headache.

She rubbed her tight right shoulder with her left hand and forced herself to breathe deeply and exhale fully. This helped, and soon she could sense an inner change taking place. She was mentally girding herself for battle, the battle of her life.

FIFTY-TWO

Madeline pulled into the driveway of the Paradise Motel on upper State Street. It was quite a step down from her last three accommodations, but it suited her purposes well. It was centrally located and convenient to everything. Yet, in all the years she had lived in Santa Barbara, she had passed it dozens of times without noticing it. It was exactly what she needed: a hideaway as invisible as her new self.

After checking in, she drove to the back of the motel complex and parked in the last slot, directly across from her room. She took her luggage in, but didn't bother to unpack. In two short weeks, she had turned into a transient, likely to be on the move from one day to the next. It was an odd lifestyle for her, but with all that was required of her to stay one step ahead of Steven, she didn't mind being ready to relocate at a moment's notice. She only hoped her vagabond days would come to an end soon.

Her current digs didn't offer much in the way of amenities or furniture. She pulled the only chair up to the bed and laid her paperwork out in front of her. She checked the time: 1:45. She studied the data she had printed in the executive lounge during her stopover in Hawaii.

Though she didn't have the benefit of knowing what site Burt had gleaned his information from, she was able to locate several sites online that provided what she needed. She had been able to search for all outstanding first and second trust deeds held by RAM, L.P. What she had netted was 67 names, with addresses, amount owed, and the date the liens were filed.

As she went over the data again, she tried to get her head around exactly what she should being doing with this information. She sat, arms across her chest, as she broke down her quest into basic components.

Burt had suspected Steven of receiving payoffs on some of these loans without returning the funds to the investor coffers. *Blind pools*, Madeline recalled from the dinners Steven had regularly used to ensnare new investors. *Okay, that part made sense.*

So, by not returning the proceeds from the payoffs to the pool, Steven had defrauded his investors, whom he had a fiduciary responsibility to protect. But the reason no one caught on was because Steven's firm continued to service these paid-off loans, sending monthly interest checks on whatever was supposedly still loaned out from the blind pools…

And, at the same time, Steven had not removed the liens on certain properties RAM, L.P. had financed, which meant some of the borrowers were also defrauded because the repayment of their loans was not recorded. Their payoffs had found their way into Steven's pockets instead. In other words, the deeds of trust had not been reconveyed and their properties were still encumbered.

What all this amounted to was embezzlement and fraud, both crimes that could strip RAM, L.P. of their licenses to do business, open them up to huge lawsuits from investors *and* borrowers, and hopefully send Steven to prison for many years.

Madeline nodded, a smile breaking across her face. *Now I understand why Burt was so eager to go after this angle.* There were real smoking guns somewhere in this list of data, and Burt had found at least five of them. All she would have to do is find out which of these borrowers had been swindled. And to do that, she would need to compare the list of outstanding liens with the actual deeds of trust filed against each property, then contact each borrower to learn which ones had paid off their loans.

Madeline rubbed her aching neck. She had flown through so many time zones, her body didn't know the difference between day and night. She felt fatigue seeping into her brain and muscles, but she couldn't give into it yet. The task ahead of her was daunting, but she didn't have the luxury of putting it off until tomorrow, or whenever she woke up. She'd pick up a coffee on her way to the courthouse and worry about sleep later.

For now, she had to work at the art of disguise. She opened the two wig boxes, laughing at her purchases. On one hand, it was kind of a charge to don a different persona. On the other hand, it felt rather ridiculous.

She held the two wig forms beside her head and tried to decide which one was better suited for a day at the courthouse. She opted for the blond; it was less dramatic and benign enough for dealing with civil servants. She pinned her hair up and secured the hairpiece, fluffing and styling it with her fingertips.

As she regarded herself in the mirror, images of a bewigged Burt flashed across her mind. She let out a huff, both sad and amused. Maybe Burt was coaching her from the great beyond. She wanted to think so, and not just because she needed the help. What she really wanted from Burt was forgiveness for getting him into this mess and getting him killed.

She shook off the reverie with effort and took the makeup she had bought out of its plastic packaging, and began to alter her appearance with a few well-placed dabs and streaks of color. She applied a nearly-nude shade of lipstick and stood back. It was good, but the clothes and jewelry had to go.

Once she had dressed and accessorized herself beyond all recognition, she took the essentials out of her big tote and put them in the decidedly inferior handbag she had bought earlier. She added the pages of borrower information, stood on the bed to check herself out from head to toe, and seized what was left of the day.

Madeline finished her coffee and dropped the cup in the trash can in front of the public library. When traffic permitted, she crossed in the middle of the street, heading for the recorder's office. She found the window she wanted behind a line three deep. She took her place behind the others and listened for clues on how to ask for what she needed.

After waiting in line for ten minutes without advancing, Madeline began pondering the likelihood of getting all the records she wanted before the office closed. It was already 3:15. From what she had observed, requested files came in small batches. She could just about imagine giving the clerk heart failure with a request for the deeds of trust on 67 properties.

So far, the man at the front of the line had asked for items individually, which was why it was taking so long. There were two others ahead of her whom she could watch and gather more about the protocol. Maybe today would have to be spent learning the proper procedure for looking at files in bulk. She didn't like the thought of having wasted a day. It gave her a knot in her stomach.

At 3:45, Madeline was giving up hope of even speaking to the clerk. There were other windows where the lines moved along more quickly, but she was apparently at the only one where she could get what she'd come for. Another person came through the door and groaned at the line. He checked his watch and left.

"Does it usually take this long to get information?" Madeline asked the woman ahead of her.

"It depends. The guy in the front seems to be asking for a lot of files." Madeline smiled grimly and reevaluated her plan.

After all she had gone through to get back to Santa Barbara early, she was aggravated to have her plans thwarted by bad timing. She reprimanded herself for wasting precious time shopping for disguises. She started to fret in earnest that she'd lost the chance to get the proof she needed. Suddenly, a fragment of the last conversation with Burt came back to her.

"Seeing as you're stuck in Guam for several more days, I'll put their statements in a safe place." Madeline froze at the recollection. Burt had already done all this leg work. He had personally gotten copies of all outstanding liens held by RAM, L.P. What she was embarking on would be duplicating steps Burt had already taken. What she really needed to be doing was looking for Burt's safe place—provided he'd had enough time to cache the borrowers' statements before he plummeted into the ocean.

Madeline swore under her breath as the line refused to move. Part of her believed the most prudent course of action would be to complete this process, take a look at the trust deeds with her own eyes, and track down the individuals who had been duped. The other part of her was all for getting the hell out of there and start searching for Burt's hiding place.

There was a distinct problem with the current game plan: somewhere in the process of uncovering Steven's illegal doings, Burt had set off an alarm that had gotten him killed. If she went through the same steps, she could trip the same wire. The man at the counter finally stepped away and she inched forward.

But ditching this avenue in favor of speeding the process along and keeping her neck out of the noose also had its drawbacks, namely, where to start looking. The obvious answer was Burt's office, which was only three blocks away. She tuned into the scene ahead of her, and sensing another protracted exchange, switched to plan B.

FIFTY-THREE

Madeline crossed behind a passing car in the middle of Figueroa Street. Now that she had abandoned her first plan, she began to see the likely obstacles of her new tactic. For one thing, how would she get into Burt's office? It would be locked, and if the coroner's report had come back showing anything but accidental death by drowning, there could be police tape across the door.

It would be too much to hope that Burt had given a spare key to one of his neighbors in the building. Besides, why would they give it to her? Even if the office wasn't cordoned off, she had left her lock picks in her other bag.

Ha, ha, Madeline thought drolly as she crossed State Street on a yellow light. Her mind raced ahead, desperately hoping to come up with a plan C. She was within 30 feet of the staircase to Burt's building when she spotted the "Space Available" sign posted above the mailboxes.

Her heart raced in tandem with her feet as another possibility occurred to her. She needed an office space if she were going to start her event planning business… It was a good pretext, anyway. She got out her iPhone and entered the number on the sign. As she waited for someone to answer, she climbed the stairs to make sure there were no other vacancies in the building. All the other offices were still doing business as usual.

She got a recorded message and hung up as she continued down the hallway. The door to Burt's office was open and she could make out the low timbre of voices, barely audible over the pounding of blood in her ears. For one split second, Madeline thought the reports of Burt's death had been a ruse, planted to throw his pursuers off the trail. But as she reached the doorway, that desperate hope vanished.

There were two men in the outer room of Burt's office, one in his late-sixties and one in his late-teens. Both looked her direction as she came to a halt at the threshold. She could either execute an about-face or inquire about the office for rent. She chose the latter.

"Excuse me," she said, stepping one foot into the office as she held onto the door frame, "is this the office advertised on the sign outside?" She smiled hopefully as she used her powers of observation to read the scene in front of her.

"It is," the older man said. "I'll be with you in a moment, if you want to wait."

"Oh, sure," Madeline said, smiling again as she backed out of the room and away from the door. She stood in the hall, back against the wall as she strained to hear what the two men were talking about. Unfortunately, their voices had dropped and she could only pick up a word here and there. But as they walked closer to the doorway, she got the distinct impression the younger man wasn't there about the space for lease.

Madeline was putting together another possible scenario as the men crossed the threshold, continuing their conversation just outside the office. She abruptly feigned interest in her cell phone, but not before catching a good look at the younger man. A chill ran down her spine as recognition hit home. There was too strong a resemblance for him not to be Burt's son.

"Okay, I'll look into renting a truck," the young man said. It was clear to Madeline that he was struggling with the added burden of taking care of his father's affairs on top of dealing with his sudden demise.

"The closest U-Haul is on upper State," the older man suggested.

"Thanks. I'll let you know when I've gotten everything out." With that, the men shook hands. The landlord placed his hand on the other's shoulder, as though he wished to say something else. After a moment's pause, he patted Burt's son on the arm. The young man gave him a rueful smile and, with head down, walked passed Madeline, in the direction of the stairs.

"Poor kid," the landlord said to no one in particular.

"If this is a bad time, I can come back later..." Madeline said. The man cocked his head toward the office as an invitation to enter.

"Max Howard," he said as Madeline approached the doorway.

"Madeline Dawkins. Nice to meet you." Mr. Howard extended his arm and Madeline passed into the front office.

"How big a space are you looking for?" the landlord asked.

"Uh...oh, about...500 square feet," she hedged.

"This is 520. It's got this reception area, the inner office, a kitchen area and a bathroom." Madeline nodded appreciatively as she gave herself the tour. The inner office she already knew about; the small kitchen area and the bathroom were a bonus. But what she cared about most were the desks and file cabinets.

"What line of work are you in?" Madeline spun around, wishing she wasn't dressed like an office staffer.

"Event planning," she said as she reached into her bag, pretending to look for a business card that didn't exist. "I think I just gave my last card away." Max didn't seem too concerned. "What are you asking?"

"It's $2.80 a foot. That comes to $1,456 a month." Madeline arched her brows reflexively.

"Hmm…seems a little steep," she said as she made a closer inspection of the premises.

"It's downtown Santa Barbara with a State Street address. Ample public parking in the back. The unit comes with one parking space. Trash and common area cleaning are included. Renter pays utilities," Max said, arms folded across his chest, his manner pleasant but aloof, as if he could show his rental property in his sleep.

"I take it you're the owner," Madeline said. Max nodded.

"Bought it in '74. I won't tell you what I paid for it." Madeline smiled.

"Have you shown it to anyone else?"

"Just hung the sign on my way up." Madeline went through the pretense of examining the space more thoroughly.

"How long a lease are you offering?" she asked.

"Two year minimum, with three two-year options." Madeline mulled this over. Her acquired propensity toward extravagance was starting to alarm her. She used to be so careful with money before she met Steven. And all she really wanted was a chance to go through every file in Burt's drawers.

"Would you be willing to come down to an even $1,400 a month if I paid a year in advance?" Max's expression barely changed as he considered the offer. But Madeline had seen the brief flicker in his eyes.

"I'm going to need references," he said.

"No problem." Madeline reached over the desk she had sat at on her first meeting with Burt and used one of his pens to write down the name and number of her bank manager.

"Charlene will be able to verify my liquid assets on deposit. Now about this furniture…"

"The kid who just left is coming back to get it."

"Oh…too bad," Madeline said, her face clouding over. "So that young man was the former tenant?"

"No. His father was. Passed away unexpectedly."

"Oh. I'm so sorry to hear that," Madeline said, adjusting her tone.

"I'd known Burt Latham for twenty years, before he started renting from me," Max said, his eyes focused on the window. "The kid hadn't seen his old man in a couple of years." Max let out a soft snort. "Anyway, he's agreed to get all this stuff out of here by Friday."

"So, the son doesn't really have any use for the furnishings?" Max shook his head.

"No. He lives up in Seattle. He's going to try to sell this stuff at a garage sale he's having this weekend. I don't envy him having to take care of matters like this. It's extra difficult because of the rift between them…"

"What if I took the furniture off his hands, save him the trouble of hauling it away? I'll pay him whatever's fair. Think he'd be okay with that? It would suit me fine for now. I'm so busy with work right at the moment, I don't have time to redecorate, and all my stuff is too large for this space." Madeline gave Max a moment to digest the offer.

"I think he'd be relieved. I'll give him a call."

"Great. How soon can I sign the lease?" Madeline asked, checkbook in hand. Max smiled slyly as he sized her up.

"What's the name of your company?" he asked, settling into a semi-relaxed stance, arms crossed, feet apart, head slightly cocked. Madeline didn't miss a beat.

"Current Affairs, Event Planning," she said matter-of-factly. Max nodded his approval.

"Like the name. Can't say I've heard of it, though. How long have you been in business?"

"Oh, I've been doing this for years," Madeline said with a weary wave of her hand. "I've done everything from intimate dinners to parties of 800 guests." Because she was telling the truth about that, she didn't seem to set off Max's BS detector. "So, if it's available now, I'd like to take it over right away," she said, all business.

"The rent was paid through tomorrow, but I guess that doesn't matter at this point."

"Great," Madeline said as she took another look around. "I can get new business cards ordered and have the computer and phone systems set up without missing a beat. I'm ready to make it official, if you are."

FIFTY-FOUR

Max Howard ran his small real estate empire from a building two blocks further down State Street. Madeline wrote him a check for $16,800 and Max filled out the lease. Madeline managed to drop enough big names to cool her new landlord's desire for other references. Charlene had verified that Ms. Dawkins had "deposits in the mid-six figures," which seemed to allay Max's fear that she might be a deadbeat.

After signing the rental agreement, Max gave Madeline a set of keys, one to open the gate leading to the stairwell that was locked after 6 p.m., and one for the office itself. Burt's son was relieved that he didn't have to deal with clearing out his dad's furniture, so Madeline was welcome to take possession immediately, which she did as soon as she left Max's office.

Her mind was seething with all sorts of mixed emotions as she walked down the hallway to her new office. *Oh, brother—what have I done this time?* she asked herself as she placed the key in the lock, triggering a new concern. It was 5:00 and probably too late to get a locksmith to come change the locks. That would be top on her agenda tomorrow.

As soon as she entered the office, locking the door behind her, the alarm she'd set as a reminder to call Mike went off, startling her. *Just what I don't want to deal with right now,* she thought, as she canceled the alarm and began her search for the evidence Burt had hidden "somewhere safe."

She got her first hint of the obstacles she faced when every drawer in the first file cabinet refused to open. They were all secured by a single lock at the top. She tried the other cabinet in the far corner of the inner office. Same problem.

She cursed herself for being so stupid as she tried the desk drawers. She stood back, exasperated by this oversight. Not ready to give up yet, she went back to the front office and tried the center drawer. It opened, exposing pens, paper clips, rubber bands and the like. She felt all around, underneath the top and under the bottom of the drawer. No keys.

She tried the side drawers. None were locked, but none contained a secret cache of keys. There were a few files and a couple of manila envelopes, which made her heart skip a beat. But none contained anything pertinent to her case. She got down on the floor and peered at the underside of the desk. Nothing.

After calling herself many well deserved names, she grabbed her phone and did an online search for locksmiths. She found a company that advertised emergency night and weekend service. She placed the call and got a dispatcher. Madeline explained her situation; a locksmith would be at her place of business within 30 minutes. She was told he would need to see her lease agreement before he could change the locks. Fortunately, Madeline just happened to have one.

While waiting for the guy to show up, the only productive thing she could do was call Mike. As she listened to the ringing on the other end, she had to wonder if talking to him would be more counter-productive than productive.

"Hey! I was wondering when I was going to hear from you," Mike said excitedly. "Are you on your way to the airport?" For one confused moment, Madeline didn't know what he was talking about. She'd been up too long and traveled too far, and now time had completely warped for her.

"You're coming home tonight, today—whatever it is where you are. It's Thursday morning where you are, right…?" Madeline tried to work the time back six hours and add a day, using her cheater's method of time conversion. But something didn't add up right. It took her a few seconds to figure out Mike had the days mixed up. She decided it was easier to just give up the charade.

"Actually…I'm not in Guam anymore," she confessed.

"Did you get an earlier flight out? That's great news. What time do you land?"

"I'm already here."

"Oh…wow…okay, um, it's going to take me at least an hour to get there at this time of day. I wish I'd known…"

"Mike, I'm already in Santa Barbara."

"What? Did I screw up?" he asked, his voice teetering on frantic.

"No. I left Guam two days early."

"What?"

"It wasn't safe for me to stay there any longer. My room at the Westin was bugged, and so was my computer."

"*Bugged?* How did you find out?" Madeline sighed.

"It's a long story," she said dismissively.

"So, what…you found out you were being spied on, so you ran to the airport and jumped on the first flight out?" Madeline hated to admit her rash behavior.

"No, yeah…sort of…"

"Why the hell didn't you come here?" Mike asked, his indignation flaring. Madeline regretted making the call. "When did you get there? Where are you staying? Jesus Christ, Maddie—if you're afraid of Steven's militia, you shouldn't be up there by yourself." Madeline tried to get a word in edgewise, but it was no use.

"What makes you think you're any safer up there in Steven's territory? You could've walked right back into a hornet's nest."

"Mike, Mike—don't get yourself all worked up. I'm fine. The whole point of leaving Guam two days early was to give Steven the shake."

"You left two days early? Isn't that going to violate your divorce agreement?" That was a question Madeline didn't want to spend much time thinking about.

"Part of the reason I returned early was to do some sleuthing on my own, see if I can find out where Burt hid the signed statements from the swindled borrowers." Mike let out a heavy sigh that conveyed exactly how asinine he thought her idea was.

"I'm coming up there," he said, the shift in background sounds giving weight to his threat.

"No you're not, Mike. I don't want you up here right now. I've got too much to deal with and I don't want to worry about you getting hurt too."

"What? You're up there by yourself playing cat and mouse with men you suspect of killing your P.I., and you're worried about *me?* That's ridiculous. Where are you staying?"

"I'm not going to tell you, Mike. I'm safe and I'm not worried. I'm flying under their radar right now. I faked a call to you from the room at the Westin suggesting I was thinking of staying with you for a few days when I got back. I rigged it so whoever has been keeping tabs on me will think I'm still safely under observation. Look, I know you're worried, but I'm not. Oh, hang on a second… Mike, I've got to call you back…I've got someone here helping me with something. I'll call you later."

"Madeline—" She ended the call, the mental image of Mike hurling the phone across the room making her wince.

"Hey, thanks for coming," she said to the locksmith. "I just moved in and I would like some locks changed and maybe a deadbolt added…"

FIFTY-FIVE

Madeline reached over the stack of files for her iPhone. 8:22. She groaned as she tried to straighten out her legs. She had been sitting on the floor for over two hours, combing through every file in Burt's drawers. She was so exhausted from the search, she could hardly see straight. She was aching from head to toe and her stomach had been complaining loudly for the last hour.

She got up onto her knees and scooted past the wreckage of strewn files, then used the side of the desk to bring herself to her feet. *I feel like a ninety-year-old woman,* she thought as she stretched her back and ambled off to her new restroom.

When she finally worked up enough strength to get off the toilet, she surveyed the damage. Looking at the mess she'd made got her to thinking about her supposition. She believed Burt was killed because of his scrutiny of certain trust deeds. If that was the case, then whoever had been tipped off would want to make sure Burt didn't have any evidence that could be found after his death.

This is what Madeline found troubling. Unless Burt had the statements from the first two or three borrowers on him at the time he was murdered, then surely someone would search his office—and his home—in order to find them. Unless they didn't know about those statements—unless the tip-off had come from Burt's fifth and final contact.

Madeline eased into Burt's chair and swiveled around to stare at the chaos on the floor. *Which was it—Steven's hit men didn't know about the statements, or did they find the evidence on him?* Madeline pinched the bridge of her nose as she willed her mind into focus.

"Okay...I don't think Burt would be carrying those statements around with him. He told me that they were in a safe place. So...either the thugs didn't know that or they broke in here and found what they were looking for already..."

This last thought further disturbed her. There had been no sign at all of any break in, but then again, the guys in Steven's employ were highly trained in the security field. Most were ex-military; she knew that much from Steven. He was quite proud of his security team. She had always assumed it was an ego thing. Boy, had she been naïve.

Now the question was where had these pros looked. "Alright…either they searched this place and found what they wanted, or they came up empty-handed like I just did and they checked his home…"

Madeline stood up and began to pace. *Where did Burt live?* She thought back through all their conversations, but she couldn't remember him ever mentioning that.

"Think, think, think…" she admonished herself. She automatically reached for her bag, wanting to spark her thought process with the books on her Kindle, but she didn't have her regular tote with her. She sat down and rapped on the side of her head, hoping to shake some memory loose.

"I can do a property search to see if his name comes up," she muttered to herself. Again, she was frustrated at not having the proper tools with her. She'd left her computer at the motel, not knowing the dramatic twist her plans were going to take.

"Garage sales!" she cried out, retrieving one clue from the conversation with her new landlord. She did a search on her phone for Craigslist, seizing on a small hope that Burt's son would have his garage sale listed already.

There were several listings for upcoming garage sales in Santa Barbara, but unfortunately none had "Burt Latham's son" in the title. Still, she had addresses she could use to trace the owners' names. But that would only pay off if Burt happened to own his own home.

Feeling more defeated than victorious after a very long, action-packed day, Madeline gathered up the strewn files and placed them haphazardly back in file drawers. She then went back to the bathroom to wash her hands, giving herself a scare as she caught a glimpse of the strange reflection in the mirror. A soft yelp escaped her before she remembered she had been parading around incognito. She laughed feebly, shaking her head at all the elaborate ruses she had put in place, the disguise being the least of them.

I must be losing my mind, she thought wearily as she gathered her things and turned off the lights. The hall lights had already shut off. She used her phone flashlight while she locked the door and then followed its beam down the eerily dark hallway.

As she approached the steps, light emanating from surrounding businesses and street lamps gave off enough glow so she could make it down the steps without falling. She fumbled with the keys and managed to get the gate locked. Three steps later, she was back on State Street.

For one unsettling moment, she had forgotten where she parked. She stood on the corner of State and Figueroa, walking her mind back several hours to where her quest began—at the courthouse. With relief, she recalled pulling into the parking garage on Anacapa between Victoria and Anapamu, which was less than three blocks away.

"Thank God," she said out loud as she crossed with the light and turned up State to walk along more brightly lit surroundings. She was dead tired, starving and vaguely disappointed with herself and life in general. When her cell phone heralded an incoming text message, she jumped. It was Mike.

Where are you staying? he asked. *What does that matter to you?* Madeline thought.

In a motel, she replied.

I'm at the Island View. I've got two queen beds and an ocean view.

You're in SB??Why?? *I told you not to come,* she typed under a street lamp. She was in no mood for surprises. All she wanted to do was find her rental car and sneak off to her motel for a hot shower and some sleep. But food would be good too…

The Marimba ringtone sounded, ending her solitary thoughts.

"I told you I didn't want you to come up here," Madeline said before Mike had a chance to speak.

"Yeah, I know. And you rudely hung up on me too, as I recall," Mike replied, nonplussed by her irritable mood.

"And I told you why I didn't want you up here…"

"Yes, and your reasoning was absurd. You somehow think you're more equipped to deal with Steven and his goons by yourself, even after all the hell he's put you through. I'm *not* going to stand by and watch you go it alone, that's all there is to it. So, get used to it and get your butt over here."

During Mike's harangue, Madeline had sputtered entreaties that had been completely ignored. In the end, she didn't have it in her to duke it out with her most trustworthy ally.

"Okay, you're here—nothing I can do about that now. But I'm in no mood to socialize. All I want is a shower and sleep—and food, if I can find something along the way…"

"Where are you right now?"

"Right now I'm in a parking garage downtown, looking for my rental car. Unfortunately, I don't know which one is mine. They all look alike."

"Use your clicker," Mike said.

"Oh, good thinking…"

"See, you do need me."

"You're right—I need you, I adore you, and I can't live without you. I'll call you tomorrow."

"Maddie, wait! Don't you dare hang up on me again." Madeline couldn't help but laugh. She was punchy from fatigue and would've laughed at almost anything. "How far are you from your motel?"

"I don't know…five minutes."

"And how far are you from the Island View?" Madeline held the car door open with her shoulder as she threw her handbag in. She stopped and sighed. There was nothing even remotely appealing about her cheap motel room. She knew if left to her own devices, she'd probably have to pass on a meal due to lack of strength.

"Does your room have a tub?" she asked weakly.

"Big tub, water jets and everything!"

"Oh, God," Madeline moaned, her resolve crumbling. "I need food."

"I'll get you anything your heart desires," Mike promised.

"You really are too good for me," Madeline said.

"Don't I know it. Now get over here before I withdraw the offer."

FIFTY-SIX

"Sorry, you must have the wrong room—I didn't order a hooker."

"Ha, ha. Let me in. It's cold out here," Madeline said, pushing her way past a gloating Mike. "Stop laughing," she said, tossing her bag on one of the queen beds.

"Is that supposed to be a disguise?" Mike chided her. Madeline gave him one of her looks that ordinarily would've shut him up. "Bleached-blond suits you. I think you should dye your hair that color."

"I think you better get this out of your system in two seconds, or I'm out of here," Madeline said, hands on hips. Mike got in one more quick smirk, then adopted a more somber attitude. Madeline gave him a stony look of warning and pulled her wig off. She tossed it beside her cheap handbag and started aggressively massaging her scalp.

"I need to wash my hair," she said, glancing around Mike's mini-suite. She wasn't going to admit it, but his plush room sure beat the heck out of her lowly motel room.

"Right this way—everything Madame requires is at your disposal," Mike said in a hammy English accent. Madeline started to follow him, but hunger won out over the need to scrub the dinginess of travel off her body. She didn't even want to calculate how long it had been since her last shower.

"Do you have anything to eat?" she asked, grabbing the back of a chair to steady herself. The sight of Madeline so wrung out softened Mike.

"You name it, I'll get it."

"I need something right now," she said gravitating toward the minibar.

"Here—we've got almonds, chips, cookies." Madeline grabbed all three, popping open the can of almonds as she went into the bathroom.

"Do you want some real food?" Mike asked through the closed door.

"Yes!" Madeline said over the sound of the bathwater running.

"What?" Mike called back.

"Mexican."

"Okay… Anything in particular? From anyplace in particular?" Madeline opened the door enough to poke her head through.

"I would kill for La Super-Rica, but that would probably be too much trouble," she said through a mouthful of chips.

"It's no problem, if that's what you want."

"No, wait—I want a chicken enchilada verde and a chili relleno from Rose Café. And some nachos. You can call the order in. The one on the Mesa is closest," she said as Mike did a search on his cell phone.

"Okay, I got it. Anything else?"

"A Negra Modelo," Madeline said, blowing him a kiss as he placed the order.

"How are you feeling?" Mike asked as he gingerly lifted a huge chicken flauta, trying to eat it before it fell apart.

"Much better," Madeline said with a smile. She took a swig of her beer and surveyed the damage. She scraped the last bit of melted cheese from the plastic plate. "You were a saint to do this for me."

"De nada," Mike replied. "Want any of this?" he asked, offering her some of his rice and beans. Madeline waved it away, taking her beer and her protruding stomach over to the sofa.

"Oh, God!" she said, referring to nothing in particular, and everything in general.

"Are you glad now that I came to your rescue?" Mike asked, joining her on the sofa with his horchata. Madeline blanched at the thought of shivering and starving in the dark, cold motel room. By way of an answer, she leaned against him, surrendering to his ministrations.

Mike smiled and kissed the top of her head. A minute later, he removed the listing beer bottle from her hand. A minute after that, her head drooped. He gently eased her against the cushion and got up to turn down her bed. He put a bottle of water on her side table, turned out the lamp and the overhead light, then lifted her off the sofa and carried her to bed.

She woke briefly, startled by the human contact and the strange surroundings, but Mike's presence reassured her. She turned on her side and was gone.

"Sweet dreams," Mike whispered, touching his fingers to his lips and placing them lightly on her cheek. He sat on the sofa, watching her sleep for about an hour, then got himself ready for bed.

Shortly after 2 a.m., Mike awoke to a terror-filled scream. He switched on the light and found Madeline thrashing against her covers.

"Maddie, Maddie—it's okay! I'm here. You're safe," he said, pulling her close and rocking her while she sobbed. "Honey, come on—I'm right here with you. There's nothing to be afraid of anymore." After a couple of minutes, Madeline became silent.

"Are you okay?" Mike asked. She nodded and blotted her eyes with the sheet. Mike got up and fetched a box of tissues. "What was it?" he asked as he sat back down beside her. Madeline shook her head. She was still trembling.

"I don't know," she whispered hoarsely. "I just remember dreaming about something…and then," she shook her head again, "…someone leapt out at me."

A knock sounded at the door, causing them both to jump. Madeline clutched onto Mike's arm and wouldn't let go.

"It's probably security," Mike said, easing away from her as they heard another knock.

"Hotel security," the man said, as Mike pulled on his pants. He peeked through the peephole before opening the door.

"We got a call about loud screaming coming from this room," the security guard said, shining his light around Mike to where Madeline was hiding behind the sheet. "Are you alright, ma'am?"

"She was having a nightmare," Mike said.

"I need to hear it from her," the guard said, stepping past Mike to stand in the middle of the room.

"I'm sorry—I had a terrible dream. I didn't even realize I was screaming until he woke me up," Madeline said. She tried to smile, though she figured her tear-streaked face and red eyes were a problem for the security guard.

"I'm going to have you step out into the hallway for a moment, sir," he said. Mike's mouth opened but Madeline flashed him a look. He left the room while the security guard gave Madeline a chance to ask for help.

"I feel terrible about this," she said. "I hope I didn't wake up the whole hotel. I've been traveling for a while, and I think I'm just disoriented." This seemed to satisfy the guard's due-diligence.

"I hope you're going to be able to go back to sleep," Mike said after the guard left.

"Would you mind if I slept with you?" Madeline asked. Mike smiled and pulled back his covers, letting her get in before he followed suit.

He held her in his arms until her breathing told him she was back in dreamland. He only hoped it was a nicer place than last time. He also hoped he'd find a way to make Steven Ridley pay for what he had done to her. He acknowledged he was no saint while they were together, but he had never treated Madeline the way Steven had. There had to be a reckoning for the hell Steven had put her through. And Mike pledged to see to it personally.

FIFTY-SEVEN

"I'm going back to the courthouse. Hopefully, I'll have better luck with the line today. But first, I'm going to City Hall to have the water switched over to my name, before it's turned off." Madeline said. The power could be switched to her name with a call to Edison, but water service had to be handled over the counter.

On Mike's insistence, she had checked out of her motel. Because she felt indebted to him, she broke down and showed him her latest acquisition. She found it both irritating and amusing that Mike had made himself at home at the desk in the front office. On balance, she supposed there was nothing really wrong with a man's presence in the office—unless, of course, Steven's posse showed up for a second look at Burt's files. Mike was big, but he wasn't armed—at least not to her knowledge.

She could "suppose" herself crazy if she let all the "maybes" and "what ifs" run wild in her head. She had to confine her thoughts to facts and the most likely scenarios until they were disproven, then she'd have to consider every possibility, no matter how farfetched. For now, all she really knew for certain was that Burt was dead and he had taken statements from at least two bamboozled borrowers. The two unknowns attached to those facts were where Burt had hidden the statements, and if Steven's men had found them already.

Distilling the situation to its essence, Madeline recognized the importance of following Burt's tracks from the beginning; it would be the only way to accurately determine who had been swindled. From there, she could take her findings straight to the D.A. The disadvantage to this plan of action was the ticking clock. The time she had stolen was quickly running out, which was why the allure of finding the signed statements from the defrauded borrowers was so strong.

Madeline worked both sides of this debate in her head as she organized herself for the day ahead of her. At least she had enough tasks lined up to keep Mike occupied while she took care of the most pressing matters.

"So, you've got my list," Madeline said as she came out of the back office to the front desk, where Mike was at work on her computer.

"Yes, Ms. Dawkins—got it right here."

"We need to have the electricity put in my name, before we do anything."

"Already done," Mike said, enjoying the look of surprise on Madeline's face. "I manage an apartment complex, remember?"

"Right. Good. And you understand how the real estate data search works? You enter Burt Latham, county, state, etc. then hit 'search' to see if his name pops up on title."

"Maddie, you may still think of me as a stoned-out slacker, but ol' Mike's actually fairly up to speed with technology," he said, eyeing her with strained patience.

"Okay, fine. Then just go through the list and I'll check back with you while I'm out," Madeline said, checking her tote to make sure she had all her essentials.

"I'd appreciate that," Mike said, his eyes not leaving the screen as his fingers tapped the keyboard. "Oh, and don't forget to take this," he said, handing her Burt's last water bill.

"Thanks," Madeline said, shoving it in her tote. "What?"

"Nothing."

"Do I look stupid?" Mike cracked a smile. Madeline stepped back to glance at herself in the bathroom mirror. "What is it?" she demanded.

"Nothing. You look fine." This time he couldn't suppress a laugh. Madeline glared at him. "I guess the blond wig suits you better."

"I'm not going to a beauty contest. The whole point of wearing a wig is so no one will recognize me." Mike wagged his head.

"Then you're in great shape. Your own father wouldn't know you." Madeline eyed him with a sulky expression. "Go on—no one's going to ever guess it's you." Mike went back to his task, maddening smile on his lips.

Madeline passed down the hallway, head down, feeling conspicuous now. Once she hit the sidewalk, she slipped on her sunglasses, held her head high and donned an aloof expression, in her mind a good match for her guise.

Mike's crack about her father had hit a sore spot. The fact that she hadn't called him in over a week weighed heavily on her mind. *Tonight*, she told herself, as she crossed De La Guerra Street and turned toward City Hall.

The line at the Water Department was short, but service was exasperatingly slow. With everything computerized these days, Madeline couldn't understand why the simple procedure of transferring the utility to her name had to be so unduly laborious.

Twenty-five minutes later, she was headed up Anacapa Street. She paused at the news racks in front of the post office and grabbed the latest edition of the Montecito Gazette. It would give her a chance to catch up on the latest goings-on while she wasted more time in another line. Not that any of it mattered personally to her anymore. She would be persona non grata in this town for a while, which didn't really bode well for her new business venture.

When she entered the Hall of Records, the office was even more crowded than the day before. Fortunately, the window she needed only had three people in line. She took the periodical out of her Prada tote—the one concession she had made to style, simply because she found it difficult to function without it. Anyone noticing the logo would assume from the rest of her garb that it had to be a knockoff. She set the tote at her feet and began to skim through the paper.

Before she could settle in, the line advanced. This hopeful sign made her smile, though she pitied anyone who fell in line behind her. Assuming she'd be successful in her quest eventually, she went back to browsing through the paper.

When she came to the "Scene Around Town" section, her heart stopped. There, front and center, was of a photo of Steven seated next to his partner, John, and his wife, Amanda—one of *her* best friends—and the future Mrs. Ridley, Elizabeth Collins-Wainwright, on the far right. If the sight wasn't enough to turn her stomach, the realization that E C-W was wearing *her* emerald and diamond necklace and matching earrings certainly was.

Suddenly, the room felt like it was spinning. Madeline fought back the powerful urge to vomit. She was sweating and her hands were shaking as she left the line and rushed out into the fresh air. She took several big breaths to get herself under control, then slumped against the stone ledge.

"That lousy son-of-a-bitch," she spat, punishing herself with another look at the photo for confirmation. It was her necklace, all right. And of course, it had to be, as hers had gone missing from the safe deposit box. She had suspected this, but it was quite another thing to see Steven's callous act broadcasted all over town. Her humiliation jumped up another notch when she discovered tears were running down her face. She wiped at them angrily and stormed over to the closest trash can to dispose of the weekly.

"I *hate* him, I *hate* him!" she hissed as she wandered blindly around the courthouse grounds. She had to get her fury under control if she wanted to go back inside. And she had to go back in—it was the only way she could retaliate against the heartless demon she had married.

Or was it? Madeline stopped pacing, trying to capture the thought fluttering around her head. *Sla… Slo… Slovich…no, Slovitch. That's it!* A hopeful smile lit up her features. *Detective Slovitch.* He was the one Burt had made an appointment with to discuss the incident at The Edgecliff.

Before she had made a conscious decision to abandon her records search, Madeline's feet were carrying her across the courthouse lawn in the direction of the SBPD. She crossed in the middle of the street and headed down Santa Barbara to Figueroa. In less than two minutes, she was in front of the police station.

She paused for a moment to compose herself. She'd had imaginary conversations with Detective Slovitch several times, one of the many drawbacks of having been stranded out in the middle of the Pacific for almost a week. But now that she was in a position to actually speak to him, she was at a loss at what to say.

She stepped back a few paces to be out of sight of the station while she ordered her thoughts. She panicked for a second, thinking she didn't have the photo with her. But she did, somewhere in the file cabinet of a handbag she lugged around. She hoisted the tote onto her knee and found what she was looking for.

As she thought about the contents of the envelope, she had to wonder if it was really powerful evidence of wrongdoing. Why would the detective be compelled to believe that she hadn't been caught cheating on her spouse and was trying to spin the situation? Madeline's hopes wavered.

Burt Latham had advised her to speak to Detective Slovitch. He knew the man and must've believed she'd get a fair shot with him. So, the believability aspect was up to her.

She took a deep breath and rehearsed her version of the events beginning from that inauspicious evening. As she went over her claims a second time, she caught sight of her reflection in an office window. She pulled the brunette wig off with a quick jerk and tried to stuff it in her bag. No luck; the tote was full to capacity. She tried to rearrange the contents in hopes of squeezing it in.

Screw it, she thought, shoving the wig in a hedge for safekeeping. She pulled out her compact and executed a little damage repair. She then ran a brush through her hair, straightened her back, cleared her throat and headed toward the public entrance.

Once inside, her courage faltered. She hung close to the doorway while she worked up her nerve. She caught the eye of the clerk at the window and was forced to step forward or back out.

"How can I help you?" the woman asked, giving Madeline a sliver of her divided attention.

"I'm here to see Detective Slovitch," Madeline said, resting her hand uncomfortably on the ledge between them, feigning assurance she didn't feel.

"Detective Slovitch is out of the office," the woman told her.

"Oh. When will he be back?" The woman checked the calendar on one of the side walls.

"A week from next Monday." Madeline's heart sank. It must've shown on her face, for now the woman had taken more than a cursory interest in her.

"Is there someone else who can help you?" she asked. Madeline stared at her. She wasn't prepared for this outcome. "What is this regarding?" the woman asked. Madeline had her full attention now and was reluctant to squander it. But still it was hard to get the words out.

"It's…uh…a personal matter—I mean, a personal matter for me, not between Detective Slovitch and me." The woman contemplated Madeline as sweat beaded up on her brow. There was something in her frank stare that urged Madeline toward fuller disclosure.

"My private investigator had set up a meeting with him, but I was called out of town unexpectedly." By now, Madeline's hand was shaking so noticeably, she removed it from the window ledge.

"Would you like to speak to Detective Slovitch's partner?" the woman asked, her tone low and sympathetic now. Madeline nodded her head. The woman gave her a small smile of encouragement and left the window, only to return a second later.

"What's the name of your P.I., hon?"

"Burt Latham." The name hung in the air between them. The woman's chin lifted slightly as the name registered.

"And your name?"

"Madeline Ridley—Madeline Dawkins, I mean. I've gone back to my maiden name," she explained. In a split-second, the woman had put the story together: private eye and name change meant imminent divorce. Madeline couldn't tell if that made her seem more sympathetic or less.

"Just a minute," the woman said.

Madeline stood at the counter, turning her attention away from the empty window as she caught sight of other personnel looking her way. Within a couple of minutes, the woman returned to the reception office.

"Detective Mitchell will be right out," she said. Madeline waited a couple more minutes before the detective rounded the corner, his left hand automatically wiping at the corners of his mouth as he approached.

"Ms. Dawkins?" he asked, extending his right hand. Madeline accepted his handshake and fell in step behind him as he led her back to the office he shared with Detective Slovitch.

"I understand Burt Latham had arranged a meeting with my partner on your behalf," Detective Mitchell said as he indicated for her to take a seat.

"Yes, that's correct," Madeline replied. "Actually, Burt was working for me at the time of his death," she admitted. She belatedly realized the police might have an interest in *her* because of her association with the dead P.I.

"I see..." the detective said. Madeline cleared her throat nervously.

"I hired him to help me find out who set me up." She reached into her bag and retrieved the now tattered manila envelope. She held onto it, hesitant to show another complete stranger the disgraceful picture. She worked up her courage and handed the envelope over. She watched anxiously as the detective pulled the photo out and turned it right side up. As soon as the image's content registered on his face, she hastily began to explain the circumstances behind it.

"So, you believe you were drugged, abducted and raped while someone took photographs...?" Det. Mitchell recapped.

"Actually, it was a video. I just recently found that out...when it showed up on the Internet." Madeline shifted apprehensively, wishing she could snatch the pornographic visual from the detective's hands. He set it on his desk and reached down to pull a new file folder from his drawer.

Madeline tensed, realizing this had now become an official case, which meant it was no longer in her control. When she hired Burt, she alone determined when and if this would become a police matter. She would have no say in how the authorities chose to pursue the incident, if they viewed it as worthy of pursuing.

But his action triggered another thought, one that made her perspire all over. When she first met with Burt, he also started a file on her. She had been through every folder in the office and not come across her own. Either Burt had taken it from the office for some reason, or Steven's men had.

"Okay, let's start with the date and time..."

Madeline took Det. Mitchell through the events leading up to waking in the room at The Edgecliff. He listened attentively, occasionally jotting notes on a sheet in her file. After she had told him everything that had transpired, he leaned back in his chair and regarded her.

"Had you consumed a lot of alcohol?"

"Not that I'm aware of."

"And how did you come into possession of the photograph?"

"They—seven altogether—were delivered to my husband's office. He brought them home and accused me of adultery and demanded a divorce."

Madeline watched the detective's face carefully as she considered telling him what Steven's motive had been. As far as anyone else was concerned, it would be supposition on her part, not hardcore facts. But she had to have a reason for implicating Steven in her rape, so she steadied herself and told the detective about the infidelity clause in the prenuptial agreement.

Det. Mitchell set his pen down and crossed his arms. His lips twisted as he let out a cynical huff.

"You realize you don't have any evidence to back up your assertion that your husband arranged for your rape so he could photograph it and blackmail you into a divorce without giving you a dime...?" Madeline could feel her face turn red.

"Look," Det. Mitchell continued, "I'm not saying I don't believe you, but you can't go after someone on rape charges without some corroborating evidence—an eye-witness, semen stains, fingerprints...something..." Hearing what she had suspected all along came as one blow too many to her fragile state of mind.

As she sat there, eyes trained on the detective, something in her snapped. The whole world could consider her crazy, but that didn't matter to her anymore. Defiance started building inside her. She didn't even bother to hide her hostility.

"Is this what you tell all the women who come to you claiming to have been raped, who've made the huge mistake of not collecting evidence?"

Det. Mitchell coughed and scooted his chair away from the desk. Madeline knew she hadn't done herself any favors, but she couldn't bring herself to apologize. What she should've asked was if he could get the footage from The Edgecliff security cameras. But something told her this man had already dismissed her as a crank.

She had an overwhelming desire to flee, but she knew if she left without somehow convincing Detective Mitchell she had been viciously wronged, she would never have another chance to make Steven answer for what he did to her. She tried to speak, but she was still so angry, all she could manage was a raspy croak.

"Would you like some water?" Mitchell asked. Madeline nodded. "I'll be right back," he said, placing a box of tissues in front of her. Since she wasn't crying, the gesture struck her as obligatory and insulting.

Once he was out of the room, Madeline began berating herself. She should've never come here. She should've never spoken to anyone other than Det. Slovitch. She should've stayed in line at the courthouse and gotten copies of all the outstanding trust deeds held by RAM, L.P.

She shook her head in dismay. Burt would've been disappointed in her, surely. She wheezed weakly at this strange thought. Burt had a lot more important grievances to hold against her, namely getting him killed.

Burt, what do I do now?

She stared at the walls in Det. Mitchell's half of the office while she tried to assess what her next move should be. She didn't see any way to salvage this line of attack. She was anxious to get out of there and back to the last hope of ever bringing Steven to justice. She reached over the desk and retrieved the incriminating photo. No reason for it to sit in a police file if no one was going to take her claims seriously.

She looked at her Guess watch, a reminder that she was still halfway disguised. It seemed like it was taking an awfully long time to get a glass of water. *The water cooler must be on the other side of the building,* she mused. *Maybe I should just leave…*

All thoughts ceased when her eyes landed on a photo on Det. Mitchell's credenza. Her heart stopped as she gazed at a group photo including the detective in military garb, surrounded by men similarly attired, all smiling. There was no doubt in her mind that Det. Mitchell was well acquainted with at least two of Steven's security team, his head man among them.

A palpable fear froze Madeline to her seat. She had tripped one of Steven's traps, and now she was in deep, deep trouble. Not only had she tipped her weak hand—connecting Steven to her rape—but she had stupidly given the enemy a head's up that she was back on the mainland well before schedule.

"Here you go," Det. Mitchell said, handing her a paper cup full of water. Madeline drank it down, hoping it would give her time to think. She sighed and set the cup on the desk and smiled sheepishly at the detective.

"I'm sorry. I never meant to come in here and lose it. I never really meant to come here at all. But after Burt's death, I've felt like it was up to me to solve this mystery. I completely understand where you're coming from. You need compelling evidence, and that's something we—I—don't have." She stood up. "Thanks for hearing me out, at least," she said, offering her hand. Det. Mitchell shook it, as both covertly tried to read the other's thoughts.

"I'm sorry I couldn't be of more help," Mitchell said, hands in his pockets as Madeline hiked her bag onto her shoulder and put on her sunglasses. "If you come across something more substantial, come back and we'll see what we can do." Madeline nodded and smiled politely, then left Det. Mitchell standing at his doorway.

FIFTY-EIGHT

Once Madeline was safely out of the building, she called Mike.

"Mad Dog Detective Agency. What's your problem?" he clowned. The humor was completely wasted on Madeline.

"I've just made a horrible mistake," she said.

"What?" Mike asked, his voice now as apprehensive as hers.

"I need you to go online and do a search. We're looking for anything that brings up the names Stewart Mitchell, Lionel Usherwood, Lance Rombach, Terry…Terry…uh…Linbald. And Rick Yeoman. You got that?" Mike read the names back to her.

"What am I looking for exactly?"

"Anything that connects Mitchell with the others. He's a detective with the SBPD. He's the one I just spilled the beans to before I noticed a photo of him with Steven's security crew."

"Oh, no…"

"I know. I couldn't have screwed things up better," she said, retrieving her tousled wig from the hedge. She shook it against her leg to clean it off and tried unsuccessfully to put it back on her head with one hand. "Hang on a sec," she said, setting her phone and tote down on a thigh-high wall bordering an office building. She got the wig on, but knocked her tote over in the process.

"Damn," she swore into the phone.

"Are you alright?" Mike asked anxiously.

"Yeah, I'm fine." Madeline took a deep breath, hand to her forehead of foreign fringe, trying to steady herself.

"I have some good news…" Mike said.

"Tell me," Madeline said as she tried in vain to reach her fallen handbag.

"I located Burt's son."

"How did you do that?"

"I called your landlord and told him I was your assistant, and said we needed to get hold of the former tenant's son—said we'd come across something that might be of interest to him. The kid was a little leery at first, but once I explained your situation, he was very helpful. He thinks his dad only kept personal records at home, but he said I could come over and have a look."

"That's great," Madeline said. It would be a huge relief to find the borrower statements and her missing file among his artifacts. Finally, something seemed to be going in her favor, though it might only lead to another dead end. "I'll go with you. At this stage, I'd much rather do this the easy way rather than the hard."

"Want me to come and get you?"

"No, I'll be there in a few minutes." She was just about to swing her legs over the wall to retrieve her bag when she spotted a black Suburban coming from the direction of Anacapa Street. Even from almost a block away, she recognized the vehicle and the driver.

"Oh crap!" she said. "Never mind about the search—I just got my answer." She averted her face, then it occurred to her she was back in disguise. All she had to do was act nonchalant and let them pass her by.

"Maddie—what's going on?" The Suburban passed and Madeline did an about-face and started walking in the opposite direction, abandoning her bag.

"Go get the car and wait by the exit!" she said. Suddenly, she heard the sound of the SUV reversing. She turned in time to see it fishtail as Lionel Usherwood accelerated out of an ungainly U-turn.

Madeline sprinted across Figueroa and onto Santa Barbara, running against the traffic of the one-way street. She looked back in time to see two passengers leap from the vehicle, which was unable to turn left.

"Maddie, what's going on?" Mike asked frantically.

"Give me ten minutes. If I'm not at the parking lot by then, go see Burt's son. It's our only hope now," Madeline said, darting out into the street between passing cars.

Rick Yeoman and Lance Rombach were already gaining on her. As soon as she leapt to the curb, she tossed her cell phone under a parked car. She ran as fast as she could in unfamiliar shoes, but it was no use. Before she could get past the vacant Hayward's building, Rick Yeoman had her by the left arm, holding her steady with a blade to her side. Lance caught up with them and held Madeline's right arm.

"Stay calm and you won't get hurt," he said under his breath as the trio passed into the deserted parking lot and took cover behind one of the small rental units. Before Madeline knew what was happening, Rick covered her face with a chloroformed cloth. She was out cold in seconds.

FIFTY-NINE

When Madeline came to, her first thought was she'd been buried alive. As she commanded her body to move, nothing responded. She slowly realized her wrists had been bound tightly behind her. Same with her ankles. She tried to open her mouth, but it was taped shut. The surface she was slumped on face-first was hard and cold. She blinked several times but she could see nothing. Wherever she was, it was as dark as a cave.

Slowly, she became aware of intense pain in her left shoulder and both knees. Whether pushed or dumped, she figured she had lain how she had fallen. With considerable effort, she managed to pitch over onto her side.

There was no way to get even remotely comfortable. The slightest movement caused her head to feel like it was going to shatter. She lay as still as possible, resting her aching body while her brain analyzed what little stimuli surrounded her.

Underneath the hush that made the place feel like a mausoleum, she picked up a soft mechanical purr, like refrigeration or air conditioning. From where she was on the floor, she did not feel any direct breeze blowing on her, but the building was very cold—cold enough to make her shiver and ache all over. It also added to her feelings of despair and desperation. It felt cold enough to cause hypothermia.

In her present state—tied up with no way to work up some body heat—she could start to feel the debilitating symptoms of hypothermia fairly rapidly. She was already shivering and stiff, and who knew how long she'd been there. Only her abductors, and they had apparently abandoned her to her fate. She could die there if she didn't get out soon.

She was on the verge of crying, but she had to use her brainpower while she still had the ability to reason. She mentally steeled herself and focused on saving her life.

With her fingertips, she examined the surface she was laying on. It was very hard, but not uniform in texture. She wiggled sideways to extend her search and discovered more crags and recesses, and then a rough, unbroken trench. Knowing her fingers' exaggerated sense of proportion, she assigned less significance to the facts they had uncovered and came up with a mental image of stone and grout. She shifted more to the left and found an intersection of grout lines to prove her assumption.

She ran her fingers over the stone surface again. She had spent a lot of time selecting various materials for interior and exterior uses when she and Steven built their house. Though that was several years ago, she had retained a familiarity with different types of stone: granite, marble, travertine, flagstone, sandstone and slate. What she was feeling now was smoother than the last three, but still pitted.

She ran her index finger around the edge of the tile again. It had a slightly irregular shape, due to the porousness of the stone. It was "softer" than most paving stones and not slick, like granite or polished marble. Tumbled marble was her best guess.

She scooted over again, picking up the grout line and following it from the corner of the tile upwards. As she suspected, the tile was large; she had to creep her bound body upwards in order to find the next corner.

Acting as a human inchworm set off painful spasms in her limbs and back. She took a few deep breaths through her nose to relax her knotted muscles enough to do more reconnaissance. This time, she laid her elbow in the groove of the grout intersection and used her forearm as a measuring stick. With her elbow fixed at the top of the tile, she squirmed until she had her forearm flush with the grout line. Using the first joint on her little finger, she rubbed around the grout joint in a circular fashion.

Finding what she had suspected made her ecstatic. What she was laying on were 13-inch square tiles. Fortunately for her, she had gotten in the habit of estimating widths and lengths with arms, hands and feet during the year and a half it had taken to build her dream home. If the tile had stopped at the first knuckle on her hand, it would've been a 12-inch tile.

This little kernel of information was helpful; 13-inch pavers hadn't been phased in until around 2000. To confirm that she hadn't missed a joint in between, she stretched her arms out as far as they would go, using her trusty finger to locate the next break.

Exhausted by her efforts, Madeline stopped to rest, the left side of her face flush with the cold flooring. As she lay there, her olfactory sense kicked in, picking up a variety of odors she hadn't noticed earlier. They were harsh smells, but also familiar. They were probably ordinary, everyday smells, but because there were no other scents to blend in with, they stood out more. She figured she was in a confined space with no windows or outside ventilation.

She concentrated on the odors while she breathed in and out. There was the distinct smell of wood—a particular type of wood... She took a deep breath, begging her brain to recall where she had smelled the odor before.

She worked herself into a sitting position and sniffed some more. From this height, she could smell something else...something musty and almost skunk-like.

Madeline sat stock-still as the realization of her most likely location hit home. Before she was frightened; now she was terrified.

Tears of anguish began to trickle down her face. But letting this happen was a big mistake. Unless she wanted to suffocate herself, she had to stop the unbidden tears from making her nose run. The gruesome thought of essentially being asphyxiated by her own snot sobered her instantly. She had to stay in control of her emotions if she wanted any chance of getting out of her own wine cellar alive.

Fear and heartache soon turned to rabid hatred as Madeline thought through the cruel way Steven had expunged her from his life. *How perfect,* she thought. *Steven's murderous lap dogs toss me in the cellar to die—no smell, no decomposition. Give me a day or two, to be on the safe side, then feed me to a wood chipper.*

Almost as soon as she had figured out where she had been stashed, she heard footfalls on the steps leading down to the cellar. She jerked herself up and wriggled in the general direction of where she had started out and slumped to the ground face-first again.

She stiffened as the key entered the lock. A second later, the room was awash in soft daylight that filtered down the steps, making the room plenty bright for Madeline's light-deprived eyes. She had only a moment to investigate her surroundings and match them to her mental image of where she had ended up.

As soon as she was able to orient herself, the overhead lights were switched on to their full wattage, temporarily blinding her. As she squinted against the glare, she heard the sound of soft leather soles coming closer.

"Hello, Madeline," Steven said casually, as he set an empty wine box on the dining table that ran through the center of the room. Madeline instinctively cowered away from him, bumping against the fully loaded wine shelving that bordered the wall. Steven bent down to get a better look at her face, pulling away in mild disgust at the sight of her.

"Haven't been taking very good care of yourself, have you?" he said, his voice light and playful. Madeline felt a sharp pain in her chest, a sign that her heart had just broken in half again. She began snuffling, unable to control her emotions any longer. At this point, she didn't even care that her death was imminent.

"Too bad you didn't stay in Guam like you were supposed to. You could've gotten some more R and R and fulfilled your half of the bargain we made. Now look at you—trussed up like an elk, close to dying on my wine cellar floor." Steven consulted his list and went about collecting wine.

"You know, Madeline, you only have yourself to blame for the way things turned out," he said as he deposited two bottles of wine in the carton. "Had you just done what you were told, you'd be safe and sound and able to enjoy the half a million I so generously gave you. That was a gift, you know. I had to go to significant trouble to come up with that kind of cash. Not that you seem to care… Looks like you wanted to have it both ways—take the money, then sic your bloodhound on me. That was a serious miscalculation on your part."

Steven looked over at Madeline. Her pathetic condition took him away from the task at hand. He went over and hauled her into an upright position with her back up against the wine rack. He may have thought he was doing her a small kindness, but it didn't feel any more comfortable to Madeline. But then again, maybe he did it for his own sense of aesthetics.

"I thought hanging out a coyote pelt would discourage you from sticking your nose where it doesn't belong. I guess I can't begrudge you for hiring someone to figure out who set you up for the photo shoot—not that anybody could ever, *ever* trace that back to me, or anyone else, for that matter. It was a waste of his time and your money, not to mention his life. But that was solely because someone had the bright idea to snoop around in my business affairs." Steven checked his list again.

"Oh, right—champagne!" he said, walking past her to the far wall rack that held his bubbly. "Can't have a celebration without champagne," he gloated. "Oh, you've been out of the loop—I'm going to ask my new girlfriend to marry me. I think she's pretty keen on the idea. Of course, your early departure from Guam has cost me more money. But I've been assured that 'Madeline Ridley' has completed her residency requirement, so it's just a matter of time before Elizabeth and I can make it official." He looked over his shoulder at his current wife.

"Poor Madeline—you just royally messed things up for yourself. Okay, the set up was difficult on you—I get that. But I had no choice. I ran into financial difficulties and had to find a way out. You weren't ever going to come into any money, and besides, I needed a quick fix."

Steven went back to perusing his list. "So, there you have it. I'm just bringing in provisions so Hughes won't have any reason to come down here until…" He let out a semi-amused huff.

"I don't suppose you named me as beneficiary on your bank accounts, did you?" he asked hopefully. "Oh well, I still have the insurance policy, though that won't pay off for a long time, seeing as how your remains will never be found."

Madeline just stared blankly at him. He had killed what little spirit she still possessed with his mercenary thoughts. She closed her eyes, willing him to leave so she could die in peace.

Madeline's defeated demeanor stirred what passed for compassion in Steven's limited emotional range. She opened her eyes to find him standing in front of her, regarding her almost ruefully.

"For what it's worth, I never wanted it to end up like this." Madeline's throat closed as she looked at the man she had honestly loved and had hoped to spend the rest of her life with. The only bright spot she could find in this horrific scenario was that she had never been able to have children. The very thought of such a thing almost did her in.

Without another word to her, Steven carried the box out of the wine cellar and deposited it on the ledge. He came back down and flipped off the overhead light, then closed and locked the door behind him.

Being back in the blinding darkness caused a ripple of panic to surge through Madeline's body. She didn't want to die like this, not in here, not at the mercy of Steven and his ghouls. She started to shake as great sobs fought against the silver tape across her mouth.

I will not let him do this to me! she thought, doing her best to control her breathing and relax the tightness in her throat muscles that ached so painfully. *I will get out of here, I will get out of here…*she repeated to herself. The more she heard the words in her mind, the more focused she became.

If I'm going to get out of here alive, I first have to cut these restraints, she thought. But how? She wished she had spent more time refreshing her memory of the wine cellar layout while she had the chance. She'd have to go off memory until—if she were very lucky—she could get the lights turned on again.

Now that her mind was geared to its mission, Madeline's instinct for self-preservation kicked in. If she could get over to the light switch, could she get it turned on? *Yeah,* she thought, *I could do that…* Being able to see would be a tremendous comfort. She had always feared impenetrable darkness. If she could see, it would make a possible escape more plausible.

She used the wine shelving to pull herself to her feet, which had become so numb she could barely stand on them. She lost her balance and tottered into the wine rack, creating a din of jostling bottles. Her heart pounded against her chest and she had to steady herself before she could concentrate on moving her feet. It was no use; her ankles were too tightly bound. She leaned against the wine shelving and lowered herself back to the ground.

Once she was lying down again, she reached her hands down toward her feet, where her fingertips just barely grazed the backs of her shoes. She arched her back as much as possible and was able to push one shoe off.

Exhausted but exhilarated, she freed her other foot. She could already tell she had more wiggle room with the shoes out of the way. She got back to her feet and was able to make half-inch shuffling steps. The process was excruciatingly slow, but it worked. She used her fingers as a rudder and a means of staying in contact with the wine bins as she worked her way to the far wall.

Once she hit the end of this section of wine racks, she would have a space of about four feet to navigate in order to reach the wall where the light controls were located. While she shuffled her feet, she used her right elbow to mark and keep track of the number of bins she passed. Though she had not been paying much attention to where she'd been situated, she had a vague idea that she had been roughly halfway into the room, which if memory served her well, was about 30 feet long. Each bin width was 20 inches wide.

Her mind was too frazzled to do the math, but she guesstimated that she had five cubbyholes to pass before she would reach the void. *One…*she counted. It seemed to take forever to reach the second divider. *Two…*

On it went, tiny gains of distance from an incredible use of energy and willpower. *Five!* Her fingers fluttered, searching for wine bottle necks to prove her theory wrong. Nothing. She rested against the flat edge of the shelving frame while she collected herself. Now she would be without a map for the four feet of space before she'd encounter more shelving—four feet that would normally be two strides. She'd have to go slow and straight to not lose her course or her balance.

The slow shuffling of her feet was accompanied by toneless humming as she scooted toward her target. Her head reached it before her feet, receiving a rude welcoming with a bump on the forehead. She groaned but wasted no time reverting to the process of letting her hands guide her to the end of this row of wine bins. She didn't bother to count or calculate this time; her goal was in reach and her anxiety demanded that she get the lights turned on before she lost what was left of her mind.

This time it was her right foot that took the impact as it collided against the step off the landing. She grasped at the side panel to secure herself while she contemplated how to maneuver up the step so she could get to the controls. The only way to do it was to sit down and swing her feet up, then lie down and get to her knees. Once she had done that, she was stuck. She had used the shelves and wine bottles behind where she had been tossed to act as handholds. There was nothing like that on the flat surface of the wine rack frame.

Having come so far and being faced with defeat, Madeline began to wail—a horrible, mournful sound that was all the more hideous because her mouth couldn't give vent to it. *Please God! Please God!* The refrain played over and over in her head, a comfort, a blanket to smother out her despair. *Keep trying, keep trying,* came the answer.

She rolled off her knees and back onto her butt, then scooted her back up against the end of the shelving. She tottered on the edge of the step while her hands grasped at the edge of the frame. Having more or less established a connection, she used every fiber in her being to scale up the side. She almost capsized, but righted herself and pushed for the last gain, ending up in a standing position against the wall.

She began to whimper, out of relief this time. She had done it. She rested against the shelving unit until she had worked up enough stamina to tackle the next step: finding and turning on the light switch. To do this, she inched her way to the corner, where the shelving unit met the wall. The controls were on the entrance wall, just before the door frame. She visualized walking in the door, usually in high heels, as hostess to a cozy dinner for five or six couples. She envisioned lifting her left arm to about elbow-height to flip on the switch for the chandelier over the dining table.

Madeline used her upper arm to locate the switch plate. She found it, but couldn't bring her hands up that high. Instead, she had to use her elbow, which was as hard as trying to pick up a dime with fireplace tongs. On the fourth attempt, she connected with the switch, her reward being the most beautiful, blinding sparkle of the crystal chandelier. If she hadn't been gagged, she would've laughed with joy.

As her eyes grew accustomed to the light, she thought out the next step. She had to find something that would cut through the hard plastic ties that bound her wrists and ankles. Seeing her extremities chaffed and bluish-purple gave emphasis to the urgency of the situation.

Okay, think, think! Down the hallway she had crossed over on her way to the door was a pantry/utility area, with an antique pine hutch outfitted with stemware and wine accessories. *Corkscrews,* she thought, though that was a rather dubious tool for her needs. Still, she had to make her way over there and see what else might be available. She managed to hop off the landing without falling over, and began her trek to the pantry.

Being able to see made the twelve-foot commute much easier. Now that she didn't have to feel her way in the dark, she was able to make small hops, which speeded up the process tremendously, but also drove the ties deeper into her skin.

She managed to turn on the light switch in the alcove and shifted so that her back was to the hutch, where her hands could do their job. She pulled open the first drawer and squirmed around to look at the contents. Mostly what she had expected to find: antique wine openers and *tastevins.* Before wasting any time on a long shot, she hobbled in front of the next drawer and repeated the process.

This time she struck gold—or rather, plastic and steel, in the form of a box cutter. Not all the wines in their cellar came in wooden crates; usually just the French wines and ports. The rest came in cardboard boxes, which Hughes opened using this very sharp blade.

Madeline was so close to liberating herself, she could hardly control her emotions. But she thought things out carefully, pushing the lever up to expose the blade, positioning it just so before picking it up, removing it from the drawer, and trying to get the blade where she needed it without opening a vein.

Once she had it all figured out, it was just a matter of time, skill and perseverance. After a couple awkward, pain-inducing minutes, she heard and felt the blade chew its way through the plastic. She continued to saw away, keeping her grip on the box cutter as best she could while pushing outward with her wrists. After another minute, the box cutter broke through the plastic binding, sending it falling to the floor. She dropped the cutter and began massaging the ligature marks on her wrists.

Then, with a quick, hard jerk, she pulled the tape off her face.

"Oh my God!" she gasped. She rubbed her face and lips gingerly, checking for blood. It felt as though she had just ripped off a layer or two of skin. No blood on her hands, but plenty of filth. She bent down and cut the ties away from her feet, and after a quick rub of her ankles, she headed back through the main room to the powder room in a second alcove, pausing only long enough to slip her flats back on.

The sight of the toilet reminded her of other neglected body parts. She scrubbed her hands and face and rinsed her mouth under the faucet and then drank like a dog until she remembered they kept bottled water in the front alcove.

She found a case of Pellegrino in one of the storage cabinets. She drank half a bottle, belched and finished it off. She also discovered a box of Carr's Table Water Crackers. She ripped the cellophane and tore into the crackers like a starving wolf. These two acts made her feel almost human again.

The problem she now faced was getting out of the cellar alive. Just feeling like a human being again had taken her mind off the real peril she was still in. This brief reprieve would be nothing more than a tantalizing interlude if her malefactors caught her here.

She had helped design this cellar under the four-car garage and the apartment Hughes now occupied. She knew there was no trap door or hatch or doorway hidden behind the wine racks. There was no reason to have a deadbolt on the inside of the door, so the only way to lock it was from the outside.

After the hard-fought reprieve, Madeline began to fear there'd be no way to save herself after all. She pulled a chair away from the dining table and sat down to think. As she sat there, she heard the sound of footfalls coming from above. Panicking, she ran to the door and turned off the light. She would need to hide and ambush her assailants before they found her.

She waited, heart pounding so hard, she felt light-headed, but no one came down the stairs. She turned the light back on and looked at her watch. 2:05. Hughes had gone to his apartment for his two-hour break for lunch and a rest. This ritual would make it possible for her to escape.

Now she had two things going for her: if Hughes was at liberty to take his break, this meant his employer had most likely left the premises. It also meant Hughes was now directly above her on the other side of the ceiling. What she needed to do was create a very loud commotion, one certain to bring Hughes running to investigate.

She had the perfect implements for generating plenty of racket, but with the reinforcements used between the two levels, a bottle of wine being smashed on the tile would be a muffled sound on Hughes's level, if heard at all. She would have to hurl many bottles to the ground simultaneously.

She walked around examining the five separate wine racks, including the narrow ones on either side of the door. It would be great if she could pitch one forward—that would surely get Hughes's attention. But she knew all the shelving had been bolted into the limestone walls.

Her next best idea was loading the dining table with bottles and tipping it over. *That might work,* she thought, hastily grabbing bottles and lining them up on the table. As she yanked absurdly expensive Bordeaux and Burgundies from the bins, she adjusted her methodology. Sure, gutting Steven's wine collection would be satisfying, but she might have a secondary round of noise if she used his vintage champagnes. She nearly giggled at the prospect of producing canon-like pops as upended champagne bottles released their corks.

When she had assembled about three cases' worth of wine, Madeline removed all the chairs on the right side of the table. Then she stood back and studied the logistics: tip table, run to the landing, cut the lights and hold herself flat against the wall until Hughes unlocked the door and came in. Then, *wham!* hit him over the head with a bottle. Madeline nodded. It was a good plan—foolproof, as far as she could see.

She took a bottle of wine and placed it to the left of the door, where she would stage her attack on poor Hughes. She didn't like that aspect of the scheme, but she had to console herself with the thought that he would knowingly put himself in harm's way to protect her. She'd find a way to make it up to him, she hoped.

With everything in place, she thought through the next few steps beyond knocking out the butler. She then took a deep breath and grabbed the underneath side of the table, and with all the strength left in her, tried to tip it over. It didn't budge.

Madeline was now perspiring all over—from exertion and dread. This had to work. She didn't have time to think of something else. *The tablecloth.* She grabbed the ends and gave it an experimental tug. Some of the bottles jiggled, but she could tell she wouldn't get the desired results with her arms.

She moved the end chair and rearranged the bottles so she could gather more cloth to tie around her waist. It would be a weird maneuver, pulling the cloth to the left with her body so that the bottles would crash to the floor and not on her heels. She did a couple practice runs without the cloth tied to her, then she fastened it with a loose knot.

"One, two, three…" She lunged forward, the bottles rocking against one another and starting to tumble. She held the ends of the cloth as she continued to lurch forward. She was rewarded with a deafening cacophony as the bottles fell off the edge of the table, most smashing on impact, some surviving the fall only to be broken by another landing on top.

It was a good execution, deriving as much racket as she could hope for. So much so, her ears rang from the sharp, explosive impact. It made much more noise than she had expected. Dark red splatters were everywhere, so were ragged fragments of glass. It was a beautiful mess, she thought, pleased with her handiwork. But she had little time to savor the ruination.

She shook her head in hopes of restoring hearing as she made her way to the door. She cut the lights and strained to hear anything above the ringing in her ears. She could hear nothing, so she counted to herself.

Even a man in his sixties would be able to abandon whatever he was doing, run out of the apartment and down the steps to the cellar in two or three minutes. Madeline would give him four, then she'd panic.

One-hundred and thirty-one, one-hundred and thirty-two, one-hundred and... Even with her compromised hearing, she could hear the key in the lock. She lifted the bottle over her head. The door flew open and Hughes stepped in. He flipped on the light and stared at the wine carnage in horror.

"Merciful heavens," he uttered, then dropped to the floor as Madeline's well-wielded bottle whacked the back of his head.

Madeline cried out as Hughes went down. She was shaking as she bent to examine the damage. She had never caused anyone physical harm before, and she didn't like the feeling. There was no broken skin, but the spot was already turning color. She knelt on the floor and felt his neck to make sure he was still among the living.

She picked up the set of keys Hughes had carried in and, taking one last look at the destruction she was leaving behind, slipped out the door, locking it behind her.

SIXTY

Madeline cautiously surveyed the grounds as she headed for the trail. Even though the sky was overcast, the glare made her head feel worse. She wished for her sunglasses as she stumbled along on feet that had almost gone dead from lack of circulation. She concentrated on each step, not allowing herself to think too far in advance.

Once she was off her property, she followed the trail that would take her past the San Ysidro Ranch. There was a more direct route to Jane's house, but Madeline couldn't risk being seen on Park Lane, especially now that she didn't have her wig anymore. She took San Ysidro Lane down to Las Tunas. From there, she turned onto El Bosque and took it to Moore Road, then turned left onto East Valley Road, where she could cross and take the back route to Jane's house.

Every car that passed as she waited to dart across the street made her paranoia rise. She kept her face hidden as much as possible while trying to make a break for safety. She crossed without recognizing any of the vehicles that passed her, and hurried down the lane to the wooded trail that was a shortcut to Jane's house.

It was now almost quarter to three. Jane would be picking her daughters up at Montecito Union in fifteen minutes. She would be gone before Madeline reached the house. Her only hope was that Jane didn't have any other errands to do afterwards. If she wasn't home by 3:30, Madeline would have to come up with some other way of getting into town.

Her mind stopped there. She had no phone, no money. She'd have no other way to get downtown except by foot, and even if she could make it that far, she'd never get to the District Attorney's office before it closed for the day. She concentrated on fording the creek and navigating the still muddy paths and the overgrowth on the trails. She hoped and prayed she'd make it to Jane's before collapsing.

When she came out onto San Leandro Lane, it was 3:05. Her timing could be perfect. Madeline forced herself to stand upright as cars passed her. She limped her way through Jane's front gate and followed the driveway toward the house. It was very tempting to flop on the porch and wait for Jane's return, but she felt too conspicuous out front, in view of the street.

Instead, she let herself in the side gate to the Emerson's backyard and was promptly toppled by their golden retriever, Max. She had no strength left to fight him off as he joyously licked her face. She laid there and took the tongue bath, gagging on Max's less-than-appealing breath until he got a whiff of the wine splatters on her pants.

He was in the process of licking her pants clean when he suddenly started barking and wagging his tail. He turned his attention to the arrival of his family and bounded into the garage as soon as Amber and Amelia got out of the car. Madeline struggled to her feet just as Jane's youngest came into the backyard.

"Aunt Maddie, are you alright?" Amelia asked, alarmed by Madeline's frightening condition. Jane and Amber appeared at the doorway. Their hands flew to their mouths in horror.

"Oh my God, Madeline!" Jane cried out. "What the hell happened to you?" Madeline tried to think of some reassuring words, but she found herself incapable of speech. "Girls, take Max out for a walk before you start on your homework," Jane said, trying to usher them away, for Madeline's sake and theirs.

"What about our snack?" Amelia asked petulantly.

"Is Aunt Maddie going to be alright?" Amber asked, unable to take her eyes off her usually glamorous godmother.

"You can have it as soon as you get back," Jane answered her youngest. "Go on—it doesn't have to be a long walk. Just make sure he does his duties." The girls quarreled over who had to carry the poop bag while Jane shepherded Madeline into the kitchen.

"Maddie...who did this to you?" she asked, tears in her eyes as she spied Madeline's wrists. "Jesus, Maddie—what is going on? Sit down, honey. What can I get you?"

"Water," Madeline croaked. Now that she was out of harm's way—at least temporarily—she felt the full impact of all she had endured. Jane returned with a glass of water and a first aid kit.

"Tell me what happened to you," she said, examining Madeline's hands and wrists.

"I will. I promise. But I need your help. I need to get downtown, immediately. Can you take me there?" The urgency in Madeline's eyes frightened Jane. "But no one can know. Swear to me you won't tell anyone."

"I swear." Jane turned her head and called out, "Lucita, I've got to go out for a bit. Will you watch for the girls? They should be back in a few minutes," Jane said, doing her best to hide her nervousness.

"No problem," Lucita said as she entered the kitchen. "Dios Mio!" she exclaimed as she spotted Madeline.

"It's okay, Lucita. Mrs. Ridley had an accident. I'm going to take her to the emergency room. But do not tell anyone. If Mark gets home before I do, tell him I had errands to run. And make sure the girls don't say anything. *Comprendes?*" Jane asked, staring at her maid so intently, the message got across loud and clear.

"I can't believe this!" Jane said, dividing her attention between her friend and the freeway. "I'm in shock."

"You're not the only one," Madeline said. Now that she was in safe hands, Madeline felt the onset of immobilizing fatigue. She had to snap out of it, though; she had to be convincing enough to the D.A. or all would be lost. She'd be dead meat for sure at that point.

"I'm just so glad you made it out of there! Jesus…I can't even imagine what *hell* that must've been. Thank God you're safe." Jane grabbed Madeline's hand, her eyes welling up. "You need to go into hiding, somewhere safe where he'll never find you."

Madeline caught herself; her eyes had closed and she was almost asleep. She blinked hard and tried to recall what Jane had been saying. *"…somewhere safe… hiding…in a safe place…you'll be safe here…"*

"Turn right here," Madeline said, startling Jane with her sudden alertness.

"The D.A.'s office is on Santa Barbara Street, across from the courthouse," Jane said.

"I know—turn here! I've got to stop somewhere first."

"Where are we going?" Jane asked anxiously.

"The Eastside Inn, on Garden Street. Turn left here."

As soon as Jane pulled into the motor court, Madeline was out of the car and headed for the lobby. After a few words with the girl at the reception desk, Madeline waited impatiently for the manager.

"He'll be right with you, Ms. Dawkins." Madeline flashed Jane a tense smile, then was greeted by the manager as he beckoned her into his office.

"After Burt's death, I was wondering if I should turn this over to the authorities," Jeff Bowen said, producing a manila envelope from his safe.

Madeline took the envelope with shaking hands. She opened it and pulled out three separate documents, each paper clipped together. All three were signed statements verifying that they—the borrowers—had paid off their mortgages held by RAM, L.P. in full and were not aware that their property titles had not been cleared of the debt. All were accompanied by copies of canceled checks, and all had the updated title reports showing the liens had not been reconveyed. It was the smoking gun—three smoking guns, to be precise. And it was enough to close down Steven's operation and put him away for years.

No wonder Steven had Burt killed and had planned the same for her. It was all over for Steven Ridley; the whole glossy charade was about to come to a halt. *If* she could get to the D.A.'s office before all hell came raining down on her again.

On the short drive to the District Attorney's office, Madeline used Jane's phone to call Mike. He was on the verge of hysteria once he heard her voice. He made her swear she was alright. She told him she was about to be a lot better and to get over to 1105 Santa Barbara Street immediately. She'd explain everything to him and the D. A. at the same time.

Jane insisted on going into the D.A.'s office with her. Madeline didn't put up a fight; she knew it wouldn't be easy getting in without an appointment, and having a credible spokesperson couldn't hurt.

She couldn't bring herself to look in a mirror, but she knew from her disheveled and wine-spotted clothing that she could've been viewed as a raving loony. She reeked and was mortified to be out in public in her condition. Nevertheless, she stated her case in a businesslike fashion.

"My husband is guilty of several felony acts, including arranging a rape, murder, attempted murder, blackmail and embezzlement, and I can prove all of it," she told the receptionist calmly. "His in-house security men abducted me this morning, bound and gagged me and left me to die in a wine cellar. If I don't get to speak with the District Attorney right now, my captors will make damn sure I do not escape a second time," she said, holding up her wrists as proof of her recent captivity. The ligature marks were convincing enough to get the receptionist on her feet.

SIXTY-ONE

"These are wicked," Mike said, playing with the assortment of spy tools Madeline had picked up from her P.O. box. "Testing...one, two, three..." he said into the microphone of the voice recorder pen. Madeline rolled her eyes but she couldn't help seeing the humor in Mike's antics, probably because there had been so little to laugh about lately.

"I think we should have the sign guy change the name on the door to 'Mad Dog P.I.'" This time Madeline shot him a disapproving look. "Hey, why not? We'd probably have greater success with that than we would with an event planning service," he said, indignant at her hasty dismissal.

What's with all the "we" business, Madeline thought, halfway amused by his assumptions. She supposed she could do a lot worse than to have a loyal friend by her side as she ventured into unchartered territory.

"Besides, you've got to admit I was rather resourceful at finding your cell phone yesterday." Madeline smiled, despite herself.

"Too bad you didn't find me, or my bag," she said, trying to provoke him for no good reason. She hoped her personality wasn't irreparably warped after all she'd been through. She regretted her words as they wiped the smug look off Mike's face.

"I'm sorry I couldn't find you," he said, looking like he had just lost his best friend, which he almost had. Madeline gave him a rueful smile meant to absolve him of his guilt.

"And don't give up on the bag," Mike said, his former enthusiasm returning. "I think someone's going to read my ad and want to get the 'BIG REWARD!'" Madeline shook her head at his indomitable optimism.

"Anyway, I still think it would be a hoot going into the P.I. business. I think you've got a remarkable aptitude for it, and well...I'm a quick learner..."

"In order to become a licensed private investigator in the state of California, you must have three years' experience as an apprentice—2,000 hours, to be exact," Madeline said, confident that would burst his bubble.

"That wouldn't be so bad," Mike said as he examined the miniature GPS tracking device. "How do you know that?" he asked belatedly.

"Through the online private investigator course I signed up for after Burt died. Besides, unlike you, I'm going to need to generate some income. Anyway, who would hire us?"

After mentioning her dead P.I., Madeline's mood became somber again. Though things had turned in her favor, she still couldn't shake the sense of melancholy and loss that had replaced her former feelings of satisfaction and contentment. In an effort to organize her thoughts, she grabbed a pen and a notepad and started a list.

Call Barry Houstein

Now that they wouldn't have any difficulty proving coercion, the divorce agreement she signed could be voided outright, along with the prenup. This time, she'd be the one suing for divorce, with cause. Lawsuits were guaranteed to spring up from all sides: swindled investors, borrowers, and her. By the time those suits made their way through the courts, there might not be anything left. She'd have to let Barry worry about that.

Go see Hughes
Hire website designer
Have business cards made
File fictitious business name

Madeline's gaze wandered away from her list. Maybe if she'd witnessed Steven's arrest, along with three of the four thugs he used to bend people to his will, she'd feel lighter inside. But there had been casualties along the way. Though Hughes was released from the hospital with a mild concussion, she would never really shed the guilt of having knocked that gentle man unconscious. She knew if she had to do it over again, she'd do it the same way, and that troubled her too.

Maybe someday she could convince herself that Burt's death wasn't a direct result of her decision to go after Steven, knowing full well they were treading on hazardous turf. Intellectually, she knew Lionel and his underlings were ultimately responsible for his plunge over the cliff. But emotionally, she felt just as culpable for putting him in harm's way.

That was his profession, one he had taken on willingly, she tried to convince herself for the umpteenth time. *He could've always refused...*

Madeline got up from Burt's chair and went to the window. There was something more troubling her than just feelings of remorse. Now that she finally felt she was out of imminent danger, her brain was able to sift through all the layers of intrigue and search for the niggling doubts and suspicions still remaining. She let her mind go blank as she stared at the parking lot with unseeing eyes.

Moments from the last three weeks replayed themselves across her mind's eye. Suddenly, there it was. Madeline stopped the slideshow and turned the incongruity over, looking at it from the dispassionate distance of time.

Russell Barnett. Burt knew from their first meeting the name of the detective Steven had paid off while she watched, unseen, from her car. He knew the man personally, and knew he was trailing Madeline like a piece of toilet paper stuck to her shoe. Yet Burt had never confronted him, even though he surely could've shed light on the events of the night she'd been raped.

Why? Why didn't Burt mine that valuable source of information? Madeline opened the window and let the cool breeze wash over her. She never doubted that Burt was one-hundred-percent dedicated to her case. *So, what gives?*

"Your sign's finished, if you want to come and take a look," Mike said from the doorway.

A smile spread across Madeline's face as she gazed at the name of her first ever business venture.

"That turned out really nicely," she said to the sign painter.

"Thanks. I like the name—'Current Affairs.' It has a good ring to it."

"Thank you. Hopefully, others will think so too," she said as she went to get her checkbook.

"It's not too late to add Mad Dog, Private Investigators," Mike said, shooting her a look of longing. Madeline wrote out the check and handed it to Mike, who gave it to the sign painter.

"So, what now, boss?" Mike asked from the doorway. Madeline had to admit she liked the sound of that.

"Grab your jacket. We're going to see a man about a job."

SIXTY-TWO

Madeline let Mike out on the corner of Anacapa and Sola. From there, he took a right and proceeded to the office of Russell Barnett, Private Investigator. Madeline drove past Mike as he went up the front steps. She pulled the rental car into the detective's small parking area, stopping directly behind Barnett's familiar silver Accord, effectively boxing him in.

As she walked up the steps, she saw Russell's expression change from guardedly optimistic to uncomfortably cagey as he realized Mike was not there to engage his professional services. When he caught sight of Madeline, he froze, his mind busily calculating his odds of disarming them versus fleeing the scene.

"What is it you want?" Russell asked offhandedly, as Madeline came in and stood next to Mike's imposing figure.

"Just some answers," Madeline said. She could tell by his forced nonchalance how nervous her presence made him. "Might as well sit down—this could take a while." Mike stood until Russell lowered himself into his chair before taking a seat across from him, closest to the door.

"I imagine you've heard the news about your client," Madeline said, her eyes never leaving her former shadow.

"Ex-client," Russell said, his voice not carrying the sense of detachment he was shooting for.

"Now that the tables have been turned on Steven Ridley—my soon-to-be-ex-husband—I think you need to tell me what exactly Steven hired you to do for him, besides following me around town."

"Would you like some coffee?" Russell asked, levitating up from his chair.

"No, and neither would you," Mike said. Russell let out a breathy snort and sat back down, an ironic smirk on his face.

"I'm not required or even permitted to discuss my cases with anyone other than my clients," Russell said, leaning back in his chair.

"That privilege doesn't exclude the D.A.'s office," Madeline reminded him. Russell tried to retain a stony expression, but Madeline didn't miss the lump of nervousness he attempted to swallow. "I spent two hours with Conrad Adams yesterday, putting all the jigsaw pieces together for him. As you can imagine, he's got a lot on his plate with all the charges against Steven. I didn't even get around to telling him about your involvement."

"I—"

"At this point, you would surely be considered an accessory to my rape, seeing as how you set up the camera, didn't report the incident and did nothing to stop it," Madeline said matter-of-factly.

"But—"

"Personally, I'd prefer to hear the unvarnished truth about your involvement from you, instead of having to tell the authorities about your role in the drama. I mean, you'd lose your license, reputation, the ability to earn a living, on top of facing criminal charges, if Adams gets wind of the part you played. A part that not only ended in my rape and public humiliation, but also the murder of Burt Latham and the attempted murder of me. So…given the choices, wouldn't you rather tell us everything you know that can help put Steven Ridley and his crew away for as long as possible?"

Russell Barnett licked his parched lips. "Your husband came to me with his suspicions that you were having an affair. Tracking unfaithful spouses is the bulk my business. His request was straightforward—simple garden-variety surveillance with all the benefits of modern technology. He said he'd found notations in your appointment book that were suspicious, and your behavior after these alleged assignations had led him to believe you were having secret dalliances with another man.

"He told me that you had the initials A.R. circled on the day of the fundraiser—the same initials that supposedly popped up in the last few months of your agenda—next to the notation 'Rm #106.' He told me he had learned from another source that you had been seen walking through The Edgecliff grounds arm and arm with another man. He wanted me to set up surveillance on that room on the night of the fundraiser. I did as he requested. Afterwards, he had me start following you to see if you'd ever lead us to the 'other man.'"

Madeline had listened to the account with an impassive expression. She could feel Mike tense up like a tightly wound coil, ready to spring. She knew instinctively he was ready to challenge Barnett, but was holding back out of deference to her. It was her show, and he was going to let her take the lead and provide backup when necessary.

"That's the PG version," Madeline said at length. "If I hadn't just been treated to three weeks of cat and mouse terror, I might've taken you at your word, simply due to ignorance of the sordid predicaments people get themselves involved in. But from my new, cynical viewpoint, I see a few flaws in your account of events.

"For starters, if you were taking a flyer at which hotel I was to rendezvous with my secret lover based on a rumor Steven 'supposedly' heard, then you are a rank amateur. Secondly, the video and stills were not taken through a pane of glass. Anyone having a secret affair would not conduct it with the draperies opened. Besides, the angle, closeness and clarity indicate the video recorder was *inside* the hotel room." Barnett coughed and tried to clear his throat. "Being inside means you would've had to break into the room to set the camera up, or have help from someone on staff. Either way, you were in the wrong. Are you willing to break the law for all your clients, Mr. Barnett?"

"Now would be the time to give it to us straight, before Ms. Dawkins calls the D.A." Mike said, eyeing Barnett the way a cat would observe a slow-witted lizard. Barnett tried unsuccessfully to clear his throat again. Madeline got up and filled a paper cup with water from the cooler and handed it to the P.I. She took her seat and waited for him to speak.

"Your husband offered me five-times my going rate to do this job. I knew what he was asking me to do was against the law, but I believed his story and I wanted the case. It had all the earmarks of adultery, so my conscience didn't bother me at all. In my business, if it walks like adultery, it's adultery."

"Right. The rape of an unconscious woman is video-recorded, and getting paid five-times the customary rate persuaded you that the woman in question— *me*—was an adulteress," Madeline said, not bothering to hide her rancor.

"I wasn't there when it was being recorded," Russell said, trying to hold his ground.

"Did you look at it before you gave it to my husband?"

"No."

"Don't you usually look at the evidence before you give it to your clients, make sure you've got what they're looking for...?" Madeline said, head cocked, waiting for Barnett to step on his own dick. His bewildered expression and lack of a coherent answer said it all.

"Look, a man walks in here and throws a lot of money at me to get recorded proof of his unfaithful wife, and a bonus if I get the goods. Am I going to argue when he tells me I'm not to preview the evidence?" Barnett said, looking to Mike this time for sympathy.

"Then how do you know it 'walked like adultery'?" Madeline asked. Russell sputtered.

"This is a waste of time," Mike said. "I say we throw this loser to the D.A. for target practice."

"Hold on…," Russell said, his agitation showing. "I'll tell it to you straight, but I want guarantees you won't go to the D.A."

Madeline looked at Mike. They had the dirt she was looking for—preserved for future use, thanks to the multi-purpose pen.

"Can't do that," Mike said. "What you did nearly cost this lady her life," he said, leaning over the desk as though he might make a grab for Barnett's throat.

"And it did cost Burt Latham his," Madeline added. Both were surprised when Russell Barnett's face crumbled into a mask of wretched shame.

"What did you think of Burt Latham?" Madeline asked. Barnett sucked in a ragged breath and regained some of his composure.

"He was a very good detective," he said with reverence. "One of the best." Madeline noticed the catch in Barnett's voice as he said this.

"Considering that I hired him the day after I saw my husband hand you an envelope on Santa Barbara Street and learned your identity when I followed you to this office, why didn't Burt pursue you as a very likely source of information regarding my rape?" Barnett half- shrugged, but Madeline wasn't going to let him off the hook. "What prevented him from exposing your part in this crime?"

"I don't—"

"Don't give me that crap. What was it that prevented Burt from following the course of action I hired him to perform? Digging up Steven's possibly fraudulent business dealings was his way of avoiding a confrontation with you. And frankly, Burt Latham was ten times the professional you could ever—"

"Burt Latham was my brother-in-law," Russell said, looking directly into Madeline's eyes. "He gave me my start in this business. I was married to his sister.

"The reason Burt wasn't keen on pursuing my involvement in your…the setup against you…was because he'd know from looking at the photos that someone would've set the camera up on the inside. Knowing I was involved—and breaking the law, again—his enormous sense of duty to his family and clients led him to shoot for sparing one while serving the other."

"You mean, taking the riskier route of proving embezzlement in order to keep you out of jail?" Madeline asked. Russell nodded solemnly. Madeline and Mike exchanged glances. Russell buried his face in his hands.

"I feel plenty responsibility for your rape and Burt's death," Russell said, his voice cracking. He was slouched over, as if he didn't have the strength to hold himself erect. "I'll testify to my part in your husband's scheme to blackmail you. In light of the way this unraveled, there's no doubt about my culpability. I'm sorry. You can call the D.A. now, if you want. I won't resist arrest."

Madeline and Mike pretended to mull this over. Madeline hoped this disclosure would lift the heavy weight of guilt from her shoulders. It should have, but too much had happened in too short a period of time. Maybe in a week she'd feel better. Maybe in a month…

"At this point, Mr. Barnett, adding one more log to the fire under my husband's feet is superfluous." Russell looked at Madeline cautiously. "I think I have a proposal which will serve to make amends—to me, at least."

"What is it?" Russell asked.

"My friend Mike and I would like to join forces with you."

"What are you talking about?" Russell asked, clearly caught off guard.

"After the up-close and personal crash course I've just taken in the world of espionage, Mike and I would like to pursue a career in private investigation."

"You're joking."

"No, we're very serious," Madeline assured him.

"What are you talking about?"

"I'm talking about allowing us to apprentice with you, with the goal of becoming licensed private investigators ourselves." Russell stared at them, his mouth open in disbelief.

"I just admitted I've broken the law, and not just once…" Mike and Madeline nodded passively. "It takes three years to fulfill the training requirement…" His audience nodded again, more enthusiastically this time. Russell pushed away from his desk, hands to the sides of his head, as if he suddenly had the mother of all hangovers.

"You're serious…?"

"Serious as a prison sentence," Mike said.

"What do you say, Russell?" Madeline asked brightly.

"Do you two know anything about this business?"

"I've started an online course," Madeline offered proudly. "And let's not forget the 'on the job training' I just received, thanks to my soon-to-be-ex."

"I'm just naturally inquisitive," Mike added.

"You're probably not bluffing, are you?" Russell asked. Madeline shook her head.

"One more criminal snagged in the D.A.'s net is one more head on his mantelpiece," Mike said. "We came to you first. Someone will take us on..." Russell blinked hard in an attempt to dispel the scene in front of him.

"Alright. You win," he said in a voice barely audible. "I'll train you to pass the exam, but after three years..." Russell paused as he grasped the dubiousness of what he was taking on. "After three years, you're on your own and I've paid my debt to you. And I want it in writing."

"Not a problem," Madeline said. "What part do you want put in writing— the part about us keeping quiet about your role in my rape...?" Russell buried his head in his hands.

"Look," Mike said, "we'll be out of your hair the minute our licenses come through. Three years is too long to hold a grudge. You're just going to have to take our word that we won't renege on the deal."

Russell studied their faces for a moment. He opened a drawer and pulled out a bottle of Jack Daniels and a glass. He poured himself a couple ounces and slugged it back.

"Okay, first lesson," Russell said, eyeing the pen in Mike's shirt pocket, "recorded conversations are illegal in California unless all parties consent to being recorded." Mike smiled and turned the pen's mic off.

"Got it, boss," Mike said, with a wink to Madeline.

"I think you better offer us a drink to commemorate this fateful occasion," Madeline suggested.

As she sipped whisky from a paper cup, she supposed that sometimes compromise was more practical than revenge.

ABOUT THE AUTHOR

Spouse Trap, the prequel to the Madeline Dawkins Series, is the fifth book by Cynthia Hamilton, and is the only fictional book to take place in her hometown of Santa Barbara, CA. Her other titles include *Lucky at Love: Some Guys Just Never Give Up...*a story about a seven-time divorced mule breeder who hasn't given up on love, and *Once Upon a Lyme...A Tale of Two Journeys,* which chronicles the author's nine-year search for the cause of her mystery illness and the unexpected by-product of becoming a writer.

Visit cynthiahamiltonbooks.com to learn more about the author and her upcoming releases.

Other books in the Madeline Dawkins Mystery Series:

A HIGH PRICE TO PAY
https://www.amazon.com/High-Price-Madeline-Dawkins-Book-ebook/dp/
B088RJSTP9?ref_=ast_author_dp

GIRL TRAP
https://www.amazon.com/Girl-Trap-Madeline-Dawkins-Mystery-ebook/dp/
B07CWHMQRW?ref_=ast_author_dp

THE TROUBLE WITH PARADISE
https://www.amazon.com/Girl-Trap-Madeline-Dawkins-Mystery-ebook/dp/
B07CWHMQRW?ref_=ast_author_dp

THE PATIENCE OF KARMA
https://www.amazon.com/Patience-Karma-Madeline-Dawkins-Book-ebook/
dp/B08CS3K8GW/ref=tmm_kin_swatch_0?_encoding=UTF8&qid=&sr=

HOUSES OF DECEPTION
https://www.amazon.com/Houses-Deception-Madeline-Dawkins-Book-ebook/dp/B08H5NRRTH/ref=tmm_kin_swatch_0?_encoding=UTF8&qid=&sr=

OTHER PEOPLE'S MONEY
https://www.amazon.com/Other-Peoples-Money-Madeline-Dawkins/dp/1648752187/ref=tmm_pap_swatch_0?_encoding=UTF8&qid=&sr=

BREACH OF TRUST
https://www.amazon.com/Breach-Trust-Madeline-Dawkins-Book-ebook/dp/B09YRZK4G2?ref_=ast_author_dp

Dear reader,

Thank you so much for downloading and reading "Spouse Trap", the prequel to the Madeline Dawkins series. I was pretty rough on poor Madeline in this installment, the reason being I wanted a heroine who comes into her private investigator role with an understanding of what it's like to live through a nightmare. I felt it was important for her to learn how helpless people can feel when things go completely awry in their lives. She takes that hard-won knowledge into subsequent adventures, along with her talent for event planning, which pays the bills while she and Mike risk life and limb unraveling mysteries.

Reviews are the writer's best friend. They are what drive sales and gain exposure for our labors of love. Sharing your thoughts with prospective readers would be so greatly appreciated!

To learn more about my inspiration for "Spouse Trap" and my other books, please visit my website: http://cynthiahamiltonbooks.com

You can also find me on Twitter: https://twitter.com/AuthorCynthiaH

Goodreads: https://bit.ly/2DKRXPi

And Facebook: https://bit.ly/2IDnLcF

With warmest regards,

Cynthia

The Madeline Dawkins Mystery Series

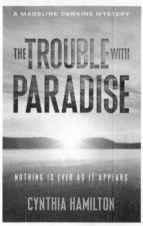

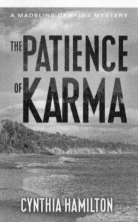

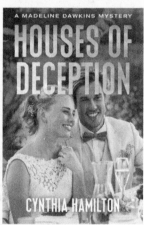

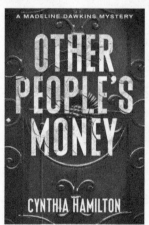

Find the entire series on Amazon at https://tinyurl.com/5n6pppnv

Made in the USA
Las Vegas, NV
15 February 2024

85772954R00177